Greed's
POISON

A Puerto Vallarta Adventure

HORATIO STREET

Greed's Poison: A Puerto Vallarta Adventure
© 2011 A Novel by Horatio Street
Published by Avantage Publishing

All rights reserved. No part of this book may be used or reproduced in any manner
whatsoever including Internet usage, without written permission of the author.

Library and Archives Canada Cataloguing in Publication
Street, Horatio, 1953-
        Greed's poison: a Puerto Vallarta adventure / Horatio Street.
Issued also in electronic format.

        I. Title.
PS8637.T744G74 2011   C813'.6   C2011-908255-1

ISBN 978-0-9878694-0-1 (e-format)
ISBN 978-0-9878694-1-8 (pbk)

Willie and Lobo
Photograph by Jaime Dale

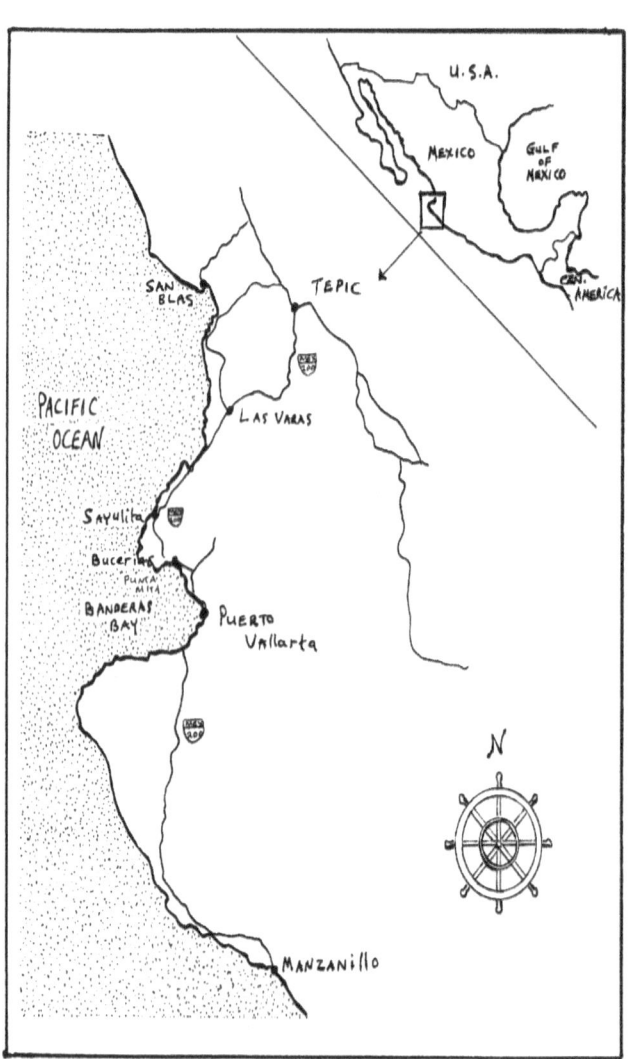

SPECIAL

ACKNOWLEDGEMENTS

We want to thank those families in Mexico who have "adopted" us. It has been a wonderful experience to watch your families and Mexico grow.

We hope the best for all of you and again, Gracias!

Technical expertise was provided by Dr. Phil Nuytten of Nuytco Research and Chris Comb of JW Fisher, Bernard Besal for his Ducati knowledge, Captain Doug Russell of the University of Washington for the "use" of the *RV Thomas G Thompson*.

Readers Note: In this story some of the historical developments had to be modified for the sake of plot. To those who know the recent history of the area please excuse the artistic license.

It is said that with every story the author puts something of his soul into the work; drawing from past experiences in his own life, or upon those of others.
This is certainly true of this story. Although a total work of fiction, the passion to finally complete it came from painful memories of the past.

As our hero discovers; although we should never forget,
we must move on.

We dedicate this story to the Carlson's and Mascarena's.
Two innocent couples murdered in the Mexican drug war.

LA CRUZ

PUNTA MITA

MARIETA ISLANDS

PACIFIC OCEAN

MORRO ROCKS

N

PROLOGUE

PACIFIC OCEAN, 1525

The impact of the spear caught Alzarro squarely between the shoulder blades, dropping him to his knees. Domingo, the only other survivor of the conquistador's land expedition turned and fired his musket. The spear thrower, the last native standing, gave an agonizing screech and fell backwards.

Domingo bent to help his captain. "Come. We are almost to the raft. We will make it."

With every fiber of strength he had left, Alzarro willed himself back onto his feet. The massive disk he carried on his back had just saved his life; at the same time it seemed to want to take it. Its weight had consumed Alzarro for nearly two days as his troop had fought their way through savages and jungle to return to the ship.

"We are almost there," Alzarro convinced himself. He staggered as he rose, yet with growing momentum he soldiered on, dragging one foot in front of the other down the sandy beach.

As they cleared a rocky point on the shore of the great ocean, their tiny sailing craft came into view. Through sweat pouring down his brow, Alzarro saw a shipmate standing on a slow moving, loosely tied log raft. The raft was halfway between the ship and the shore. White water splashed around the raftman's feet as he paddled furiously towards them.

Inspired by the sight, Alzarro and Domingo trudged forward.

The raftsman jumped into the waist-deep surf to help Domingo support Alzarro as he staggered forward. The men bodily lifted Alzarro and his heavy load onto the deck of the water-swept raft. They climbed aboard, picked up crude paddles and dug deep into the water.

They were not thirty yards along when another band of natives emerged from the dense jungle. The natives raced down the beach to intercept the foreign monsters who had spread so much death and thievery. The natives waded into the ocean, drew their bows and fired.

Even though arrows rained down around him, Alzarro could not move. His head lay on the rough wooden planks. He gasped for air; the bitter taste of salt water splashing on his face refreshing him. He did not flinch when an arrow dug deep into a log, only a hand's breadth from his face.

Suddenly, an arrow pierced Domingo just where his thick, leather tunic separated from his belt. The obsidian arrowhead sank deep into the back of his abdomen. With a scream he fell to his knees.

Alzarro twisted to face his loyal servant. "Can I help you?"

Domingo writhed in pain. After a minute he took a deep breath and focused his eyes on his master. "I will be all right, Captain," he gasped.

The raftsman was panicking. "They will kill us! We must keep moving."

Using his paddle as a crutch Domingo rose, his face a portrait of agony. Weakly, he started paddling. Although the raft was not going straight, it was moving. Had the native's supply of arrows not been exhausted, the men would surely have been killed.

Alzarro turned his attention to their tiny ship. It was a sorry collection of rough, axe-hewn planks and braided vine ropes. The jib and mainsail were nothing more that woven palm fronds. The jib was raised, but sloppily, spilling wind as the pilot prepared to raise the mainsail.

Domingo soldiered on. With each pull of the paddle, the razor sharp flint dug deeper into his soft internal organs, slicing his spleen and liver. He sagged, as the mortal wound sapped his strength, but he did not stop.

As the raft came to rest at the side of the ship, Alzarro dragged himself onto the deck of the ship. He untangled the ropes that secured his load and then rose to help Domingo. The men gently lifted Domingo onto the ship. He cried out in torment as his body twisted.

"Are there no more?" the pilot asked.

"All lost," Alzarro sighed.

As the pilot and raftsman concentrated on getting the ship under way, Alzarro focused on Domingo's wound. He gently pulled the heavy leather tunic back and cut away Domingo's rough shirt. The arrow was deep. Around the opening, acrid stench of yellow liver bile assaulted Alzarro's nose, as blood seeped out in increasing volume. It was obvious the wound was fatal.

He knelt by Domingo's face. "We will cut out this arrow and you will be fine. Take heart."

Domingo wreathed in pain. With each breath, his body began to settle. He looked over at the man he had served for so long.

"I am spent, master."

His body sagged. With one last breath, his eyes stared vacantly into space.

Alzarro gently pulled his faithful servants eyelids down.

"Domingo," he lamented.

They wrapped Domingo in a mat with a few of the ballast stones from the bottom of the ship.

"In the name of our Holy Father and Savior and our Great Guidance, we give you back our faithful companion, Diego Juan Maria Domingo of Seville. He has obliged me as servant, protector, and friend for many years. These three months since we left the camp of Guzman, we have pursued these devils in the hope of returning to you the treasures of this heathen country. Dear Domingo's sacrifice was for you, oh Great Father. We commit him to the sea to return to you."

Silently, they slipped the body over the side of the boat. After the impromptu ceremony the men gathered around the satchel. Alzarro pulled the ragged cover back. All had to shield their eyes from the sun's glare bouncing off the gold. They quickly shifted their bodies, shading the treasure from the light.

Alzarro's companions gasped in disbelief. It was nearly as thick as a man's thumb and wide enough to cover a grown man's chest. In the center was a square hole where Alzarro had strung ropes to strengthen his grip throughout the journey. The wheel was covered with finely-scribed etchings of the savages from the great city that Cortez had first conquered. The strange etchings made no sense, but this didn't matter as they were nothing but the work of the devil. What mattered was the gold.

The three men looked at each other, their eyes taking on a wild look. The pilot reached to lift the disk and was astounded by the weight.

"You carried this all the way?" He looked at his captain with awe.

"Nearly so. Two carried it at first, they were cut down one by one. None were left by yesterday. I finished the job, but am sorely spent."

The raftsman helped the pilot turn the disk over. In the middle, just a fraction from the square hole, was the mark of the spear. It had struck with such impact it had almost penetrated the entire thickness of the disk.

"It saved my life."

They extracted several other small gold pieces from Domingo's leather travel bag—all that was left of the hoard they had first come upon when they caught up with the natives.

"These pieces are nothing of what we first discovered, but one by one the men were lost to the savages. I, for my part, could only carry the wheel. It has been a desperate fight. These savages are wild. Only the power of our muskets saved us—the savages ran in fear of the death they delivered. Had they attacked at once, we would never have survived," Alzarro explained.

The pair listened in fascination, yet their eyes kept returning to the shine of the Aztec symbol.

Five years after the conquest of Mexico City, Cortez had dispatched a large army to the west to explore and search for treasure. Alzarro and his small company of twelve had been separated from the main expeditionary body for three months now. They had hunted the savages further and further west in pursuit of the treasure of the Aztec priests.

The pilot breathed a sigh of relief as the afternoon breeze pushed the awkward craft further to sea and safety. Yet as the sun set, the pilot looked anxiously at the southwest skies,

"I do not like the look of the clouds."

Alzarro saw the pilot's concern; great white clouds towered to the heavens, their bases dark-gray and leaden.

Before midnight the storm was upon them. The ship, built in haste at the guidance of the old Canary Island pilot, had never been meant for more than the pursuit of the retreating natives. Made of planks fixed with wooden pegs and caulked with the bark and gum of strange trees, the pilot was surprised that it had lasted this long. Several times he had to re-braid the vine ropes that held the woven palm-frond sails together. The natives they had drafted at gunpoint to help, had marveled at the floating creation—yet it was much to their credit that the ship sailed at all. Their skill with weaving the sails and braiding the vines amazed the pilot. When this adventure was over, he vowed to return and learn more of these native's strange seamanship.

The storm bore down on them with violent vengeance. As the hours of darkness continued, the pilot knew that something would soon decide their fate; either the ship or the storm would break.

During the last watch, they sensed the change. The tempest wind was coming to bay. The waves came in different, confused patterns. The pilot called the men to take heart. The small jib was raised halfway to aid steerage. Faint light could be seen through the thick gloom.

As quickly as hope rose, it plummeted. Coming out of the murkiness was a rock wall covered in white foam. A giant wave of water drove down onto the stern like a massive fist. The raftsman vanished. The tiller, unmanned, swung wildly.

The rock seemed to rise and fall, like a monster opening and closing its mouth, gasping for air. Slowly, as if pulled by a magnet from hell, the ship moved toward the beast.

"If we can pass the rock, the waves will settle," the pilot yelled. He pulled the jib higher for steerage and raced back to the tiller.

A boiling cauldron of white water fumed as wave after wave exploded on the deadly rock. By sheer force of will, the pilot tried to steer the ship away. Life and death hung in the balance. Suddenly the wind snapped the jib ropes like spiders' threads. Steerage was lost.

With all the force the pair could muster, they held the rudder over. The sea opened to feed the ship to the rock. Just as abruptly, a wave surged between rock and ship, throwing it skyward, denying the rock its appetite.

They stared in disbelief as the rock emerged close enough to touch. But the sea had moved them. They were past!

No sooner had their hearts stopped pounding and the sea opened once more. The ship slid down into the waiting teeth of another rock. The bow smashed, the mast snapped like a dry twig. The sea rushed in to raise the wreck again.

"We are lost," the pilot screamed just as he was crushed into the stub of the mast.

Alzarro grasped his oilskin-wrapped diary and the rope tied to the golden wheel. Loading the diary down his breeches, he looped the rope around his neck, just as the ocean took him. Tumbling, he fought against nature, against death, against sea. Suddenly he broke the surface and was granted another breath.

In his desperate flailing his hand caught hold of a strand of rope attached to a broken shaft of wood. He pulled it to himself and held on. The disk was gone.

In the growing light he saw surf pounding on the shore of dry land. With what strength he had left, Alzarro kicked toward the land. It was the waves, more than effort on his part, that spat him onto the stones of the shore.

Dazed but driven to live, he crawled out of the sucking vortex and onto dry land. Blackness took him.

For the first few days, worthless pieces of the ship drifted up to the shore. When natives paddled out to collect the bits of driftwood, Alzarro hid in one of the many caves worn into the limestone of the island.

For weeks, Alzarro survived on seabird eggs and brackish water from shaded pools. Miraculously, his tattered oilskin-wrapped diary survived inside his breeches. As the loneliness engulfed him yet more-and-more along with the loss of his men and the great treasure, Alzarro's mind drifted. He wandered the small island, talking to Domingo; telling his servant what they would do upon their return to Spain. He talked about how they would be honored and gifted by the king for their great accomplishments.

Then one morning, Alzarro couldn't believe his eyes. On the horizon was the silhouette of a ship. Alzarro frantically ran up and down the shore, waving bits of the scrub-brush to get their attention.

After an eternity, the craft slowed, men came overboard and rowed towards him.

1

SEATTLE TODAY

"You make me feel like a kid again, Mrs. St Julian." Jack gave his wife a wry, loving smile.

"You make me feel like a woman again, Mr. St Julian." His wife responded with a lecherous grin.

The Greek restaurant was crowded, but the pair was in their own world. For a long moment, they gazed transfixed, into the depths of each other's eyes.

"It's been a long time coming..."

"...But worth it." Pat St. Julian finished her husband's sentence.

"First time we've been out for dinner since I got home." Jack smirked.

"And that was because of the tiramisu. I figured we were due." Pat laughed.

The sound of her happiness was pure delight to Captain, Jack St. Julian. It was something he had missed terribly during their long separations, caused by his duty in the US Navy. Now that that duty was over, he looked forward to much more laughter.

"Don't know why I never learned how to make it... Oh, I know." She giggled, slightly tipsy. "Didn't have any studs, least none worthy of my cooking, while my husband was off saving the world."

"You minx." Jack smiled, knowing full well that nothing of the sort had ever crossed her mind. "You will now be held to that domestic duty by your own cognizance."

"Yes, sir, Captain, sir... er, Ex Captain, sir." She corrected herself with a cheeky smile and an impertinent salute.

"It's Captain, Retired... If it matters to you."

"All that matters is that you're home." Her look softened.

The couple's faces were highlighted only by the glow of a single candle. The bottom third of a bottle of Retsina and two nearly empty wine glasses, were the only obstacles between their hands. Jack moved the bottle away reached out and engulfed his wife's hands in his big paws. Other patrons secretly stole jealous glances.

"I can't count the nights; waiting in that endless heat, or in the darkness of a chopper, waiting to go into another hellish challenge, that I didn't dream of this moment... to be home again, safe, with our whole lives ahead of us."

Tears glazed Pat's eyes. Her man's last assignment had been drug interception out of Guantanamo.

"I am so proud of you...of what you have done--and you care for me so much." She squeezed her husband's fingers. "It had to be a hard choice."

Jack stroked her fingertips.

"I gave the Service good years but it's our time now."

He let go of her hand and took a sip of wine. Through the window Jack saw the rain. His lips tightened. They had come by motorcycle and though they were dressed for it, it would be a cold wet ride home.

Jack looked at his wife's reflection in the window. Her mother had been part Native American, giving Pat high cheekbones and a wholesome, honey-toned complexion. Her big brown eyes were framed by long eyelashes, tipped with a golden glow that matched her dark, brunette hair.

"Whatever comes, we'll work it out." Her smile deepened as she looked into his Paul Newman-like, ice-blue eyes.

He took a deep breath. "Not really sure where to start, now that it comes to it."

"Well, you've talked yourself out of a job, putting your younger brother in charge of the St. Julian Foundation."

"I'm not a white-collar kind of guy. Ben's the man for the job--he's great." Jack said.

"Maybe so, but your love of the sea hasn't changed, my love. The foundation needs you Jack. There's much to do."

"...things we both can share in." Jack finished his wife's thought.

"What's money if you don't use it? Do something good. We can do that now."

"Together." Jack added, gently rubbing his wife's arm with the back of his hand.

"Could start by heading back to Puerto Vallarta," She gave her husband an enthusiastic look, "...and sail the *Heavenly Daze*. I'd love to do that. Besides, Charlie is waiting for us."

"Now you're talking. Sailing Banderas Bay for a few weeks would be great." Jack said, his mind skipping over the times he had returned to his favorite haunt; first as a boy, fishing with his dad, then sailing with his wife.

"How many times have I gone to rest and recuperate? It was a shame you couldn't join Charlie and I as we sailed the *Daze* home."

Charlie was Jack's shipboard cat that had kept him company when he used his sailboat as his residence, while stationed in Guantanamo.

Jack's smile widened, "Let's head home, the rain's getting heavier. We can discuss this there." He waved to the waiter for the bill.

Outside, May weather in Seattle was typically annoying. When they had come into the restaurant, it had been cloudy. Now the rain was coming down in earnest.

As they stepped outside, Jack said, "I'll get the bike, you stay dry."

He trotted off without looking back. Pat stood outside under the protection of the restaurant's canvas awning.

Wearing his motorcycle helmet and red leather jacket to keep reasonably dry, Jack jogged the two blocks to the parking lot to retrieve his 1100 Ducati motorcycle.

He paid the parking lot attendant and swung his 6 foot 3 inch frame over the big Italian machine; one of the most powerful motorcycles in the world. Jack gave the accelerator a couple quick twists, loving the feel of power under him, as the more than 100-plus horsepower machine warmed up.

As he pulled out onto the street, Jack heard the sound of a gunshot from the direction of the restaurant. He instinctively popped the clutch and accelerated. As he approached the restaurant, he saw two scruffy-looking young men wearing hoodies, running toward him. Something was wrong.

The lead runner half-turned, raised a pistol and fired at the follower. The follower didn't stop. Instead, he returned fire.

Jack snapped the accelerator. The Ducati went airborne, jumping the curb onto the sidewalk. His rear tire burning the wet concrete as he gained speed.

The lead runner's feet never stopped moving, but Jack saw his eyes widen at the sight of the screaming motorcycle coming straight at him.

The distance between the bike and the runner closed. The man had just enough time to raise his pistol and fire. Jack felt a searing flash of pain through his arm.

Just before impact, Jack dropped two gears, snapped the clutch and accelerator. The front tire was three feet in the air as it collided with the stomach of the young thug, throwing him viciously onto the concrete.

The bike reacted as Jack knew it would, only slowing a fraction as it climbed over the man's chest and back onto the sidewalk.

The second runner broke into a panicked run across the street. He fired towards Jack. The Ducati leapt off the sidewalk searching its prey. The runner headed for a clutter of parked cars. He never made it. Jack closed the gap, drifted the bike into a side spin, crushing the back of the man's legs. The runner's head ricocheted off the front grill of a pickup truck, like a basketball off the backboards.

Jack stopped in the middle of the street and looked in the restaurant's direction. His heart stopped. Pat was half-leaning against the window; half-kneeling on the sidewalk. The window was smeared with blood where her back had slid down the pane.

The Ducati's rear tire burned blue as Jack flew to her. Bystanders offering assistance flinched with fear as the Ducati came to a tire-streaking stop, five feet from her body.

Jack was instantly at her side.

She tried to speak but couldn't. She looked into his eyes, "I love you" she mimed. Blood began to drip out of her mouth.

Jack grasped her head in both hands, pulled her to his heart and sobbed. "No! No!"

The sound of sirens grew louder. A crowd gathered. Jack heard nothing.

*   *   *

"Captain St. Julian...Sir?"

From a hard-back chair in the chapel of the hospital, Jack looked up at the Seattle Police uniform.

"Terribly sorry. Need to ask some questions--you okay with that?" the officer asked respectfully.

"Sure." Jack answered soberly.

"Why did you confront those men?"

"They were firing weapons, people could get hurt." Jack shook his head at the obvious irony.

After a long pause the cop continued. "From what I hear, you are pretty good on a motorcycle."

"Raced 'em when I was younger."

"How long you had it?"

"This one, three years. Don't get to ride much lately. Been on active duty...Was." He corrected.

"Yeah, we know."

"You know?" Jack looked up at the officer.

"It's a crime scene, sir; you know the drill. We have to check out everyone. Captain, US Navy. You recently resigned?" The officer asked. "That's not on file."

"Just last week. 'Been married 6 years... Was." Jack corrected again. "...'bout time I started building a new life."

"Understand getting a late start with marriage because of duty—did a 20 myself, in the Coast Guard."

After a long pause, Jack looked into the officers eyes, "It was drugs wasn't it?"

The cop nodded. "Crack cocaine."

Jack's mind wandered back to a month before; the nights spent commanding a naval cutter intercepting drug shipments bound for America. He hated drugs before. Now it was personal.

"Which one was it?" Jack asked.

"Sir?" The cop responded.

"The bullet. Which shooter?"

"Don't know yet, sir. But because of your actions we got both pistols. We're running ballistics; it'll take a while. How many shots did you hear?

"Four or five for sure. The lead guy fired behind him as he was running toward me. Then he fired at me." Jack looked down at the fresh bandage on his left arm.

"I felt something--didn't register, you know?" Jack shrugged.

"The other guy fired twice...maybe three times." Jack continued, "One shot wild when I started after him, another sort-of straight up, while he was running... just before I caught him from behind."

"That one's got seriously broken legs and nose. The other guy's in a coma; should recover."

" Lucky him." Jack said bitterly.

Jack was numb. His thoughts were bouncing off the walls of reason. Why had they gone out that night, why *that* restaurant, why take the bike, why...why...why?

*　　*　　*

The weather was as somber as the occasion. Clouds filled most of the sky. One minute it was drizzling, the next, the sun would peek through, but only for a short time.

Many of Jack's maritime outfit attended. Jack's brother Ben, his wife, and the entire staff of the St. Julian Foundation came, along with Pat's family.

Surrounded by friends, Jack was alone. He had been to too many funerals. He couldn't remember how many, but could remember the faces of all the fallen comrades in action he'd been with. That was different. They knew the score. It was combat, kill or be killed. The price a soldier pays.

His love had died an innocent, standing outside her favorite Greek restaurant, in what was supposed to be a peaceful Seattle neighborhood. But there was no place in America that was peaceful anymore, drugs had seen to that. The hollowness of the reality sickened.

As Jack was walking back to the limousine, a man in a dark suit approached him. It took Jack a moment to realize it was the cop from the hospital. The officer offered his hand.

"My condolences, sir."

"Thanks." Jack returned the handshake.

The man stood there silently looking down at his shoes. "Not supposed to tell you, but think you deserve it. Ballistics confirmed that the bullet that hit your wife was from the lead guy's pistol and... he didn't make it; some complication. Don't have all the details yet, but sort of thought...you know." His words tapered off as he tried to find the justice in it all.

"Oh, and there will be no charges laid against you. It's been deemed self-defense."

"Thanks" Jack said with an empty heart as he stepped into the limo just to get away from the reality of the world around him.

2

MEXICO CITY

"What you two are doing is wrong!" Ramon Vegas slammed his fist in to the palm of his other hand.

"My sons." He sneered. "You have everything…yet you risk it all on drugs."

"Father, I will not defend our actions. Our returns are ten times anything the business generates. Security is covered. Our transportation business provides the perfect cover." Ernesto Vegas said calmly.

"I came to this country out of Franco's war and built a life for my sons. Yes, there were challenges."

"Challenges!" Ernesto Vegas spat back. "How many suffered from challenging you? It's no secret—what happened to anybody that crossed you, Father."

"That is business." The old man looked at his eldest son through cold eyes. "Those who competed with us were always offered a buyout. Some made poor choices." He shrugged unconcerned. "I had to take care of business. What you are doing will destroy your own futures."

"You have made us who we are. We too, have 'taken care of business.'

"I never beheaded my competitors and hung them off bridges." The father growled.

"We have not done that."

"No but you have had those two *gorillas* do it."

Ernesto Vegas fell silent. From the backseat of their

bulletproof, armored Mercedes Benz, he watched the cars cruise along Avenida de Los Insurgents; one of Mexico City's major thoroughfares. In the distance, Mexico's World Trade Center rose majestically. Ernesto Vegas turned to look behind. One car back, was his 'gorilla', Jorge Ortega—in their chase car with a number of other bodyguards. It was true, they eliminated competitors in the fashion his father accused him of. That was just the nature of the business.

"You have played us off each other for years. Miguel and I are not drug lords like those murdering savages up north. We are only supplying the transportation," his son lied smoothly.

"You will regret this." The father said flatly. "Look at your failed attempt on that federal narco, that was pure stupidity. Your future ended there."

"We had nothing to do with that. You speak of futures, what is the future of Vemexa? Tell me father, who will lead this company when your time is over? The more ruthless? The cunning? That is what you taught us, seize the opportunity—not to fear a challenge. So, don't speak to me of virtues!"

Ernesto Vegas continued, "For years you have been asked to name a successor to your 'legitimate' business. Yet you have done everything you could to make my brother and I enemies. Vemexa is worth billions. We have eight divisions. Tens of thousands of people depend on us for their livelihood and millions for their daily bread—literally."

"Yet you name no successor. You control all with that Yankee bean counter, Hamilton, while doing all you can to make your sons enemies. Now you criticize us when we join forces. You speak like a hypocrite!" Ernesto Vegas growled.

"How can I trust my sons," the old man spat. "Hamilton could have saved you. Your arrogance will destroy you. Enough of this!" His hands chopped the air, signaling an end to the conversation.

Ramon Vegas watched through the window as the tree-lined streets of the high-end Benito Juarez district of Mexico City, slid by.

Both the chauffeur and the bodyguard in the front seat of the

Mercedes noticed the unattended wheeled garbage can, so familiar to Mexico City streets, set unusually far into the street. It was the last thing they ever saw.

The bomb blast lifted the front of the car five feet into the air. In spite of the unique reinforcing, the windshield shattered into a million fractured missiles. The bodyguard took the full impact and was dead before the car came back to earth.

The driver, fatally wounded, and half blind from glass slivers, floored the accelerator, only to run the car up the curb and directly into a large tree.

The bomb shattered windows for half a block, and three stories high. Several pedestrians were blown to pieces.

The Vegas' security chase car that had been directly behind the Mercedes was shielded from the worst of the blast. The security detail was out of the Ford Explorer before it screeched to a halt—just behind the Mercedes.

While glass was still falling from smashed building windows, Jorge Ortega raced for the back passenger door. Reefing it open, Ramon Vegas literally fell into his arms. As if lifting a child, Ortega pulled Vegas out and laid him on the grass-covered curbing. One of the other security men took over from Ortega as he raced around to the other side of the car where Ernesto Vegas struggled to open his door.

The other three security men had their .38-caliber revolvers, recently purchased from an American middle-man, drawn as they surrounded the car and scanned the area for any other threat.

Ernesto Vegas slowly eased himself out of the car and gingerly placed his feet, one at a time, onto the pavement. His head pounded like a bass drum. His eyes refused to focus. Everything around him was taking place in slow motion, as his mind tried to grasp what had just happened. He saw Ortega shouting at him, but couldn't understand the words. He turned to see through the car, that one of his security detail personnel was caring for his father on the other side of the car. He wanted to go to him, but was too shaken to take his hand off the stability that the chassis offered. He wiped blood from his forehead.

He slowly shook his head, as words from his bodyguard, Ortega, began to penetrate his brain. Ortega grasped Vegas "Are you okay?" He nodded gently, for fear his head would explode from the pounding.

The sound of rapidly-approaching sirens penetrated his consciousness.

Vegas looked into the front seat. His father's driver and bodyguard were both dead. The worst impact had been on the passenger's side, his father's bodyguard lay motionless, obviously dead. The driver's face looked like some kind of surreal pincushion; pockmarked with tiny shards of glass. His father had been sitting on the passenger side too—in the back seat.

"Supposed to be bulletproof?" Vegas mumbled, looking at Ortega. His mind was clearing now. He took tentative steps around the car to where his father was lying. The older man had several severe gashes on his head; he was unconscious and looked terribly vulnerable.

As the first police car pulled into view, Ortega turned to his men and hollered, "Cover me."

He stepped into the street and waved to attract the police cars' attention. They pulled to a fast stop beside the Mercedes. Two officers jumped out. Ortega exposed the palms of both hands in a sign of peace, then reached into his breast pocket and pulled out a business card—behind which several 1,000 peso notes were folded.

"I'm Jorge Ortega, security for Ernesto Vegas of Vemexa Corporation. We have federal licenses to carry arms. We are not the threat. We need help immediately. Señor Ramon Vegas is seriously injured"

He looked the first cop in the eye. "Immediatamente!" He commanded.

The cop scanned the card and his eyes widened with recognition. "Si Señor." He pulled his walkie-talkie up and called in.

Ernesto scanned the scene, his senses returning. Across the street screams and crying were emanating from victims on the sidewalk. Some people were walking around in a daze; others were helping the victims.

More sirens filled the air. Police cars and ambulances arrived from every direction. The lead cop frantically hand-signaled the first ambulance to the Mercedes. The crew jumped out and attended to Ramon Vegas.

The scene quickly became a whirlwind of activity. While all of this was happening, one of Vegas' security detail walked back to the chase vehicle and punched the speed dial on his cell phone.

Shielding his mouth with the palm of his hand, he scanned the crowd to see if anyone was watching him make the call.

"The father is serious, but alive. Ernesto only slightly injured—nothing serious. The bomb went off too soon, or was not strong enough." He listened for a moment, then hung up, and casually slipped the phone back into his pocket.

Hanging up his cell phone at the other end of the call, Garcia Santana looked over at his master sitting beside him in the back of a black Mercedes and shook his head negatively. The other man's face turned to stone.

"Come, we must pay La Serpiente a visit" The man said. "This is one snake that will crawl."

Thirty minutes later Santana punched a number on his cell phone. "Cover the back. If he runs, don't shoot to kill, but stop him... on your life."

The driver of Santana's Mercedes watched in his rearview mirror as their chase car slowed behind them and turned down a side street, as ordered.

The Mercedes pulled up to a seedy tequileria. The entire street was just a long line of the same one-story buildings; different doors were surrounded by different colors. The crumbling adobe building was covered with vulgar graffiti between the broken neon signs for various beers and cigarettes. Men and prostitutes stared as the big, black car slowed to a stop.

Three prostitutes and a pimp standing near the door of the tequileria, jumped when Santana emerged from the car. They scurried like cockroaches for shelter.

Santana reached into his jacket and freed his pistol from its holster.

Suddenly, two men came out of the tequileria, herding a third man between them. The look on the middle man's face was one of abject terror.

The pair led the man to the back door of the Mercedes. Santana opened the door and pushed him roughly into the car. Santana followed instantly, closing the door behind him. The car sped away.

The man's eyes bulged as he realized who he was sitting next to.

"You have failed me a second time. Suarez lived. Ernesto Vegas lives. You will not be so fortunate."

The chase car quickly pulled up behind the lead car. The entourage drove the four blocks to La Serpiente's home. The man cried and pleaded, knowing his family had only moments to live. He looked up as the chase car sped into the lead, and screeched to a halt in front of the solid steel gate to his house. Three men jumped out and sprayed the gate's bolt with machine gun fire. They kicked the steel door open and charged in. Moments later, screams and automatic fire filled the air. In less than a minute, the three men were backing out of the gate and jumped into the car. The car burned rubber as it sped away.

*   *   *

Todd Hamilton, Chief Financial Officer of Vemexa, strode into the private emergency room just as the doctors were finishing the stitches on Ernesto Vegas' face.

Two Mexico City detectives sat watching.

"What happened?" Hamilton asked.

"I don't really know." Vegas glanced over at the cops. "One

minute we were talking, the next I'm standing by the car and all hell is breaking loose."

Vegas turned the cops. "You tell me what happened?" He commanded.

"It is early to know, Señor, but we suspect it was some sort of bomb. Might have been a gas explosion, but not likely. We are treating it as a crime—not an accident, Señor."

"Damn right." Hamilton said.

"I've got nothing else to say." Vegas looked at the cops.

The two officers looked at each other and got up. "We will be in touch if there is anything we learn, Señor Vegas. It is an honor to meet you," one cop fawned, as they left the room.

Once alone Hamilton continued. "Miguel called. He is furious. He has our people looking into it. He said he would be here as soon as possible. How is your father?"

"Let's find out amigo." Ernesto said.

The two men approached the public emergency ward, the chaos was like a war zone. Beds and chairs were filled with bleeding people, most moaning and crying in pain. Blood-stained bandages and dust-covered people were everywhere. Doctors and nurses worked at a fevered pitch.

Ernesto spotted Ortega standing at a discreet distance from the chaos. Upon seeing them, Ortega approached immediately.

"*Jefe*, it is not safe for you to be here." Ortega said, scanning the crowd.

"Where is my father?" Vegas asked ignoring the warning.

"He is upstairs in an operating room. No word yet on his condition. Some of our people are outside the door."

Ernesto Vegas looked Ortega in the eye and nodded.

"Is there a place to wait up there?" Vegas said.

"Si, Señor, we have arranged a private room. The hospital has been very accommodating." Ortega looked at the crowd of people milling around.

No matter how rich you are hospitals only move so fast.

Ramon Vegas had been the first to arrive and first to be attended to, but many others had followed.

"Let's go." Vegas commanded.

They followed Ortega to the elevator and up four floors, to a private waiting room.

Entering the elevator, Vegas turned to Ortega. "What did you see?"

"A flash of light came from the curb, just before your father's car got there. The Mercedes took the worst of it. The shock wave pushed us backwards. Your men up front were killed almost instantly."

"Who did this?" Hamilton demanded.

"We do not know yet, but we are looking hard." Ortega said.

"My father accused us of trying to bomb that federal narco, what was his name?"

"Suarez." Ortega answered. "We have no information of who did this, it wasn't anyone on our side."

"First thing we need to find out is who knew which route we were going to take to the office." Vegas said.

"You were only a block from the office. But we will check anyway." Ortega reasoned.

"Miguel has called in and is calling all our contacts. He said he will be here as quickly as he can but his first job is to find out who did this." Ortega continued.

"Yes, I'll call him soon as I talk to the doctors." Vegas answered.

Once Ernesto Vegas and Hamilton were alone in the VIP hospital room, Hamilton closed the door.

"So who do you think did it? Hamilton asked. "Could your brother be that ruthless?"

"It is possible, but there are so many easier ways. I don't think so, father had many enemies. We were talking of exactly that, when it happened."

"You think it was one of the cartels?" Hamilton asked.

"That would be my first guess. The government war is

constantly stirring the pot. One never knows who is coming after who anymore. But why go after my father? This will attract the law—big time."

"Well, maybe the target wasn't your father." Hamilton looked Ernesto Vegas squarely in the eye.

After a moment Hamilton continued. "Miguel could know that we know."

"Si, I thought of that. We must be very careful compadre. We must show no sign of suspecting Miguel. Things must appear to continue as if we are going to follow through with our plans together."

The American nodded. "Totally agree. But I'll put my auditors on notice to be extra careful."

* * *

Worldwide, the next day, newspapers read:

"At 8 am Wednesday morning, a bomb exploded in an apparent assassination attempt on the life of well-known business magnate and multi-billionaire, Ramon Vegas. His limousine was travelling along Insurgents Avenue, when the bomb apparently hidden in a garbage can, went off. Mr. Vegas survived the attempt, but is in serious condition in Hospital Angeles de Jesus. A personal bodyguard and Mr. Vegas' driver were killed in the explosion. Three people standing nearby were also killed. Several buildings in the vicinity were damaged, and reports indicate the falling glass and debris seriously injured 18 people; 50 others were treated and released. A passenger in the limo believed to be Vegas' older son, sustained a minor head injury and released. Nothing is known yet by police—as to who the perpetrators might be. The investigation is ongoing."

On the third page of most local papers, was the story of Jose Garcia Montoya, also known as La Serpiente—an individual known to the authorities, was found dead. He had also been badly beaten. The cause of death was believed to be a single, thin puncture wound through the chest, into the heart. Montoya's wife and two children were gunned down in a brazen raid on the family's home at 9 am Wednesday morning. An investigation is being organized.

*   *   *

Three weeks had passed since the car bomb. In a sterile, darkened room on the top floor of a private hospital, three men and two women sat waiting. All faced the bed of the now-wizened relic, Ramon Vegas, his leathered face fixed in a permanent scowl. He continued to breathe superficially, for a short while—for what would be his last few breaths. No priest was now in attendance, the padre had come and gone.

The two sons of Vegas were dissimilar in stature. Nevertheless, they could be easily recognized as Vegas' lineage. The eldest by two years, Ernesto, was a short 5 foot 7 inches in height, but full-chested, like a bull. The bruises on his forehead had faded, but the stitches were still covered by small bandages. His eyes were closed; he was waiting patiently for the inevitable.

Miguel Vegas, five inches taller and leaner than his brother, sat silently staring at the floor. His right hand was in his jacket pocket, repeatedly rolling a silver-and-pearl handled switchblade, between his fingers. His pleasant, good-looking features belied a cruel and monstrous side, cunning and calculating. He never forgot a slight.

Both men were in their early thirties. They sat dry-eyed and stone-faced as they waited for destiny.

From their earliest memories the pair had been rivals— Miguel's game had always been to "bait and trap" an opponent. Using the opponent's anger or pride, he got them to react in a way of his choosing. It was then, like a mongoose that Miguel would strike.

Ernesto was no less intelligent and had a confidence born of strength. His style was that of a pit bull, grabbing hold and not letting go until he had crushed his opposition.

Both approaches had proven deadly efficient in the past, and would again.

Todd Hamilton, 39, with light brown hair that was showing the first signs of graying, sat in the background. His lanky frame didn't fit in the standard issue hospital armchairs. His legs stuck out. He was uncomfortable, but he resisted the desire to get up and walk about. He was there at the behest of the old man.

Through the past three weeks, Ramon Vegas had only gained consciousness a few times. Internal complications had slowly but steadily mounted. Doctors explained that operations were necessary, but the procedures would likely kill him. The sons agreed to let nature take its course. It hadn't been a difficult decision.

The old man's wife, frail and robed in black, sobbed quietly at the side of the bed. No one paid her any heed.

The old man let out a feeble groan. The nurse looked at her watch and scanned the faces of the two brothers for direction. They paid no attention. She deemed it was time and prepared the syringe.

The two Vegas brothers shot each other a glance. Ernesto Vegas raised his eyebrows, Miguel Vegas nodded. Both men got up and quietly left the room.

In the hall of the hospital, Ortega and Santana rose as their masters approached.

"We will have privacy." Ernesto Vegas commanded the pair of body guards.

Santana looked to Miguel Vegas. Vegas nodded and the man turned and followed Ortega down the hall.

"Well brother, the time has finally come." Ernesto Vegas stated unsympathetically.

"He is truly done." Ernesto Vegas said.

"True, and it is as we suspected. I knew he would not forgive or bow." Miguel Vegas said.

"We will carry on as before." Ernesto Vegas agreed.

"We will, brother." Miguel Vegas responded with confidence.

"My sources tell me that the federales still have no case against us. Although they say we are being watched."

"Si. Mine say the same." Miguel answered, not wanting to concede the point that his brother's intelligence-gathering was getting better than his.

Neither would admit that as the deceit born of dishonesty grew between them, so did the corruption of others.

Todd Hamilton watched the brothers re-enter the hospice room. Ernesto shot him the briefest eye-contact.

Hamilton had been the financial adviser to the old man for over 10 years. He was now the chief financial officer of a multibillion dollar company. Under his direction, the family's legitimate wealth had grown astronomically. Their empire now spread to many areas of Mexico's daily life, most notably in real estate.

The old man's breathing became choppy, as if he were trying to bite off pieces of air. His breaths gradually came further apart. The breathless interludes grew intolerable. The sobs of his, soon-to-be, widow increased.

Experience told Hamilton that with the old man's death, real terror would begin—it was always that way when a dictator died. Just as the false front of the family's years of integrity were being used, so too was the deception between the brothers. Now the battle for power over Vemexa would begin in earnest. All talk of cooperation would be nothing but political spin. Miguel Vegas' inevitable drug-fueled war chest had to be neutralized. This was the same high stakes poker Hamilton had experienced in his earlier financial experience in Europe and the Middle East. Only now it was personal. His own life was on the line.

The stilled sounds in the room were hypnotic. Time slowed.

Suddenly, the old man's body jerked and the entire room

jumped in reaction. In unison, the brothers stood and took a step towards their father. They all watched as the old man drew in a ragged breath, tried to speak, but was too weak. He tried again, but the sound was meaningless gibberish. Neither looked at the other as they resumed their sitting positions.

The nurse moved in to check his pulse against the monitor by his side. Then she proceeded to the prep table and loaded another syringe of morphine.

Finally, there was one last sigh.

*   *   *

The funeral procession somberly traveled through the city. Mexico City Police had the streets cordoned off near the Panteon del Carmen cemetery. Todd Hamilton rode with Miguel Vegas. Santana was in front with the driver. A chase car followed the black stretch limo.

"My brother and I have decided that we need to take a low profile for a while. There is nothing unusual in the pipeline coming north at the moment," Vegas lied. "We think it is best to slow things down."

Hamilton remained silent for a long moment, absorbing what he knew was a bald-faced lie. The relationship between the two men had never been good. The old man had meant it not to be. Now with his death, the only things that stood between Hamilton and a violent end was his knowledge and capacity to make money for the Vegas'. But even these attributes had limits.

"You're the boss. I have the hotel in Puerto Vallarta to open, that's my focus. There will be few adjustments on the business side of things. Everything is in order on that end."

As much as it annoyed Miguel Vegas to know that a gringo had been brought in, the profits didn't lie. Hamilton had been particularly capable in finding funding sources from rich Europeans and Saudis for many of Vemexa's projects. In spite of the current market problems, Hamilton found ways to make money.

"You say 'adjustments,' there are no issues with our finance?" Miguel Vegas said.

"No. My contacts in Europe are nervous about everything these days, but they are taking the long-term approach with us, me, actually." Hamilton made the point whilst gazing confidently at Vegas.

"You will be coming to the opening? Many of your financiers will be there. Good PR." Hamilton continued.

"I'll be there."

The poor, rich and powerful attended the funeral. Security arrangements were tighter than any for politicians, of which there were many. Police directed traffic. Hundreds of green and white VW beetles surrounded the neighborhood around the cemetery. Many Vemexa vehicles filled with employees were present.

A trio of brass instruments blared out traditional Mexican music. An entourage of Catholic priests and their acolytes provided the pomp and ceremony.

The press was well represented, with television vans sporting satellite dishes and transmitters. All the major news outlets were scurrying for photo opportunities.

In one car, with local Mexico City newspaper markings on it, sat United States Drug Enforcement Agency senior officers Tom Bollen and Larry Diaz. Bollen scanned the crowd with binoculars. Diaz focused his telephoto camera and took half-a-dozen rapid-fire shots.

"It's a shame, really, that so many of the world's sins could be resolved with a well-placed explosion in the middle of this crowd. A few innocents would die; but on balance, it would be worth it." Agent Bollen shook his head and looked over at his partner with a wry smile.

Larry Diaz smiled back. "Well, there's a rumor it was someone in the Vegas organization that was behind the bombing of the federal narcotic department a few months back."

Bollen smiled conspiratorially. "Well there you are then. Dare we call it justice?"

"I suppose," Diaz answered. "But it's those 'innocents' as you call them, that we are sworn to protect. These guys may be the suppliers, but it's America that's got the problem. Seems to me we got things kinda' backwards."

"Wow! look who's running for office." Bollen retorted.

"Look there, it's Bellini!" Diaz went tense.

"It's touching that the Cabello drug family would send their love," Bollen joked caustically.

Fabio Apollo Bellini, Luigi Cabello's top Lieutenant, was a tall, angular man in an immaculate black, silk suit. The agents watched as he stepped slowly and deliberately down the line of well-wishers. Taking Ernesto Vegas' hand, he solemnly offered his condolences. He then walked to the widow and did the same. When he came to Miguel Vegas, the two men looked soberly at each other, their expressions never changing.

"Tomorrow," was all the Sicilian-American whispered.

Miguel Vegas nodded silently.

The movement was not lost on Todd Hamilton.

Inside the car the DEA agents also caught the gesture. "How touching," Bollen said.

Bollen's camera cycled smoothly as he got several close-ups of the two men together. They watched as Bellini walked away from the receiving line and vanished into the crowd.

"Probably ordered a couple of tons of dope," Diaz added. "Cabello seems to be letting his dog have a lot of leash."

"Interesting," Diaz responded.

Both DEA agents knew the Cabello reputation all too well. The family controlled organized crime from Texas, up the Mississippi river, and over to Virginia—the entire south. Cabello's base of operation was Miami. In spite of the growing power of Columbian, Russian, and Vietnamese gangsters, the "old mob" was still at the top of the heap. But no heap was as slippery as the drug trade.

"There's the Vegas' boys personal bodyguards" Bollen said sarcastically, "…standing by the hearse."

"Right." Diaz's camera caught several clear shots. "Big fellas. What's the 'sheet' on them?"

Bollen punched up his laptop. "The big one's Garcia Santana. Says here he graduated from the University of Texas, had a football scholarship—pretty good at it from what this says."

"Umm, don't doubt it. He must go 6-4; 240. Looks nasty." Diaz responded.

"The report says he got a knee blowout, ended any chance of a pro career. Got into some sort of trouble after that, but the details are sketchy. No visible markings, other than being a big bruiser."

"What about the other one?" Diaz asked.

"Jorge Ortega. Mexican military rank Lieutenant; Special Forces, intelligence. Skilled in just about everything they got. Resigned five years ago. Not much since then. Must have come into the employ of Ernesto Vegas. Born in Ciudad Juarez, Chihuahua. Identifying marks, dagger and snake on the right forearm, some regimental thing. Both are said to be very intelligent and ruthless. Suspected of numerous murders, but no one lives long enough to investigate. Got all the political protection billionaire's can buy."

"What a pair of book ends."

Bollen watched a group of women dressed in black, weeping together. "There's Miguel Vegas' wife. Can't make out the other one's wife."

Diaz brought the camera up and captured the women.

"The widows, past, present and future. Weeping more for themselves than the old man, I'd wager," Bollen observed.

"There'll be more widows soon," Diaz agreed.

"If this Vegas family is getting into the drug trade, there'll be a turf war like nothing we've seen yet. With a conglomerate like Vemexa behind them, these brothers are more than any cartel can handle. Imagine how many politicians they already own. Yep, things are going to get very interesting in Mexico." Bollen said.

*   *   *

Todd Hamilton left the funeral with Ernesto Vegas.

"Bellini seals it." Hamilton said dryly.

"Yeah, there's another shipment in the works." Vegas agreed.

"With your father's death, this one will be the coup d'état. He'll have capital to bribe or buy the muscle he'll need to take over Vemexa," Hamilton predicted.

"Yeah. Well, we just can't let that happen, can we?" Ernesto Vegas looked over at what was now his partner for life.

Hamilton had known of Miguel Vegas' subterfuge for nearly two years.

Five years ago the brothers agreed to ship drugs for one of the cartels. They knew that Hamilton would have to be involved. Back then he had willingly agreed. The trio had schemed to keep everything from their father, and to keep a pretense of animosity toward Hamilton.

Their illegal enterprise had started slowly, but had grown meteorically. Marijuana shipments had expanded to cocaine and heroin. The Vemexa Company's shipping division's reputation, and their skill with packaging and containment, had made for an ideal fit. The splintering of the various cartels, because of the government's assault on the drug trade, had led to more opportunities. A few busts had been made, but each time, either the truck driver or shipper had taken the rap. Vemexa had disclaimers on their contracts and a huge staff of lawyers that had thus far kept them at arm's length from the law. It was one of the benefits of being a multi-billion, multinational corporation, and one of Mexico's largest employers. There was no shortage of politicians lining up to curry favors from the company for their district.

But the Vegas brothers and Hamilton knew it wouldn't last. The bloodshed of the government's war had to stop. That meant that drug traffic had to be controlled. The trio had agreed that they had to get big or get out. Greed won out.

Methodologies, routes, carefully cultivated connections with Columbian and American cartels and a network of corrupt officials had been developed, but there was always a 'side' to the contact; some were Miguel's, others Ernesto's. That was when Hamilton discovered the subterfuge.

Miguel Vegas was stealing from the partnership to finance his own clandestine drug-running operation. It was not difficult to reason that his motives were to build a surplus that would, at the very least, remove Ernesto and Hamilton from Vemexa.

Hamilton had watched Miguel Vegas' money as it moved through the banking channels. His ability to understand and control the flow of funds had been the very reason the old man had allowed him to get so deep into the family business—that and the fact that it caused division between his sons.

Hamilton's strongest suit was land development, and Mexico was becoming ripe again. The contractions of the markets over the last few years had brought real estate back into vogue. Even the killings in northern Mexico hadn't stopped North Americans from wanting the sun and easy life style. Ironically, the drug lords had to find a place to put all their profits, why not in tourism and land.

A student of history, Hamilton recognized the evolution of things, similar to the development of the Mafia in the States. Mexico's illegal activities were changing, becoming more sophisticated. But the cohesion was still missing. Like the American crime families of the last century, the Mexican families had yet to understand the power of cooperation. Vemexa and Hamilton's knowledge were the keys. Soon all would come together.

Hamilton had initially hoped Miguel Vegas would approach him, but that had not happened. The American realized that he would not be part of Vemexa if it was controlled by Miguel Vegas. The capital that was being fueled by the clandestine shipments was going to buy that sort of power.

Hamilton had decided to approach Ernesto when, much to his surprise and relief, the older brother had come to him. It was decided that, rather than expose Miguel, they would set up their own fund. With Hamilton's knowledge, it had been a simple fiscal exercise of larceny. A couple of the family's auditors had received titles to large tracts of land, purchased at bargain-basement prices. They were told that the tracts would be developed as industrial sites only after Ernesto was firmly in control. Miguel Vegas didn't know it, but his finances were controlled by men loyal to his brother.

When they discovered the younger brother's treachery Hamilton had told Ernesto.

"There's old adage 'You can lie to your wife, but not to your accountant.' Miguel has made a serious mistake if he thinks he can cover this up. If you know how to follow the money, everything will be exposed."

And so it was to be.

*   *   *

In the penthouse suite, in one of the family's premier hotels, Miguel Vegas entertained Bellini. Santana waited in the foyer.

"Don Miguel, my condolences on your loss," Bellini offered.

"Thank you, Señor Bellini. It is better this way. My father did not want to live under those circumstances. It is no way for a man to live."

Just then Miguel Vegas' mistress walked in the room. Vegas enjoyed the admiring gaze Bellini paid her, sweeping his eyes up and down her gorgeous body. The only flaw was a slight purple swelling around her left eye.

"I'm going into the city?" She said looking at Vegas for permission.

"Si Brazil. Fix your face first." he commanded.

Both men were silent, studying her lovely derrière as she sauntered out of the room.

"Better a heart attack in the arms of a beautiful woman, ah?" the Sicilian smiled wolfishly looking toward the woman.

"Umm." Vegas responded.

For a long moment they stood gazing out the floor-to-ceiling windows—it was a rare, pollution-free day in Mexico City. Fabio Apollo Bellini could have been cut from a fashion magazine; his black hair was perfectly groomed and his handmade, silk suit fit him like a glove. His classic Roman facial features could have landed him a job as the lead in romantic movies. Women were attracted to him for more than just his power. He enjoyed many of the social perks that being young, handsome and wealthy provided.

The men sat down together on the white leather sofa. After the small talk, they got down to business.

"You're ready?" Bellini probed.

"Si, very soon."

"How long will this delivery take to get to me?" Bellini said.

"I have to bring it together. It is stored in small quantities for obvious reasons. I estimate about six weeks, maybe less." Miguel continued.

"I will be ready."

For the past three years, each February, they moved a shipment of cocaine north. Each year the shipment grew in size as they reinvested the profits.

"You have your resources in place?" Vegas asked.

"Yes. Everything will go smoothly in my area. Things will be not so in others," Bellini said.

"How do you mean?"

"Don Cabello is getting soft. The feds are closing in on him. It is an old story," he shrugged. "First they are tough and sharp and then they get rich and soft. With this shipment, I will take over," Bellini said with certainty. "However, to be cautious, we will bring the shipment through in Tucson, yes?"

Vegas nodded. "Somewhere near there," he said cryptically.

That was business. They both knew the risk—you win or you die. Both men had been party to the termination of other, would be usurpers-of-power. They understood the price of failure.

La Serpiente had failed Miguel Vegas twice. He had spent his last hour begging Vegas to spare him. Even after seeing his family murdered, the coward had been more concerned with saving his own miserable life. Vegas' switchblade had pierced the man's chest.

"What about your brother?" Bellini asked.

"I missed my chance. If he finds out who was behind the car bomb, it will be a problem. But he won't. He can continue working on the legal side, him and that gringo bean-counter."

"And if he does not?" Bellini asked with cunning interest.

"Well, then you will provide me a service," Vegas smiled coldly at Bellini. As the men looked at each other, they both knew this was going to be the only answer.

"Have your people put on 48-hour notice," Vegas stated flatly.

Bellini nodded. "You have been smart, my friend," Bellini said. "With the other families fighting the war for control at the border, all sides will eventually lose against the Americans. When that happens, we will quietly fill the void."

"Agreed. Angering the Yankee beast is not the answer. Use stealth and guile, and the Americans will slip back into apathy. They are easily outmaneuvered if we proceed cautiously. It will not be long now."

*   *   *

Miguel Vegas drove the darkened Mercedes through the streets of Mexico City. Santana sat in the passenger seat, ever watchful.

"It went well," Vegas said, smiling over at his bodyguard.

The big man nodded.

After a couple of blocks Santana asked, "And your brother and his shadow?"

"Bellini has promised two of his best to remove them."

"Too bad. I was looking forward to doing it. Ortega particularly. Then again, we have not been entirely successful with car bombs have we, Jefe? First Suarez, and then missing your brother."

Vegas snorted at the caustic sarcasm. "You are right my friend, car bombs don't seem to be our specialty."

Both men laughed at the irony.

"Well there are other ways." Santana said.

"Too true, 'practice makes perfect,' the gringos say." Vegas laughed.

"Have to keep this outside the family." Vegas continued. "We must be very careful with this last shipment. Word of it too soon, could be very dangerous. Once done, the men's loyalty will be easily purchased and secure. The cartels will think twice before taking us on."

It would soon be time to challenge the status quo, first in Mexico, and then beyond.

3

PUERTO VALLARTA

"It's tuna time, Jack!" Deni yelled.

Both men's reels screamed and lines scorched as the tuna ran. Jack let the fish have its head as he watched a pod of Pacific Bottlenose dolphins entertaining themselves. Over 50 of them were pirouetting and jumping as part of a giant aquatic ballet. Many spun completely out of the water, two at a time, in an exotic dance of the ocean. To Jack St. Julian, it was pure heaven.

Just then, Jack felt the fish give just a little. He gently tightened his thumb on the spool, increasing the drag. The fish slowed and Jack began reclaiming his line. With the increased tension, the tuna changed tactics, and was off again. Jack held the pole high, increasing the pressure, as he looked over at Deni —who was also joyfully struggling. Both men shared a quick, satisfied smile.

The dolphins were thinning as the school of bait moved in its constant effort to escape the predators. Jack could see the few that remained darting under *Carmen I*, Deni's little fishing boat, or "panga" as they are called in Mexico.

Jack pulled hard, his powerful arms not letting the fish take anything until its last possible ounce of effort was consumed.

Out of the corner of Jack's eye, he saw Deni hand his pole to his son, Israel, in exchange for a gaff. Israel expertly held the pole high as Deni's fish surfaced at the side of the panga. The gaff came down with practiced, deadly efficiency. Just as they cleared the tuna over the side, Jack caught sight of his leader coming in from out of the deep.

"I'm coming up, amigo."

Deni released his fish into Israel's care and came forward. He expertly tagged the big tuna at the back of the head with the gaff.

Not tall, even by Mexican standards, Deni was barrel-chested and had legs like trees. In one fluid motion, he pulled the 60 pound fish out of the water and into the boat. Before Deni had the hook cleared, Israel leaped behind the wheel and pegged the throttle, chasing the school.

Jack pulled a pair of Pacificos out of the ice cooler. He popped the caps with the back of his knife and handed one to his friend.

"Great stuff," he smiled, taking a swig.

"Si, amigo. Good size, this school."

Jack drained the beer and then double-checked the leader and the edge on his hook. They were five miles out in the Pacific, due west of the Bay of Banderas. Jack looked southeast toward the bay where he could just make out the Sierra Madre Mountains. At the base of the mountains, well beyond their view, was the city of Puerto Vallarta.

As Israel sped north dolphins again appeared under the boat. With a quick bark from his father the young man turned the boat and stopped, all in one fluid motion. Jack and Deni quickly cast their lines.

Jack never ceased to be amazed that dolphins did not take the bait. "How could they tell the difference between herring and lure?" he thought. The tuna, on the other hand bolted ravenously at the plugs.

Jack gave the line a hard jig at the same instant the tuna hit. The game was on again. This catch was smaller, not more than 20 pounds, Jack estimated, as he handled it with ease.

As the leader cleared the surface Jack noticed that Deni was occupied. Israel was standing by with the gaff. Jack gave him a nod and lifted his pole. The lanky young man took the line in one hand to steady his blow, and gaffed the fish. Jack smiled at Deni's son, another master fisherman in the making. Israel dislodged the jig hook as he carried the fish to the back of the boat.

Without wasting a second, Jack cast back into the boil of the sea. Again, a tuna took the plug. But this time the feel was different. St Julian knew he was in for a real fight.

"This one is running big time Deni!" he yelled as his spool shrank.

"You've got a big one, amigo," Deni stated calmly.

Jack nodded. His focus was on saving as much line as possible without breaking it or damaging the reel.

"Rapido!" Deni commanded his son. Israel brought the boat around to the tuna's heading. He gently applied power, but the fish kept taking. On Deni's command the lad added more power until Jack was able to regain a little line.

The fish changed directions and headed off to the right, again taking. Israel followed the line, judging the power needed just to keep pace, he had to make it a fair fight.

The tuna's next tactic was to go deep. The men watched as the pole, like a divining rod finding a source, pointed straight down. Israel dropped into neutral, a big smile spreading across his face, as he watched the game.

Deni came up behind Jack and wrapped a support belt around his waist while Jack placed the pole in the cradle. Carefully, Jack reached his fingers to the star drag of the big Penn reel and increased the tension a fraction. His effort was met with equal pressure from the fish. It was a draw. Jack knew that with his full strength he could easily break either rod or line, but that was not the game. Balance was everything. Both fish and man refused to give.

Jack gave a quick glance over the side of the boat. The fish was actually pulling them sideways. Suddenly, the line went completely limp. Not fooled for a second, Jack reeled, his hand a blur.

"He's coming at us!" Jack yelled.

Jack walked along the side of the little craft, heading aft. He ducked his 6 foot 3 inch frame under the sun awning as he moved back.

Israel stood at the wheel, alert to his father's instructions. Deni waited; he knew from years of fishing with Jack, that he could handle the situation. Few gringos could fish as Jack could. Deni had seen him lose few fish, yet each time he lost one he had been pleased for the fish, as it should be.

Like a silver torpedo, the fish zipped under the boat. Jack lifted his pole high, and deftly swung it past the big twin Yamaha outboards, and over to the other side. The line now ran cleanly away in the opposite direction. The fish took and the reel screamed. Jack looked down at the old Penn Senator reel to see how it was holding up. It was a good reel, but it had seen a lot of action.

Deni, too, sensed the change in tone and quickly commanded Israel to give chase. Again, Jack reclaimed some line.

The early afternoon sun glared down. The battle raged for over 20 minutes as fish and fisherman took turns giving and taking. Jack was strong, but the strain was showing in the massive shoulder muscles that bulged through the sweat of his faded old shirt. His floppy hat was soaked with sweat.

"Gonna take all day?" Deni stifled a false yawn. "I think I'll take a siesta."

Jack gave him a wry look. "You'd better be worried about this reel. I think it's giving up the ghost."

"It's not my reel, it's yours."

Jack looked down at it closely and saw that the Mexican was correct. "I guess I'll have to be more careful who I lend my stuff to."

"Amigo, you do me dishonor," Deni grinned.

Just then the pole jerked violently as the fish began another round. Jack could tell it was tiring, as he slowly won back more line.

"Israel, the .22," Deni commanded.

The young man began rummaging through the forward hatch. After a time, the lad came back to his father. Jack listened as the fisherman let loose a venomous string of Spanish blasphemy.

"I'll take that 'as no pistol,'" Jack said. His Spanish was above average.

"It is not here. We did not expect the big fish this early in the season."

That was a problem, a fish this size was dangerous. "What do you think?" Jack asked.

"We try with the gaff, or we let it go."

A silver shadow appeared in the deep as Jack reeled.

"Momma Mia!" Deni whistled, looking into the water. "We better tire it out first."

"Tire it out?" Jack asked dryly, continuing to pull.

Deni stood ready with the gaff.

"I don't think he's quite done yet," Jack said.

"I think you are right," Deni agreed.

As if on cue, the fish took off.

"Yeah, it must have seen your ugly face," Jack said, straining. Jack babied the reel, using his thumb, instead of the reel's gearing, to create drag. Very carefully, he slowly increased and decreased pressure on the spool. The last thing he needed was a 'bird's nest' of tangled line.

The fish slowed. Jack reeled. The gears were begging, grinding—the crunching sounds more obvious with each rotation. Finally, the leader returned.

"You better get it right the first time," Jack stated flatly, with a flash in his ice-blue eyes.

The Mexican shot him a look of wounded pride mixed with a foxed smile. "Maybe I just might miss this one. The baby should be returned to its mama."

Israel came back from his pilot position amidships to get a look at the object of the two men's attention. As he saw it, his brown eyes widened. He flashed Jack a big white toothy smile and a thumbs up.

Deni looked down at the fish. From long experience, he knew the fish had given its all, and whether caught or released, it would not survive.

Deni's leathered fingers lightly held the leader to balance his blow. In a great arch he drove the gaff point into the fish. He lifted, but for all his strength he could not get the huge fish over the gunwale. Furiously displeased with being removed from its native environment and pierced by the gaff, the re-energized tuna snapped its head, nearly freeing the gaff. Jack acted on instinct. He reached down and wrapped his arms around the great fish, lifted, and stepped backwards.

The fish gave a mighty slap, freeing the gaff completely. The full weight of the fish fell on Jack, sending him down onto the deck onto his back, while embracing his catch in a bear hug. Jack lay there spread-eagle while between his legs, the fish pounded the deck in wrath. Jack quickly pulled himself back into a sitting position, staring at the still-protesting tuna.

Deni and Israel jumped to help, fearing Jack had been hurt, but when they saw his compromised position and the startled look on his face, they burst out laughing in unison. Jack raised an arm and Deni hoisted him out of harm's way while the fish continued pounding the deck. Jack was covered with sweat, seawater and slime, but the laughter was infectious, and with a shake of his head he looked at his friends and joined in, too exhausted to do anything else.

Deni, sitting on the gunwale said, "I think it is not done with you, amigo. You best get down there and show it who's boss."

Jack just waved an arm at him, pulled off his sweaty light shirt, reached over the side and washed it in the ocean. He headed for the cooler and grabbed a beer. Lifting his floppy soaked hat, he rolled the icy bottle across his brow and damp, light-brown hair.

When Israel stepped back to knife the fish, it almost knocked him out of the boat, generating more laughter at the young man's expense.

Everyone, including the fish, began to settle down as Deni finished the knife job. Israel hauled a bucket of water in and washed the deck clear of the blood.

"This is a nice one, amigo. The biggest I've seen this season," Deni said.

The two men looked respectfully at the fish for a few moments in silence.

"It almost had the last word. I've never seen a fish want a man so bad, and you so ugly."

"Well, if someone else wasn't getting so old and weak and forgetful…" Jack retorted. He picked up his pole and looked at the reel. Winding and unwinding a couple of turns, he could feel and hear the grinding within the gearbox. "This one's had it for today."

Deni looked out across the horizon. "I think we should call it a day, anyway. It will take us a good two hours to get back in, and we have a lot of fish to clean."

"Works for me," Jack sighed, "it's been a good day."

With a quick command from his father, Israel headed amidship and put the small boat in motion.

Jack and Deni worked in smooth rhythm as they prepared the fish for market. Overhead, seagulls squawked, calling for handouts. The men threw the hides into the air; rarely did one hit the water before it was claimed by an aerial wiz. Many times, two gulls would grab at the same hide and the mid-air wrestling match would stop the men's work as they watched the commotion.

Years of fishing had made Deni's hands tough, and his arms like iron. He could pull the thick hide of the tunas off all day, without tiring. Deni looked across at his North American friend and smiled—not many of his clients helped with the dirty work. Jack's arms bulged as he pulled the hide off a fish.

"You are still in good shape, amigo."

"Thanks, but I'm getting soft."

"Not so soft, I am thinking." Deni responded. "Not many

would help with the catch, especially after that last one." Deni chuckled again at the antics of the fish.

As Jack sat bare-chested in the shade of the canvas awning, Deni could see the straight line of the bullet scar across the back of Jack's left arm and abdomen; a bullet he had picked up years ago. Deni noticed Jack's latest puncture wound, a freshly healed, wrinkled scar, again on his left arm; the one he'd received during the murder of his wife. Since he had been down, Jack had refused to talk about any of it. Deni knew this was not a good thing, but…

The butchery complete, Deni covered the meat with a woven mat and doused it with salt water to keep it cool.

"Amigo, remind me to show you something when we get in," Deni said, surveying the growing pile of plunder. The fish would more than pay for the day's fuel and provide young Israel and his fiancé with a good day's wage.

Jack sat in the front of the boat, aimlessly watching the Marieta Islands slip by on their starboard side. The two uninhabited islands stood like guards to the northern entry of the Bay of Banderas. He had sailed around them many times—the last time with Pat. On his port side was a point of land called Punta de Mita, it was the northern tip of the Bay of Banderas. The bay was literally a sailor's paradise, one of the largest bays in the world. It offered safe sailing, boating and diving.

Jack somberly watched a gull flying overhead, squawking its displeasure that there were not more offerings. As much as Jack enjoyed the fishing and his friends here, the emptiness wouldn't leave. "I had fun today. Can't remember the last time I've come out of the fog," he thought.

He was supposed to be assisting in whale studies in Cabo San Lucas, aboard the University of Washington's research vessel, *MV Juan de Fuca*. It was his casual arrangement with the university that allowed him the freedom to be in Puerto Vallarta.

The university was studying the migration of these magnificent mammals. Jack had been assigned to test a prototype of a new model of a special deep-diving suit, but his heart just wasn't in the work.

During the months since the funeral, Jack had been bumming around, working on odd jobs for the Foundation, but nothing mattered. Jack knew when he volunteered for the research project that he'd end up in Puerto Vallarta. The need for additional parts for the deep diving suit had given him the excuse he needed to come back to the Bay of Banderas. He hadn't been back since the death of his wife.

"As painful as the memories are, it just feels right." He told himself.

Jack came out of his reverie and noticed Deni watching him. Deni offered a smile, Jack nodded, and turned back to watching the shoreline. As they approached La Cruz, the number of sailboat masts grew. La Cruz de Haunacaxtle had been a sleepy little village but now was like all the areas around the bay, experiencing the effects of tourist growth.

They slowed as they wove through the harbor, full of American and Canadian sailboats and yachts. Jack surveyed the lines of his own sailboat as they passed. It always gave him a feeling of freedom just to look at her. *Heavenly Daze* sat content on her mooring, waiting peacefully for him to come home.

At that moment the skinny body of Jerry, Jack's deck hand, appeared in the wheelhouse. He spotted the panga and gave them a wave.

It had been Jerry who had sailed Heavenly Daze over to Cabo to pick up Jack.

Jack thought, "How long ago was that?" He couldn't remember; his life was still a vacuum.

Jerry was a true beach bum. He had been hanging around La Cruz for the past five years. Because he was honest, and handy with tools, Jack and others let him stay on their sailboats' in return for repairs, running errands and keeping an eye on things.

After the fishermen secured the panga, they off-loaded the catch onto the old concrete wharf.

"I'll see you at Rosa's," Jack said, as he jumped into his little skiff and started rowing out to his sailboat.

Deni waved good-bye.

"Gracias, amigo!" Israel hollered.

4

Deni gave his wife Rosa a soft pat on the behind as she rushed by, her arms loaded with ingredients for dinner. The restaurant, simply known as Rosa's, was renowned as the best place in town for seafood; and why not, it was supplied by the best fisherman in the bay. Located a block from the wharf, it was a two-story building that took up a quarter of the block. Nearly the entire front opened up to the street, with the second floor ringing the open courtyard below. It held two living quarters accessed by a stairway that led from the back of the kitchen. One was a multi-roomed apartment for the family. The other was a studio suite Jack had purchased when they first built the place.

The center courtyard of the restaurant was open to the sky. The walls were decorated with plants, artwork of local artists, and, of course, several mounted trophy fish. In the rear was the kitchen and storage.

Rosa caught up with Deni in the rear of the restaurant as he and Israel unloaded fresh fish that would soon be on the plates of diners.

"Good day?" She asked

"Si, good day. Deni and Israel looked at each other and simultaneously started laughing. They related the tale of Jack's adventure. The woman rolled her eyes at the men's' foolish sense of humor.

"How is he?" she asked with sincerity.

"I saw that look again," her husband said.

Rosa shook her head sadly, "Poor man, he must learn to go on."

Later that evening Rosa made Jack a meal of fried tuna, refried beans, guacamole and rice. After finishing, he had the Penn torn apart on the table, picking through the gears.

Deni came in and sat beside his friend. He lightly dropped a beaten-up old satchel on the floor between them. Angelo, the bartender, came up with an unbidden Pacifico.

"The gears are gone. I was lucky to get that one in."

Deni looked over the damaged guts of the reel and nodded sagely. The two men sat in silence for a long minute, enjoying the feel of the end of a great day.

"One of my friends, an old lobster diver, brought this to me a couple weeks ago. I thought you might be interested," Deni finally said. Out of the satchel, he pulled the corroded frame of what looked to be an antique, flintlock pistol. The weapon had a heavy layer of nondescript marine life covering it.

The butt was beaten and crumpled. Jack gently took the relic and weighed it in his hand; it had the feel of something fragile, yet sturdy. Rolling it around in his hands, Jack focused on the top of what was left of the grip.

"Just a minute," Jack said as he got up and left. When he returned, he set a powerful underwater flashlight, diving knife, and a small magnifying glass on the table. "Here, hold this," he said, giving Deni the light.

Jack very carefully used the tip of the knife and a tiny wire brush to worked away some of the filth from a small area of the weapon's handle. Slowly, faint script-like letters appeared stamped into the metal.

"I think you have something here, amigo," Jack said softly to his friend as he concentrated on the script through the magnifying glass. "There is some kind of writing." Looking up he said, "I better not do anymore or old Professor Torres will box my ears."

"Who?" Deni asked.

"Professor Antonio Garcia Torres, head of archeology at the

University of Guadalajara. He was a friend of my father's. When I was a kid, Dad's foundation sponsored a number of explorations around Central America. For three summers, I tagged along with the two of them; I picked up a little understanding of Mesoamerican pre-Columbian history. Interesting stuff. You remember, we were either coming or going from those trips when we stopped here to go fishing with your dad."

He paused briefly, refocusing on the pistol. "Yes, I really think you have something here." He gave Deni a conspiratorial grin.

"What is the best thing to do?" Deni asked, swept into intrigue of the potential.

"I would strongly suggest that you get this over to him. He'll be able to tell you if it is the real thing."

"Could it be valuable?" Deni asked.

"Yes and no. It isn't worth much as a collector's item. It's too beat up. But it could be invaluable as part of your history."

"This professor…he knows his stuff, hey?" Deni asked, suddenly apprehensive of letting the treasure go, yet trusting in Jack's opinion.

"Oh yes. His students say he knows so much about archeology because he was there when they buried the stuff," Jack gave Deni a wry smile. "What do you know of ship wrecks around these coasts?"

"There have been many, but the oldest is… more legend, really… is said to have been before Buenaventura. He discovered the bay, you know. Anyway, they say, before him there was another ship. It wrecked and only one man survived. It is said that he was part of some exploration that found the last of the Aztec gold treasure. It makes for a better tale," Deni chuckled. "It is an old legend. The fishermen say the ship was wrecked off the Morros rocks south of the Marieta Islands"

Jack nodded, knowing the area well.

"The man was found by Buenaventura when he sailed out. Little was made of it because Buenaventura was the nephew of Cortez, and he wanted credit for being the first to make discoveries all up the coast. Having someone else there first, sort of stole his thunder—at least that's the legend, you understand." Deni gave a most typical Hispanic shrug.

Jack understood.

"Since then, a couple of small things have been found. But for more than 450 years these waters have been used by pirates and others who did not announce their presence. So these things could have come from any of the ships wrecked or plundered."

"This is pretty cool. Do you know where this was found, exactly?" Jack asked feeling the infectious excitement in Deni' voice.

"I thought you would ask that," Deni smiled. He gently pulled an old folded map of the bay out of the same bag. "This was my father's, from back in the '50s. He put small dots with numbers where he and others found bits and pieces of wrecks."

Jack looked over the small, scratchy Spanish handwriting along the edge of the map that corresponded to the numbered little dots.

"Since this map was made, we know many of the soundings are not perfect, but they were pretty close," Deni said.

"These fresh dots are yours?" Jack asked.

Deni nodded. "I've kept it up. I've always had dreams of finding some old wreck and making a fortune. An old romantic," he admitted. "This is where the pistol was found," Deni stated, pointing to a small rock outcropping that made up the Morros Islands, a series of rocks jutting out of the ocean to the south of the bigger Marieta Islands. The rocks and islands made a coarse guard over the northern entrance to the Bay of Banderas.

"What are these circles?" Jack asked, looking at faint pencil marks on the map. The word *langosta* could be faintly seen. Jack gave his partner a knowing smile.

Deni nodded. "Some of my father's favorite fishing spots. This one is a lobster bed, not as good now as in the old days…but what is?"

Jack studied the map for a long minute. "Are you busy tomorrow?"

"I have a charter of gringos taking out the cabin cruiser." After a rather long pause Deni smiled and added, "Nothing Israel and Ivan can't handle."

"You know, I haven't had any lobster on this trip."

"Well, we mustn't disappoint our North American guest!" Deni laughed.

"I have a commitment in Puerto Vallarta tomorrow afternoon. I was going to give it a pass, but now, if you'd like, we can take a look around where this was found. Afterwards, I'll ship this piece to the professor." Jack stood up and stretched. "Well, enough for one day. I'll see you in the morning."

"You staying here tonight?" Rosa asked, coming out of the kitchen.

"No. I promised Jerry I'd give him a hand on the boat tomorrow. I better tell him there has been a change of plans. Thanks for supper, delicious as usual." He gave Rosa a squeeze and a quick buzz on the cheek.

Jack walked across the cobblestone street and down onto the beach to his little dinghy. Throwing his sandals in the boat, he pushed the small craft out into the bay. He methodically rowed back to his sailboat. He had only been back in the apartment three times since he got back. It just reminded him too much of Pat. Rosa had been kind enough to keep it clean and ready. Jack smiled at the love these folks showed him—like family. Nevertheless, he really didn't want to talk—hadn't since that night.

As he climbed aboard, the first sound to greet him was a "Yeow!" and "Rawoo!" as Charlie, the ship's cat, expressed her dissatisfaction at being left unattended.

Jack attempted to give the cat a pet.

"Hey puss, how you doing?"

This only earned Jack a swat from a paw.

"Oh, come on!" Jack reached down behind the cat's ear and

rubbed gently. After a few more choice growls of dissatisfaction, the cat allowed herself to be scratched. She maneuvered her head and shoulders to get the maximum effect from the man's attention. Soon an audible purr could be heard. After a moment, she was simultaneously licking Jack's hand and rubbing up against his leg.

If Jack tried to keep petting her, he would have been left in contortions. Reaching down to pick her up got him a kiss on the nose as the cat smelt beer, her favorite beverage. Charlie wrapped herself around his neck as Jack continued to scratch behind her ear. He pulled a beer out of the fridge and poured a very small amount into a saucer.

The cat immediately forgot about him and wanted down. Jack dropped her on the counter and she turned her full attention to the liquid. Jack reached in his pocket and took out a small piece of tuna fish, rolled up in a paper napkin. He set it on the edge of the plate. Charlie gave the fish a discerning sniff and then looked up at him in expectation.

"Sorry buddy, no shrimp today. That's the best I could do."

The cat gave him a look that spoke, "I really expected better of you," then proceeded to chow down. Jack petted her one last time. She arched her back but otherwise ignored him.

"Jerry! Where are you?" Jack called.

In a moment, a sleepy young man in his twenties came out of the side cabin, scratching his tousled head.

"Umm, hi skipper," he responded sleepily. "Just takin' a nap."

"It's nine o'clock at night."

"Umm, maybe I'll take a longer nap," Jerry stated groggily. He turned to go back to bed, but not before grabbing the beer.

"How did you do on the engine?"

"Okay. But we're going to need a couple of parts. I'll know better tomorrow," he said as he closed the cabin door.

*   *   *

After Deni helped Israel and his younger brother Ivan get organized with a group of tourists in the cabin cruiser, *Carmen II*, he and Jack got underway in the panga. The previous night, Deni had sent Arturo, his third son over to visit the old lobsterman who had found the ancient pistol. Deni made arrangements with the old man to go out in his panga and lead them to the area where the artifact was found. Deni promised to compensate the old man, but he would have none of it; Deni had been good to his family. A final bargain was struck to cover the cost of fuel and reloading the man's air tanks.

The two pangas quickly passed Israel in the slower diesel cruiser. Deni allowed Arturo, a lanky boy of 14, to steer. They ran at half-throttle so as not to lose the slower lobsterman.

Jack watched Arturo. The lad was pleased to be out with his papa and in command of the ship. Rosa had objected only a little over the lost school day, but knew the boy would be better for the chance to be with his papa, on the water for a day. Jack remembered when Arturo was a toddler. Jack had just been badly injured in a dust-up with pirates in the South China Sea. Jack had come down to Puerto Vallarta, his second home, to recuperate. It seemed like such a long time ago and yet, like yesterday.

His thoughts flashed back to Pat. She had been gone only eight months. The pain was still very fresh, yet the fishing the other day and the excitement of the dive was making him feel alive again

He came out of his reverie to see Deni watching him. Their eyes met. Deni broke the awkwardness by lifting a thermos in an offer of coffee. Jack shook his head and returned his gaze out over the horizon. He watched beams of dawn spread over the Sierra Madre Mountains behind Puerto Vallarta. The star-like lights along the shoreline of the city were slowly eclipsed as the new day grew.

With the arrival of the sun, the air warmed. "Another perfect day in paradise," Jack said to himself with a sigh.

His mind was distracted as a family of humpbacked whales

emerged a hundred yards off the port side of the two pangas. The humpbacks arched above the surface a couple of times and then in slow rhythm, their huge tails cleared the water as they plunged down into the depths of the bay.

It took a little over an hour to arrive at their chosen dive site. They approached the northernmost rock that constituted the Morros. It was nothing more than a 30-foot- high piece of gray-black granite. It was covered from the top, down to the high watermark, with thousands of years of bird droppings. The Marieta Islands were clearly in view to the north. The weather was fine, the light haze slowly melting under the rising sun. The seas were mild with a light chop, and the swells surged rhythmically against the rock as the ocean current worked its way to shore. Around the rock the water changed colors with the varying depths; the water under the boats was dark.

Jack checked his GPS and carefully marked the reading on maps he had brought. Deni's father's map was quite accurate; the size of the rocks had been exaggerated, but the positioning was right.

Arturo watched with rapt attention as Jack took the satellite readings. After confirming the rock's location, Deni had Arturo steer over to where the lobsterman's panga was bobbing peacefully.

The fisherman was in his late seventies, and couldn't have weighed more than 120 pounds. He was as skinny as a rake, and the flesh on his arms hung loose. But first appearances were deceiving; he was as tough as wire from years of fishing. His coffee-brown complexion told of years under the hot Mexican sun; his near toothless smile was light and cheerful.

The water visibility was 30 feet on the surface, normal for the time of year. Once suited up in diving gear, they performed a quick check and were over the side, working their way down their respective anchor ropes. Jack's gear was more sophisticated than the others. Besides the dive bag that they all carried, he had a dive light, inflatable marker buoys, a JW Fisher

8X underwater metal detector, and a buoyancy control device or BCD that allowed him to hover motionlessly, in place.

At a depth of approximately 35 feet, they broke through a thermocline, a layer of water where there is an abrupt change in temperature that separates the warmer surface water from the colder deep water. With the drop in temperature the visibility improved to near-limitless. The current was gentle as they approached the bottom at 55 feet. The old man swam to his right. The others followed, fanning out on either side behind him. They walked with their hands along the rocky bottom, working slowly into deeper water. The terrain consisted of large outcroppings of rough rocks, crevasses and valleys that created thousands of places for fish and lobsters to hide. The old man and Deni fell naturally into their old routine, exploring every crevice in every ledge for any tender morsels they might hold.

Jack's first encounter with sea life was with a large moray eel. The eel not accustomed to seeing these strange bubbling sea creatures, nevertheless made very little effort to avoid them. It coiled itself into a sharp, dark crevasse with only its snout protruding, and stared back at the alien in its world.

Jack watched the creature gulp water, as if taking big bites—its gills fluttering as it expelled the used water.

The trio worked along the bottom edge of an outcropping. Deni pointed and signaled Jack to stop. Jack's gaze followed Deni's finger. There, a few feet ahead, was one long, thick, hair-like strand, rising above a crack in the rocks. Deni slowly worked his way behind the antenna and in a flash, grabbed the lobster from behind. Even with the mask and regulator in his mouth, Jack could see the big smile on the Mexican's face.

Once they had a lobster in the bag, Jack focused on the metal detector. He slowly swung the round disk of the coil at the end of the shaft of the Fisher, back and forth.

The detector's needle quivered when the device was waved over a small pocket of sand, trapped between a series of large rocks. The little beach of sand was an irregular space—not more than three feet by five feet. Jack gently probed the sand with his knife. Six inches under the surface, he struck something. Carefully brushing away grains of coarse sand to avoid creating a cloud, he exposed a small, corroded ball of metal. He slipped it into the dive bag.

Jack dug with his hands and discovered an ancient glass vial. His short but studied examination, determined it might be an interesting object, deserving a longer inspection. He carefully nestled the vial in his dive bag. One last pass over the area with the detector revealed no other treasures. Satisfied, he lifted up, relocated Deni's rising bubbles, and headed in his general direction.

Fifty feet from Deni, Jack hovered over a dark canyon of rock. Using his light, Jack lit up a serpentine river of sand at the bottom of the ravine. He checked his depth gauge: 95 feet. His computer told him he didn't have much time left. He tapped his tank with his knife to draw Deni's attention. Deni stopped, turned and headed Jack's way.

Jack showed his computer to Deni and then pointed down into the ravine below. Deni nodded, checked his air, and gave Jack an "okay" signal. Deni would wait higher up to conserve air in his tank as Jack went deep. Jack now headed into the crevasse, working along the sandy bottom of the ravine. In most places it was wide enough to drive a car through. Occasionally it would narrow, and Jack would have to waste valuable time rising above the ravine to get through. As Jack came to a fork in the ravine, the computer on his console started screaming. But a sixth sense told him that something important lay ahead. Jack checked his gauge, his safety margin was gone. If he wanted to explore the ravine, it would be another dive. He quickly tied a marker on a jagged piece of rock and released the pressure. A tethered balloon headed skyward. It would make it to the surface, from there Jack could get a GPS reading.

He rejoined Deni 50 feet above. They spotted the lobsterman floating well above them to their left. He was pulling a large bag full of lobsters behind him. It had been a good day for him.

Jack showed Deni his gauge, and the Mexican nodded. Jack would be out of air before a safe ascent to the surface. Deni gave an encouraging "okay" signal. The two of them headed slowly upwards. At 30 feet, they stopped. The warmer water of the upper thermocline was a welcome relief from the colder, clear bottom water. They took their time, buddy-breathing from Deni's tank. While they waited, Deni lifted a bag containing several lobsters. Deni looked like a happy young lad with his day's catch. Jack gave him a thumbs-up.

On the surface, Jack handed Arturo, the metal detector and then the dive bag.

"Easy with that," Jack cautioned.

Once aboard, Jack gingerly extracted the encrusted vial and lump of metal. He handed the vial to Deni.

"Any idea what it is?" Deni asked, rolling it around in his fingers. Arturo looked on intently.

"Not really. Maybe some kind of medicine bottle."

Bouncing the ball in the palm of his hand, Jack said, "This is a musket ball."

Arturo's eyes widened.

"You are right amigo," Deni agreed as he examined the ball.

Jack handed it to Arturo, who looked at it with wonder.

*   *   *

After a break they moved the panga over the floating buoy marker. Jack recorded his GPS reading on the map. They donned their gear and headed back down, swimming well about the ravine to conserve bottom time. From above they could see that what started out as a thin crevasse quickly opened up and plunged deep. Returning to his tied marker Jack worked his way to the sandy bottom. He followed the programming in his computer back to where he had previously left off. It dawned on

Jack, that sophisticated detection technology had likely never been used in the area. The potential for finds could be quite impressive. He began his search anew, but all too soon his air was low. Just then the needle of the detector came alive. Jack quickly pinpointed the most active spot in the sand.

He set the detector down, using his hands he burrowed into the sand. After creating a two-foot hollow his fingers came across an object. Gently scooping it out of the sand, Jack studied his reward: an oval the size of a robin's egg. In the beam of his dive light it gleamed as bright as the sun. He was bouncing it in the palm of his hand and it was obviously made of pure gold. Examining it closely, he could see faint inscriptions. Jack's experience told him immediately it was Aztec. With a smile, Jack put the treasure in the velcroed pocket of his BCD and double-checked to ensure it was secure.

Jack methodically moved the detector back-and-forth, around the area, but got no further signs. Checking his computer, he knew it would start screaming any second now. He had to make a choice. He decided to take a quick peek ahead and moved further down the canyon. After some distance it fell deep into the ocean, there was no way he could continue. Securing another marker he headed up to Deni.

Back in the panga, they stripped off their gear. "Well, any luck?' Deni asked.

"A little"

Jack watched his partner's eyes widen as he pulled the golden egg out of his pocket.

"Madre dios!" Deni exclaimed as he took the orb in his hand and felt the weight "got to be close to 2 ounces. It's worth thousands!

Arturo looked on in amazement. "Wow!" he whispered. "It's beautiful. It's got funny writing on it."

"It's worth a lot more than that, I'm positive it's Aztec." Jack said.

Deni grinned at the American, letting the full impact of what they had found wash over him. "You really do have to get to your professor," Deni said.

Jack nodded, his mouth twisting up at the corners.

*   *   *

By the time they arrived back at the dock in La Cruz, it was just before one o'clock.

"Great morning, guys. I'll have just enough time to get this off, with a few minutes to spare," Jack said. He was holding up the golden treasure so the group could sneak another admiring look. "I'll take the bike, if it's okay with you?"

"Yeah, sure. You're going to miss a lobster dinner," Deni teased.

"You never know, I might be home early."

"Your foundation thing?"

"Yeah, my brother emailed the foundation has stock in some company that deals with hotel management. This is one of the hotels they are covering. And being that I am here… Duty calls. We call it 'showing the flag.'"

"We have a similar expression in Spanish. Too bad for you." Deni laughed.

5

Ben, Jack's brother had practically begged him to attend the grand opening of the new Vallarta Pacifico Hotel Maria Elena. According to Ben, some very influential people were going to be there. As the newest hotel in town, it was managed by the Inglis Hotel Group, of which the St. Julian Foundation owned a respectable share. Jack had reluctantly agreed to be the foundation's 'pretty face.'. First though, he had to pick up his wheels.

As Jack walked through the restaurant kitchen Rosa was busy with her usual duties, an apron wrapped around her waist, knife in hand.

"Look what we turned up out at the Morros." Jack concealed the egg in his hand as he drew it out of his backpack, and placed it on the cutting board. He withdrew his hand with flair. He enjoyed the look on Rosa's face as it went from confusion to amazement.

"Is it real?" she whispered, as her hand instinctively reached out to touch it.

"Pick it up."

Gingerly she rolled the egg in her hand and gently hefted it for weight. She looked up at Jack. "It's solid. Feel the weight. Where did you find it?"

"Just off the Morros," Jack repeated. "We're sending it to the professor to get it analyzed. Look at it closely."

She said, "It's got writing." She looked up at Jack again.

"Aztec."

Again her eyes widened. "Aztec."

"Yup. If true, then there's some serious history going on. As valuable as the thing is, it may be worth more to your history."

She nodded and slowly handed him back the egg. He rolled it up in a clean kitchen towel and added it to his backpack.

"Got to run. Hopefully be back in time for dinner, we got a few lobsters," Jack said, grinning, as he headed out the backdoor.

Just to the right of the kitchen door, under the stairs that led up to the apartments, was a storage area. Within, Deni kept an old Honda 500 XL motorcycle. It was a serviceable workhorse, but no steed.

Pulling away from the old cobblestone streets of La Cruz, Jack headed for Puerto Vallarta. Puerto Vallarta, a growing tourist site, had prospered after a number of famous actors had shot films and had taken up residence in the city back in the 1950's. Its natural beauty and friendly people had taken care of the rest.

Cruising down the rough, two-lane asphalt road out of La Cruz, Jack felt fresh and alive. He loved the feel of the wind in his hair, whether on a motorcycle or out on the water. The 500 Honda was no replacement for his Ducati, but any motorcycle brought him pleasure.

Deftly working his way through traffic, he watched the countryside go by. The whole area was growing. Although much of the area was still jungle and farms of guava and coconut palms there were signs of development everywhere. Turning onto Highway 200 confirmed it, the new interchange through Bucerias ushered vehicles onto the four-lane highway that led to Puerto Vallarta 30 kilometers to the south.

Traffic slowed as the city's inbound lanes were diverted over to the old, two-lane bridge. The new bridge over the Ameca River had opened, and almost immediately needed to be repaired. Jack didn't mind. The slow travel gave him a chance to spot alligators in the river, something that had fascinated him ever since he started coming down here.

His first stop was at a courier service. He addressed his package directly to the professor, and slipped a note inside the envelope.

Doc, Jack St. Julian here in PV. You're going to love these. Found them in about 60 feet of water off the Morros. Will be around for a while. Can be reached at…
He wrote the phone number to Rosa's restaurant.

On the outside he wrote "*Personal*" to ensure only the professor would open it.

Next, he dropped off his damaged reel at the old tackle shop his father had used for years. The aged man behind the counter looked at the reel and clucked disapprovingly. He didn't say a word, but the look he gave Jack spoke volumes. The old man's weathered hands skillfully handled the reel as he crouched over it to get the best look. Watching him fuss over the old reel gave Jack a flush of nostalgia, remembering a time when 'good enough' wouldn't do. Thousands of reels had been brought to the old man before Jack's, and Jack knew there were generations of happy customers out there.

Jack meandered through the city streets toward the majestic new hotel. The shocks on the bike weren't what they once were; offering a bumpy ride over the cobblestone streets of Puerto Vallarta. He joined a column of taxis and other vehicles as they slowed near the protective gates, set in the walled enclosure that surrounded the exclusive hotel property. Each taxi waited on the street as their guests were pre-approved, before being allowed to enter the grounds.

When Jack pulled up on his modest motorcycle, a large guard stepped in front of him. Without a word, Jack pulled the slightly tattered invitation out of his back pocket, and handed it to the guard. The guard looked down at Jack's meager means of transportation, but the gold inlayed invitation left no question as to the rider's credentials. He waved Jack on, with a bow.

Cars, taxis and a few limousines lined up to get into the grand breezeway—to disgorge their passengers. High arches and palm trees created a shaded avenue over the sculpted brick driveway. The walks on either side were flanked with flowering bougainvilleas, birds of paradise and more. The vine of greenery flowed up into a variety of trees—jacaranda, almond and others.

Driving up toward the lobby entrance Jack spotted a parking section for motorcycles. As he was dismounting and trying to tame his wind-blown hair, another guard came up him and politely asked for his invitation. Jack coolly offered the card again. The guard waved over to a petite, sharply-dressed young woman.

"Good afternoon, Señor," she said brightly.

"Buenos tardes," Jack said, with a smile.

The guard handed her the invitation. She became instantly alert.

"Please follow me and we will arrange a special badge for you, Señor St. Julian."

He followed the young woman into the lobby. At a special registration desk, another bright-looking young woman took the invitation.

"Mr. Jack St. Julian, it is our pleasure that you are here. May we see some identification?" she smiled disarmingly.

Jack handed over his driver's license.

In quick order they had confirmed his identity and handed him a gold-colored badge with his name boldly embossed on it. Smiling up at Jack, the young woman at the desk proudly and officially announced, "Señor Jack St. Julian, let us be the first to welcome you as a very special guest to the Vallarta Pacifico Maria Elena hotel, the newest member of the Inglis Group of resort hotels."

Jack bowed at the honor and gave them a gracious smile.

"Would you like a personal tour of the property, Mr. St. Julian?" she asked.

"No thanks," Jack said. "I'll just wander around a little, but you could look after this for me…"

He handed them his backpack.

"As you wish, Mr. St. Julian."

The girl signaled an eager-eyed porter with a tiny flick of her wrist. He placed Jack's backpack into the short-term luggage storage.

"The executive party is on the penthouse level. It is in progress now," the clerk smiled.

Jack gave them a nod and departed.

The cavernous lobby was five stories high with a woven palm ceiling—the effect airy and spacious, cool and breezy. At the front desk, a mob of people was checking in for the gala-opening weekend. Jack ignored the crowd and headed through the lobby. He passed a bar, not yet full with eager guests. Next, he climbed over a bridge that led him under a natural stone waterfall and then outside. Jack stopped and looked down a long, covered corridor that continued to a pool. Beyond that he could see the beach. There were people everywhere. He doubled back to the bar, deciding he had time for a bracer before facing the ordeal.

The VIP invitation had included an all-expense paid weekend, but sitting alone in a hotel, luxury or not, was the last thing he wanted to do. He had promised to put in an official appearance and that was all he was planning to do.

He ordered a vodka tonic with a couple of twists of lime, and made idle conversation with the bartender. Jack spoke in Spanish while the bartender practiced his English.

"Well, I have to see a man about a horse." Jack nodded goodbye and left, leaving a generous tip.

"Derecha," the bartender pointed to the right, down the corridor to the washrooms.

Just as he spotted his destination, he was hit on the side of his arm. Turning, he saw a small elderly lady wielding an umbrella, like a pointer.

"Young man, I need my bags taken to my room." She stated matter-of-factly.

With only an instant's hesitation Jack smiled, reached down, and grabbed the two ponderous bags, "Si, Señora."

He obediently followed the ramrod-straight woman toward a bank of elevators. As if realizing the oncoming threat, the elevator door opened just as she reached the threshold. She marched straight forward, Jack in tow. A few other new arrivals entered before the doors closed.

"The seventh floor, please," she commanded.

Someone pushed the number.

Jack glanced around, sizing up the group. With the exception of his new mistress, the others were yuppies who appeared, from their bleached 'blanco' northern skin, to have arrived within hours.

As the elevator rose Jack quietly hummed *La Paloma*. By the sixth floor the blancos had all cleared the elevator.

"Your first time in Mexico, Señora?" Jack decided to take a stab at a conversation.

The old lady gave him a quick questioning look but after a moment responded, "My first time out of the United States."

When the door opened, Jack asked, "Your room number, Señora?"

"7121."

He did a quick read of the directory board and headed left. "Where are you from?"

"Nantucket, Massachusetts," she announced with considerable pride. As an afterthought, "And you?"

"Seattle, Washington."

"Oh! You are American. I didn't know the hotel employed Americans as bellboys. That is a very good idea. Are you all Americans?"

"No, some are Canadians," Jack panned.

She gave that some thought as they shuffled down the hall towards her room, then reasoned out loud, "Yes, I suppose that is logical."

When they reached the door the woman hesitated. She

looked at the credit card-like key in her hand, then back at the door.

"May I, Señora?' Jack asked.

With a slight reluctance she handed him the card. Jack slid it in and the door opened.

Her mouth pressed in frustrated disgust, she complained, "What is wrong with an old fashioned key?"

"This is for your safety, Señora," Jack said. "Please remember your room number."

"Of course I know my room number, young man," she stated defensively. Hastily, her eyes flicked up to the number on the door.

Upon entering her room, Jack continued the charade. He opened the drapes and stuck his head into the bathroom to see that, in fact, it was there. He thought to himself it was a very nice suite—large for a single person.

"Are you traveling alone?" he asked.

She gave him a cool stare, which softened as she looked at his face. "Since I lost my Morgan several years ago, I decided it was time to get out and see the world. So I decided to come on this trip."

Jack nodded knowingly. "Will there be anything else right now?"

"No. Thank you, young man." She slipped a five peso coin in his hand. "That will be all."

"Oh, thank you Señora." He smiled at her thoughtfulness, then humbly backed out of the room and closed the door.

Walking back to the elevator he flipped his newly-earned wealth in the air, grinning at how he would spend his 50 cent worth of hard-earned tip.

As Jack waited for the elevator to arrive, he studied the hotel map. Deciding the 14th floor washrooms were probably closer than those in the lobby, he headed up the additional floors. He stepped out into a gaily-decorated foyer and turned to the right, where he found what he was looking for.

Jack was leaving the bathroom when a gorgeous young woman walked in. She gave him a startled look.

"You're in the wrong room," she stated in a condescending manner.

Jack looked at her calmly and replied, "I don't think so." He stepped aside and gave her a clear view of the row of urinals.

"Oh dear, excuse me!" She was flustered. Quickly, she spun in retreat, succeeding only in plowing into an unsuspecting male, as he entered the room. The impact knocked her off her feet. Instinctively, Jack grasped her slender waist and arrested her fall.

"She gets confused when she forgets her medication," Jack glibly announced to the stunned male as they pushed past him into the hall.

Regaining her composure, the woman gave a quick twist of her hips, signaling Jack to back off. He complied, but managed to point out a small drawing of a Spanish girl in a dress, located over the door of the adjacent ladies' room.

"I don't know why they don't put up a decent sign," she fumed, spun on her heels, and departed without paying a visit to the room Jack helped her find.

As she walked away, Jack noted that the rear view was just as good looking as the front. She was wearing a light sundress that suited her lithe figure and it show-cased lightly-tanned, shapely, long legs.

Wistfully, he turned and thought to himself, "Well, let's go get this over with."

*   *   *

In the foyer a trio of violins played softly beneath a canopy of company logo-ed balloons and a marquee banner announcing *Welcome To All!* in English, Spanish, French and Japanese. A crowd of well-dressed people milled about, lost in conversations. No one noticed Jack.

Jack drifted over to the bar and picked up a lime-wedge-crowned bottle of Pacifico. As he looked over the crowd, he noticed a number of men trying to blend into the scenery. Any one of these guys could have played professional football, and all of them were sporting communication earpieces. "There's some serious money in this room. I wonder how much is legal," Jack though with a sarcastic scowl.

Just as quickly he chided himself for his prejudice. He made a flippant mental note to be careful not to offend anyone.

Jack gravitated to the balcony. It provided a majestic view of the Bay of Banderas and the Sierra Madres mountains east of the city. Jack looked over the water and envied the boaters enjoying perfect conditions.

"I guess I owe you an apology."

Jack turned. The beautiful woman he'd encountered moments ago had found him.

"An honest mistake, Miss… Hamilton," he noted, reading her badge.

"It's Jan. Anyway, they should make the signs clearer. I'll tell Todd," she said defensively.

"And Todd would be?" Jack asked.

"My brother, this is his hotel."

A light breeze off the ocean lifted her shoulder-length, light brown hair, up and over her face. She instinctively moved it away.

"Really. Well if you are assisting him, there is a very sweet elderly lady in room 7121 that doesn't have a clue what she is doing here and could easily get herself in trouble."

"That's kind of you, Mr. St. Julian." she looked at his badge and gave a light and cheery smile. "Excuse me."

Jack watched the back of her shapely body merge into the crowd. His conscience instantly bit him as Pat came to mind. He let out a deep sigh and returned his gaze to the sea. Just then someone slapped his shoulder. Jack turned to see Dave Houston, the district manager of the Inglis Group, the reason for his being here. He was with another man.

"Jack, old buddy! Glad you could make it!" Houston announced a little too loudly. "Let me introduce you to Miguel Vegas, one of the owners of the hotel. He's with the Vemexa Group."

Jack offered Vegas his hand. In return he got an overly-challenging handshake as the Mexican tried twisting Jack's fingers. For just a second, Jack applied his full crushing strength like a vise and then remembered the promise he made to himself and released the grip.

"Mr. Vegas," Jack nodded politely, noting that his point had been made.

Vegas' eyes flashed, he had not expected the challenge, however brief. A cold, calculating smile spread across the Mexican's face.

Houston sensed the tension and jumped in. "Jack, have you had a look around the property? It really is spectacular."

"I haven't. Perhaps later." Jack glanced back toward the water again, showing his disinterest.

"Miguel, will you excuse us?" Houston placated the other man with a smile.

Vegas turned and walked away without a word.

Houston leaned closer to Jack and whispered, "I'd be careful with people like Vegas, Jack. He's got a lot of power."

Jack looked squarely at the man. "What do you mean by that?" Jack feigned innocence.

"Just rumors, you know. It doesn't pay to ask questions down here." Houston flushed.

With penetrating ice-blue eyes, Jack looked at Houston. At that moment, he decided to sell all the stock his family held in the Inglis Group at the first opportunity.

"I'll remember that," Jack said coldly.

As Jack made to leave, he saw Jan Hamilton with another man. The family resemblance was clearly evident, although the man was considerably older. The Mexican 'handshake' came up to them. He bowed and kissed the lady's hand. From across the floor Jack could see Jan's blush. After a few words Vegas bowed again and took his leave. Jack could see the woman was smitten by the courtesy.

Jan and the other man walked toward him.

"Todd, I want you to meet Mr. Jack St. Julian. He's been most helpful today." She shot Jack a polite smile.

"Mr. St. Julian, you're with the Inglis Group? Glad you could come. What do you think?" Todd Hamilton appeared tired and haggard.

"Very impressive," Jack replied. "I especially like the grounds. Very well laid out; gives a nice feel as you come in, sets the mood so to speak."

After a pregnant pause both Houston and Hamilton set off to welcome others.

"You haven't seen any of the grounds, have you?" Jan asked.

"Just what I saw coming in," he shrugged.

"Well, the best view is here, from the balcony. Can I offer to show you from there?"

"I make it a rule always to be nice to beautiful women."

Jan noticed the man wince at his own remark, then his composure went blank as a mask. She saw he did not realize she'd seen his reaction.

From the vantage of the ledge, she pointed out various features of the hotel. For a long moment, they stood silently; both lost in the panorama of the view.

He spied her looking at him out of the corner of her eye.

"Peso for your thoughts," he said.

"I was just thinking how you don't seem to belong here, yet you look so at home."

"What? Underdressed?" He flashed her a cock-eyed smile as he spread his arms showing the cut of his well-tailored tropical shirt.

"No, not that. More like…" she hesitated, "…fresh versus stale. I know these people are all about money and power. You seem comfortable in the surroundings, but don't seem to care, or be impressed."

"Pretty and insightful," Jack thought. "Best be careful."

He said pointedly, "What I don't care for is the way some of these people probably got their money in the first place."

She stood silently turning pale.

Seeing her reaction, he realized, "I've broken my promise again. She must be one, too."

After a long stillness, Jan inhaled sharply and said just above a whisper. "I've thought the same thing, but have never dared say anything to Todd."

"Call it a strong suspicion. What's your brother got to do with it?"

"He's Vemexa's chief financial officer, has been for years."

"Ahh," Jack said, maintaining a neutral look.

Jan's gaze was caught by something far out in the bay. "What's that?" she pointed.

Jack followed her aim into the bay. A white spray of water rose out of the sea. "A whale."

"Really? A whale?" She touched his arm in innocent excitement, his darker mood evaporating like morning mist.

"Yes. This time of year you'll see lots of them in the bay."

They watched, as a thousand yards out to sea, a fin slapped down creating a spray of white water. Others on the balcony began turning their eyes towards the ocean. Not far from the first whale, a second started slapping the water.

"What are they doing?"

"Well, either feeding or calling attention to themselves for mating, it depends. I can't tell from this distance."

He watched her as she viewed the scene with rapt attention. After a minute, the black backs of the whales became visible. Their tail fins emerged out of the water momentarily pointing straight up, and then sank down into the deep.

"They're diving now," Jack said.

"How long can they stay under?"

"Oh, up to 10 minutes."

"Really?" she said, revealing genuine wonder. "Where did you learn about whales?"

"Bit here and a bit there," he answered obliquely.

Jan's look penetrated him. "There's more," she called him out, expecting a full answer.

To his own surprise, he responded. "I've been on or by the sea, most of my life. In fact, I'm sort of playing hooky from a whale research project that the University of Washington is conducting off the Sea of Cortez."

"Isn't the University of Washington way up north? What are they doing here in Puerto Vallarta?"

"They have a very large marine biology department. And they're not here, they're over near Cabo San Lucas, at the bottom of Baja California," he explained. "You know that long arm that comes down off California?"

"Of course. It's one of the longest peninsulas in the world. Cabo San Lucas is a vacation destination. I think it was one of the Van Halen band members that opened a club down there and made it hip. Beautiful beaches."

"Where'd you learn about Mexico?" Jack looked at her, impressed with her knowledge.

"Just because I haven't got to go anywhere, doesn't mean I haven't dreamed…Bali, the Bay Islands, Honduras, Amalfi, Italy. One day I'll get there. I love researching places I dream about visiting one day, but family first," she said, giving a determined nod. "How far is Cabo from here?"

"About five hundred kilometers, that about 400 hundred miles."

Jack wondered what exactly she meant by "family first."

"How did you get from there to here?" she continued.

"I have a sailboat. We sailed across."

She gave her head a slight tilt as she processed this new information. "Okay," she concluded, as if pieces of a puzzle had fallen into place.

Jack liked the self-confident poise of this woman. "Where are you from?" he asked.

"Indianapolis."

"And this is your first time in Mexico?"

She nodded.

"Okay," he responded in like manner.

The pair stared at each other for a long minute. Finally a smile grew on her face. "Okay, what is it, Mr. St. Julian?" she asked as her smile turned mischievous.

"Okay, I don't quite know, Miss Hamilton, but it would appear to me that conclusions are being jumped to."

"You think? Mr. St. Julian?" she stated firmly. "How about 'strong silent type, prefers to be outdoors, doesn't like crowds, and definitely doesn't like presumptuousness'." She paused. "So far so good?"

Jack checked himself at the flattery directed at him and gave a shrug.

"Not comfortable with flattery, either," her smile widened.

"Okay, that's enough." He held up his hand and conceded. "What about you?"

"Oh. Well, let's see. I'm a nurse. I look after my—our," she corrected herself, "…mother fulltime. She has Alzheimer's. And yes, this is my first trip to Mexico. First trip, anywhere. Todd promised me I could come out to one of his openings and I finally got the chance. I practically had to threaten him," she confessed. Then realized she'd conveyed too much.

Jack noted her discomfort and changed the subject. "How long have you been down?"

"Just three days. It really is a beautiful place."

"You mean the resort?"

"Everything. I saw on TV this morning they were having a snowstorm back home. Here you're in shorts. It's just lovely." She gave him a deeper look. "Really, let me show you the grounds."

To his surprise he agreed.

The rest of the afternoon passed quickly. Jan acted as his personal guide, as they toured the hotel and grounds. Along the way, Jan related more of her life story to Jack. He learned that her brother, Todd who was much older than her, had supported her family after her father had died, and had paid for her education. When their mother developed Alzheimer's, he paid for a private nurse in the home. Soon afterwards, he built an entire nursing home for Alzheimer patients. Jan technically owned it, and while professional staff ran it, she focused her time on their mother.

"She obviously thinks very highly of this brother," Jack thought.

Characteristically, Jack said little about himself, telling her only that he was in La Cruz, and spending his time fishing with an old family friend.

"So, tell me about this sailboat."

"It's a classic, built in the late '30s in Denmark, for one of the royal family. Made of stainless steel, 55 feet long with a beam of 15.5 feet."

"What's a beam?"

"That's the width of the ship. She has three staterooms and can sleep 12 in a pinch. We can sail for weeks, if we want to."

"We?"

"Charlie and I. She's the mistress of the ship."

"Charlie?" she asked.

"She's my cat. She's an 'it' really, with long hair, black and white. Got a black mustache that looks like Charlie Chaplin. The name just stuck."

At that moment, Jan and Jack nearly collided with Jan's brother who had been deep in consultation with another man.

"Hi, Jan," Hamilton paused for only a second before rushing off.

"Man, he is under a lot of stress," Jan noted, watching him scurry away.

"How long does this grand opening business go on?" Jack asked.

"Through the weekend."

"Well, maybe after it's over, you could invite him to join me for a sail," he said.

"Just him?" Jan gave him a challenging smile.

"Oh, he could bring others," he returned the smile.

Jack noticed that the sun had started to close on the western ocean. "I better be heading home."

"Really?" she seemed disappointed. "We're having a fireworks display and all sorts of live entertainment this evening."

Unexpectedly the thought of live entertainment intrigued him. The last time he had seen a live performance had been with Pat. He suddenly felt guilty standing next to another woman. He realized Jan was looking at him and quickly commanded his composure back in line.

"No," he said firmly and then realized his manner had wounded her. With a soft smile, he continued, "Besides, I'm afraid of the dark."

That earned him a raised eyebrow. "You're putting me on again. That can go both ways Mr. St. Julian." She gave him a confident, conspiratorial smile.

He took her arm. "But you can walk me out." Jack let Jan lead him back through the lobby to the check-in desk. Things were quieter now that the rush was over. Jack retrieved his backpack and let the desk girls know he would not be using his hotel room.

"Tell your brother I expect to see him Tuesday," Jack said.

"And my brother's friends." She gave him an impish smile.

"If you, or he," Jack corrected himself with a grin, "can't make it, call this number." He gave her a card for Rosa's restaurant. "Any cab will know the way."

They reached the parking lot. "My trusty steed," Jack announced regally, pointing to Deni's old Honda. "It's a friend's."

"Is it safe?" she asked with concern.

"Only if you're carefully aggressive. Riding a small motorcycle on Mexican roads is always an adventure."

"I see your point," she agreed, sad to see him go.

Jack threw a leg over the bike and gave a swift kick on the starter. As the machine sprang to life he gave the throttle a couple of quick twists to warm it up.

"Thank you for a nice afternoon," she said above the motor.

"Thank you too," he nodded. "I look forward to seeing you soon."

He gave her a smile as he backed out of the parking lot. And with one last nod he headed down the cobblestone drive.

*   *   *

On the drive home Jack's mood was decidedly melancholy. The pain and vacuum of the loss of his wife, mixed with the fresh floral scent of the living pulled at his conscience.

It had only been eight months. How could he consider looking at someone else? A kaleidoscope of memories flooded his mind, always ending with the tragedy of those last few minutes.

He still couldn't fully grasp that she was really gone. Their relationship had seen a number of partings, but there'd always been reunion, not this time, never this time.

Weaving through traffic he passed the airport on his way north. Inching his way across the bridge in the slow traffic, he once again looked down to spot alligators in the Ameca River that separated the state of Jalisco from the state of Nayarit.

As he waited, Jack remembered some of those "second honeymoons" with Pat. He recalled the feverish passion as they gave themselves to each other each time he'd returned from a tour. They'd had barely six years of marriage, yet Jack knew it was a lifetime, an eternity that could never be replaced.

The congestion finally gave way. The warm fresh air with the promise of another beautiful sunset, clear the dark cobwebs of his mind, as he bounced down the rough cobblestone of La Cruz. He secured the bike under the stairwell and entered the rear of the kitchen. The aroma of cooking lobster pleasantly assailed his senses. He joined Jerry and Deni, each with the remains of lobster before them. Angelo brought over an unbidden Pacifico with a wedge of lime jammed in the top.

"You get the package off to your professor?" Deni asked.

Jack nodded.

"Hope that's not the last one," Jack said, looking at the remains on Jerry's plate, suddenly realizing he was hungry.

"As a matter of fact," Deni stated dryly, "we figured you weren't coming back so we each had seconds."

Jerry gave Jack a smug "cat-stole-the-canary" smile as he dug out the last morsel of the succulent, buttery crustacean.

"You are tired amigo?" Deni asked, studying his friend's face.

Jack cast a worn smile. "It's nothing."

Rosa placed a welcomed platter of lobster, rice and refried beans down in front of him.

"Thanks Rosa," he looked up with a smile and gave her a gentle squeeze.

*   *   *

The next day they approached the dive site. "Let's locate the marker and start deep. If you search higher ground, I can get more deep-bottom time," Jack suggested.

"Sounds like a plan," Deni answered. The thought of more discoveries had been with him since yesterday.

From the surface, using his GPS, Jack located the coordinates of the marker that he had logged the day before. Then they headed down. Jack followed the cord of the buoy to the bottom and resumed his search.

The top ridges of the canyon were at a maximum height of 130 feet. Jack moved up and down along the jagged ridge, staying in a 130 to 150 foot depth. At one point he swam out over the top of the canyon; the steep walls plunging steeply beyond sight. Whatever it is that might be down there, would require much more sophisticated equipment. Jack smiled to himself at the thought of more sophisticated diving equipment; that was what he was supposed to be working with on the *Juan de Fuca*.

On the second dive, he methodically worked the narrower, shallow end of the crevasse. The detector remained motionless. The two men probed sandy pockets trapped between rocks. Deni uncovered a bottle in perfect shape, but it was doubtful any ancient crew ever got to enjoy Coca-Cola. He spotted a couple of lobsters. But after last night's feed, they left them for the lobsterman. After two dives at these depths, they were forced to call it a day.

On the way back to La Cruz, Deni said, "I have charters tomorrow and Sunday."

Jack nodded. "I think we'll have to wait for the professor before we do any more. Besides, I think I have an idea of how to get deeper, but let's wait to hear back."

6

At the Vemexa Mexico City headquarters, relations between the two camps were anything if not cordial. Both Ernesto and Miguel supporters played a game of blind chess, each side looking for position without wanting to bump into the other.

Ernesto and Miguel, both masters at the art of deception under normal circumstances, continued the charade of working together. But everyone knew it was only a matter of time—time and opportunity.

Ernesto had reasoned with Hamilton that it was best he be with Miguel at the opening of the hotel in Puerto Vallarta. Hamilton had not liked the idea of being so close to Miguel Vegas, but acquiesced.

The hotels were Hamilton's projects. It would look strange if he were not there. More importantly, the opening gave Ernesto time alone in Mexico City to subtly politic. He encouraged any staff that might be willing to stand by him, with small offers of advancement—vague promises, all depending on circumstances and loyalties.

*   *   *

Sunday morning beamed bright and sunny. Jan woke up to the sounds of her brother talking on the phone. She couldn't make it out, but it sounded like another issue with the opening. She stretched and slipped out of bed, and donned her robe. In the living room, Todd was just finishing up.

"That's right, we'll have the mechanic double check the fans right after breakfast; don't worry about it." He hung up.

Jan raised an eyebrow at him inquisitively.

"Just some problem with the exhaust fan in one of the kitchens. It's not working right. No big deal. Don't know why they had to call me on it. What are you doing today?"

"If you're free, let's get out of here."

"I can't, not yet."

"Oh." Jan gazed out the window, taking in the morning light. "Hey, you remember that guy that was at the opening party? The one that told us about that little old lady who was sort of lost?"

"No."

"I showed him around the grounds. 'Jack'."

"Oh, yeah, I think so."

"Anyway, he invited us to go sailing. What about Tuesday?" Jan said.

"No can do. I have a meeting on Tuesday."

"Oh," Jan sighed.

He thought for a minute. After a moment of silence, Todd looked up his sister. "Jack, that Inglis big shot you say. You know, that might be a good idea."

Jan gave her brother a hard look. "What's with the turn-around?"

"We want to get a closer look at the coast, north of the city. What better way to do it?" He hadn't noticed her tone. "Let me double-check, but I think it'll be fine with him."

"You and I were invited. Who are you talking about?" This time her raised voice snapped him to attention.

"Vegas, of course. I've got a meeting with him. But I could arrange it for the boat."

"It was supposed to be you and me!" Jan shrilled, her voice rising with each word.

Todd stepped back at the fire in her voice. "I have to work," he said defensively then his voice softened, "You should get to know Miguel, sis. He could be a lot of fun."

"Are you nuts! He's got a mistress."

"Who told you that?"

"What difference. A mistress presupposes a wife!" She snapped caustically. "Where's your head Todd Hamilton?

"Look sis, things are happening with Vemexa. The old man left me as the executor. The two sons will get his shares, but not before there is a lot of legal wrangling. My European investors have given me a commitment to their proxy, if I need it. Basically it means you and I could end up the winner of a multi-billion dollar company."

Jan looked at her brother anew. There was actually a gleam in his eyes when he talked of riches. "Can you hear yourself, Todd Hamilton?" She scolded. "What good is such money? Your mother is fading away and you are down here playing Monopoly! Do you know what people are saying this Vegas is into?" she pointed her finger at him. "Drugs! Do you have anything to do with that?" she accused.

"What are you talking about?" His voice turned harder with every word.

"Drugs!"

"That's right. Anyone who succeeds down here can only do it illegally." He retorted sarcastically. "We have our critics, and all they can come up with is 'drugs.' You're living on my success. I make you and mother a lot of money."

The words burned Jan. She wanted to say more, but realized it would only make matters worse. She spun on her heels, and grabbed her purse. Unanswered pleas from her brother followed her out the hotel room door.

*   *   *

The taxi dropped her off at the McDonald's restaurant, opposite the Malecón, the unofficial start of Puerto Vallarta's downtown shopping area. Jan's anger cooled as she strolled along the concrete boardwalk that followed the coastline along the downtown core. She spent the morning watching people. Many were tourists, but the majority were local Mexican families, enjoying the day together.

The surf rhythmically rolled up along the beach in front of the raised walkway. In some places the beach was gray grapefruit-sized boulders, others were pleasantly sandy. Jan purchased ice cream, sat on a bench, and watched little kids squealing with delight as they chased the waves on-and-off the sandy shore. Jan bit her lip as she watched the family relationships. In just the few days she had been here she had come to appreciate the importance Mexican's put on family. She didn't understand it but felt a kindred spirit.

Opposite the Malecón, Jan recognized several international designer shops. She stepped into several but mostly just lazily window-shopped.

"Hola Señorita. How are you today?"

A well-dressed man in his early twenties was smiling directly at her.

"Would you like to take a free day-trip to Yelapa? Free boat ride, lunch included." He paused.

Jan focused on the curious little stall built right into the building wall. The man moved out from behind a waist-high, concrete counter. It was covered with colorful brochures of various tourist attractions around the city. She immediately realized that he was one of the timeshare salesmen that she had read about in her research of the city—pushy, always trying to get you to their presentations. She was momentarily torn between not wanting to be impolite and not wanting to waste her time. She turned to go.

"Where you from?"

"Indiana," she surprised herself by answering. "You've been there?"

Instantly he replied, "Home of the Colts, Indy 500, capital of the state."

Jan looked at him with renewed interest. "You've been there?" she asked again.

"No, but always wanted to go." He looked her straight in the eye.

Jan huffed. "I doubt it. Not if you live here."

"A person's got to get out and see new things," the young man retorted, looking her directly in the eye. "You got someone you can take the tour with?" the man asked quickly.

She gave him a sharp look and was about to give him a piece of her mind, when his hand came up defensively.

"No, Señorita," rightly reading her indignation, "it is that the tour is for two people, just that you could take a friend."

Jan didn't care to play his game and was turning to leave when she saw a brochure for the Hotel Maria Elena. She reached out and took one. "What do you know of this hotel?" she asked.

"Very beautiful. Newest in the city. I know the owner. Can get you a personal tour if you like."

Jan gave him a smirk. "Know the owner, do you?"

"Si, Señorita," he said convincingly. "I can get you a personal tour this afternoon, and we can still go on the Yelapa tour the next day. I promise you a good time." He smiled. "You know where Yelapa is?"

She looked him square in the eye. "Yes, the remote little town, inaccessible by road, on the south-end of the bay."

He didn't flinch. "So, tomorrow," he continued to press. He pulled a pen out of his breast pocket, and in a twirling motion that was much too slick, picked up a form and had it in front of her instantly. "Just sign here," he smiled.

Jan ignored him and looked at the brochure. It was artfully done. She had not seen it before. It opened up, showing colorful, professional pictures of the hotel and grounds. Two scantily-clad lovers were sitting in one of the pools, looking up at her as they sipped something cool out of coconuts—all very appealing.

She tapped the brochure against her fingertips. "I don't think so." She turned and walked away.

Jan didn't want to admit it, but the picture of the couple in the pool struck a nerve. She'd always been happy keeping her own company, but the photo surprised her. For the first time in a long time, she wondered what it would be like to be with someone.

In college, many of her girlfriends had been men-crazy. She had focused on her grades always concentrating on being the best in the class. Beyond excellent grades, her aloofness had actually attracted a few men whose company was appreciated, while it lasted. She'd had a couple of significant relationships, but they did not stand up against her resolve to finish her schooling and get back to being of help to her mother. Family mattered—her mother had needed her. The dark, sad journey into Alzheimer's Jan witnessed day-by-day over the last few years had made her all the more determined to do all she could to help.

Now Todd needed her. She shouldn't have gotten all wound up over this sailboat trip. She stopped in her tracks. "I can make this all work," she said to herself. "We'll still have a nice day. After all, Todd's my brother." She took a deep breath, gave her head a little shake and tightened her jaw, resolution made.

She eventually found herself in the local crafts market called El Mercado. It was housed in a large, bland, three-story, concrete building that sat on the edge of the Rio Cuale, the river that flowed through Old Vallarta. The Mercado reminded Jan of the old-fashioned farmers' markets they used to have out in the country towns of Indiana, only Mexican.

It was a veritable storehouse of local handicraft. The workmanship of the silver and other crafts wasn't on par with the shops along the Malecón, but the articles were priced to draw the interest of the average tourist. Several vendors approached her with offers of, "Special prices! Just for you!" in thickly accented English.

Jan smiled and gently turned them down.

The smells of cooking drew her to the top floor. She realized she was hungry. She had never seen such chaos. There were at least 10 small kiosk eateries, each with its own small kitchen and a dozen or more seats. She found a spot where she could sit by a window and watch people, both inside the building, and walking along the river boulevard below. A waitress came up and handed her a tattered plastic-coated menu. Jan briefly toyed with whether or not it was safe to eat in such a place. Then again, hundreds of others were doing so, so she trusted to luck and ordered the only thing on the menu she recognized: hachinago, fish.

When the fish arrived, she was aghast to see it came whole. It filled the dinner plate; head, eyes and all. She carefully picked away at the flesh, eventually pulling out the bony spine. The meat was excellent, in spite of the presentation. But the head and eyes were just too much.

Toward the end of the meal, she looked out at her surroundings. Through the glassless windows, Jan could see that a small river made its last path to the sea, a couple of hundred yards from where she sat. Jan's view was filled with banyan trees towering overhead; their horizontal branches attached to vertical roots that dropped down to the ground. The thick roots twisted and wove around each other, thicker than trees back home. Amongst trunks and hanging roots were intertwined strangler vines that Jan recognized from her research. She suddenly realized she was finally living her dream of travelling. "This is what it's like, and I like it," she thought to herself with a smile. She gave a contented sigh.

After lunch, Jan wandered the crowded stalls. Everyone had 'special deals' just for her. Before she realized it, Jan was loaded down with two T-shirts, four pairs of earrings, a bracelet, and a serape—none of which she needed—all of which was simply fun to buy.

Walking back in the center of town Jan saw a big Catholic Church with an ornate top. The bells chimed two o'clock, it was time to head back to the hotel.

*   *   *

It was eight o'clock Sunday night. Rosa's was empty with the exception of a couple of lovebirds sharing a dessert and Jack and Jerry talking with Deni.

"Let's close early," Rosa told Angelo. "Close the bar and you can head home."

No sooner had she said the words when a pair of friendly faces stepped across the threshold. Rosa's face brightened.

"Willie! Lobo!" She rushed to wrap each of them in a motherly embrace. Both shied from the affection, loving it all the same. In her next breath the scolding began, "Where have you been? You always come in December—that was over a month ago!"

"Working," was all Willie got out.

"Why are you late? What have you been doing?" She reached up and fondly patted Willie's cheek, continuing to rebuke them like a pair of truant schoolboys. "You will eat, then you will play." She shifted gears as smoothly as an Italian sports car. It was a command, not a question.

The pair looked at each other. They had known what they were going to get when they arrived—a scolding, a meal, and love—such was the way of home.

Willie Royal, violinist and surfer. Wolfgang Fink, flamenco guitarist and surfer. The pair had found each other in Mexico years earlier, and their passion for music had merged. As time passed, that passion was shared with millions. La Cruz was one of their many home bases. They came for the surf and the solitude.

Willie had the look of a lanky leprechaun; his bald pate accented by prominent ears. His mischievous smile and face made you think he was the bearer of some secret joke.

Wolfgang Fink was formerly of Bavaria. Wolfgang was a name that just didn't work in Spanish, so he was hung with the handle "Lobo" which means wolf in Spanish. The name secretly pleased him although he wouldn't admit it. Lobo let his music do the talking. His deeply carved face showed years of sun and the 'salts' of life.

As Rosa rushed back to the kitchen to put together a meal for her new guests, the pair sat down with the gang.

"How you guys doing?" Jerry asked.

"Good," Willie said. Lobo just smiled.

"Good?" Jack pressed.

"Yeah, albums are selling," Willie continued in his soft Texas drawl. "*Fandango Nights* has made the top ten on the world charts; although the Americans haven't really found it yet."

"That's fantastic!" Deni glanced at Jack and chided, "I'm sure the Yankees will come around sooner or later." Jack rolled his eyes in humor.

"Are you back for a while?" Deni continued.

"Yeah," Lobo piped in. "Actually, we're looking for a little quiet time to finish a new album. We've written it, but haven't been able to get it down."

Deni and Jack looked surprised. It was the longest statement they had ever heard from him. "You must be really into it," Jack said with a grin.

"Yeah," Lobo answered, returning to typical form.

First, a pair of Pacificos arrived, then chili rellenos, and a large bowl of beans, one of Willie's favorite meals. Duly fed, bellies round, chins wiped, the pair prepared to sing for their supper.

Willie looked to Jack for a little guidance. "What'll it be?"

"The new stuff."

Jack sat and listened as the duo embarked on a voyage of sound that, until he heard it, he hadn't realized how much he'd missed it. The music drifted into the still night air. Their musicianship was deep, intense; a creation of numerous musical roots, including gypsy, blues, eclectic, Moorish and more. The new set was truly inspired and original.

Soon, like the response to the calling of the pied piper, locals filled the café. Rosa beamed, though it was hard to say if she was happier with having the two musicians back within her reach, or at the steady stream of customers who dutifully ignored the closed sign. The locals knew the sound, Willie and Lobo were family many in La Cruz followed their career.

*   *   *

Later that night, after the music and beer stopped flowing, Jerry rowed Jack back to the sailboat.

"On Tuesday we're going to have company," Jack said, Jan's breezy hair filling his mind.

"Okay. We sailing?"

"Hope so. I met some people at the hotel opening the other day."

"Roger. Anything special?"

"No," Jack paused, "but let's get things shipshape."

Jerry nodded and continued to row.

"Why don't you hook up the motor to this thing?"

"What for? I got you." Jack cast him a wry smile.

As the moon led the way to the boat, Willie and Lobo's music continued to course through their minds. Jack had heard the pair for the first time at Rosa's, a few years ago. Since then, he had caught their act in Seattle twice, both times with Pat.

Jack and Jerry spent most of Monday getting the boat ready for their guests. For a couple of bachelors, they kept things pretty tidy. But with company coming, only the naval standards would do.

7

Tuesday morning Jack opened the ship's cabin door with caution. It was a rare occasion that Jack drank tequila, and this morning was a reminder why. The hangover negated the bright beautiful morning. He and Jerry had spent the evening at Rosa's listening to Willie and Lobo and relaxing with the locals. It had been a great party.

Jerry's coffee smelled better than it tasted. The bitterness and heat scorched Jack's coated tongue. "Well, there's nothing to be done," he thought as he pulled off his shirt, set down the mug, and jumped over the side. The cool saltwater seared every nerve ending, but now he was wide awake.

He cleared the water and wiped the grit from his tequila-reddened eyes. The saltwater dutifully stung. Squinting towards the dock, Jack caught sight of the slow, ominous approach of two dark green Ford Explorers, with darkened windows. They cautiously bumped along the deeply rutted, dirt road that led to the wharf. They came to a stop. Dunking his head one last time, Jack gave a strong kick and made for the sailboat ladder. As he toweled down on deck, he watched his shore party organize and head for the pier.

The size of the crowd was a disappointment, six instead of two. Jan, her brother, the belligerent 'handshake' Miguel, and some hired lackey. Walking in between Miguel and the lackey was one of the most beautiful, statuesque women Jack had ever seen. If she wasn't an actress, she should have been. The sixth person was a fat, short-set man who was removing day bags from the rear of one of the vehicles.

Jack stuck his head into the companionway. "Jerry, we have guests."

Jack decided his guests would have to take him as he was. He slipped his shirt back on and stepped down into the dinghy.

"How you all doin'?" he called out and smiled up at the group as he rowed up to the wharf. He tossed the bowline up to Hamilton. The tide was out and the dinghy sat a good three feet below the deck of the old concrete pier.

Hamilton secured the rope to a big rusty cleat on the wharf. Jack hauled himself up and shook hands all around. "Miss Hamilton, Mr. Hamilton, nice to see you both." This time as he grasped Miguel's hand he gave no pressure at all—mustn't insult the guests.

Close up, the Latin woman was even more impossibly beautiful: tall and lithe, with light coffee-mocha skin; and professional poise. Whereas Jan was good-looking in a wholesome, girl-next-door sort of way, this woman was royalty. Her only blemish was the sad, vacant look in her eyes.

"Buenos Dias, Señorita," Jack said cautiously.

"Buenos Dias," she said coolly, giving no name. By her accent, Jack guessed her to be Brazilian.

Jack heard, and forgot, the name of the lackey the moment it was given. The man looked like a weasel. His skin was pulled tight over his face. He had a pinched nose, sharp chin, and beady, dark eyes. His hair was oily and combed back in a ponytail. Jack instantly christened him "the Ferret."

"It's going to be a two-tripper, getting you to the sailboat," Jack stated. "Your call, gentlemen. Who's first?"

Vegas gave the orders, sending the two women and the Ferret with Jack in the first load. He ordered the fat one to stay with the vehicles.

Once aboard they weighed anchor and moved out of the harbor under diesel power. Jerry brought up coffee and fresh fruit. Charlie made a fashionable entrance. She allowed the women to scratch her ear and make the usual fuss over her. She paid the men little notice.

Jack headed west along the coastline. The low bank of morning mist slowly melted. He decided to stay close to the shoreline, which kept the men occupied. All had binoculars glued to their eyes, scanning every inch of the coastline. They paid special attention to the few houses and mansions along the beach and cliffs that lined parts of the shore. The buildings were stunning Moorish and Mediterranean architectural designs, with rich natural accents and overtones that worked well with their surroundings. From the snippets of conversation he overheard, the men's' singular motive for the trip was to review real estate and the present state of land development.

The women sat on the sunny, seaward side. As the sun's energy increased, they pulled off outerwear, revealing excellently filled bikinis. It wasn't long before they stretched out on towels side-by-side on the deck.

Not to be outdone Charlie got up from where she was sitting next to Jack in the wheelhouse and joined the other ladies. She moved in between the pair, looked in Jack's direction, gave an exaggerated stretch, then a couple of turns, and settled in for a little sunbathing of her own.

Jack could not help but look at the cat's companions. The images of a panther and leopard flashed through his mind. "Sorry puss, but you are totally outclassed," he smiled to himself.

Things settled smoothly into "cruise mood" as Jack called it, when suddenly Jan snapped up into a sitting position. "Look!" she pointed.

Jack saw the spout of spray an instant later. He swung the wheel hard.

Both women jumped to the edge of the boat and held the mast's guy line, as they peered across the ocean. Jack estimated the advance of the whale's progress. A hundred yards from his quarry he shut off the engine and drifted silently.

"What's that?" Jan yelled, as a pair of dolphins appeared from under the ship.

"Look, Look, Look!" Both women jumped in excitement as Pacific bottlenose dolphins paralleled the sailboat, 10 feet from where they stood. The dolphins darted back-and-forth under the boat, and then were gone.

The women's disappointment was only momentary, as a huge humpback whale broke the surface no more than 30 yards away. A moment later the whale was joined by another. Everyone watched as the whales breathed in unison, exhaling with a wet, hissing sound as they emptied, then filling their enormous lungs. Then with a smoothness and grace capable only for creatures born of the ocean, the pair arched their backs and dove. Last to see the sun was their massive tail fins as they slid into the deep.

Jack watched Jan's rapture. She was completely oblivious to anything else, her mouth was open in awestruck amazement. His heart was pierced by a vision of his wife. Pat had stood in the same spot, holding the wires and watching the whales. He pressed his lips together hard as the pangs of loss and guilt, past versus present, tore across his heart.

Jan turned and looked at him, an enormous toothy grin on her face. He smiled back.

Her brows furrowed, "I didn't get a picture!" She threw her hands up in disgust. "Will they come back?" she asked.

"No, they're long gone. But we'll see more."

"Really? You promise?"

"Money back guarantee, Señorita," he laughed. "But, you have to spot them."

"Okay captain," she saluted, before turning and scanning the horizon.

Jack watched the dynamics of the group. Jan's brother seemed edgy. Jack saw Hamilton twice have words with the Ferret at what Jack guessed, was the way he had been ogling his sister. Jack also wasn't fussy for the way either Vegas or the

Ferret were staring at the women, but it really wasn't his affair. After the first conversation with Hamilton, the little greaser laughed and retreated to the protection of Vegas. The second time it happened, Hamilton, obviously struggling for control, wandered back toward Jack at the wheel.

He took a deep breath and looked at Jack. "Nice boat."

"Thanks," Jack nodded.

"You come down here often?"

"Not enough."

Jack noticed the gaunt look on Hamilton's face. "Working for the Vegas family must be stressful," he said off-the-cuff.

"I don't work for them." Hamilton snapped. Immediately realizing his error, Hamilton said, "Sorry, not your issue."

As if Jack point were proven right, Hamilton's body stiffened as Vegas ambled back, but not before spending ample time observing the two females, as if examining artwork.

The Mexican ran his hand lightly over the sleek, teak rail. He stepped down into the wheelhouse, turned and surveyed the boat. "This is a beautiful craft," Miguel assessed.

"I like it," Jack responded.

"I have an eye for beauty," Miguel glanced back at the women lying on the deck, 20 feet forward. "I think my resort could have a boat like this and take clients out." He smiled thinly.

"Good idea," Jack returned amiably, one eye on Hamilton's reaction.

After a long pause Miguel looked at Jack. "Maybe I'll buy this one."

"Not for sale," Jack replied coldly, not liking the man's tone.

"No?" Miguel paused before continuing, as if instructing a child, "Well, maybe I don't really need to buy it." He let the statement hang, until he had Jack's attention. "This is Mexico, after all, Señor." His smile grew as he saw the anger flash in Jack's eyes.

Before Jack could respond, the man turned his back and

casually sauntered away. Jack stared at the retreating back. He had been ready to get up and throw him overboard, when he caught the eye of the Ferret. There was a knowing smirk on his pointy face. Jack suddenly realized Miguel's game: "goad and entrap." A sucker-punch guy.

Jack's face went blank; he looked through the Mexican as if nothing had happened. "So, you want to play a little poker?" Jack thought. "Well, two can play, pal."

Jack looked over at Hamilton and got a knowing smirk.

"Yes working, with that Vegas," he nodded towards Miguel Vegas, "is stressful."

Jack looked the man in the eye. "She's your sister." Seeing through what was really bugging the man.

"Yeah, didn't realize the mistake it was to bring her down here. She shouldn't be around these types. Never saw the animal in Vegas before."

Jack was going to say something, but figured it wasn't his place.

For a long minute, Hamilton looked pensively out on the horizon as if trying to come to some sort of a conclusion. Jack left the man to his reverie.

Jack finally changed course taking them further out to sea towards the Marieta Islands. "I'm going to anchor at the tip of that island and give you all a chance to take a swim, okay?" Jack nodded to Hamilton.

"Suits me," Hamilton said.

"Would you like to try snorkeling?"

"I don't think so, thanks," Hamilton said.

"You want to help out a bit?" Jack asked.

"Sure."

"We're going to drop anchor at the island coming up. Tell Jerry we're about 10 minutes out."

"Aye, captain," Hamilton smiled lightly. He headed down the companionway to find Jerry.

When the pair returned, Jack sent them forward to drop

anchor. Jack watched his depth-finder and stopped 100 yards from the northeast tip of the island. The activity attracted the attention of the women, drawing them back to the wheelhouse.

"We're going to stop here for lunch. But first, would you like to snorkel? It's quite good here." Jack said.

The Brazilian looked over at Miguel and got a disinterested shrug in return. Jack had figured she was some sort of appendage to the "great man" and that action removed all doubt.

"Have you ever snorkeled before?" Jack asked Jan.

"No. But I'm a good swimmer and use goggles in the pool."

"That's enough," Jack smiled. "If you're comfortable in the water you'll have no problem. You game?"

"Okay." She looked over at her brother, hopeful. "Come on Todd! It'll be fun."

"No thanks. I'll stay on board and guard the women and children," Hamilton gave her a quick wave of his hand.

"Come on. The women will be in the water and I don't see any innocents up here," she said sarcastically. She looked over to where Jack was standing. "No offence."

"None taken," Jack said looking her squarely in the eyes.

She could not hold his gaze.

"Look!" Jack pointed to the black tip of a fin moving stealthily through the water, about 30 yards from the back of the boat.

"A shark?" Hamilton asked.

"No. A manta ray. A good sized one too. That's just the tip of one wing."

"Is it safe?" Jan asked with apprehension.

"Quite. In fact, sometimes they will let you grab their shoulders and you can ride them down. It's quite a rush."

Jan cast him an eye of disbelief.

"Seriously, it's quite an experience," Jack answered her unspoken question.

Jerry dropped a number of fins, masks and snorkels onto the deck for the women to try. As they sorted things out, Jack asked the other woman, "Have you snorkeled before?"

"Si, many times. A long time ago," she said. The air of sadness about her made her quite mortal, in spite of her stunning beauty.

"I never asked your name," Jack inquired genuinely.

Her eyes grew suspicious. She looked for Vegas. He was at the bow of the ship looking out over the horizon with binoculars. "They call me Brazil," she said coolly.

"They?" Jack asked.

She just shrugged, averting her eyes.

Jack nodded and gave her a kind smile. Wanting to change the mood he said, "Here, you'll have fun with this." He handed her a Ziploc plastic bag filled with bread.

Brazil looked at the contents inside and gave him a ghost of a smile. She took the bag and stepped down the ladder.

Just before she let go, she looked up at him. "I will look out for your Señorita," she smirked as she pulled on her mask.

Jan, looking up from putting on her fins, asked, "What did she say?"

"I didn't catch it," he lied, and winked at Brazil.

Jan stepped down onto the ladder. "Just tell me it's safe," she stated bluntly to him.

"It's safe. You have my word on it," he smiled. "Honest." and arched an eyebrow mischievously.

Jan gave him a sour look. "This is serious."

"No, it's not. You'll have fun."

She shook her head, steadied herself and slipped into the water beside Brazil.

"Just keep this in your mouth," Brazil said, showing her how to hold the mouthpiece, "and breathe normally. If you get water, just blow it out."

Brazil lowered her face into the water. Jan imitated the moves and stuck her face under. Almost instantly, she was back up, pulling the snorkel out and yelling excitedly, "There are all kinds of fish down there!"

"Really! In the ocean?" Jack smiled.

She gave him a dirty look, put her mouthpiece back in and

went under again. The two women floated in place for several minutes.

The giant manta ray glided 30 feet below them for a full minute, then arched gracefully away into the depths and out of sight. The women surfaced in unison, congratulating themselves on their viewing accomplishment.

"Is magnificent, no?" Brazil said, genuinely excited.

"Really!"

As they worked their way further over a huge outcropping of rock, a veritable aquarium of harlequins, sergeant majors, clown fish, angelfish, along with a host of others, swam beneath them. The swells lifted them high up above the outcropping, 20 or 30 feet below. Then they would drop down, creating the sensation of floating on air. Jan was mesmerized.

A particularly beautiful blue-flame colored fish poked its head out of a crevice. Jan grabbed the other woman's hand and directed her attention Brazil squeezed acknowledgement. The pair watched as the fish played peek-a-boo before it darted off into the deep. The ice broken between them, the two spent the next 20 minutes sharing sightings as one then the other discovered new undersea wonders.

Taking a break, they removed their snorkels and masks. Jan was amazed. "Wow!" she said with a smile.

After a brief rest, Brazil motioned for Jan to put her gear on again and said, "Watch this."

Ten feet below was a school of damselfish. Brazil opened the plastic bag and removing a piece of bread, she crushed it in her hand, letting the soggy crumbs cascade down. The fish reacted instantly, swimming for the food.

Jan watched in fascination as the colorful fish swam around them. The sun's reflection on them was mesmerizing. She looked around nervously, not sure if bigger fish might come for the bait. None did.

Brazil handed Jan a piece of bread, but signaled her to just hold it. Soon, the small fish were pecking lightly at her hand, trying to pull pieces of bread through her fingers. In no time, the bread was gone.

Coming up for another break, Jan noticed that the current had slowly drawn them toward shore. On the beach before them, rose a natural limestone arch, like a tunnel. They could see the sunlight shining brightly on a sandy beach beyond the arch. They began working their way towards it. Jan popped her head out of the water and waved back at the boat to signal that they were going in. Jack waved back. Brazil looked for permission, but her master was not paying any attention. She looked at the other woman and decided to take the risk.

In the sandy shallows they stood and tried to remove their fins. Just as they bent over, a swell came up, slapped their backsides and pushed them both face first, into the water. Laughing, they crawled on hands and knees, up the soft sand to the beach. Hand in hand they ran up the shore a few yards, turned and marveled at the secret spot. It was a magical, tiny, natural wonder. They were alone in the world.

"Can we sit here for a few minutes?" Jan asked.

Brazil cast an anxious look back towards the unseen sailboat. Then she shrugged and sat down. Jan sat beside her.

"Is Brazil your real name? You are so beautiful. Are you an actress or something?" Jan asked amicably.

The woman turned and looked at Jan with her large, sad eyes. "My name is what they give me," she said.

Jan was taken aback by the sudden sadness in her voice. They fell silent, and watched tiny waves lap the sand of their hideout. Brazil finally reached over and gently patted Jan's arm.

"I'm sorry. This is fun, really. I have not done anything like this in a long time." She gave a sad smile. "Yes," she continued, "I was an actress, once and a model."

Brazil paused and looked up into the sky. "I was quite famous in my country. I thought I could make it in America, but it was not to be." Her eyes fell and she looked at the sand at her feet.

Jan gave the woman an understanding smile, not that she understood.

"I came to be in service to Miguel Vegas," she stated, as if it was perfectly obvious. "He is tiring of me," she continued. "I saw what happened to the one before me. The one I replaced, you would say."

Jan's throat tightened at the realization of what the woman was saying.

Brazil looked into Jan's eyes. "I have seen the way he looks at you, Señorita. Avoid him. He is worse than death itself. It seemed such fun in the beginning. How quickly that changed."

Jan shook her head. "You could leave," she stated emphatically.

"No, Señorita." Brazil turned her arm and exposed the crease of her elbow. The nurse in Jan saw the tiny punctures, and she knew what Brazil meant.

Jan stared silently into the water. Brazil wrapped her arms tightly around herself.

"They call me Brazil, because that is what they want to call me. What I was no longer exists. I am only what he wants me to be and will be so only for as long as he wants. Then I will be passed down, maybe to that pig on the boat," she said, her voice fading. "It matters little now," she said with a sigh of resignation.

Brazil stretched her long legs and stood. "I should get back in his sight. Already, I have gone too far. Please take care." She walked back into the water, her beauty diminished by the defeat in her posture. Jan followed.

As they swam back, Jan noticed Vegas and his man, standing on the deck above them. She pretended not to notice, but she could feel their eyes on her. She felt naked, vulnerable, and angry.

At the stern, Jan let Brazil climb the ladder first. Jan lingered in the water for a moment, looking down at the outcropping below, trying to collect her wits. "Let the pigs look," she decided. "That's all they'll ever get."

As she lifted her face out of the water, she saw Vegas and his man staring down at her. In anger she took a deep breath and dove deep, her powerful legs driving her for all they were worth. She came to within inches of the rock below, but could not quite reach it. Inextricably she was pulled back to the surface, back to waiting eyes. When she broke the surface of water, the first thing she saw was Vegas a shark-like smile on his face. She saw his pleasure at her discomfort. Jan gave another powerful kick and came around, out of sight, to the rear of the boat. Jack was waiting at the ladder.

"Don't let this man have the same look," she prayed. She cleared her mind of all else but to stay in control. She intentionally took in a mouthful of salt water. She tasted the bitterness and spat it out. Purposefully grabbing the ladder she looked up, her gaze fixed on Jack's ice blue eyes. "Where are they going to wander?" she thought angrily daring him. All she saw was concern.

He reached his arm down and whispered, "You okay?"

She lengthened her gaze for a second longer, trying to read him. Her mind told her: "This one was not the same." Jan said to him, "Hand me a towel, please?"

Jack complied. As she climbed up the ladder the towel engulfed her and shielded her body from any prying eyes.

The mood, never jovial, was even cooler than before. While the women were in the water Jerry had laid out a lunch prepared by Rosa the night before. It became a rather somber affair. After lunch, Jack motored around the two main islands that made up the Marietas. Ocean swells increased noticeably when they cleared the point, where the women had been diving.

"We're entering the real Pacific now," Jack said.

"Is it like this all the time?" Hamilton asked.

"No, this is a bit heavy but nothing special. When she gets a mood you better beware."

Hamilton held on tight to the gunwale railing as the sailboat heaved back and forth. Jack worked them around the second island, and then headed back into the bay. The swells died down to little more than a choppy lake. When they got further around the outer island they saw a sailboat anchored.

"Between the two islands is a natural anchorage. The water is usually as calm as glass," Jack informed them.

With Hamilton's help Jerry raised sail and they caught a crisp afternoon breeze. During their trip home, Jan made a point of covering herself and staying to the back of the boat which was fine with Jack. After the sails were up, Hamilton too, returned to the wheelhouse.

"Would you like to steer?" Jack asked.

"Sure. What do I do?"

"Just keep this heading on the compass, and watch out for icebergs," Jack pointed to the large glassed compass in the front of the wheelhouse. He sat with the man for a few minutes as he got familiar with the movement of the wheel, and the surges of the sea.

"Would you like to see the rest of the boat?" Jack asked Jan.

"Okay."

They stepped down into the companionway.

"Thank you for being kind to my brother. Bunch of stuff going on with their company, kind of stressful."

"I noticed," Jack said without getting overly familiar.

"He should come home."

"Yeah," Jack thought, but said nothing.

Changing the mood, Jack did a comical sweep of his hand. "So, here we have the main cabin—kitchen on the right, dining on the left." He gave an exaggerated wave, playing the TV tour guide. "Every modern convenience, if you're resourceful. Three burner stove, oven." He pulled down the door, exposing the oven.

Jan looked in and found it spotlessly clean, actually shining back at her. She stepped back and looked around. "No dishwasher?" she teased.

"That's beside the oven." He opened the matching stainless steel door. "Three-way fridge, small but useful, freezer and ice maker." He opened all the doors. Everything was tidy and evenly stacked. The kitchen was very modern brushed stainless steel and wood. It looked very efficient and user-friendly.

"How do you keep things cold?" she asked.

"We have batteries, an onboard generator, and wind and solar generators, that automatically recharge and supply extra power, if we need it, like when we are out at sea for an extended time and want to save diesel. I had the whole thing modernized about five years ago. We tried to keep all the original styling and materials."

"So you could sail around the world?"

For an instant, Jan saw that look in the man's eyes again.

He and Pat had thought of doing just that.

"You could, you know." He gave her a quick smile before moving on. "Anyway, the dining area, the table and all the wood was originally teak from East Asia. We replaced some with Mexican. It's from a friend of mine's ranch actually, not far from here." Jack passed his hand along one of the stabilizing railings that ran along the edge of all the counters.

He escorted her to the companionway. "Up front, we have the head and three staterooms, one on either side and the master up front."

Jan passed her hand over the wood. "It's very nice," she commented earnestly.

"Yeah. She's a little dated, but that's the point with a classic."

From the wheelhouse, they heard Hamilton shout, "There's a whale!"

Jan rushed up the stairs to the outside. "Where?" she asked excitedly.

"About eleven o'clock, 300 yards out!" Hamilton pointed, quickly getting both hands back on the wheel.

Jack came over to him and quickly assessed the wind. "Bring her over a little, towards them."

"You want to take it?" Hamilton asked, slightly nervous.

"No, you're fine. Just do it smoothly."

The boat slowly turned as another wisp of spray appeared on the surface, closer now. All eyes were on the ocean. But for nearly five minutes nothing happened. Then suddenly, a whale shot straight up out of the water 100 yards away. Three-quarters of its huge body was visible above the water. Jan couldn't believe her eyes as the enormous creature paused in midair, as though it was posing specially for her. Then, in slow motion, the whale turned and came crashing down, causing a massive wave to cascade on either side of its body.

Jan grabbed Jack's arm and squeezed. "Is that normal?" she squealed in delight.

Before he could answer, another whale rose out of the sea. Even the Mexicans were impressed everyone watched the incomprehensible power of 25 tons of sea mammal thrusting itself toward the sky.

The pressure on Jack's arm increased. "Why do they do that?" Jan asked in awe of the spectacle.

Jack looked at her and with a straight face answered, "I hired them for the afternoon, just for you."

Her eyes shot skyward and she gave an exaggerated sigh. "No, really?"

"They're feeding. They'll come down on a school of fish. The concussion stuns the fish; then the whales sweep them up. But I did pay them," he deadpanned, giving her a cock-eyed grin.

She gave him a smile in return. "You don't take much seriously, do you?'

"Try not to."

Before the spray of the second had settled, a perfect miniature copy of the previous adults shot out of the ocean. It did an exact imitation of the big ones, but on falling back into the water, its splash was comical in comparison.

"Aw! I didn't get a picture, again!" Jan chided herself.

"You saw it. That's the important thing," Jack said.

Jan looked at him. "You're right."

The trio blew a couple times before surrendering to the deep. The show was over for today.

"Well," Jack said reluctantly, not wanting to break the magic, "I'd better spell off your brother."

*   *   *

As they approached La Cruz, Jack called for the sails to be drawn, and they motored the final mile to the anchorage.

Just before they got organized to leave the boat, Jan approached Jack. "Thank you for a really memorable day. I enjoyed it very much." She gave his arm another squeeze.

"Thank you," Jack returned. "You and your brother are welcome anytime."

Jack took the two women back in the dinghy with the group's gear. At the wharf, the rotund driver met them and helped the women up and out.

"Thanks again," Jan waved as she scrambled to organize her belongings.

Jack focused on the silent Brazil. She looked back at him with an aloof air, until he gave her a big wink. She gave her head a shake at his foolishness, but couldn't conceal a smile.

"Made you look," he chided. "Anytime you ladies need a sailor, you just have to give a whistle. You do know how to whistle, don't you?" Jack laughed.

As Jack set out to row back, Brazil leaned over and whispered to Jan. In unison, they put their hands to their lips and threw him big kisses. He jumped up and grabbed one, then another, out of the air, pulling them to his heart, and swooned intentionally. He almost tipped the boat when he sat back down. With a final wave, he rowed back to the sailboat.

Jan stood there watching him make his way back, and shook her head. "What a goof."

"You should let that one catch you," Brazil said.

"He's nice. But there's someone or something else in his life."

"Maybe, but he is, as you say, a keeper."

"Umm."

The short, heavy driver returned from delivering their bags and led them back to the vehicles.

Jack returned shortly with the men in tow.

As they disembarked onto the wharf, Vegas turned and looked down at Jack sitting in the dinghy. "I left money with your boy to pay for the day."

"You were my guests," Jack snapped. "Guests of Miss Hamilton really."

Vegas flicked his hand in disregard, and then added, "Maybe I'll have to repay her, somehow."

Jack's eyes flashed. He saw Hamilton on the verge of losing control.

"At least I don't have to drug my woman," Jack said with a crocodile smile. He watched Vegas' face melt with rage. Jack flipped him a one-fingered salute before rowing away.

8

The day after the sailing excursion, Miguel Vegas' treasonous plan swung into action. Santana was dispatched with Pablo Perez, the fat driver who had stood guard of the vehicles at the La Cruz wharf, to organize the shipment. Seven hours south of Puerto Vallarta, lay the city of Manzanillo.

In the hills, 25 miles north of the city, Santana oversaw the gathering of the drugs. Small amounts had been stored in several locations: remote huts in the hill, storage lockers, and a dozen other hiding places. The cocaine had been methodically repackaged into boxes labeled *Colima Ceramica Tiles.*

Under Santana's direction a four-man transport team was assembled to drive the shipment north. The team consisted of Perez, Jose Esparza, Juan Meza and the mechanic, Samuel Vásquez. Nothing was going to go wrong with this shipment. Santana was satisfied that fear alone would make the men do his bidding, but what he did not understand was that there are different types of fear and different types of men, it wouldn't be long before he learned.

9

UNIVERSITY OF GUADALAJARA

With weathered old hands encased in fine white gloves, the professor slowly opened the atmospherically-controlled vault in his University of Guadalajara office. He withdrew a cover letter and a thick, rich, leather-bound, three-ring binder. The binder bore the title: *The Diary of Heraldo Santa Anita Alzarro.*

The cover letter read in Spanish:

From: Bureau of Archeology and Antiquities, Mexico City. DF
To: Professor Antonio Garcia Torres: Head of Archeology Antiquities Department, University of Guadalajara
Herein are the results of the forensic testing for the enclosed parchment (with noted text).

Dear Professor Torres,

We return to you the Diary of Heraldo Santa Anita Alzarro and accompanying research.

It is our opinion that these archives are genuine. However, as no other substantiating evidence exists, the Board of Antiquity cannot accept the hypotheses that another European predated Domingo Cortez de San Buenaventura in the Pacific.

Signed,
Dr. Jose Franscalo Degato

There was a hand-written Post-it note slapped hastily to the bottom of the letter that stated: *Sorry Doc, but you are getting close. JD*

Torres remembered Jose Degato, he'd been a bright student. Now he held one of the highest positions in the Mexican Board of Antiquity.

Over the years Professor Torres had read the letter a dozen times. His face, still registering disappointment, Torres rose from his desk, walked over and stared out his fourth-story window. A jacaranda tree was in full bloom, the yellow blossoms filling his view of the beautiful University campus. The walls of Torres' office were lined with shelves, covered with rare pre-Colombian artifacts. A few faded black and white and color photographs sat propped up against priceless carvings— along with small pieces of pottery from Olmec, Mixtec and other Mesoamerican cultures. A number of books covered, what was left of the shelf space.

Torres walked over and picked up a silver-framed photo. A much younger Torres smiled back at him. On Torres' right was his old friend Fred St. Julian. To his left was the American's young son Jack, smiling up at the camera. Even at a young age, it was apparent that Jack was going to be a tall man like his father. All three were adorned with khaki trousers and shirts. The Americans wore canvas hats to protect them from the Mexican high-desert sun. Torres' head was bare.

The photo had been taken the day they had found the diary at the ruins of the mission of San Ignacio de Oquitoa.

His old friend was gone now, like so many others. Torres remembered hearing something about the son, Jack—and some tragedy about the loss of his wife.

Fred St Julian's family foundation had generously financed the expedition that had excavated the mission at Oquitoa. At the time, the importance of the diary had not been realized, but over the years, Torres had become fascinated by the mystery of a man, Captain Heraldo Alzarro. Torres had spent years with the indigenous Indians along the Pacific coast from Manzanillo in the south, through Puerto Vallarta to Mazatlan in the north. His research had revealed that the oldest legends of plundering conquistadors told that they had come from the sea. Pillaging was nothing new to the natives of Mexico, but to have come first from the sea—that was a mystery.

Torres set the picture back on the shelf and returned to his desk.

The condition of the diary was thought to have been beyond recovery, but the work of Professor Torres and his students at the University, had brought the book to life—to a degree.

The professor opened the rich, leather binder containing the shards of the original diary. Each plastic sleeved page was serial-numbered and contained a single remnant of the ancient parchment. In some cases a note of the probable writing on the original parchment had been inserted. In other cases, there was no text that could be recovered.

The professor stroked the enclosed parchment as if *willing* the writing to appear. The notes of the first few scraps read only: "*No discernable text.*"

"What stories could you tell?" Torres asked himself.

Several sleeves into the binder, parts of sentences (barely discernable), could be seen.

"*...reached the great salt sea...*"
"*...a ship.*"
"*...unhappy ... They are ...*"

Then, the part that the professor felt was all the proof he needed:

"*We head inland from the sea...*"

What followed was three further pages that could no longer be translated, until:

"...*They attack again*..."
"...*thirst for the golden objects especially the great wheel...*"

A footnote on the insert stated: "Possibly one of the Aztec Calendar wheels xiuhpohualli (year count) or tonalpohualli (day count)."

And, on a single page:

"I alone dare carry the wheel over my back...saved my life...
mark....dead center that would have skewered...
...back to the ship...
great storm has taken us. We..."

That was all there was.

The professor put the archive down and stared absently out the window. The many tribes of Mexico had hated the Aztecs. They did not know that the Aztec yoke would prove to be nothing compared to that of the Spaniards. Yet power conquers—that hard fact, the brave people of Mexico understood.

Torres turned back to the diary. His theory had been that Buenaventura, nephew of Cortez, and known for his arrogance, chose to preserve his pride and not acknowledge that another man—Alzarro—had been first to sail the Pacific waters off Mexico. Rather, Buenaventura had used his powerful influence to have Alzarro dispatched to a remote convent to live out the short end of his days, concealing the truth from history records.

Torres set the leather binder down and picked up the golden egg, laying on a bed of soft, black velvet on his desk. Since receiving the package from young St Julian, his staff had performed every conceivable test on the remnants. The professor took his magnifying glass and peered at the filigree script on the egg—Aztec, most certainly.

He picked up the note "...*Found them in about 40 meters of water off the Morros.*" The professor picked up his phone and dialed the number on the note.

*   *   *

Jack sat with Jerry and Deni at Rosa's, enjoying the end of the day when the phone rang.

"Is for you, Señor St. Julian," Angelo said.

Jack smiled as he recognized the reedy voice on the other end. "Professor Torres, good to hear from you."

"Yes, Professor, we… Yes, we'll… No problem, I'll…" Jack's voice petered off as he pulled the dead phone away from his ear. He shook his head and handed the receiver back to Angelo.

Jack sat back with a smile. "That man never did like to talk on the phone. I remember him and my dad years ago. What a character."

"What's happening?" Deni asked.

"Oh nothing, apparently a couple of jokers," Jack's finger flicked from Deni to himself, "found something that could wreak havoc on the Mexican history books. The professor is in a dither. He says if what we found is accurate, he could have proof that Buenaventura was not the first to sail these waters."

"Is that important?" Jerry asked.

"Not in the grand scheme of things, but it is an important piece of history for the Mexican people and their heritage," Jack answered.

"If that's true, then maybe the bit about the treasure is true—like my father always believed," Deni added excitedly.

"Well," Jack leaned back and crossed his arms above his head, "the professor is dropping everything and coming over. He wants to get an expedition going immediately. From what I know he has the political pull to make it happen. He ordered— ordered, mind you—that I contact the University of Washington and see if they will assist." Jack shook his head as if to somehow organize the details.

Jerry and Deni, hanging on to Jack's every word, looked expectantly for him to continue.

"He has officially filed for an archaeological site. He says we'll get cooperation from the government through the Port Authority here in PV. I'm to see one Señor Zillia and let him know what we are doing. The Professor will be over as soon as he can. He also said that his department has informed this Zillia, to have papers ready to protect the site."

Jack took a long pull on his beer. "Oh, and he wants to know why we're not diving right now," Jack said, dead-faced.

Deni looked out at the dark night sky.

Jack got up. "This just might work. Remember when we were too deep the other day, out at the Morros?"

Deni nodded.

"There is a Newtsuit on the *Juan de Fuca*. It's what I need to really explore."

"A what?" Deni looked inquiringly at Jack.

"In a minute," Jack answered, heading for the phone. "I need to make a long distance call, okay?"

The Mexican just waved off the comment.

When Jack returned after a few moments, he sat, silent in concentration.

"Well?" Jerry asked.

"I got in touch with Captain Erikson on the *Juan de Fuca*, that's the University of Washington's research vessel I was on before Jerry picked me up in Cabo. The Captain wasn't sure what to think of the idea. Has to call the university. I said I'd do the same in the morning."

"That's good?" Deni asked.

"Yes, that's very good." Jack said. "And they have a Newtsuit on board."

The other two looked at him, not understanding.

Jack looked up from his musing. "Oh, sorry. A Newtsuit... actually, they call it an atmospheric diving system now, ADS for short. It's a high-tech, one-man deep-dive suit; totally self-contained, communications—everything. You remain at one atmosphere inside the suit… which is sea level, so no decompression."

"How deep?" Deni asked.

"Like, a 1000 feet, plus."

Deni let out a whistle. "You could really treasure hunt with that."

"Well, you'd better be pretty sure of your treasure. The thing goes for, like, ten thousand dollars a day. The one they've got on board is a new prototype for the Navy. They gave it to the university to practice with. I used it on a rescue mission on an oil rig in the Gulf of Mexico after Katrina."

"Where did they come up with the name, Newtsuit?" Jerry asked.

"The inventor's last name is actually Nuytten—Phil Nuytten—but Newt sort of stuck for the suit. Officially, they don't call it that anymore though. The guy is a genius, my dad knew him pretty good. I've used it a few times, definitely high-tech."

* * *

The morning sun glowed behind the Sierra Madres Mountains, yet to make its full presence known. The sky was cloudy for a change. It was at the wharf where Jack caught up with Deni. In spite of the Professor's wishes, clients had to be served. Deni was organizing two groups of fishermen between Israel and Ivan, in *Carmen II* and Arturo, and himself in *Carmen I*.

"Where you headed today?" Jack asked.

"I think we'll try La Corbeteña. They want tuna," Deni said.

Jack watched with a tinge of envy, as the groups boarded. Deni's voice boomed over the idling motors, half singing and half encouraging his charges, as they embarked on their day of adventure.

Jack walked back to the restaurant, pulled the Honda from

its resting place and headed for Puerto Vallarta. Zigzagging through the early morning traffic, he again enjoyed the freshness of the morning and the freedom of the ride.

As much as he tried to get Jan Hamilton out of his mind, she just wouldn't leave. His thoughts kept going back to yesterday's sail. It had been disconcerting to have the scent and presence of a female that close.

Again, he chastised himself. He was just not done, loving Pat. He never would be. "She had been enough for one lifetime," he kept telling himself. But just as quickly his thoughts turned to Jan, remembering how her eyes filled with wonder as she watched the whales, and her enthusiasm with snorkeling. She showed a zest for life, just like…

"Stop it!" he said out loud.

Jack made his way to the Port Authority parking lot. "*Gilberto Zillia—Harbormaster*," was written proudly in Spanish on the empty double-parking space, closest to the door. Just as Jack dismounted, a Mercedes pulled in, "*Harbormaster*" displayed on the license plate.

The harbormaster's smile dissolved when he saw the American. Zillia disliked Americans, but he disliked anyone telling him how he was going to run his affairs even more—most particularly, one professor Torres. Gilberto Capilla Jose Zillia thought himself a righteous man. Through careful cultivation of family and acquaintances, he had come to enjoy the fruits of his labor.

In reality—though a legend in his own mind—his position held little power. He had become adept at delegating all but the most critical and pivotal assignments. He strongly believed it was who you knew, not what you knew, that led to success in this world. And one of his best acquaintances was Miguel Vegas of the Vemexa Corporation.

Zillia had studied at the University of Guadalajara. He remembered in particular, the disgusting semester he had spent sifting dirt, looking for broken shards of pottery in some ancient dumpsite. The only thing beyond the misery of the dirt and heat had been the constant lecturing of Torres. It was an experience he had long tried to forget.

Subsequently, it was less than a pleasure when he got a phone call the night before, from the old buzzard. A very official-looking fax, signed by the head of the Department of Antiquities in Mexico City, had arrived shortly afterwards. It named a Captain St. Julian, US CG Retired, as Torres' authorized representative for some dive site or some such thing. An American! Yet the letter was approved at the highest level. "What was a man to do?"

Zillia dallied in the car, letting the American wait outside. Finally, not wanting to appear foolish, Zillia opened the door.

Jack stood patiently. He had seen this attitude before. Regardless of the nationality some bureaucrats couldn't stop power from going to their heads.

"Señor Zillia?" Jack asked pleasantly.

"Si."

"My name is Jack St. Julian. Professor Torres sent me to pick up some documents."

"I know a Professor Torres," was all the acknowledgement Jack received. Zillia locked the car and proceeded toward the building without another word.

Jack bit his tongue and moved to catch the man before he entered the building. He leaned heavily on the glass door, preventing it from being opened. His ice-blue eyes bored squarely into the man.

Zillia was affronted by the crass American attitude. "They are being drawn up," he lied. "They should be ready within the week. We will call."

Jack stared at the man for a long minute, then let go of the door. The Mexican quickly opened it and escaped into the building.

Jack stood, considering his options. He did not believe the peacock for a second. The way the professor had put it, this whole issue was all very important. Jack was to do all he could, to get things started and the Mexican government was behind it 100%. "So, what's the deal?" he thought. The site had to be protected. The professor had told him to get the whole area off-limits, immediately. Jack pondered the situation for another moment and decided to give Zillia a couple days.

Zillia was shaking by the time he got to his office; he had never been so threatened. He opened his briefcase and reread the fax from the professor. There was no question, something was important here. But why hadn't he been informed earlier? He realized what he had to do. It was at times like these that he thanked his great wisdom for cultivating important contacts. He would start at the top. He would call Señor Miguel Vegas. Whether Señor Vegas knew anything about this Torres business or not, was not as important as the excuse to call him.

Over the phone in Mexico City, Vegas listened with little interest to the pompous harbormaster as he droned on about some dive site, and ancient professor. Then Zillia mentioned St. Julian.

"St. Julian?" Vegas snapped.

"Si, Señor Vegas. Captain Jack St. Julian, US Coast Guard. He is supposed to be on some whale research in Baja, but he is here."

"Tell me again what this is all about."

The harbormaster repeated his tale, but this time in a more conspiratorial tone. Anything that involved the US Navy and archeology of Mexico had to have political overtones. Zillia recognized there were advantages here, the question was, where?

Vegas made notes as Zillia spoke. "I will call you back," Vegas said and hung up.

Vegas made a few calls. No one had any idea what was going on. There didn't seem to be any secret about the expedition—it just wasn't important. But they all promised Vegas that henceforth, they would listen.

Vegas called the harbormaster back and told him to stall as long as he could, weeks if possible.

When Zillia put down the receiver, he was white. "What have I done?" he said aloud. He now found himself between a direct order of his government and Señor Vegas.

If that was not enough, his secretary walked in at that moment and dropped an official government overnight courier parcel on his desk. Numbly, he opened it. He found the official letter from the director of antiquities in Mexico City within, along with maps and specific instructions. There, in bold black and white, it stated: "*Immediate Attention for Captain Jack St. Julian, US Navy, Retired.*" Below that was two paragraphs about the importance of cooperating with this US officer.

Zillia dropped the papers and fell back in his chair.

*   *   *

Jack went to the tackle store to see about the progress on his reel, and was told that damage like this was not a quick-fix. The parts were coming, maybe tomorrow.

Deciding the day had been a bust Jack headed back to La Cruz. He was half way home when he realized he was wrong; it was a beautiful day in paradise, and he was free and on the back of a bike. It came to him that his frustration was coming from Jan, a woman he figured he'd never see again. "Well, that's the way it is. There's no reason to get all maudlin," he told himself.

As the miles rolled by his mood brightened. There would be no better cure than a good sail, and that's what he did.

*   *   *

That night, Jack found himself relating the actions of the harbormaster to Deni.

"I do not know this man," Deni said, "but he sounds like so many who have a little power. What will you do?"

Jack shrugged. "The *Juan de Fuca* is going to take a couple days to get orders and then wrap up what they are doing in Cabo. The professor, too, needs some time. So, I guess the key thing is that we see that the site is protected. No one besides us and the lobsterman know anything is up."

"And Zillia," Deni added.

"Yeah. That's the rub. If somehow he thinks there is something to gain, then he could be telling... I don't know who," Jack shook his head. "But it doesn't make sense. To mount any sort of expedition would take time and money. All this has fallen out of the blue. What's this guy going to do with the information?"

"I don't know." Deni thought for a moment. "But here's what we can do... I will tell Israel and Ivan that every day, we will take our charters around near the Morros. The fishing is better to the north, but our clients will not know that. We will make a pass of the rocks in the morning and the afternoon. If we see anything funny we will report it."

Jack grinned at his friend. "Thanks, amigo."

*   *   *

Over the next couple days, Deni and his boys took their fishing parties trolling south of the Morros. To their pleasant surprise and their clients' delight they picked up a number of nice dorados and wahoos. In the afternoons they headed up to where the other boats were having even more luck, north of the Marieta Islands and Punta de Mita. Their clients never knew the difference. Each day the report was that the lone lobsterman had been the sole worker at the Morros.

10

It was just before midnight when the phone rang beside Ortega's bed. He answered it before the second ring.

"It is happening," José Esparza, from Santana's truck team, whispered over the phone.

"When?"

"They are gathering the shipment now, outside of Porto Escondido, on the west coast."

"How are they going to transport it?" Ortega asked.

"By truck. We have been checking over vehicles for two days now, making sure everything is in perfect condition."

Ortega smiled. Shipments normally went by sea. The local fishermen south of Mazatlan, who moved drugs for the Vegas family, had been loyal to Ortega for years, especially around San Blas, north of Puerto Vallarta. That area had literally hundreds of square kilometers of mangrove swamps, offering ample hiding places. Nothing would get past San Blas by sea, not without Ortega hearing about it.

"Miguel must know we have contacts throughout the coast. Nothing will get past them by sea."

"Si, Señor. So, I think we take the highway, at least north to Tepic," Esparza said.

"How many are there?"

"Five. Santana is here," Esparza answered.

"Describe the vehicles and license plate numbers," Ortega demanded.

"A blue five-ton Dina diesel with Colima Ceramica written on the doors, and a white Ford, three-quarter-ton pickup with a white canopy, no other markings on it," Esparza squeezed out, barely above a whisper.

Ortega wrote down the details and license numbers. "Is Vásquez there?"

"Si, but he is scared. Santana's presence is dreadful, but they need Vásquez. Only he and I can drive the big diesel—and he's the mechanic."

"He is a coward who will do as he is told. We needn't worry about him. When do you think you will move the drugs?"

"Day after tomorrow. I will not be able to call again," Esparza informed him.

"You have done well. Remain calm and watchful."

"Si, Señor. I must return before anyone suspects." The line went dead.

Ortega immediately called Ernesto Vegas. "It is on."

"What do you know?" Vegas asked, suddenly awake and alert despite the late hour.

The bodyguard recited what he had been told.

Vegas hung up, thought for a minute, then and called Hamilton in Puerto Vallarta, outlining the situation.

"We have to get Santana back to Mexico City," Hamilton reasoned. "But we'll never get him away from that cargo."

"I have an idea," Vegas said and hung up.

*   *   *

Just before dawn, an attempt had been made to break into Miguel's hacienda. An hour later the security system of Ernesto's downtown apartment had been set off. Neither attempt amounted to anything, but with everyone's heightened anxiety, they had had the desired effect.

At mid-morning the same day, the Mercedes-Benz owned by Miguel's wife was blown up in a shopping mall. No one had been hurt, but the explosion made the major news.

That afternoon Ernesto stormed into his brother's office. "Something is going on."

Miguel turned off the television news report. "Si."

"Who is it?" Ernesto paced back and forth nervously.

"I don't know, brother," Vegas said tersely. "Whoever it is, they are pretty clumsy."

"Or they are testing us," Ernesto shot back. "I am calling Ortega back to the city. Clumsy or not, whoever's doing this will not catch me napping."

Miguel studied his fingernails for a long moment. Ortega was a problem, and at this stage of the operation, knowing his brother's goon's whereabouts would be reassuring. "Yes, brother, maybe you're right." A smile grew. "I shall call in Santana. Together we will find out what is going on." He looked innocently into his brother's eyes.

"Si, hermano, and together we will fix it." Ernesto coolly stared back. Then he spun on his heels, striding down the hallway. A smug grin spread across his face. "Yes brother, we certainly will fix it." He said to himself.

Miguel sat contemplating the recent events. "What was going on?" he asked himself. Was his brother setting something up? Or had one of the cartels got wind of something?

Vegas was lucky to reach Santana on his cell phone. Much of the mountainous region of Mexico still did not have cell coverage.

"We have a problem," Vegas stated calmly.

Santana waited for the rest of the message.

"There has been a series of attempts on our security in the city."

"We have people." Santana answered.

"They tried to kill my wife about two hours ago."

"Who?" the killer asked.

"We don't know yet, but Ernesto is calling Ortega back from Tijuana. I don't know if this is some sort of trick on his part, or if someone else thinks it is time to come after us."

"This cargo is important."

"These men you have chosen, they are the best?" Vegas asked.

"Si."

"Who is in charge?"

"Perez, then Esparza," Santana answered.

Vegas thought for a minute. These were good, long-time servants. He remembered something favorable about Esparza, put couldn't place it. "Well, get them organized and moving. You get back here. If everything calms down, then you can rejoin them in Tepic."

"As you order, sir." Santana didn't like it, but if that was what his master wanted, it would be done.

*   *   *

High in the mountains outside of Manzanillo, from a hiding spot between a series of large boulders, Esparza watched a cloud of dust approach. He turned toward their hidden camp and blew a shrill whistle. He cushioned his large, stocky frame into the shooting platform he had made for himself.

Shortly, a pickup truck came into his view through the trees. Esparza shouldered up to his 7mm magnum rifle and pivoted the tripod the gun-barrel rested on. He focused the scope, identifying the driver. He placed the cross hairs of the scope squarely on the head of the man. Gently, he slipped the safety off and continued to follow the head as it drew closer. He wanted very much, to pull the trigger, but did not.

Santana pulled the pickup under a large palm-covered shed next to the camouflaged tents that had been the men's base for the last few days, and stepped out.

"Call the men," Santana ordered Perez.

"Si. Esparza, too?" Perez asked.

"Yes. We can do without a guard for a few minutes."

Esparza joined Perez, Santana, and two other men, Meza and Vásquez. They made up the transportation team. Esparza, the guard, was dressed in full jungle camo, complete with a painted face, to hide his presence. The others were dressed in work clothes. Meza and Vásquez were covered in dirt and grease from working on the vehicles.

"You will leave in two days. Until then you must not leave each other's sight, you understand?" Santana spoke directly to Perez, the tactical boss, but all heard the command.

"Any of you go near a phone or try anything I will rip your guts out with my bare hands." Santana looked each one in the eye.

"Perez is in charge. You will do anything he says. You got a problem with that?" Santana scanned the group. Slowly his gaze fell on Esparza.

Esparza looked the killer directly in the eye. "No, Señor, none." It was quite likely the bravest thing he had ever done.

"I have been ordered back to Mexico City. There is trouble. You need not worry, just get this truck up the 200 Highway," he commanded. "I should be back before you go. Leave early. If I am not here, go, I'll join you on the road. Only Perez is to communicate."

* * *

Two days later, well before dawn, they started without Santana. The first ten kilometers were excruciating, as they worked themselves down off the steep mountain road. The five-ton truck was loaded with cases of ceramic tiles, each case weighing nearly forty pounds—basically solid rock. The boxes were two rows deep at the back, and one row, all the way around the sides. The real cargo was within; it too, was in the same cartons as the tiles. If they faced an inspection, it would be only the most industrious inspector that would muscle all that stone weight around to get to the heart of the cargo. The drug runners' immediate fear was that the weighty ceramics would shift while they drove on the remote dirt path to the highway. As a result, they crawled slower than a man could walk. A mistake would have cost them time and worse, the wrath of Santana.

A hundred yards from the pavement, they stopped and double-checked the load. They were exhausted, but relieved, when they finally pulled out onto Highway 200—the main and only road along the Pacific coast of Mexico. Perez and Esparza rode in the pickup, and Vásquez drove the big Dina diesel, with Meza. It was just before noon when the trucks cleared Manzanillo.

The four men had worked loosely with each other in the past. This was the first time no senior supervisor was present. Both Perez and Esparza took this opportunity as very important for their career, but for very different reasons.

"How long have you worked with Vásquez?" Perez asked of Esparza as they cleared the heavy traffic of Manzanillo.

"Maybe five years. He is a good mechanic."

"He gets on my nerves, with his twitching, nervousness, and smoking," Perez confessed.

"You are right," Esparza placated. "He is like a nervous weasel. If I ride with him, I have to have a window down or I would choke." Esparza looked over at the other man and gave a knowing smile, neither were smokers.

In fact, the thing that kept Vásquez on the team was his knowledge of diesels. He could fix anything. With the importance of this load, his presence had been an immediate choice.

The Ford pickup stayed roughly a mile ahead of the big Dina diesel, just in case any traffic issues came up. The men stayed in communications over CB radio; just two of the hundreds of trucks moving products up and down the coast.

North of Manzanillo were the resort towns of Barra de Navidad and Melaque. Before leaving the congestion of the twin resorts, the road turns off. To the left was Melaque, and to the right Highway 200 continued up into the mountains, towards Puerto Vallarta. The military regularly used the intersection as a checkpoint. As the turnoff came into sight, the men in the Ford nervously approached the checkpoint. Esparza slowed and looked at Perez for instructions.

"I have an idea," Perez said. "Turn off at that food stand. Go buy some pollo for the road while I take a walk."

Over the CB, Perez cryptically told the others what they were doing and for them to do the same.

Esparza pulled the Ford over onto the dirt parking lot and walked over to the chicken stand. Perez headed down the highway on foot. A couple minutes later, the Dina arrived.

Returning to the Ford, Perez said to Esparza, "All clear. Let's go now... and stay together!" Perez looked back at the Dina, caught Vásquez's eye, and gave his head a jerk.

At the guard post there was a lone, young, uniformed guard. He didn't bother looking up as they passed. Perez and Esparza shared a collective sigh.

Slowly, the little caravan crawled up the winding hills north of Melaque. Vásquez pulled over to the edge at every possibility, so that traffic could pass them.

The fact that Perez was in charge was a further insult to Esparza. He had been with the family longer and had been passed over for promotion, before. The reality was that he had slighted Santana. Two years ago Miguel Vegas had taken a tactical suggestion from Esparza, over Santana's objections: to expand by flying drugs over the border. The killer had never forgotten it.

Esparza's recommendation should have been rewarded with an opportunity to work in the United States. This would have meant his kids would have a chance at a better life in America. The chance never came, because of Santana. "Well, that chance would come soon," he reassured himself.

Esparza didn't like what he was doing, but what choice was there? He grew up in a family of nine kids in a crowded, rough neighborhood of Mexico City. He had lived on the streets as long as he could remember. He had been young and tough, and all this led him to a life of crime. Now he had a chance. Just after he'd been refused the chance of his American dream, Ortega had approached him and made promises of a real future in America. What he asked in return was for Esparza to risk his and his family's lives. Esparza agreed.

Esparza continued to soldier on in Miguel Vegas' camp, while keeping the older brother's bodyguard posted. Esparza had been surprised that he was chosen for this mission, given Santana's distaste for him. The fear that somehow he was being used was always in the back of Esparza's mind.

The convoy reached the southern edge of Puerto Vallarta by late afternoon. There they stopped for fuel.

"Stay with the trucks," Perez ordered. "I must phone in."

Miguel Vegas' secretary put him through immediately.

"Everything is fine?" Vegas asked.

"Si, Señor. We are in Puerto Vallarta. We will make Tepic tonight."

Vegas thought for a moment. He had locations all the way up the highway, where the big diesel could be concealed for the night. There was one in Puerto Vallarta, and another in Tepic.

"All right. Make Tepic and then get some rest. Santana will join you there in the morning. Call him when you arrive."

"Si, Señor," Perez said. He tried not to sound disappointed at the loss of his position.

"Anything else?"

"No, Señor. All is fine."

"Keep your eyes open." Vegas hung up.

Returning to the truck, Perez said to Esparza, "We make Tepic tonight."

Esparza nodded.

As they cleared the tunnel through Puerto Vallarta, Esparza said casually, "About an hour from here I know a good restaurant. Good local seafood but you're the boss."

Those were the words Perez wanted to hear. Esparza knew his place. "Sure," Perez agreed.

Esparza bit his lip to avoid a smile. The bait had been taken.

*   *   *

Earlier that same morning, Ortega had quietly left the commotion in Mexico City and had flown to Puerto Vallarta. The 200 Highway was the only road coming north along the Mexican Pacific coast. Ortega had posted lookouts at the south end of town.

Ortega took the call on his cell phone. The trucks had been spotted. Immediately, he headed to the rendezvous. Months earlier, he and Esparza had worked out half a dozen places they would attempt to meet. The next rendezvous offered an excellent location; it was a remote restaurant north of Puerto Vallarta, just past the town of Bucerias. Ortega headed north with a purpose.

Ortega sat in his nondescript pickup truck and surveyed the remote restaurant. The roof was made of woven palms, supported by raw trees and branches. Loudspeakers located in the rafters bellowed taped mariachi music.

The kitchen was framed with cinder-block walls and fronted by a large, open mesquite grill. From his vantage point, Ortega could see the staff working further back. There was a back door to the kitchen, and next to that, the door to a bathroom. The only place of concealment was to be found at the back of the building, near the bathroom.

Dark, black smoke from the mesquite-fired grill billowed up into the rafters and then out of a hole at the top. Ortega knew that the cook and his wife were the owners. There was one waiter and an assistant in the kitchen. Presently, there were six customers; four at one table, and two at another. Ortega waited as long as he dared, then made his move. He walked directly up to the owner and nodded in a friendly manner.

"Buenos Dias," Ortega said.

"Buenos Dias," the owner smiled at the new customer.

"I will need your assistance tonight, amigo."

The owner looked at the man but did not comprehend.

Ortega leaned closer to the cook. "Some men are coming. Bad men. You will do as I say and there will be no trouble."

He pulled his jacket open a fraction. The cook's eyes widened as he saw the large handle of a pistol.

"Don't do anything stupid, and no one will be harmed. Do you understand?" Ortega hissed. "You must stay calm."

The man nodded woodenly.

"Go about your business. Do not say anything to anyone." He looked the man in the eye. Ortega let the threat hang in the air for a moment, then turned and sat at a table near the kitchen and waited.

It took about an hour, but Ortega immediately recognized the white pickup. The pickup's slow advance into the dirt parking lot allowed him time to nonchalantly walk through the kitchen and into the concealed area he'd discovered earlier.

He saw Perez step out of the Ford and jog toward the washroom at the rear of the restaurant.

Ortega pressed himself further back. As he waited he flicked off his pistol's safety and prepared to fire if Perez recognized him. He watched as the door to the bathroom slammed closed and he heard footsteps receding back to the Ford.

Soon after, as darkness approached, the Dina arrived. Ortega risked a look. He didn't need to worry about being spotted because the others' attention was focused on the diesel's arrival.

"Vásquez, you stay with the truck. We will bring you something," Perez ordered.

The other three walked casually into the restaurant and chose a table with a clear view of the Dina.

From the kitchen door, Ortega watched the waiter take their order. Then he saw Esparza casually get up and walk back to the washroom. Ortega stepped behind the door and waited. Esparza jumped as he saw him.

"You're here," Esparza sighed with relief at the fact that the plan was working.

"What are they ordering?" Ortega demanded.

"The Diablo shrimp," Esparza said.

"Both?"

"Si."

"Perfect. And you?"

"Fajitas."

"Good. Don't eat the soup." Ortega quickly stepped back out of view.

Scared, Esparza had to concentrate on walking normally as he moved back to the table.

The kitchen staff knew that something was wrong, but they were too frightened to do anything. Ortega stirred white powder into two bowls of bean soup. As a last thought, he added a dash of hot sauce to each. The woman sneered at the destruction of her cooking.

"Serve these to the pair out there not to the man who just sat down. Understand?"

The woman silently nodded and told the waiter.

Ortega watched with satisfaction as the waiter got it right, the pair immediately started in on the soup. When Esparza's soup arrived he ate little. Ortega was satisfied when the two bowls returned empty.

As hungry as Esparza was, he found it difficult to focus on food. The die had been tossed, his actions would spell success or death for his family. All three men ate in silence, finishing their meals quickly.

Ortega watched as Esparza stepped behind the wheel of the pickup and Vásquez, into the big Dina. The pickup moved out first. After half a dozen minutes, the Dina rumbled north into the darkness. Ortega followed.

Within five miles, Ortega came up to the two vehicles that were now parked beside the road, with engines idling. Esparza was standing next to the open door of the Dina. Ortega jumped out of his pickup and raced for the open door of the big truck. With a quick jab he stuck a hypodermic needle into Meza.

Vásquez stared in disbelief. "What is happening?" he screamed.

"Shut up and live," Esparza hissed.

Ortega now raced to the pickup and jabbed Perez with a

needle. When he returned to the two men standing by the Dina, he pulled his jacket back and exposed the .44 to Vásquez. "You will drive, or you will die right here and now."

The man nodded his head furiously. What choice did he have?

"There's a turn-off a couple of miles ahead. We will dump these two." Ortega commanded Vásquez.

Turning, Ortega yelled to Esparza, "Let's get moving!"

Esparza led in the Ford, with Vásquez and the big Dina in the center. Ortega was right behind. In a short time Esparza turned right off the highway and led them up into the hills.

A mile off the highway the dirt road became impassable for the big truck. They loaded the unconscious pair into the back of Ortega's pickup and took them a mile further until the road ended.

Ernesto and Ortega had agreed that, if at all possible, they would not kill. These men were loyal members of the family and to kill them would create bad blood. Killing your own was what Miguel Vegas would have done.

The trio manhandled the sleeping men out of the truck and leaned them up against a large tree. Ortega handcuffed them together at their wrists and feet and then set a plastic gallon jug of water beside them.

The plan was to have someone pick them up the next day and keep them in hiding until it was all over. They would not be comfortable, but they would be alive.

Returning to the highway, the truck caravan turned south back from where they had come. There was an anxious moment as they passed the restaurant but all was normal. At the overpass north of Bucerias they turned off the highway and drove past La Cruz, then headed toward Punta Mita.

It was several miles past La Cruz when they stopped at a gated dirt road that led north, away from the sea. A barbed wire fence spread in both directions from the chain-link gate. Ortega unlocked the padlock on the gate and they drove through.

The old rutted road slowly led them high into the hills. After several minutes they came to a dry riverbed. One hundred yards upstream their headlights reflected on a man standing beside a dilapidated hut. Esparza recognized Todd Hamilton, standing in the white glare of headlights. The caravan stopped. All three got out and joined the American.

"Well done, gentlemen, well done," Hamilton said excitedly in Spanish. He shook hands with all of them. "Any trouble?"

"None," Ortega said, patting Esparza on the back.

Vásquez stared from one man to the other as he tried to light a cigarette. His hands would not cooperate. He did not dare say a word.

Ortega steadied the match and looked at him. "You are now with us," he said matter-of-factly, "or you and your family are dead."

The man only stared, nodded, and took a long drag on the cigarette.

Hamilton watched. "Good. Let's get the truck up here under cover."

"Move," Ortega commanded Vásquez.

Vásquez remained still. There was a long silence. The cigarette hung from his mouth. They all looked at him, expecting some sort of trouble.

"Señor," Vásquez stammered, "the truck cannot go up that slope."

"What do you mean?" Ortega snapped angrily.

Vásquez cowered at the threat and pointed to the riverbed. "I am sorry Señor, but the load will not take that sort of ride. We packed it tight but that will shake it loose, I am sure." Vásquez's hand swept to take in the riverbed and the bank in front of the truck.

Previously, when Hamilton had shown Ortega the site, they both thought it perfect. A hut sat under a ceiling of a pair of giant avocado trees. The trees spread their leafy branches 40 feet in every direction, ample space to conceal the truck. At the time it had been daylight and anything looked possible. Of course, neither man had ever driven a fully loaded five-ton diesel up a sandy embankment.

Now, in the moonlight, standing next to the monstrous truck filled precariously with a valuable load, both Hamilton and Ortega realized the bank posed an awesome challenge.

Under the glow of the headlights and moon Vásquez walked up and down the slope. Then he backtracked along the riverbed. Pointing, he said, "I am not sure, but I think we can go up the bank back there...the slope is less, and the bed is harder."

"Let's get some light on it," Ortega commanded. In unison, the men turned the pickups around and gave Vásquez all the light possible.

The group walked back down the riverbed where Vásquez had shown them the bank was firmer. Vásquez stomped the ground to prove his point. "The earth here should hold the truck, Señor. Even so, it will be close," he said, looking expectantly at Ortega.

Ortega nodded. "Do your best."

The others walked beside the big truck while Vásquez gently guided it back down the riverbed. Then carefully, as if driving on eggs, he worked it up the slope. The others walked beside the truck, willing it up the hill. Although the angle wasn't severe, they could see the shifting of the cases in the rear, under the plastic tarp. The load barely held.

Once up the slope, Vásquez eased it along the top of the bank and under the pair of big avocado trees. When Vásquez stepped out of the truck the others pounded him on the back for a job well done.

The men crawled over the big Dina covering it with camo-mesh and palm branches. The truck soon looked like a newly-roofed hut under shading foliage of the avocado trees, a common sight in the area. Lastly, using palm branches like brooms they swept away the tire tracks in the riverbed.

With the aid of the trucks headlights and a couple of Coleman lanterns, they unpacked food and camping gear from Hamilton's truck.

Once all had been done Ortega commanded the pair, "Do not move from here. That is an order. We'll return in a day or two."

The eastern sky gave off the faintest glow, as Ortega and Hamilton closed and locked the gate at the paved road.

"I wish we had more notice to get the San Blas boats organized," Hamilton sighed.

"I'll be in touch with them today. It should not be more than a day or two before all is ready," Ortega replied.

Ortega and Hamilton separated and headed south to Puerto Vallarta.

*   *   *

After returning to his hotel suite, Hamilton stepped under the stream of a long, hot shower. As tired as he was he couldn't sleep. The enormity of what they had done and the risk he was taking twisted in his mind like a cyclone. Having Jan here had been a terrible mistake, he realized that when he was out on the American's sailboat. He had to get her out of here and fast.

*   *   *

Just before midnight in Tepic, Santana called Miguel Vegas. "Something is wrong. They should have been here by now."

Vegas tapped his pen on his desk nervously. "I will wait here in case they call."

"Si. I will call you when I can but there is little cell phone service in that whole area."

11

Just as Ortega had locked the gate, Pedro Lopez de Silva had lifted his tired old bones off the hard mat in his palm-covered hut. In the light of a single candle he began his day.

He saddled up his horse, Colorado, a tired old pony but his only companion for many years. When Pedro mounted, the little horse huffed, even at the frail man's weight. The darkness was of no consequence to the pony. It knew where they were going as they headed up the dirt path out of the jungle.

Today Pedro was going into the high country to gather palm nuts. They would earn him a couple of pesos, to buy a few beans and keep him from starving one more day.

Plodding along in the slowly-growing light they reached the coastal highway. Following the edge of the pavement for a few minutes they crossed over and headed up a dirt road into the hills. Once on the dirt Pedro stepped down out of the stirrups giving the old horse a break. Pedro stretched his tired and weary bones. As he lifted the braided rope reins over Colorado's neck he paused at a strange sound. He looked around but saw nothing. Just as he began to lead the horse up the rocky path, he heard it again. This time, unmistakably, a low moan. Cautiously, walking towards the sound, he reached a large mahogany tree on the side of the road. There he spotted a man's boot and to his amazement the boot moved slightly.

He walked slowly around the tree. Two men lay together, one partly covered by a blanket. The uncovered one's head rolled from side to side. Pedro stared not sure what to do.

"Hola?" he whispered hesitantly. "Are you okay?".

The moving one jerked his head and mumbled something Pedro could not understand. Pedro continued cautiously around the tree until he could get a closer look at the moving one. As Pedro came around, the man's eyes opened for a moment. The man was struggling to say something. Pedro realized they must be drunk.

The man mumbled again. Pedro made out the word—aqua. Aqua? He wanted water. Looking around feverishly Pedro spotted a jug of water at the base of the tree. He carefully stepped toward the pair picked up the container and handed it to the man. When the prone figure tried to bring his arm up the blanket fell away exposing handcuffed wrists.

"Madre Dios!" Pedro gasped. He stepped back and almost dropped the jug.

Out of mercy Pedro moved beside the man and tried to cradle his head. He gently poured a small amount of water onto the man's lips. The man licked at the water like a parched animal. Pedro carefully poured a bit more into the now-open mouth. The man's eyes opened wider. Pedro saw they were dazed and distant.

"Who are you?" the man mumbled.

"Pedro Lopez de Silva, Señor."

"Pedro?... Pedro?" The man repeated, not making any sense of it. "Where am I?" The man slurred.

"Under a tree, Señor."

"Under a tree?" the man repeated. "Why?"

"I do not know, Señor."

"What is wrong with my wrists?"

"You are chained to another man."

The man struggled to turn his head to see who it was.

"Meza? Meza!" Perez said in a weak voice, beginning to come to his senses.

Meza began to stir.

Perez looked back at Pedro. "Where is the truck? What did you do with the stuff?" he demanded.

Pedro pushed the man's head off his lap. It landed with a thud on the base of the tree. "I know nothing of a truck," he said, scrambling to his feet in fear.

Perez lifted his head and shook it. "Don't go. Please. We need your help Señor," he begged.

Pedro afraid now, looked down at the pair; he didn't know what to do. He looked at his horse and said. "They must be dangerous, or why would they be here? If I help them, they might take you."

"I did not steal your truck," Pedro managed to say to the man.

"No, no, of course not. You are going to help us," Perez mumbled apologetically.

"Shall I get the police?"

"No. No police. That won't help."

"Then a doctor?"

"No. You must get us free," Perez said, more alert. "And there are two others."

Pedro jumped at the thought that there were more men nearby. Ignoring the prone man's rambling, he cautiously looked around the big tree and in the sparse bushes nearby, but saw no one.

Pedro heard the word 'reward' coming from the man as he returned to the pair. The second man was waking. He too asked for water. Pedro gave it to him.

Perez asked, "Is there no one else here?"

"No, Señor."

"Where are we?"

"In the hills, about a mile from the highway."

"Where in the hills?"

"In the state of Nayarit, Señor."

"There is no truck here!"

"No, Señor. Only me, Pedro Lopez de Silva and my horse, Colorado."

"Do you have something to break these?" Perez lifted up his arm weakly and showed the handcuffs.

"Si. I think so."

He grabbed a hatchet and his ever-present machete out of his saddlebag. Searching, he found a large, flat rock and carried it back to the pair. He set the rock down between the men's hands and laid the chain over it.

"You want me to break this?" Pedro confirmed. He didn't want to make the man angry by breaking his chain.

"Si, Pedro. I want you to break the chain," Perez explained simply.

The steel was good and resisted the pounding of the hatchet. The two men were now fully awake and watching intently.

As the pounding continued, Perez reasoned, "We have to get to a phone. Do you know of someone with a truck?"

"Si, Señor. I have a cousin, Heraldo. He has a truck. It works good most of the time."

"How long will it take you to get it?"

"I can ride there in under an hour."

Finally a link yielded. The two men gave a sigh of relief and climbed stiffly to their feet.

"Pedro de Silva, you have earned the appreciation of some very important people. When we are out of this you will be rewarded. You have my word."

Pedro nodded wearily.

Perez reached into his front pocket and pulled out a couple of large bills. Pedro's eyes bulged at the sight of such an amount. Watching the man's reaction, Perez stated clearly, "I will see you get much more when we get out of here, but now get this cousin here, quickly."

"I will be as quick as I can, but my old horse has no speed left."

The two men watched as he mounted and slapped the horse's rump. Reluctantly, it tried to trot but, almost as quickly, fell back into its plodding walk.

After de Silva was out of sight, Perez turned to Meza. "We were set up. It must have been Esparza. I'll kill him with my bare hands," Perez snarled. "Do you remember what happened?"

"Not exactly," Meza said, trying to remember. "We were at that restaurant, then I got so sleepy and woke up here. How could they have done this?"

"Some drug, you fool," Perez snapped. "My mouth tastes like a ditch, and I have a splitting headache."

"Me too," Meza said in his own defense.

"Help me and we will get our legs free."

In short order the chain holding their feet together, broke. Wasting no time they headed back down the dirt road to the main highway. They stopped just out of sight of the traffic and waited.

After what seemed like hours a beat-up, rusty, old pickup truck turned off the highway. Perez recognized the old man and stepped out onto the dirt road. The truck ground to a halt, the brakes squealing in protest.

The driver stepped out of the truck with a swagger. The old man's cousin was short and fat with a drooping mustache and a scraggly wisp of chin hair. His black hair was matted with oil and dirt. Perez instantly sized the man up as a machismo oaf.

Perez walked directly up to him and offered his hand. "Glad you could get here so quickly, amigo. Now we must hurry." Perez smiled benevolently.

"How much?" the oaf demanded. "I don't do nothing for free. Pay me now."

Without responding, Perez walked past the man and climbed into the passenger side of the truck. The man scrambled back to the truck and reached for the key—it was gone. Perez sat there key in hand. Still smiling, but in an icy voice, Perez said, "My employer is a very generous man but he can also be very cruel."

"Give me my key," the driver commanded, his bad breath making Perez's empty stomach churn.

"I do not have time for games, amigo. You will be rewarded, generously, if you cooperate," Perez looked the man in the eye.

The cousin weighed the situation. He was strong but these two would be more than he could handle, and to what end? He smiled showing a row of unkempt tobacco-stained teeth. With a shrug he climbed behind the steering wheel. Meza jumped in beside Perez. The old man obligingly climbed into the back bed of the truck.

"We need these off," Perez waved the remains of the handcuffs. "And a phone."

"I'm a mechanic and have a small shop down the highway, but no phone. The nearest is in San Francisco, three kilometers."

"Cuffs first. Let's go." Perez shoved the key into the ignition.

They headed north. In a short while they came to a rude building with walls that were made of part brick, part rough-cut slabs of wood; the roof consisted of corrugated steel sheets and palm branches. Old tires lay haphazardly in the dirt. Two dirty children were playing near the old horse. The horse stood dejected, covered with sweat.

Against a cold chisel, small sledgehammer and anvil, the handcuffs latches yielded quickly.

"How much to drive us to the phone?" Perez demanded

"A thousand pesos!" the man said.

"For that much you will drive us to Tepic. Get in."

They pulled into the small town and stopped in front of the public phone. Perez was relieved to hear a dial tone.

*   *   *

Just after nine o'clock in the morning the phone rang on Miguel Vegas' private line in Mexico City.

Vegas answered after barely a ring.

"Yes?"

"It's Perez."

"Where are you? Why haven't you called?"

"Esparza has hijacked the truck. We are in the state of Nayarit, about 200 kilometers south from Tepic."

"What have you done?" Vegas' voice turned Perez's blood cold.

"They drugged us somehow. With some food, I think."

"Who's us?"

146

"Me and Meza."

"When?"

"Last night when we stopped to eat. We woke up handcuffed in the hills somewhere. This is the first phone I could reach." Perez knew that his and his family's lives hung by a thread. "Señor Vegas, we have been doing all we can to get out and reach you," he pleaded.

The phone was quiet. Beads of sweat rose on Perez's forehead. He knew not to speak.

"Get to the Tepic airport. How long?"

"We have transportation." Perez looked at the beat up truck. "We can be there in maybe two hours, maybe less."

"Call me back in ten minutes. You can do that, can't you?" Vegas sneered.

"Si." The line went dead. Perez backed away from the phone. He couldn't swallow for fear. He wiped his brow with the back of his hand.

*   *   *

Vegas immediately ordered a helicopter to meet him on the top of the building. Then he called the airport to contact the corporate jet, only to discover that his brother had it.

"Where?"

"His flight plan called for Guadalajara," the receptionist said.

Slamming the phone down, he told his secretary to hire a private jet immediately for Tepic. Next, he called Santana.

"The truck has been kidnapped. Ernesto is behind this, I am sure."

Santana's jaw tightened. "Si, Señor," he managed to get out. "When and where?"

"Last night, north of Puerto Vallarta. Perez says they drugged him and Meza. Perez is on the way to Tepic. I am leaving now to meet him at the airport. Start calling everyone you know who's loyal. See what you can find out."

"Si, Señor."

Next he called his brother's office. "Have you seen him or Ortega?" he demanded of his brother's secretary.

"He has not come in this morning, Señor Vegas."

He hung up as his private line rang. It was Perez.

"Hold," Vegas commanded.

Punching his secretary's line again he shot, "Have you got the plane?"

"Si, Señor Vegas, as soon as you get there. The helicopter is coming now."

"Thirty minutes. Have it ready the instant I arrive." He hung up and punched the other line.

"I'll be in Tepic as soon as possible, two hours. Santana will be there to meet you at the airport." Vegas killed the line.

*　　*　　*

Perez went numb at the thought of Santana. He willed his legs to move to the truck. "We are going to Tepic."

"Tepic. Tepic will be extra," The fat driver demanded.

Patience gone, Perez grabbed the man by the throat of his filthy tee shirt and snarled, "Does the name Miguel Vegas, Vemexa corporation mean anything to you, you fat stupid fool?"

The man grabbed Perez's hand and tried to break the grip. Then the name, Vegas, saturated his brain. He stopped struggling and stared at Perez.

"Madre Dios! Vegas?"

"Vegas," Perez repeated, releasing his shirt.

"Madre Dios." The man slammed the accelerator and dropped the clutch. Gravel sprayed as the truck fishtailed out of the parking lot.

*　　*　　*

"Brother, if you are behind this you are a dead man." Miguel Vegas spat.

Vegas unlocked the lower drawer of his desk and withdrew his Browning 9mm pistol in its heavy leather, hand-tooled, Jim Brown holster and shoulder harness, along with a box of shells, and put them in a black carrying bag. He patted his pocket for his ever-present switchblade.

"I'm going to Tepic. Tell no one. If you need me, contact Santana, and only Santana," he commanded as he passed his private secretary.

On the roof of the building the chopper was waiting. From his cell phone Vegas chartered two additional helicopters to head to Tepic.

The jet was warmed and waiting when he arrived at the airport. The pilot was cleared and they were airborne in short order. In just over two hours from the first call Vegas met Santana.

*   *   *

After a nightmarish drive Perez and Meza arrived at the airport. As they stepped out of the truck Vegas and Santana emerged through the front doors of the airport. Perez was so terrified at the sight of the two that he didn't hear the sound of the old pickup truck speeding away. They stood there trembling as the killers approached.

Vegas, seeing the look on the men's faces, made his decision, at least for the immediate future. He strode up purposefully and extended his hand to Perez.

Perez nearly collapsed at the offered hand, unsure of its meaning.

"Perez, you did right." Vegas purposely showing admiration while looking directly into the man's eyes.

Perez forced his knees to hold. Vegas gave Meza the same treatment.

Santana just stared at them in deadly silence.

As they headed out of the airport, Vegas demanded, "All right, tell me again what happened? You think they acted on their own?"

"I do not know Señor, honestly. I thought there was someone else," Meza volunteered meekly, his voice tapering off as he realized the others were listening to him. Just above a whisper, he continued, "I thought someone was watching us at the restaurant and I heard a strange voice when I was sleeping. But I thought I was just dreaming. Then I found this when I was washing in the airport." He undid his shirt and on his upper arm was a small bruise with a pinprick in the center.

They all looked at it. Perez pulled his shirt off the shoulder. He too had a similar mark.

"They shot you with something," Vegas said looking at the wounds.

"Why didn't they kill you?" Santana asked bluntly.

Perez looked at his master's enforcer. "I don't know, but if we ever meet again they better not expect me to return the favor."

"We'll start with the restaurant," Vegas stated. "How long to get there?"

"Two hours," Perez said.

"Let's go."

When they were half way there, Vegas received confirmation from his secretary that the arrival of the helicopters in Tepic would be later that day.

After about an hour they passed the road where Perez and Meza had been abandoned. They commented on each point of their recent journey north, trying to verify the reality of their claims.

It was just after lunch when they arrived at the restaurant. There were a few vehicles in the lot. The restaurant owner froze upon recognition of the pair from the previous night. Then he nearly fainted when he saw the well-dressed man and the threatening bodyguard that accompanied them.

"We will talk," Vegas said to the owner.

Santana took the man's arm, led him to a table and forcibly sat him down. The others surrounded him.

"What happened last night?" Vegas demanded, towering over the man.

Everyone in the restaurant stopped and watched.

Santana scanned the crowd for any threat, then headed slowly to the kitchen.

"Please Señor," the man begged. "A man came in threatening us. He had a gun. He said no one would be hurt. What could I do?" The sound of his wife made him turn. Santana was dragging her over to the table. "Maria!" the owner cried, trying to get up.

Perez pushed him back in the chair.

The owner desperately turned back to Vegas. "Please Señor, what could we do?"

"Call the police?" Vegas suggested sarcastically.

"We have no phone. The trucks, two of them, arrived not that long after the man." The man nodded at Meza and Perez.

"What did the big man do?"

"He put some powder, white powder, in their soup. He made me serve these two first," he said nodding at Perez and Meza.

"That's right, we got ours first," Perez confirmed.

"Two Diablos, si?" the owner said, encouraged by Perez's confirmation.

Perez continued. "As I remember, Esparza didn't eat much of his soup. I don't remember anything about Vásquez. Esparza took something out to him…" Perez's voice trailed off as he tried to think. "I had him guarding the tr…" He stopped again, not wanting to say too much.

Vegas's attention returned to the owner. "What did this man look like?"

"Solidly built, not as big as that one," he pointed at Santana, "but still big and strong. He grabbed my arm at one point and I felt the strength in his hand. On his forearm was a tattoo—a dagger and serpent."

Perez jumped when he realized who it was.

Vegas weighed the situation. He had a misplaced truck with a very valuable cargo. More importantly, he now had the opportunity to defend himself against his brother; everyone that mattered would see that. If he acted quickly, all matters big and small would be rectified.

"That is enough," Vegas commanded. "Let's go."

The men headed for the car. The owner was barely able to keep his feet as he staggered back to his fearful, crying wife.

As the men headed back to Tepic, Vegas checked his cell phone. Still out of range. He ran through his options with the others.

"It's been 16 hours. How far north could they have gotten?"

"Quite a ways, but not out of Mexico." Santana answered.

"Would Ernesto make a run for the US border or stash the cargo until the dust settled?" Vegas figured he had to cover both options. He would notify all his contacts along the border, and he would start the search locally with the helicopters. Lastly, it was time to call Don Bellini and hire his associates.

Consistency was not necessarily a wise thing in the drug trade. In fact it could prove quite deadly. For years the Ferret had been in charge of the family's affairs in Puerto Vallarta. It was he who had provided the services of a particular young woman to Ortega when he was in town. The Ferret was well aware of the apartment where she now stayed and the company she kept. It was with little difficulty that he had arranged for another girl to befriend her. Often, when not on call to Ortega, they would heat up the town. Together they made good money, providing the services that some of the wealthy tourists were looking for.

Thus, when Vegas called the Ferret, he was able to act quickly. It took one call to Donna Maria, his contact, and a simple, innocent question: "What are you doing tonight?" And that was it. She had said that Ortega and his boss were visiting town. They were to meet them and an American couple, later at Cristobel's nightclub.

"How very nice," Miguel Vegas smirked as he hung up from the Ferret. "Well brother, your time has come."

*　　*　　*

Miguel Vegas recalled the beatings his older brother had administered upon him during their youth. Their mother had worked at reconciliation, their father had not. It was as if the man wanted the two sons pitted against each other from birth.

The pain his brother had inflicted burned in Miguel's memory. Ernesto was older, stronger, and out-weighed Miguel by a good 10 kilos at the time. It had not been until his early teens that Miguel discovered that speed and cunning could give him an edge. He had waited for his opportunity and baited Ernesto into a confrontation. On that occasion years ago, it had been easy. As the conflict had progressed, Miguel kept giving way, trying to take as few blows as possible. Ernesto had tired of the feinting game. When Miguel saw the frustration in his brother's eyes he was ready. Ernesto charged, and pulled Miguel in, expecting to easily pummel him. But as Ernesto did, a searing fire cut across the side of his ribs. He violently released his brother. Miguel saw the startled look on his brother's face; it had been one he would cherish for years. Ernesto had pulled his hand away from his ribcage. It was covered with blood.

Miguel raised the switchblade knife. "More?"

Enraged by the insult, Ernesto advanced, but it was different, he was no longer the master of the conflict.

Miguel watched Ernesto's hands. If Ernesto got hold of him, he would be in serious trouble. The knife flashed, just missing Ernesto's outstretched fingertips.

"I will kill you," Ernesto snarled.

"Not if I kill you first," Miguel challenged. He swung the blade again as the combatants venomously eyed each other.

Miguel determined it was enough. "You ever try to beat me

again and I'll use this…only more," he spat, and slowly backed away.

It was good that they were alone or the humiliation would have driven Ernesto to continue the conflict. The wound, although painful, was not deep and there was no scar, except on Ernesto's pride and that burned hot.

Yet, the beatings stopped.

Miguel learned years later, that after that day, his brother had tried to use a knife but found he was not fast enough to guarantee an advantage. Before a rematch could develop, the school season had begun and Ernesto was sent away to a finishing-school attended by all of Mexico's "high-society" families.

Miguel's education had also continued. Since that day he had discovered that he was very good at enticing others to react in a way of his choosing. He found that he gained immense pleasure from manipulating people. North Americans called it "pushing your buttons." Miguel liked the expression. He learned how hard to push, and when, in order to elicit a particular reaction. In the jungle, it was called a trap.

*   *   *

Miguel's calls were rebuffed by Ernesto's office staff throughout the day. They swore that they could not reach him. Miguel was sure the staff was walking around in soiled clothing. He smiled at the fear he was creating.

Once this was over, he would make a point of forgiving most of them. A couple would have to be sacrificed, so the others could see how fortunate they were—and where their loyalty was best placed. Terror was such a useful tool.

As soon as Vegas was alone in Tepic, he made the call. "Señor Bellini. Miguel Vegas calling," he told the gangster's secretary.

The phone was answered in under a minute. "Miguel, how are you?"

"The shipment has been stolen."

There was a long pause. "What can you tell me?"

"We know when and where it was taken." Vegas waited before adding, "We also know by who."

The man on the other end of the line, who rightfully thought of the cargo as his property, waited.

"We have planes in the sky and people on the ground. We believe we have them at a stalemate. We haven't found it but they can't move it."

"What do you propose?"

"It is time that I engaged your specialists." Vegas paused. "If we cut off the head the body will wiggle."

"When and where?" Bellini asked.

"I will make arrangements. Where are they now?"

"Phoenix, waiting for the shipment."

"Excellent. How soon can they be at the border, at Nogales?"

"It is one in the afternoon local time. Under five hours I would imagine. What do you have on your side to get them there?"

"I'll call you back. I think it is best to bring them across by car with their equipment. I'll get them flown down after that."

"You will ensure their absolute safety." It was a command, not a question. Both men knew the retribution they would suffer if anything happened to these two professionals.

"Si, their crossing will never happen. As to their time here, we will make it worth their while. I will get back to you with details."

Just before they hung up, Bellini stopped. "I almost forgot, they will want to know how many and who."

"Three. Jorge Ortega, Todd Hamilton, and," Miguel paused, "Ernesto."

"It will be done."

12

Jan sat in the hotel restaurant having breakfast and watching people go by. They wore shorts and light shirts, enjoying gentle weather. She had seen on TV that it was -5°F back home, with an icy front coming off Lake Michigan and another snowstorm predicted. The thought of going back to Indianapolis made her sour.

Todd had promised an early start, but she knew better. She figured he had been out very late the night before. There had been a note on the table: *"Wake me at 10. T."*

After her leisurely breakfast she wandered back up to the room and peeked in. He was on the phone and jumped when he saw her. He looked terrible.

Todd cupped the phone. "I'll just be a minute, then we'll get going. Shut the door. I'll be right out." He turned and went back to the caller.

"Todd, you promised," she stated firmly refusing to leave.

He looked up and waved, "Yeah, yeah," then went back into the phone. "Look, I'll have my cell on. We're going out to Punta de Mita for the day. Anyway it's probably best if I make myself scarce."

As he hung up he turned and gave her a big smile. "Things are cooking. If all goes well we'll be out of the woods in a couple of days."

"And that's good?"

He suddenly realized what he had said. "Uh yeah, never mind. I'll have a quick shower and be right with you." Allowing no room for further conversation he raced into the bathroom.

*　　*　　*

They drove out of the city in one of the hotel's Jeeps. The warm sunshine and the wind in her hair reminded Jan of how little time the two of them had spent together while growing up. Todd had been practically grown by the time she was old enough to remember, and he came home only for holidays and the summer months. To a little sister he always seemed so busy, always doing something terribly important. Todd had helped out so much after their dad was gone and both she and their mom had never wanted for anything. Nowadays it felt good being able to do her bit, helping her mother and others, as they dealt with Alzheimer's. And as much as it grieved her she knew she was in Todd's way, and should be getting back to their mom. But for now, riding beside her big brother in that beautiful place, with the wind blowing her hair, things couldn't be better.

She looked out onto the Bay as they passed the turnoff to La Cruz. There was a flotilla of sailboats in the harbor.

Todd followed her gaze. "Thinking of someone in particular?"

"Just wondering if I could recognize that sailboat again."

"Yeah, right. The boat not the guy, right?"

"Well…" she smiled.

"I thought you sort-of had the hots for him."

"He was nice, but…I don't know," she paused. "One minute he seemed friendly, then the next minute he cooled off. I think maybe he's married or got someone else. I don't know."

"I'll have him checked out," Todd stated bluntly.

"You'll do no such thing. You can't go snooping into someone else's life."

"The hell you say. I can't have someone leading my baby sister on without checking his pedigree. Besides, he seems a bit of a rogue to me." He baited her.

"He's not, and you know it."

"So you do have the hots for him!" He gave her a devilish smile.

"Todd Hamilton! How can you say that?"

"Hey, go for it. Faint heart nar' won fair…what?" He tried to find the right word, "Brute? Stud? Hunk? I don't know. You tell me."

"I'd like to think the strong, silent type," she smirked. "Of course, stud has a nice ring to it too." She gave her brother a wanton smile.

"I'll not only have to check this guy out, I'm going to have to warn him of what he might be getting into," he laughed. With that he down-shifted and passed a slow-moving bus. "We're coming up to Rancho Banderas resort. It's a beautiful hotel. They've got one of the most beautiful stretches of beach on the whole Bay. They have big plans for this beach. I know the guy who runs the place, you want to go down and take a tour?"

"Definitely not! You'll just start talking business. I want you all to myself."

"Okay. You're the boss. I do have one place I want to show you though, and I can guarantee that there will be nobody there."

They breezed along for a number of miles around tight, winding bends on the narrow paved road leading out to Punta de Mita. The road was treacherous, buses passed by so closely that Jan could have touched them. There was no shoulder, no protective fencing of any kind along the edges of cliffs that fell hundreds of feet, towards the ocean.

Jan was amazed to see that in some spots, trees on either side of the road provided a complete canopy above their heads. It was like a park.

Todd gave her a running commentary on the development of the area. She was amazed at the details he knew…like how the Bay of Banderas was going to be the next Gold Coast. The recession had slowed things down, but also gave everything a chance to get consolidated. "Sort out the weak," as Todd had put it. As sure as time, baby boomers were going to retire down here. They didn't want Mexico the way it was, they wanted all the comforts and security of home brought here, and more importantly they were willing to pay for it. Jan really didn't care. She dreamily watched the beautiful scenery flow by.

All of a sudden Todd turned left off the road onto an old rutted bit of dirt. In front of them was a padlocked chain-link gate. Jan watched in fascination as her brother jumped out of the car unlocked the lock and drove through.

They bounced down an old, unkempt, dirt road for a couple of hundred yards and came to the ocean.

"Look at the vines!" Jan exclaimed, craning her neck as they drove along under giant trees covered with foliage. She had never seen anything like it.

Todd pulled the Jeep up in front of a run-down old building. The concrete flooring remained but the rest was in shambles. And, true to his word, there wasn't a soul in sight. Todd bounded out of the car.

"Come on! I want to show you something," he said excitedly.

Jan was surprised at his enthusiasm. She quickly hopped out and took his hand as they navigated the broken surface of the old floor. When they came around the building she saw the beach. It was completely private and formed a perfect crescent. They watched as the gentle surf rolled in and washed soft white sand.

Jan turned to her brother, who was watching for her reaction. "Oh Todd, it's gorgeous!"

He smiled and savored the look on his sister's face.

"What's it called?"

"Paradisio Escondido… Hidden Paradise."

"It is," she agreed heartily.

She kicked off her sandals and walked down onto the fine sand. The place had a this-is-our-little-secret feel. She ran along the shore and stood at the edge of the water. The surf spent itself at her feet. She gazed as the waves formed out in the ocean, crested, then formed again as they reached the shore.

"Is there a shallow spot out there?" she asked.

"Yes, more's the pity. At the moment that's a bit of a problem."

"Really. Why?"

"Oh, it's nothing." He changed the subject. "What do you think of the place?" Without waiting for a response, he continued, "This is going to be a very exclusive resort. Very small, so it keeps the feel of privacy. We're not hurrying anything."

They sat there for a while watching the surf ebb and flow along the crescent. Sometimes the waves would come in as bold as brass, while other times they slid softly up the sand like a whisper. Brother and sister walked to the far edge of the sand and up onto the rocks bordering the beach. Jan crawled along the edge, observing the aquatic life in the tidal pools in the rocks.

"Be careful, you'll get torn up pretty bad if the surf catches you on the rocks." He offered his hand as Jan cautiously navigated the water's edge, seeking out flat stones or sandy pockets, safe for bare feet.

For a brief moment their eyes met, and Todd's face brightened at the happiness he saw in his sister. Just as quickly, her eyes focused back on the rocks. Jan took a few steps back, for safe measure. They watched the surf roll up onto the shallow rock outcropping, then reform as it surged towards the shore, then gently curl as it reached the sandy beach. After a while they walked back to the safety of the sand.

"The rocks are what make this so private," Todd explained. "But they can be dangerous."

"I can see that," Jan agreed.

"We should be going." He tugged at his sister's shirt, encouraging her to chase him across the soft sand toward the Jeep.

Todd double-checked the padlock on the gate before they left. As they pulled back onto the road, Jan commented, "That must have been a very expensive piece of property."

Before answering he hurried to pull out ahead of a slow moving construction truck. They had yet to drive fifty yards, when he slowed and pulled off to the right.

"Yeah, it was," finally acknowledging her comment. "But there's a bit of land just up there that's worth a whole lot more."

Jan looked to where Todd pointed and saw another set of corroded cement pillars and another chain-link gate, complete with padlock.

As they cruised further down the road Todd pointed out the entrance to the Four Seasons Punta de Mita resort. He kidded her again about going in and meeting the manager. Jan gave him an evil eye. He laughed and they sped forward to the Punta de Mita area, the northern tip of the bay and the little town of El Anclote at the very end of the road. This is the only place along the whole area where the general public could enjoy the beach. The rest of the Punta de Mita area had been carved up by developers. They grabbed their day bags and walked along the street. Jan gave Todd a sour look as he pulled out his cell phone.

He tried it. "Out of range."

"Good," she noted.

As they passed each restaurant that lined the beach, a waiter would come out and invite them in, each offering the best food and prices. Todd ignored them and headed toward the end of the beach. Stepping into the last restaurant in the row, Todd greeted the owner like an old friend.

"Señor Hamilton, Señorita," the owner greeted them and bowed to Jan.

"Alfredo, my sister, Jan."

"Hola, Señorita. Welcome to my restaurant." He shook her hand. "I am honored that Señor Hamilton would bring us his beautiful sister. Come. We will find you a perfect table for the day."

The man led them to a table at the edge of the beach where the pristine, white, powdery sand enthralled Jan. Little fishing boats lined the edge of the breakwater and a row of pelicans sat idly on their gunwales and sterns. Jan wiggled her toes in the sand. It was the softest, whitest sand she had ever imagined, even softer than at Hidden Paradise.

To Jan, the rest of the day evaporated like mist in a dream. Waiters fussed over them. Little native girls came up trying to sell souvenirs. The girls were shooed away until Jan asked to see their wares.

Todd laughed. "You're paying about twice as much as that stuff is worth, you know."

"I don't care. They need it more than I do. Especially these cute kids with the Chiclets."

"You got a year's worth," He chuckled and shook his head.

When she finished buying, Jan lined her treasures up on the table, assigning each as a souvenir for a particular friend. It was all very organized. She had great fun.

"Come on, let's go in the water," Jan said.

Todd made an ugly face.

"Come on!"

Much to her surprise, he got up and took his bathing suit to the change room. She couldn't help but giggle at his pale white legs.

"For a guy that lives in Mexico, you don't get out much," she teased as they stood hip deep in the water.

Todd grabbed her arm and twisted. They both collapsed into the water. When Jan came up, Todd playfully pushed her head under. At that, she grabbed his trunks and gave a strong pull.

"Okay, that's enough," he laughed, "If you're going to pick on me, I'm going in."

"You started it!" She made a grab for him, but he was too quick for her.

"You go for a swim," he called out, retreating.

Jan floated on her back for a while and then turned and did a hard, fast breaststroke for fifty yards, back to shore.

She ran up the beach, puffing. As she neared the table, she saw her brother was fast asleep. Quietly, she sat and read a book until he came around.

"Mmm, I needed that." He rubbed his eyes. All too soon, the sun arched over the sky. "We better be heading back if you want to catch the sunset from Señor Mister Pepe's."

"You'll take me then?" she smiled as she squeezed his forearm.

"Sure. I said I would, didn't I?"

"Yeah, but you said on the phone you had to do something else tonight."

"Oh. We're invited to a little celebration at Cristobel's. It's the hip nightclub in town. I didn't think you'd be interested, but we can go if you'd like."

It was the last thing she wanted to do, but she could see that he wanted to go. "Let's see after Pepe's," she answered diplomatically.

"Reasonable."

On the drive back, he again slowed at the gate in the woods and checked the lock before he sped home.

Todd surrendered the Jeep to the valet. When they got to their suite, Jan headed straight to the shower, and Todd, to the phone.

"How are things?" Hamilton asked Ortega.

"Not good. The tide's too low during the night to get the boats to shore. It'll be two more days at least before they can get in, and then only for a short time."

"Yeah, I was there today. It was close to high tide and the waves were still cresting on the rocks. We'll have to wait. I'm taking Jan to the airport tomorrow at noon, so that will be one less worry. I promised her we would go out to dinner tonight, just the two of us." Todd said into the phone.

"We are all meeting at Cristobel's. I made arrangements. If she doesn't want to come, fine, but you should be there." Ortega responded.

"Amigo, I've had a long week. Don't push me. I'm spending time with my sister, then getting her out of here. This thing is getting on all our nerves. Besides," he placated, "how safe is it for all of us to be seen together? I understand Miguel thinks you are in Guadalajara and Ernesto is in Mexico City."

"Miguel has his head up his butt. He's in Tepic. He's got helicopters and planes flying all over San Blas and into the interior." Ortega laughed sarcastically.

"Be careful. He's to be feared." Todd pleaded.

"You worry too much, Hamilton, but that's what we pay you for, amigo. You will miss a good time tonight."

"Thanks, but no thanks." Todd looked up and saw Jan coming out of her suite, already dressed. He hadn't started yet. "I've got to go," he said and hung up without another word.

"Just be a minute," he yelled running from the phone like a boy caught with his hand in the cookie jar.

*   *   *

On the way into old town where Señor Mister Pepe's was located, Todd confessed, "I had to check in. Something big is coming down and everyone is a little on edge."

"Right… like I hadn't noticed." Jan paused, "When was the last good sleep you had?" she scolded.

"Well, mother," he looked at her with a grin, "to tell the truth, and I always do, I could use a good night's sleep."

"We can have a quick dinner and head home early."

"We are not going to McDonald's, little sister. This guy puts on a nice spread, sort of a Mexican full-course dinner thing. It's the perfect place to watch a sunset."

"Sounds romantic."

"Ah nuts!" Todd exclaimed. "I should have invited your sailor boy."

"Whatever gave you that idea, Mr. Hamilton?"

"Oh, I saw that look again as we were coming home through La Cruz. I think my little sister is smitten."

"Brother, you are starting to make Indiana look good," she stated in mock disgust. "Even in February."

He gave a hearty laugh as the taxi worked its way up the steep, rough cobblestoned hill that led to Señor Mister Pepe's restaurant.

At the top of the long flight of stairs, the proprietor met

them with enthusiasm. "Mr. Hamilton! How are you?" The short, rotund owner happily clasped Todd's hand.

"Hola, Mr. Pepe, como esta?"

"And this is?" Pepe said.

"My sister, Jan Hamilton."

"The beautiful Miss Jan Hamilton, very glad to meet you." Jan watched in amazement as he bowed and kissed her hand. "Come. I have made a very special table right in the corner just for you." He led the pair out onto a roofless patio.

It was, by far, the best table in the house. The view was panoramic and breathtaking. They were three stories above the street, and the street was one of the highest in Puerto Vallarta.

"It's lovely Todd. The view alone was worth the walk up those stairs."

"He has a great spot. Across there," he pointed across the valley to the central ridge behind the center of the town, "is the church tower that you see on all the posters. See it there? Looks like a crown, huh?"

"Yes. I saw that the other day when I walked the Malecón."

"Just up the hill from it—I don't know which one—is where Liz Taylor and Richard Burton lived."

It was another perfect sunset in paradise. A number of other couples came near their table and had their pictures taken in the sunset, many with Mr. Pepe. Everyone chatted as they shared the gorgeous view. Once the sun was down the patrons returned to their tables and back to enjoy their meals in privacy. The owner buzzed by making small talk with each table.

"Quite a showman," Jan observed.

Todd smiled. "Doesn't bother advertising. The neat thing is, you come back here in a year and the guy remembers your name. He's a great salesman."

"How does he remember?"

"I don't know, but he does. I've brought people here over the years and that's what he does, makes people feel important. Plus it's great food, so you get it all."

It was a great meal with a surprisingly decent Mexican wine. As evening settled into night, the pair lingered over coffee, listening to the owner's two daughters—one on the piano, the other a very good singer.

"I want to thank you for this time we've had together," Jan said.

"You're very welcome. I apologize for having to send you home so quickly, but there'll be more times—I promise you."

"I know, and I'm starting to feel guilty about being away from mom. It's just that, well, I've never really had a chance to say thanks for so many things—helping out with mom and everything," she stumbled.

"Hey, that's what big brothers are for. Besides, I only did what I could. You put a lot into this too, staying home and all. You haven't had much of a life yet, but I promise that will change."

She smiled at the thought. "I have no complaints."

"To tomorrow," he said, lifting his coffee cup.

*   *   *

As Todd opened the door to their suite he said, "I'm bushed. I think I'll take a sleeping pill. You want one?"

"No, I have to pack a bit. Besides, I can sleep when I get home."

13

A hearse pulled up to the border crossing at Nogales, Sonora. Within was a uniformed driver and two assistants. The coffin carried Pedro Morales. The paper work showed Morales had died of hepatitis—the result of a blood transfusion. The Mexican border guard had been alerted to contact his supervisor immediately on their arrival.

The supervisor, Bernardo Vallejo, had a bad habit—gambling. He had been pretty lucky, too. But as is the way of all gamblers, he finally lost—and lost big. The debt he owed the Vegas family could never be repaid on a border supervisor's wage. So when the offer of forgiveness had come, only hours earlier, there was no question of "why" or in "return for what." Only, "Si, Señor. No problemo!"

The border guard knew something was up when Vallejo rushed to the vehicle and escorted the driver into his private office. Paperwork was quickly dispatched and the hearse was on its way.

Fifteen miles south of Nogales, on a dirt runway, a fast, twin-engine Piper had been waiting. The two assistants were airborne minutes after arrival, and they made the trip to Puerto Vallarta in just over three hours.

Just before sunset, the plane taxied to a private section of the airport where the two men and their tools were unloaded into a windowless white van. The men spent the rest of the evening at the house of the Ferret in Nuevo Vallarta, ten miles north of the airport. They studied drawings of the interior of Cristobel's, and memorized the faces of their subjects before double-checking their equipment.

Once they analyzed the situation, they agreed that the best weapon would be the Glock 9mm subcompact. It was small, fast and accurate.

Through his contacts at the hotel the Ferret learned of Hamilton's dinner plans and conveyed the information to Vegas at his warehouse in Tepic.

After hanging up, Vegas turned to Santana and said, "Hamilton has taken his sister to an early dinner. I am told they will be joining the party later."

Vegas quickly called the Ferret back and commanded, "Give instructions that none of the women are to be harmed, especially not the Hamilton woman, you understand?"

"Si, Señor. Not the Hamilton woman."

"At least not yet," Vegas added.

The Ferret had engaged the services of two young toughs to hang around Cristobel's and signal when Ernesto and Ortega arrived. One thug remained inside and the other waited in the back loading bay. The one out front recognized Ernesto and notified the Ferret as soon as he and Ortega arrived, women in tow.

The Ferret called Vegas. "Your brother and Ortega are here. There is no sign of Hamilton. What do you want to do?"

"How long will it take for our people to get there?"

"Twenty minutes, no more," the Ferret said.

"It is ten o'clock. Have them execute the plan at eleven. In one hour be at Cristobel's. You understand?" Vegas commanded.

"Si, Señor. It will be done. Eleven o'clock. I will tell them."

Just after ten thirty the two men stepped back into the white van. Each was dressed in black pants, crisp white shirts, black bow ties, and dapper short, black jackets—like the wardrobe of waiters at Cristobel's. They both carried black canvas tote bags.

From their bags they took small earplugs and tough, laser-thin, skin-toned gloves. Methodically, they counted out the number of rounds in the magazines—nine in each. Although these particular magazines would hold ten, it was safer not to apply full pressure. As professionals, both men were confident that one bullet was all they really needed.

Pulling into the restaurant's loading bay the Ferret flashed his headlights. The punk guarding the back area stepped up.

Just before eleven o'clock the place was jumping. Waiters rushed back and forth from the kitchen. No one noticed two extra uniforms stepping into the kitchen, even though they wore shaded glasses to protect their night vision.

The lead man grabbed a pitcher of ice water from a shelf in the kitchen as they made for the darkened lounge. Back in the darkness, their eyes readjusted. Another harried waiter rushed by and yelled at them to get moving. The killers bowed their heads to avoid recognition.

Disco music pounded the walls. Beautiful people were gyrating everywhere. The oppressive sound would make the assassins work easier. They both spotted the table where their quarry sat and they gave each other a nod. After scanning the area for any sign of extra security they moved in.

The targets were sitting beside each other in a large booth. The women were on the outside of either man. It couldn't be simpler. The lead man set the pitcher down too close to the edge of the table and gravity took over. All eyes watched as the pitcher slowly arched over onto the lap of one of the women. Ortega tried to catch it.

The waiters counted the number of times they fired. Any chance of survival ended with the first shot; four more prevented miracles. In the briefest of seconds, each confirmed the other's work. They turned, concealed their weapons under their jackets and purposefully moved back through the kitchen to the outside.

The two women stared as blood enveloped the bodies and wall behind them. When they finally found their voices, their screams, were lost in the blare of the music.

Before anyone realized what had happened, the hit men were in the moving van.

The pair immediately stripped and stuffed their costumes, gloves, and pistols into a thick plastic bag. They washed their faces and hands with wet towels, each surveying the other for any sprayed fluids, then deposited the towels into the bag.

Finally they changed into fresh outfits; designer pants, light shirts and jackets, finished off with deck shoes. They looked every inch, the part of wealthy yachtsmen.

In less than five minutes, the van pulled up to the Iguana Marina. Unhurried, the killers walked down the wharf and stepped onto a waiting launch. Before the police had arrived at Cristobel's, the pair were motoring out on to the Bay of Banderas, heading for a chartered luxury cabin cruiser that would take them fishing for a few days to the south towards Manzanillo.

After they departed the Ferret called Vegas. "The job is done."

"Any problems?" Vegas asked.

"They got your brother and Ortega—guaranteed. Hamilton was not there."

Vegas sneered, "I win." He said to himself.

Over the phone he asked, "Hamilton?"

"Do you want us to go and get him now?" the Ferret asked.

Vegas thought for a moment, "No. We will leave for Puerto Vallarta now and will pick him up in the morning. He may be useful in helping us find our truck. Have him watched," he commanded.

Vegas turned to Santana and smiled. "It is done."

"Hamilton remains?" Santana deduced from the one-sided conversation.

"Yes, and I'm sure it is for the best. If he knows anything, he will tell, especially to save his precious sister."

"And if he doesn't?"

"Then it will be all the more fun to make him watch." Vegas gave a cold smirk.

*　　*　　*

At the nightclub all hell broke loose. One of the women at the table screamed until she fainted. Once the crowd realized what had happened, half stampeded to the exits while the other half tried to get a closer look. Several took pictures. Others vomited. The music kept playing.

As soon as the police arrived they closed the place. It wasn't until this point that it became clear that this wasn't just a random shooting, but rather an assassination. Even though the police knew the victims, they refused to issue a statement until the bodies were officially identified. Their caution didn't stop the news and pictures from hit the outside world the following morning.

*　　*　　*

A newly-employed security man had been assigned to watch Todd Hamilton's room. No one told him what to do if a woman departed.

Jan was up early that morning, fresh from a peaceful night's sleep. She gathered her clothing and readied to leave. She lingered by the bay window for a moment looking at a couple of early sailboats heading out to sea. Before she left she jotted down a brief note for Todd and left it on the coffee table.

Shortly after Jan left, Vegas and his Tepic entourage met the Ferret in the loading bay behind the hotel.

"Santana and you will come with me," Vegas said, pointing at the Ferret. "Perez, you and Meza wait here. Be ready to leave quickly."

The trio rode the service elevator to the top floor. The security guard approached as they came out of the elevator.

"Is Hamilton still in there?" the Ferret asked.

"Si, Señor. A woman left a short time ago."

The Ferret addressed the security guard. "You are dismissed.

You can go home. Say nothing to anyone, no one…you understand?"

Santana withdrew his pistol as the Ferret used a master key to unlock the door. Santana and his pistol led them into the suite followed closely by the Ferret. Vegas waited until Santana signaled him to enter.

On the coffee table, Vegas picked up the note: "*Gone to the Plaza Marina for some shopping. Back in a couple of hours. J.*"

Vegas slipped it in his pocket. He nodded to Santana, who cautiously opened Todd's door. Todd, groggily coming around, looked up as the light changed with the opening of the door.

"What the hell!" He snapped to alert. "What are…" He got no further.

The Ferret strong-armed him back down and Santana pushed the muzzle of the pistol deep into his cheek. Hamilton froze.

Vegas gave him a crocodile grin. "You made a deadly mistake, amigo. Ernesto wants to see you."

Hamilton only stared.

"No harm will come to your sister if you come quietly. Otherwise…" Vegas said coldly.

"Where's my sister?"

"We have her already," he stated. "Get dressed."

The Ferret dug through Hamilton's closet. After emptying the pants' pockets and removing a belt, he threw some clothes on the bed. Santana's aim never wavered.

"We are going to walk out of here quietly, as friends," Vegas stated with deadly calm.

As they led him out of the suite, Hamilton desperately searched for any sign of his sister but he could hear and see nothing. Vegas scanned the hall and then moved down the emergency staircase. Hamilton was book-ended between Santana and the Ferret.

When they reached the loading bay, the others were ready. Hamilton was in the van within seconds. When he realized his sister wasn't there and that they were taking him away, he started to struggle. Santana seized his throat and slammed him to the floor. They quickly tied his hands and gagged him.

Vegas instructed Perez, "You remember the woman from the sailboat the other day?"

Perez nodded.

"Take Meza and get her. Go to the Plaza Marina. Find her," Vegas commanded. "Bring her to the farmhouse. Don't cause a scene. If she is not there, come back to the hotel and wait in her suite. Tell her you are taking her to her brother. Be very helpful, very polite. Understand?" Vegas cast the men a deadly stare of finality.

Perez jumped into the passenger side of the dark green Explorer. They waited for Vegas to pull away and then headed for the Plaza Marina.

14

Hours earlier, as the sun had been making its presence known behind the Sierra Madres, Jack had sat over his coffee thinking about Zillia and the permits.

Now, he wiped the moisture off the little sailboat dinghy.

"Here's the bushings for the generator; we need new ones." Jerry handed him a plastic bag.

"Okay." Jack stuffed them in his backpack.

Jack caught up with Deni at the wharf where he was organizing two groups of fishermen between Israel and himself.

"Where are you headed today?" Jack asked.

"I think we'll try La Corbetena again. Did good the other day." Deni said. As usual, Deni' voice boomed over others in his jovial, Latino fashion.

The motorcycle ride in the fresh morning air, with the sights and sounds of the country coming alive for another day, was invigorating. At the bridge repair, Jack moved ahead of several cars in the lineup much to everyone's chagrin, until he settled behind a newer Cadillac that wasn't puking out exhaust smoke like so many cars in the city.

Try as he might, Jan came back to his mind. For the umpteenth time, he had to forcibly change his thoughts. Jack had contacted the University of Washington and Captain Erikson on the *Juan de Fuca*, and after a series of exchanges between the three, it had been agreed that the publicity resulting from being part of this exploration, outweighed the inconvenience of lost research time in Cabo. The ship was heading toward Puerto Vallarta, shortly.

His first stop was the machine-parts store for new bushings. Next stop was the Port Authority, where he sat waiting for the harbormaster's arrival.

Jack was pleased to see Zillia's smile dissolve when he saw who was waiting for him.

"I'm here to pick up the permits," Jack said bluntly.

Zillia had thought of simply not coming to work, but his absence might have allowed others to make decisions for him. The harbormaster gave a hint of a shrug and walked towards the building, without a word.

Jack had had enough. He followed the man to the door. "Señor, your government has asked that I assist in a certain project—which I am happy to do. I understand instructions have been forwarded to your office."

"Yes, yes," Zillia interrupted. "We are working on it, Señor St. Julian, but we are not as efficient as you Americans," he said caustically. "This all takes time."

"Here we go again," Jack thought. "Señor," Jack continued in Spanish, "this project is not mine. I have only been asked to help. You mentioned time. Well, Señor," Jack's tone matched Zillia's, "I don't know your game, but I'll put my money on your government's displeasure if something should go…" Jack hesitated, looking for the word, "…missing."

Zillia knew he was beaten and changed his tactics. "I understand, Señor St. Julian. We all want to do our best. It is all being looked into and appropriate action is even now, under way. Please leave a number where we can call you as soon as everything is in order. We appreciate your time and concern, and we will contact you."

"In a pig's eye," Jack thought. He took one of Rosa's cards out of his pocket and shoved it into the harbormaster's pocket.

"We will be in touch amigo," Jack said caustically as he turned and left.

Once Zillia was able to stop shaking, he dialed Vegas' number again. He had been dialing for two days now, but had been unable to get through. The secretary took his name again and said her boss would call.

Jack's anger subsided as he parked at the tackle shop in the mall, and waited while the old man unlocked the door. Jack told himself he really didn't have a dog in this fight… the ship wouldn't get here any faster, and if Jack knew anything about the professor and Mexican politics, the fool harbormaster, would ultimately pay. It would be a shame, however, if Mexican history was plundered. Jack made a mental note to keep surveillance going on the site.

Inside the shop, Jack accepted the reel and was pleased with its action. With a smile, he told the old repairman he would be more careful who he let play with his toys in the future.

As Jack stepped out of the tackle shop, a row of newspapers caught his eye. Each screamed a different Spanish headline: "*Vemexa Head Assassinated; Asesinado!*" and "*Local Nightclub Scene of Murders*." The last one stopped him cold: "*Vegas Assassinated*."

Jack picked up a newspaper, handed the little Indian newsboy some change, and stood digesting the article. The sub caption read: "*Ernesto Vegas, Vice President of Vemexa, and another man, were assassinated last night in Cristobel's nightclub*." Jack studied the gaudily-colored photograph of two men with their heads covered in blood. It wasn't the Vegas brother he had met. "Too bad," he thought. He folded the paper and slipped it in his backpack. He kick-started the motorcycle and started walking it back out of the parking stall.

Just then a dark green Ford cruised by nearly hitting his taillight. Jack was about to confront the driver when he recognized the Explorer from the other day in La Cruz. It came to a stop 30 feet from where he stood. A passenger stepped out and scanned the crowd of shoppers. He looked familiar. Then Jack placed him, he was the fat one who had stayed behind at the wharf that day.

The man's gaze flowed over Jack without recognition. The

cold, purposeful look on the man's face told Jack he was looking for somebody. The man walked into the mall out of Jack's view. The Explorer moved slowly down the lane.

Jack killed the engine, stepped off the bike and searched the crowd. Instantly, he spotted Jan leaving the mall through another door. She was wearing a long, loose sundress, sandals and a straw hat. She was casually swinging two plastic shopping bags as she walked. Jack knew instinctively it was her they were after.

He moved swiftly towards her. At ten feet away she recognized him, but her big grin of recognition quickly faded as she saw the grim look on his face. "What?" she asked, confused by his rapid, businesslike approach.

"Walk with me," he said as lightly as possible, taking hold of her arm and leading her toward the bike.

"Something wrong?"

"Not sure." He gave her a disarming smile. "Remember those guys the other day on the sailboat? The one that stayed with the trucks?"

Jan nodded. "The fat one?"

"He's cruising around looking for someone." Jack nodded toward the green Explorer now at the far end of the parkade in the other one-way lane but heading back towards them.

Jan recognized the truck with a start.

Jack jumped on the bike and kicked it to life. "Get on."

"What are you doing?" she demanded.

Jack saw the other man step out of the mall. The sound of the bike drew his attention. Perez started trotting toward them.

"Get on, now!" Jack commanded.

Without another thought, Jan hiked her dress high up on her thighs, and straddled the seat.

"Hold on!" Jack yelled as he gunned the machine.

Perez lunged, grasping one of Jan's plastic bags, his leverage nearly toppling them. The bag split open, loosening the man's grip. Perez stumbled forward and slammed face first into the concrete sidewalk.

Stability reestablished, Jack popped the clutch. The bike jumped forward, its front tire still off the ground as he slammed into second gear.

"Lean forward!" he yelled as he weaved, between the slower-moving traffic, in the wrong direction. Jack cast a quick glance back, only to see that the fallen man had gained the truck. However, the parking lot's high concrete row-divider, kept the truck away from them. Jack used the maneuverability of the bike to jump a curb, and ended up in the same lane as the truck, several cars behind, but now going in the opposite direction.

Mexican drivers have little regard for others, unless it is in their best interest. Jack's driving incurred the ire of several. True to form, a cacophony of horns sounded. Jack reached the parking lot entrance, where he exited, turning into oncoming traffic, and running a red light; cutting left across the four-lane highway that led to the airport.

The truck finally cleared the parking lot and charged onto the four-lane road, leaving a trail of burned rubber and snarling traffic, in its wake.

The light traffic on the highway provided Jack with little chance to get ahead. Winding expertly between cars and onto the narrow shoulder, only put a couple of dozen cars between them.

"Keep your head right behind mine for balance. Don't look back!" he hollered.

Jan's arms were locked around his chest. Several times, she was certain they were going to crash as he pitched the bike far over on its side. Yet by some miracle, he was able to pull the machine back each time. She closed her eyes against the oncoming blasts of warm dusty air, and tried to hide behind his backpack. Jan had long given up trying to hold her skirt down, offering the mostly male audience, an excellent view of legs worth talking about later.

When traffic began backing up from the bridge repair, Jack gained more distance as he skillfully cut down the middle of the bridge, slicing past vehicles in both directions. Jan opened her eyes for a second and her heart froze; they were flying past cars that were only inches away. He was threading a needle with their lives at 60 miles per hour.

Jack knew his top speed would never match the Explorer's. The old Honda was no Ducati, and although maneuverability was on his side, sheer speed was not. Their only slim chance of escape was to get ahead far enough, to give him time to think of other evasive actions.

Stuck in the slow moving, two-way traffic on the bridge, Meza saw the bike driving dangerously, down the centerline. "They are getting away!" he yelled.

"Just stay with them. Watch to see they don't pull off. If they stay on, they are ours," Perez said, as he tried to get the blood to stop flowing from his broken nose.

After the bridge congestion, Jack's only advantage, evaporated as they returned to separated lanes. The highway had been built to hover twenty feet above the surrounding fields; and the steep embankment was covered in grass and coarse stubble. The slopes led down to ditches at the base of the roadbed. Only a few years earlier, the farmers of the area would regularly drive their livestock down the road at night; a practice that made night-driving very dangerous in Mexico.

Along the edge of the pavement ran a near-continuous concrete curbing that acted to protect the slopes from washing out during the rainy season.

In his mirror Jack saw the truck coming fast. He tried to create confusion by wildly whipping in front of cars and forcing them to swerve and brake. It was a deadly game—gambling on the other drivers' reactions.

Up ahead, Jack saw a cluster of cars, then a clear spot for at least a couple of hundred yards. They would make their move in that bare section. Once Jack was in the cluster of moving cars, he eased up on the gas a fraction. Mentally measuring his RPMs he slipped down into fourth gear to let the Ford catch him.

Little did the attacking driver know his opponent's talent with a motorcycle. Jack let the Explorer gain. He drove along the shoulder of the road, gaining on a slow-moving, old Toyota pickup. The Explorer was only feet behind the old truck and only feet away from Jack when Jack slowed down, just enough to give his opponent a chance to hit him. Meza hesitated, trying to figure out what he was going to do. At the last second, Jack turned to the men in the Explorer and grinned.

Meza swerved into the bike's position, hitting nothing but air, as Jack popped the clutch and buried the throttle. The bike pulled alongside the old car again, and the Explorer had to back off. The driver of the old Toyota laid on the horn. If he'd hit the brakes, the Explorer would have been finished.

Inside the Explorer Perez was screaming at Meza. "Be careful, you idiot! You will kill us!"

"I will have this man," Meza snarled as he slammed the brakes, to avoid the little truck.

"We must get the woman safely!" Meza yelled.

"She will live."

Meza's grip on the wheel tightened and he pressed the accelerator, passing the truck on the left.

People in the traffic just ahead, had seen and heard the near miss. Like children in a school ground not wanting to get involved in a fight, the cars moved to distance themselves from the two combatants. There was nothing left that Jack could hide behind.

"Now we have him," growled Perez.

Meza pulled into the right lane, removing Jack's chance to maneuver.

Racing along the narrow shoulder, Jack saw a break in the roadside curbing. It was going to be close.

"Hang on!" Jack yelled.

He almost touched the Ford as he pulled the bike suddenly over to the left. Meza and Jan couldn't believe what he was doing.

He jerked hard to the right. The Explorer followed. The

bike shot through the drainage break in the curbing. To Jan's total disbelief, they went airborne.

Meza, focused on making contact with the bike. He realized too late that he had over-committed. He tried desperately to pull back, but the dice had been thrown. The truck's right front tire slammed into the curbing and the momentum carried the truck over the bank.

Jack soared five feet above the ground. His luck held as the descending bike matched the incline of the bank perfectly, and the tires found a solid patch of grass. They raced down into the bottom of the slope.

Jan experienced the full hardness of Jack's upper body as he used every muscle to control the machine. With brakes locked the tires cut a deep groove in the dried grass. By sheer force of will Jack dumped enough speed to sweep the bike up the other side of the dry drainage ditch.

Like a missile only yards behind them, thousands of pounds of truck corkscrewed down the bank and rolled over twice before stopping upside down at the bottom of the ditch. A cloud of dirt and sod sprayed skyward.

The action caused a five-car pileup on the road above. For a long moment, the earth and life itself seemed to stand still, as the dust cloud rose over the scene.

Jack pulled the bike hard around. "Hold the bike!" he yelled, giving Jan only a brief second to get her feet down and the bike stabilized, before he jumped off. Jack ran to the truck.

Through the open passenger window, Jack could see both men were past help. One hung in his seat belt with his head at an impossible angle. The other one's face was half way through the windshield, blood flowed down the glass from a severed artery.

Jack raced back to the bike, "Let's go!"

They turned north, negotiating the ditch until it came to a dirt crossroad. Turning away from the highway, Jack followed a secondary paved road for several miles.

When Jan dared reopen her eyes, her mind was in a daze.

Numbly, she watched as pastoral farmland flowed by. She had no idea what was happening; only that this man felt safe.

As they crossed under a bridge spanning a dry riverbed, Jack pulled up and onto a paved, secondary road. They were soon in the middle of the town of San Jose; just another commuter in a lineup of cars and trucks. After a few blocks, they pulled down a side street where he parked in front of a large, two story nondescript building, with a high, solid metal gate.

"Jump off. I'll just be a sec."

Ringing the buzzer, Jack waited.

Jan stared down at the bag around her wrist. It held a bathing suit. "What was in the other one?" She didn't have a clue.

"What is this place?" she asked.

"A friend works here. Anyway, I think she's here today. I want to stash the bike in case anyone is looking for us."

After a long, impatient minute, a stern female voice addressed them on the other side of the solid gate. When Jack announced himself the sound of a heavy bolt could be heard and the door swung open a few inches. A wrinkled, heavyset woman gave them a cool appraisal.

"Que? What do you want?" she shifted to English.

"Need to see Carmen," Jack stated, his tone just under a command.

The woman looked at him for a moment, turned and walked back into the courtyard.

Jan watched through the partly opened gate, as a good-looking young woman in a pretty aqua-colored medical smock sauntered out. When the young woman saw who it was, her eyes lit up.

"Jack!" she squealed, grabbing him and planting a big, demanding kiss on his lips, at the same time wrapping her arms and one leg intimately around his body. Jack's efforts to restrain the woman were only partly successful. After a moment, he gained the upper hand and set her firmly on her feet.

"Woman, give me peace!" He gasped, and at once she settled

down. He held her at an arm's length. "Carmen, I need a favor."

"What can I…" she stopped in midstream as she spotted Jan. Her demure look changed completely as she looked Jan over coolly.

"Carmen, this is a friend of mine and we're in a little trouble."

Returning her gaze to Jack, she nodded. "What?" her lips forming an unmistakable pout.

"Stash the bike for a few days. Your dad'll pick it up."

"Sure. Okay, Jack," she stated flatly, but didn't move.

"And we're in a bit of a hurry,"

The woman swung the gate open fully, as Jack pushed the bike through. He wheeled it across the courtyard to yet another wire-mesh gate, which the young woman opened, exposing a small storage area. Jack wedged the bike in and covered it with the remains of a tattered canvas awning. He leaned a few garden rakes and tools up against the machine to obstruct it from view.

"Don't tell anyone the bike is here, Carmen," he instructed.

"Si."

"We have to go."

There was a long, pregnant silence as the two women eyed each other; neither sure of the lay of the land. Jan was confused, Carmen obviously jealous.

"We have to move," Jack repeated.

As they arrived at the outer gate, Jan looked up to find several scantily clad young women looking down from the second floor windows at all the commotion. Jack reached down and gave Carmen a quick peck on the forehead. She scowled at the childish affection.

15

Miguel Vegas would have been pleased to know how restless the night had been for Esparza and Vásquez. Twice during the previous day, they had seen small planes flying slow circles around the area. Both men knew it had to be Vegas looking for his lost drugs. When Ortega had called them on the CB the day before, and cryptically told them that it would be one more day, Vásquez almost bolted.

During the night Vásquez had talked endlessly of Vegas' "monster" Santana sneaking out of the bushes, slowly carving pieces off of them and roasting them in the fire.

Esparza finally woke to sunlight pouring through an open hole in the hut's roof. Half alert, he started coffee on the Coleman. He checked the cell phone, no messages. He listened to the CB, nothing but fishermen talking about where they were heading, and for what.

Bored, he turned on the portable radio for a little music. Vásquez was just rousing himself when the news came on. The two men turned to stone as they listened to the murderous events at the nightclub. When the announcer speculated who the murdered pair were, Vásquez let out a cry of terror. He tore the bedding off and started throwing on his clothes.

"We are dead! Dead!" he screamed. "We have to get out of here!" He began hopping around, trying to get one leg into his pants while pulling on his shirt.

Esparza couldn't agree more and quickly gathered his few belongings.

Taking the big truck was out of the question. If it held all the gold in the world, it was worth nothing with all eyes looking for it. They threw their gear in the back of the Ford pickup and jumped in. They both stopped simultaneously and looked at each other, then at the bigger truck. Greed overtook them.

"If we take some, we can sell it," Esparza said. "How much money have you got?"

"Not much."

Without another word, they raced to the back of the big diesel. They cut away the camouflage webbing with machetes and unlocked the padlock that held the two swinging, wooden-rail gates closed.

Like men possessed, they threw cases of ceramic tiles behind them. The flimsy cardboard casings exploded on impact. Case after case of tiles flew into the air until they reached the cocaine.

After several trips, they slammed the tailgate shut on the Ford and jumped in. Racing back down the riverbed and out onto the dirt road, they came to the locked gate. Vásquez slammed to a halt.

"I'll just drive through it!" he yelled.

"No! Wait!" Esparza jumped out and looked closely at the gate. It was solid. The truck could undoubtedly break through, but at what cost to the truck? It was their only transportation. It wouldn't pay to get stopped by the cops for a broken headlight. He looked to the left of the gate. Two strands of barbed wire ran to one fence post and then ended. The dense jungle growth covered the fact that there was no more fence; the whole gate had been a ruse. He jogged to the fence post and looked at the bush. There was a small shallow ditch between them and the paved road. The truck could easily make it. He waved Vásquez over. The man needed no prompting as he saw Esparza walk through the bush and out onto the pavement. Vásquez backed the truck up and followed up and out of the ditch, and onto the road. They were free in less than a minute.

They followed the coast road back past La Cruz and turned north on Highway 200. Getting out of Mexico was their only hope.

"I have relatives in Tucson," Esparza said. "We would be safe there, at least for a few days."

Vásquez didn't care. He just wanted out.

They stopped at the first pay phone they came to and told their wives the news. They told them to get the kids, all the money they could grab, and to get out, immediately. They arranged to contact them later in the day. Both women screamed at their men for being so stupid and putting all their lives at risk.

The men suffered serious apprehension as they passed the shrimp restaurant, but it was early in the morning and the place was deserted. As the miles streamed by they began to relax.

About 40 miles north of Tepic, Vásquez found himself following a slow bus that was crawling around the last curves of a mountainous section of the road. Seeing a straight stretch ahead, Vásquez prepared to pass—falling back, then picking up speed. As he pulled out he saw, in the fast approaching distance, an Army truck parked in the middle of the road and soldiers standing around it.

"Road block!" he screamed. Esparza had seen it too.

"Pull back," Esparza commanded. Vásquez complied, terror written across his face. "Be calm," Esparza demanded, himself no portrait of tranquility.

The bus ground to a slow crawl and the soldier in the road waved it through. Thirty yards past the roadblock it pulled over to take a group of people on board.

When Vásquez stopped in front of the soldier, he was visibly shaking. The young soldier looked at him for only a second and then lifted his head and called to an officer who was standing with another group of green-clad soldiers near a Jeep.

The tall, stern-looking officer in a distinctive, blue uniform cast a glance at the truck and took one step forward.

Vásquez buried the accelerator. The soldier fell backwards getting out of the way. The other soldiers stood frozen in disbelief watching the truck's escape. The officer however reacted instantly. As the pickup sped by, the officer unclasped his holster and drew his pistol. The truck was a good twenty yards away and gaining speed fast. The officer calmly lifted the pistol, using both hands for accuracy, aimed and fired.

Inside the truck, the first shot went through the windshield. Vásquez instinctively swerved and turned his head to look behind. Esparza grabbed the dash to steady himself. He heard a popping noise just as the entire driver's side windshield exploded in a sea of red. A second later something like a bolt of fire hit him in the back, pitching him forward. The truck swerved violently and left the road at full speed, rolling over as it dropped into the coarse ditch.

The blue-uniformed officer barked to the others as he jumped aboard the moving army Jeep. They reached the overturned truck as dust and steam rose skyward. The officer stood watching as the young men in green jumped out and raced to the cab.

"Captain! One is still alive!" a soldier yelled up. Others joined in to try to get the man out of the passenger side of the truck.

The officer picked up the transmitter. "This is Captain Heraldo Suarez. We need an ambulance."

Another soldier dug through the mess in the back of the truck, turned and signaled to the officer. Suarez worked his way down to the back of the truck where several ceramic boxes lay split open, exposing black plastic bags. One had burst on impact and a small cloud of white powder filled the air. Suarez took out his knife and cut open another carton; it too contained a black plastic bag.

One of the young solders stepped up to him. "What is happening?"

"Two men making a run for it within twelve hours of Ernesto Vegas' assassination. Things aren't going well for the bad guys today." Suarez said with a cold smile as he fingered the wrinkled scars that covered much of the right side of his cheek. The wolfish smile broadened across his face as he looked over the scene and contemplated the possibilities.

He worked his way to where the soldiers had the man on the

ground. Blood was spreading on the man's shirt. His breathing was ragged and short, but he wasn't spitting blood, yet. From experience, Suarez doubted the man would last long, but nothing was certain.

16

The streets of San Jose were busy under the midmorning sun. No one gave Jack and Jan any notice as they headed towards the center of town. Jack grabbed the backpack and marched as fast as he thought Jan could handle it. As they reached the road at the village church, an old, blue, beat-up transit bus squealed to a stop.

"Come on! We want that bus!" He grabbed her arm and trotted forward. "Watch your step," he warned as they navigated the broken concrete that made up the crude sidewalk.

Climbing aboard, he paid the driver a few coins and they took seats toward the back. As the old bus ground forward, the staccato exhalation of its exhaust resonated through its metal frame. With each shift, the gears sounded as if the transmission was coming apart. Jack looked over at Jan.

"I…" She stammered, shock beginning to settle in.

Jack gave her a reassuring smile and put his finger to his lips.

She looked into his eyes, searching for meaning. What she saw was a calm strength that she had never experienced in another human. "He is in total control." She thought. His calmness reassured her. She gave a deep sigh, and tried to concentrate on the scenery and postpone reality for just a little while.

The bus ride through the dry delta countryside was a new experience. She had only seen the tourist side of Puerto Vallarta. The diversion kept her mind from places she didn't want to go.

After several stops, a young teen-age boy got on, carrying an old relic of a guitar. He had a brief word with the driver, walked to the middle of the nearly-full bus and began strumming and singing.

To Jan's ear it sounded like someone was pulling the tail of a cat, but after a bit she could pick out the melody and a few of the words like "*Corazon*" and "*Amour*." The sound of the tune made it sad somehow.

"A lost love?" she asked Jack.

He nodded, giving her a little smile.

"A little young to know about that, don't you think?" Jan said lightly. Jack's smile widened. He raised an eyebrow at the irony.

Jan suddenly realized she'd been holding Jack's forearm during the entire ride. Sensing her awareness, he gave her a hand a reassuringly pat. Self-consciously, she released her grasp.

The young troubadour followed the love song with a bouncy number that included a lot of palm slapping on the guitar—and mercifully few words. During the song, Jan noticed the guitar had only three strings and the sound box was covered with stick-on logos. It softened her attitude toward his pitiful effort.

She concentrated on her surroundings, the bus's worn wooden flooring and the bare metal seats, were like nothing she had ever imagined. On the driver's dashboard was a wild mosaic of small, religious artifacts, statuettes of the Virgin Mary and small crucifixes of Jesus. In the middle of the grouping sat a miniature of Snoopy on his back atop his doghouse.

The top of the entire windshield had been painted to look like a lacy lattice fringe. In the middle of the passenger side, painted in what looked like white shoe polish was a large cross and the words "*Pte. Mita* and *Valle*." Jan concluded that this most likely signified the two end points of the bus route.

"Punta de Mita?" she asked.

Jack followed her gaze and nodded.

After a third song the musician decided it was time for his audience to show their appreciation for his talent. He made his way through the crowd collecting small change. Jan started when she realized her purse was still hanging over her shoulder and she clutched it guardedly. Jack gave the kid some change. The kid jumped off at the next stop.

A few minutes later the bus neared the town of Mescales and the intersection of Highway 200, leading south to Puerto Vallarta, north to Tepic. Traffic was backed up heading south. There was little congestion heading north.

As they turned north Jack noticed Jan holding her purse for dear life. He didn't know her story, but the attack was deadly serious. Last night's assassination had to figure in somehow. Looking down he could see her trembling slightly. He put his arm around her shoulders and gave her a reassuring squeeze.

"Hold on," he said gently. "We don't have far to go and we don't want to be noticed."

Jan again deeply searched Jack's eyes and nodded comprehension. She ran the back of her hand over her moist eyes. "I can handle this," she told herself.

With a determined will born of years of self-reliance she set her jaw and nodded, "I'm okay."

"You're great," Jack reassured.

Surprisingly, he found he had to fight an overwhelming urge to wrap her in his arms and comfort her.

"I have to call my brother!" she shouted.

Several passengers looked over at them. Instantly, she ducked her head in silence. Jack squeezed her hand with a pat. "It's okay."

As the drive dragged on, Jack tried to put things in perspective. He sensed no malice in this woman. Or was he blinded by his own emotions? What her role was he did not know, but his overwhelming feeling was that she didn't know what was going on. That didn't change facts; someone was willing to kill to get her, and wherever he took her, it would put innocent people in danger.

The palm trees and fields gave way to the bustling town of Bucerias. A couple of miles past the town, Jan recognized the overpass Todd had taken only yesterday. "Todd, are you okay?" she whispered to herself.

Neat rows of trees passed on one side of the bus. Jan could see that they were following the curve of the ocean shore. On the other side were hotels and apartments.

Jack calculated their next move. He figured the bad guys wouldn't know where they were but the meter was running fast. If her brother was involved, and Jack couldn't see any reason why he wouldn't be, then he was beyond any help they could offer. Jack figured Jan must be some pawn in all of it. If the brother was safe, he'd be going nuts worrying about her. But the brother's anxiety was of little importance compared with the woman's safety. Getting Jan to see that logic might be another story. She could easily blow the whistle on herself trying to find the guy. Any phone calling would create interest and that put everyone around her in jeopardy.

Then again, he admired the way this woman had remained cool under fire. Although there had been angst and confusion on the surface, underneath he sensed real steel. His mind flashed back to Pat, she too had possessed those qualities. Memories came flooding back the sense of love she could convey with just a smile. He took a deep, controlling breath.

Jan noted the brief flash of pain on Jack's otherwise-restrained face. Was it fear? She'd just witnessed his courage in the face of danger. She knew nothing of motorcycles, yet what he had just done was impossible. The woman inside her sensed his reaction as something else; something deep and something vulnerable. She stole another look at him. Fear was the last thing she saw. His eyes were alert yet calm, in total control.

"We have to get going," he said, readying to get up. The bus slowed noisily. She followed his lead, standing but holding onto the rails as the bus lurched to a final stop.

The pair exited calmly with a few other passengers. As traffic cleared, they crossed the road and walked down the quiet cobblestone street that led to the center of town. Being off the beaten path, up to now, La Cruz had been a quiet little fishing village but that had changed. Hotels had sprouted where only a few years ago bush had grown.

They walked toward the beach. Jan spotted one of the few phones in town.

Reading her thoughts, Jack stayed a step ahead by offering, "I have a friend with a phone, more private."

Jan looked at the phone and back at Jack, seeing the logic and putting one more degree of trust in the man she signaled silent agreement.

As they walked down the street he casually asked, "What did you do last night?"

"It was my last night. Todd insisted I go home. I didn't want to but I agreed, as much as I like this place I have responsibilities. There was this restaurant that friends back home had talked about, Señor Mister Pepe's. We went there, just the two of us."

"Yeah, great sunsets," Jack nodded. "Pepe's one of the old-time restaurateurs in the city before it got famous. He's a fishing nut."

"I remember Todd saying there was some party we were supposed to go to at a nightclub but he agreed to spend our last night together."

Jack kept his face calm. Whatever future Todd Hamilton had ended.

Rounding the corner, they came to the back door of the restaurant. Rosa looked up from her work and as the pair entered. She immediately sensed something was wrong, "Que pasa, Jack?"

"Small problem," Jack answered lightly. "Deni here?"

"He is out at the rancho. He'll be back in a couple of hours," she answered, scanning the woman's filthy clothes and red eyes. She followed as the pair walked into the restaurant.

"Are you all right, Señorita?" Rosa asked.

"Yes," Jan answered, giving the woman a weak smile. "Thanks to Jack."

"Sorry," Jack said. "This is Rosa. Rosa, Jan Hamilton."

"Mucho gusto, Señorita," Rosa offered with a warm smile.

"Nice to meet you, Rosa," Jan shook Rosa's hand as she collapsed into a chair.

"Jan was on the charter we took out the other day," Jack said.

Rosa knew the story. She looked at Jack for more.

"We had a bit of an accident." Jack said.

Rosa's look deepened. "I didn't hear the bike."

"No, we left it with Carmen."

At that information, Rosa's face darkened. Jack walked over to the bar and grabbed a couple of cold beers. He opened them and passed one to Jan. She drank deeply.

After a long pause Jack said, "Maybe you'd like to clean up a bit?"

He looked directly at Rosa who took the hint.

"Come on now," Rosa commanded gently. "We'll get you cleaned up. Look at your beautiful dress! What has this beast done to you? Men, you can't believe them sometimes," she purposely prattled as she led Jan up the stairs to the apartments.

Minutes later Rosa returned. "The lady's dress is a mess. It is torn. The grease may never come out. I have sent Arturo to my niece Tina's—she has dresses in her shop." Rosa gave Jack a look of concern. "What happened?"

"We had an accident," Jack began. "But there's more… she's in some kind of trouble. We'll sort it out."

Jan shortly reappeared at the kitchen door; her hair still damp, wearing a Mexican-style dress that was quite becoming. "I want to call my brother," she stated firmly as she sat back down, taking another sip of the unfinished beer.

"Look," Jack started cautiously, "these guys may be waiting for just that and when they find out where you are they could try again."

"Try what?" Jan asked.

Rosa sat silently, absorbing the conversation.

"I don't know," Jack stated in mild frustration. "What is going on? Those guys wanted you bad enough to get themselves killed. They'd have killed us if they had even touched the bike at that speed." He sighed heavily. "Do you have any idea what they wanted, or why they were after you?"

"No! None." Her irritation mounting.

"While you were in the shower, I called a friend in Puerto Vallarta and had him contact the hotel, asking for your brother. There was no answer in his room. We don't want to put other people in danger, do we?" It was a statement, not a question.

She sat, looking dejectedly from Jack to Rosa. With reluctance, she shook her head.

"Look," Jack said calmly, "I'll organize a way to reach him. It will take a little while but we can do it. Do you understand?"

Jan nodded in resignation. Then without warning the weight of the recent events caught up with her. She dropped her head into her hands.

Jack stood and reached for her. She let herself be drawn into his arms and rested against him. He stood still as grief engulfed her, her anguish coming in waves. The smell of her freshly washed hair intoxicated him.

Her sobs slowly subsided. When she looked up again she was in control but her eyes continued to brim with unshed tears. "What am I going to do?"

Without an answer, Jack just tightened his embrace. His eyes hardened. "Why don't you let me worry about that?"

As her grief ebbed he gently drew her away into Rosa's tender care. "You will be safe here if we are careful," he said, nodding at Rosa to take over.

Holding Jan's arm, Rosa grabbed several napkins off the table and handed them to her. "You sit down. I'll get something for your face." Rosa patted her arm and led her back into the chair.

Jan wiped her face and drew a deep, ragged breath.

"What do you know about that guy in the truck?" Jack asked hoping to get her mind refocused.

Jan shrugged. "He was with Vegas, a servant or something. He drove the truck out here and stayed with it when we were sailing."

"Did you know the other Vegas? The brother of that Miguel, guy from the other day?" Jack asked.

Jan shook her head. Rosa handed her a wet towel. She wiped her face again and gave a heavy sigh.

"Look, there's no easy way to say this..." Jack looked her squarely in the eye. "Last night, that other Vegas—Miguel's brother—him and his bodyguard, were gunned down at a nightclub in Puerto Vallarta."

She stared at him, stunned. "What!"

"It's been on the radio all morning." Jack watched her reaction carefully.

"How can that be?"

"The news says two guys dressed as waiters walked in, went up and emptied half a dozen rounds into each of them. No one else was hurt—including the women that were with them. All this tells me it was a professional hit."

Jan's anxiety peaked. "We have to call Todd now! We have to! He could be in trouble!"

"Why?" He said, continuing to concentrate on her body language.

She looked up at Jack, her face as white as a ghost. "We were supposed to go to some party at some nightclub last night. Todd had been talking to someone about getting together but..." she trailed off, her mind unable to take in so much so fast. After a long pause she blurted, "We would have been there!" She paced back-and-forth, her nerves in tatters.

"Jan, look," he took her gently but firmly by one arm, "It wouldn't surprise me if the Vegas' were dirty, very dirty. If your brother was supposed to be there then they are after him. You too, judging from what they did this morning."

Wide-eyed, she looked up, "Todd couldn't be..." she stopped and her glance fell to the floor.

"No, of course not," Jack placated. "Maybe they can't find him and they want you as bait or maybe as a hostage. Who knows? One thing is sure, you're at great risk. Jan, if they are into drugs, life means nothing. We can't let them find you."

Jan sat down, her head bent to her knees as the words sank in. "We would have been there last night," she repeated hollowly. "We have to find him."

"Where?" Jack responded. "We have no idea where he could be. No way of contacting him. They have people everywhere, in all kinds of places." He spoke in a gentle, tender whisper.

Jan anxiously scanned the restaurant. "I don't know but we have to try something."

"Will you trust me?" he asked bluntly, looking her straight in the eye.

"What can you do?"

"We are not without assets. Will you trust me?" he repeated.

*   *   *

A couple of hours later, from a phone booth in Puerto Vallarta, Jack placed a call to the Maria Elena Hotel and persistently asked for Todd or Jan Hamilton. There was considerable delay, but finally an operator came on politely asking more questions than giving answers.

In a thick, put-on Texas drawl, Jack explained he'd come down to talk to Todd about real estate. He blustered and insisted he only had a few hours and "where was the young fella?" When he was pressed for details, Jack became righteously offended and told the listener this was his "nickel" and he'd "do the talkin'." That earned him the response: "...they had checked out and would be back from Mexico City next week, please leave a number and Todd would call." The caller swore and slammed the receiver down.

Grim-faced, Jack walked away from the payphone.

17

Later that afternoon Deni sat listening with deepening concern as Jack related their dilemma. From time-to-time Jan nodded in acknowledgement.

When Jack finished, Deni said. "I know a good cop. Name's Suarez, Captain Heraldo Mexia Suarez, distant cousin of Rosa's. He's with the Federal Narcos. Top dog in this region of the coast. Death on the druggies."

Deni looked from Jan to Jack. "It's your call. What do you think?"

"It's not my call. It's Jan." Both men looked at her. "What do you want to do?"

"Mexican police?" Jan asked suspiciously. "Aren't they corrupt?" she looked at Deni.

"I understand, Señorita. Most yes, but not all."

"I have to find my brother but am I not putting you all in danger, if what you say is true."

Jack and Deni exchanged a look. Jack delicately answered: "I'm familiar with risk—that's not the concern. But we do have to consider Deni's family."

They looked at the Mexican. "Let's get more information, then we will see," Deni stated calmly.

On the TV above the bar the news came on. The lead story was the assassination. In rapid Spanish the announcer spelled out what was known. The screen showed pictures of the murder, sparing no visual detail—everything in gruesome color, typical of Mexican coverage. Next, they shifted to file film of a living Ernesto Vegas and Jorge Ortega, with their names in captions under the pictures. A picture of Todd Hamilton suddenly flashed onto the screen.

Jan rocketed from her chair. "What'd they say? That's Todd! What did they say?" she demanded.

Jack was trying to catch it over her yelling. "They said he is missing. The police are looking for him. He was reported to have been with them last night."

Jack looked over at Deni to confirm he got the rapid translation right. Deni nodded.

"But he was with me!" she shouted at the television.

"No! No!" She walked around the room like a caged animal. She stopped abruptly and fell into a chair. "He was with me last night," she repeated. "We went to a restaurant, home by 10. He took a sleeping pill, he was too tired to go out. Oh Todd! Please be okay, please!" Her hands covered her face.

Jack spoke in a low tone in Spanish to Deni. "They make it sound like he's the guy that did it and now they are looking for him."

"That's what I got."

"Back home we call that spin-doctoring, twisting the truth to sound like something else. It's a politician's game."

"Is the same here," the Mexican nodded.

"There was no mention of any grieving Vegas brother. Nothing. That tells me more than I need to know. Look at her. You think she's putting that on?"

"No amigo."

"I think you should make the call but we need her on board." Jack looked Deni in the eye. "I know how she feels."

Deni saw the pain in his friend's face.

The two men didn't have to wait long. Jan gathered herself together and took a couple of deep breaths. "We gotta call this cop of yours. I've got money, at least Todd has," she stumbled. "I have access to it. I'll pay anything but please just find him."

"He's straight you figure, this cop?" Jack asked.

"As straight as there is. He's lost a kid brother and a niece to the druggies. Kid got mixed up with a gang, selling dope, and was killed in some turf war—up in Mazatlan. That was years ago. The girl… well, you know."

"They tried to kill him with a car bomb. Two of his men died. He bears the scars," Rosa said as she joined them.

They looked at Jan for final approval.

"I want my brother back."

Jack nodded agreement.

As he got up to phone Deni said, "From what I hear of this Vegas family, the father figured the meanest one would sort things out, even if that meant the death of one of his own sons." Deni's voice trailed off. "I'll bet you anything the other one did it—or had it done."

"From what I saw of that guy on the boat, I'd have no trouble believing that," Jack agreed.

They all listened as Deni phoned and tried to work his way up the chain of command. He did not want to say why he was calling until he knew he had Suarez' ear, so he was forced to leave a vague message.

After the call the three of them sat in silence. Rosa returned to the kitchen where she and her assistant worked furiously. Willie and Lobo were playing later and the place would be packed.

"You said he took a sleeping pill," Jack asked, "But you didn't actually see him this morning?"

She shook her head. "That was just this morning? We said good night, I saw him take the pill. He offered me one but I wanted to shop in the morning. I even left him a note so he would know where I was…" her voice trailed off.

"That's how they knew where you were," he stated, the pieces falling into place.

"He's taken my brother. Ever since I got here I didn't like those slimy greasers." She stopped realizing the insult. "Sorry."

Deni laughed. "Señorita, I can't believe you could even imagine words low enough to fit the scum bag. Do not worry."

"That business with the towel on the boat…?" Jack looked her.

She lowered her eyes. After a long pause, she said, "That lady, Brazil, told me that he was tiring of her. She thought that I would be his next victim. I saw the marks on her arms. She was trying to warn me. I just saw all men as pigs. My prejudices are getting the better of me."

"Enough of this. We need to hide her," Jack concluded, slapped his thighs and stood up.

"Si," Deni agreed.

"She should leave. Go back to America," Rosa stated firmly in Spanish as she made a pass through the dining area.

"These guys are there too. If they want her, they'll find her. Besides, would you go home without your brother?" Jack spread his hands.

"My guess is she'll be lucky if she sees him again," Deni said gloomily in Spanish.

"You're probably right but let's not go there. Keeping her close is our only option. What about the boat?" Jack said in Spanish.

Jan cast them a look of curiosity. "What are you saying?" she snapped.

"We were discussing the best way to protect you for the time being," Deni lied. "Jack thinks it's the boat. I'll get a couple of the boys to keep lookout tonight."

"If we hurry we can be ready for tomorrow. We have to fix the generator. I have parts in my backpack," Jack said, "Can you get Arturo to take them out to Jerry?" Jack stepped behind the bar and retrieved the backpack.

"What's tomorrow?" Jan asked.

"That I don't know but it's time we took command of everything at our disposal," Jack stated firmly.

Just as Jack was heading for the door the phone rang. Deni waved Angelo off and took the call on the third ring. They all saw Deni's body stiffen as he turned to look at Jack with raised eyebrows. Hanging up Deni signaled Jack to walk with him outside, alone.

"That was Suarez from the hospital in Tepic. Something big must be happening. This morning two guys were stopped at a routine road check. They ran it and were finally stopped in a shootout. One bought it there and the other just died in the hospital. They had a pickup packed with cocaine. He suspects they were part of a rumored drug heist. No one seems to know exactly what is going on but he is very interested in your story. But he can't get here 'til tomorrow."

Jack had a sinking feeling, the situation was very quickly getting complicated.

Shortly after the call, Israel and Ivan returned from fishing. Their father filled them in on the basic details. The young men did not hesitate to take care of Jan. Together with Israel's young fiancé, they escorted her around town where she picked up a few articles of clothing and some sundries.

Arturo, Deni' number three son, and his younger brother Roberto along with two cousins, showed up at the restaurant just after dark. Deni told them that someone was after Señor Jack and they had to protect him. Their chests puffed with pride at the honor of the assignment. Deni handed them each a flashlight and a whistle and told them they must keep each other awake and watch out for any men or vehicles driving slowly or acting strangely. If they saw anything they were to run away blowing their whistles. The boys were scared before he finished his instructions but they swore they would stay awake and do their duty.

*   *   *

Later that night Jack quietly rowed Jan out to the sailboat. "I'll just take a quick look around the boat before you get aboard," Jack said as he unzipped the backpack. He unrolled a sheathed hunting knife.

In the lights reflecting off the water, Jan gasped as he strapped it around his waist. "You... you know how to use that?" she stammered, shocked at the sight.

"I've had a little experience."

Jan's mouth dropped as the man seemed to change before her eyes. like ninjas she had seen in the movies, his body fairly flowed over the stern of the sailboat and slipped into the wheelhouse.

Charlie gave him a welcome meow at the cabin door. The sound of the cat was reassuring. The tone was her typical, selfish, "where you been, I'm hungry" meow, which meant there was no alarm. But just in case, Jack ignored her protest and searched the craft. Coming back to the cockpit, he saw the hind end of the cat as it looked down at Jan in the rowboat.

"Didn't have to worry," he said lightly. "Our guard cat was on the job."

As if on cue the cat meowed again looking for her reward. Jack helped Jan into the sailboat and secured the dinghy.

They sat around the main cabin table drinking coffee as the cat ate.

"You seem to know what you are doing around things," Jan ventured.

"I was in the military, Coast Guard—saw some combat. You'll be safe tonight."

"'Combat', what does that mean?" Jan thought. As much as she wanted to know more, she said nothing.

"Well, it's late," Jack said. "Let me show you a couple of things." He led her to the sleeping quarters. "You remember how to use the head, right?" He pointed it out again as they walked down the narrow corridor between rooms. She nodded. "There are towels in there. We have some water on board but I want to save it. It's best if you shower back at the apartment." He opened the door to a stateroom. "You can sleep in this one. Jerry put new sheets on."

He stepped aside as she looked into the room. The bed took

up most of it. There was a small teak shelf with drawers under it for personal gear, and a small chair. "Okay," she stated tentatively, and stepped in.

He poked his head in to be sure everything was organized and available to her. "If you want any company just keep your door ajar."

Her head snapped back.

Jack took two steps down the corridor and froze. "I meant the cat."

She grinned and Jack shook his head as he walked away.

Stepping up on the deck Jack pulled in a deep breath of the freshness of evening air. From Rosa's, the sounds of Willie and Lobo drifted through the night air. It should be a wonderful peaceful evening, but it wasn't. Evil had come to this place where before, he had found so much peace and healing. He let out a deep sigh.

*　　*　　*

Several times during the night Jack flashed the boy's positions to ensure they were awake. Each time he got an answer back. Returning to the cabin, Jack walked down the corridor and smiled at the cat standing by the closed bedroom door.

Charlie kept Jack company off-and-on during the night. She sensed something was up and jumped on his lap, climbed up his chest and looked at him as if to say, "Is there something you need me to take care of?" She allowed her ear to be scratched until she figured he'd calmed down. Then she made a couple of turns around his lap, kneaded out a likely spot and gifted him the opportunity to be her mattress, it was the least a cat could do.

Charlie woke Jack from one of his own catnaps. She had sensed Jan's movements and jumped to investigate. Jack started at the motion. A second later he heard Jan.

The sun's light glowed behind the Sierra Madres. At the wharf Israel and Ivan were organizing the panga for another day.

Jack rubbed his eyes, mentally chiding himself for sleeping. Through binoculars, Jack saw Deni looking back at him from his second floor apartment. They exchanged waves.

Jack stuck his head in the entryway. "We'll head in as soon as you're ready. We can get breakfast at Rosa's after you shower."

"Okay."

He was wiping the heavy dew off the dinghy's seats when Jan appeared. He couldn't help noticing she looked pretty good so early in the morning.

Jan was holding the cat. Charlie lay upside down and seemingly spineless, letting her belly be rubbed, her paws kneading the air in sheer ecstasy. "Some life," Jan said, looking down at the antics of the cat.

Charlie rolled her head over, looking down at Jack as if to tell him he could be replaced.

"How'd you sleep?" he asked.

"Okay, except for someone scratching on the door." She looked down at the cat, who ignored her. "I assume it was the cat," she added with a wry smile.

Jack ignored the comment. "We should get going."

She put the cat down and accepted his hand as she stepped down into the dinghy.

As they rowed to shore Jan looked Jack over. "You don't look like you got much sleep."

"Umm, some. I'll be okay."

*   *   *

At his hotel suite headquarters in Tepic, Miguel Vegas continued the search. He too had been getting little sleep. The people that worked for him were getting even less. Losing the Hamilton woman had made him furious, yet the news of the shootout at the roadblock gave him renewed hope. He had cut off the head—and the tail had in fact, wiggled. Early this morning he had received confirmation that it was Esparza and Vásquez who had been killed. Vásquez had died at the scene; Esparza last night in the hospital.

Pouring over maps, Vegas concluded that the truck had to be somewhere between Tepic and Vallarta. They wouldn't have had time to unload it. His informants told him that there were only a dozen boxes of cocaine found at the shootout. "The rest must be together," Vegas reasoned.

Vegas tapped a pencil on the map. "Where did you put my treasure, brother?"

Vegas knew the fishermen around San Blas had been in Ernesto's pocket. Santana's presence in the area was changing that rapidly. At last report the Vegas camp had received numerous expressions of regret for the loss of his brother, but more importantly, clear willingness to do business with Miguel Vegas. The callers had been told graphically: "find the truck and turn it over."

Vegas had also learned that Suarez was in charge of the government's pursuit of his property. It had been Suarez who had shot the pair of traitors. Suarez' presence was unfortunate for Vegas, as he could not be bought.

Vegas savagely rubbed his scalp with both hands, exorcising his demons as he concentrated on the task at hand. "When will people learn? It's only the living that matter. The dead are nothing, only the living win!" He snarled.

Vegas bit the end of the pencil, "Where are you woman? How could they have failed to capture her?" He heard about the accident, but her escape didn't make any sense. His people were investigating a rumor of some motorcycle being involved.

The answer came almost immediately. His phone rang, it was his personal secretary.

"Señor Vegas, I realize you are very busy but a Señor Zillia has been trying repeatedly to contact you."

Vegas had to think for a minute before recalling the situation. "The number," he commanded.

Zillia answered his cell on the second ring.

"Hola."

"Zillia, Vegas. What do you know?"

"Ah, ah. St. Julian was here yesterday, Señor. I must release the papers. The government has a record of sending them three days ago," he stammered nervously.

"Shut up!" Vegas yelled. "Tell me about the Yankee."

"He's in La Cruz. I have a card."

Vegas took the information and hung up.

He phoned the Ferret. "We've found the American sailor. This is what I want you to do."

The Ferret sneered as he took the instructions.

18

Jack and Jan met Rosa and Deni sitting over their morning coffee.

"Que pasa, amigo?" Deni asked.

Rosa poured them each a cup and headed for the kitchen.

"Not much," Jack answered. "The kids did a great job last night. They were there every time I checked."

Deni smiled. "Si. I checked them too. Now one day they will be able to tell their friends they guarded the beautiful Señorita and the great Jack St. Julian, as they spent the night on his yacht."

Jan cast Deni a pert smile as Jack rolled his eyes and changed the subject. "Jan will take a shower and then we'll have some breakfast and figure out our next move."

"Other way around I think," Jan said as Rosa approached with platters of food.

As they ate, Deni said, "Suarez called. He said he would be here this morning. He's very interested in talking to Señorita Hamilton."

Jan cast a frightened look at both men, "Did he say anything about Todd?"

"I'm sorry. He did say that he had notified the American authorities."

She nodded and picked at her food.

"When?" Jack asked.

Deni only shrugged. "One other thing," Deni said. "Your crash was on the news last night."

Both waited for Deni to go on.

"They say both men died and that someone on a motorcycle was there. They didn't say any more about it."

After breakfast Jack took Jan out the back of the kitchen and up the stairs to his second floor apartment. He opened the double sliding, glass doors at the top of the staircase, pulled back the thin privacy curtain and ushered her in.

"This is your place?" Jan asked.

"Yes. You showered up here yesterday, didn't you?"

"No, I was in Rosa's." She looked the place over with interest. It was only a studio suite but the colors were bright, cheerful and airy. The floor was tiled in bright aqua, sea-blue and a rich green. A tiled counter held a stainless steel sink and a new two-burner gas stovetop, next to a small refrigerator. The king size bedspread matched the tones of the tiles. It was all very tasteful.

"Not exactly a grass shack on the beach," she smirked.

He gave her a neutral smile. "Shower's in there." He pointed to the bathroom.

The bathroom was fresh and vibrant. The shower was directed back towards the wall so no door was necessary. The counter top and sink were made of small hand tiles that were designed with inlaid sailing ships and dolphins. Opaque, square glass blocks, created a window that brought in light. She suddenly realized that the whole place had the feel of a feminine hand.

She looked at him again. "You didn't design this, did you?"

"No. My wife did. She's gone now." He didn't elaborate.

Jan was silent.

"I want to look after a couple errands," he changed the subject. "You going to be okay?"

"I'm sure. And Jack," she paused, "thanks again. I didn't mean to pry."

He shrugged. "No problem."

He stopped at the sliding entry doors. "Oh by the way, there's no lock on the door. In fact, it hasn't got a latch."

She walked over to him, a concerned look on her face. "You don't have a lock on the door?" she asked.

"Never needed one. It wasn't built with one in the first place," he said, and then continued. "This is what we use for security." He slid the sliding glass doors together and from the handle of one of the doors he unwound a thick red rubber band and fitted it over the opposite handle so both sliding doors were joined. He looked at her—she looked at the rubber band.

"If you want real security, you wrap the band twice." Which he did.

She looked back at him. "You're kidding."

"You want me to stay?"

Her mind yelled yes. "No, that's okay. I guess."

"You won't have a problem. No one will bother you." He unwound the band and opened the door.

After he stepped out, Jan pulled the rubber band over the handle, twice. She looked at it and back at him. She couldn't believe the absurdity of it all. "You are something else, Mr. St. Julian," she said through the door.

"Yeah," He said as he turned to leave.

Jack trotted down the stairs and back into the kitchen. He gave Rosa a peck on the cheek.

"Thanks for breakfast."

As he headed through the dining area he saw Deni slaving over his accounting books, trying to make sense of them.

"I'm going to get some of Jerry's stuff off the boat. Be back in 20 or 30 minutes." Deni nodded but was totally distracted by the books.

*   *   *

Deni was in deep concentration when a shadow crossed over his table. Looking up, he saw the snide face of the Ferret standing over him. Another man stood beside him. Before Deni could move he felt the pinprick of the knifepoint just under his armpit in the back of his rib cage.

"Buenos dias, amigo." The Ferret smiled coldly, holding the blade firmly against Deni's ribs. Pulling a chair up so that he was still behind Deni, the man spoke quietly into Deni's ear. "We are looking for someone. Maybe you can be of help for a change."

Deni held his cool, looking at the man out of the corner of his eye. His mind was in overdrive, trying to remember where everyone was. He saw Rosa glance suspiciously through the breezeway from the kitchen.

The men saw her.

"Check it," the Ferret commanded.

His companion headed to the kitchen.

Deni saw the man move towards his wife and made a move but the pressure of the knife deepened, lifting him partly out of his chair—cutting off any ideas he might've had.

The Ferret continued, "There is an American woman that was in La Cruz the other day, on a sailboat ride. We just want to talk with her."

"What's that got to do with us?" Deni glared.

"We know about you. You have kept your nose out of things, but this needs doing. I know you were at the wharf, and you know the gringo sailboat owner." The Ferret looked over at his partner who had been standing at the kitchen door and nodded. His companion moved slowly into the kitchen.

Deni tried again to get up but the edge of a knife painfully dug into his ribs. The Ferret's other hand grabbed traction at Deni's neck. "We are just going to look around a little. Nothing stupid, amigo, and no harm comes to any," the man warned.

Deni froze.

The other man moved into the kitchen where Rosa was busy chopping tomatoes for salsa with a very large knife. He cautiously checked every corner to ensure they were alone. Rosa watched him while continuing to chop. He walked over to the cutting board and picked up a piece of tomato. The knife came down with a snap and missed his finger by a whisker, his hand flinched back. He reached under his jacket and pulled out his own knife.

Rosa stood her ground venomously staring at the man. Her knife was defiantly leveled at his belly. He hesitated and stared back at her. A smile crossed his face and he moved off. He pointed up the stairs to the apartments. "What's up there?"

"Our apartment."

He slowly moved towards the stairs.

"So is that American sailor still in town?" the Ferret asked of Deni.

Deni didn't answer. The pressure on the tip of the knife moved. Deni felt the pain as his flesh opened.

"No, he's not here. He went out today, fishing." Deni stoically absorbed the pain.

"Well, we'll check his boat next."

Jan stepped out of the shower humming to herself enjoying a fresh feeling of cleanliness when she saw movement through the screen doors. Someone was coming up the stairs—the stealthy movement screamed trouble. She backed up, out of sight. The intruder would be on her in seconds.

At that same moment Captain Suarez, his driver, a guard and US DEA agent Larry Diaz drove around the corner to the cantina. Suarez recognized the dark Ford suburban. They rolled silently to a stop. Suarez looked at his driver. "Go around the back. Take Agent Diaz."

The two men quickly and silently slipped out of the car.

Suarez and his bodyguard exited the car, drew their pistols and headed for the front of the restaurant. He cautiously looked around the corner of the doorway and saw Deni with another man standing too close to him. The body positions were all wrong for a friendly conversation.

Suarez signaled his guard to be alert and then holstered his own pistol. He casually walked into the restaurant. He watched the standing man's eyes bulge at the sight of the Federal blue uniform. Suarez loved that look of terror when the bad guys saw him.

Suarez saw the man quickly pull something away from Deni and conceal it in his jacket. The man began to move but a flick of the guard's pistol froze him where he stood.

Walking up, Suarez announced affably, "Good morning, my friend Deni. Como esta?" He saw the spot of red stain on Deni's shirt. In an ice cold voice he commanded the Ferret. "Move away from my friend, amigo, and sit,"

The Ferret complied. Deni was about to smash the man's face in when he saw the gun in the guard's hand and decided to be patient.

Out on the patio, the Ferret's accomplice had reached the top of the stairs. He pulled on the sliding door. It didn't open. He tried again with more force. It gave a little but still would not open. He looked through the screen and saw the rubber band. Someone was definitely inside. He lifted his knife.

"Freeze!" a voice snapped behind him.

He slowly turned and saw the gun in the officer's hand. The criminal spread his hands away from his body and dropped the knife.

Rosa couldn't believe her eyes as a uniformed cop led the man slowly back through her kitchen door. A white man followed, obviously an American. He nodded as he passed.

Watching them enter the dining area, Suarez commented caustically: "So, a twin. Sit."

The driver saw that his boss' order was carried out.

"What are you doing here?" Suarez asked the pair, receiving silence in return.

After a minute, Deni said, "They are looking for some American woman."

Suarez looked at the pair. "Is your boss sending you to attack little old ladies? And you can't even do that right?" he sneered. "Were these two bothering you, amigo?" he asked Deni.

"I don't have what they want," Deni answered flatly.

Suarez slowly looked the pair over so they knew he would recognize them again then warned, "You are going now and you are not to come back. If I hear that you come into La Cruz for so much as a fish, I will find you. Comprende, amigos?"

As the Ferret began to move Suarez grasped his wrist exposing the knife. "I could make you eat this, or better yet, give you to Deni. Drop it."

The power in Suarez' hand forced the man to obey. The knife clattered on the tile floor. With his other hand on the Ferret's shoulder Suarez lifted him out of the chair. His guard grabbed the accomplice and with the barrel of his pistol under the man's ear forced him to rise.

"This officer will see you out. Search their car, take their cell phones. See they get out of town." Suarez ordered his staff.

As they departed Rosa came in from the kitchen still holding her knife.

"Hola, tia," Suarez greeted his cousin gravely.

Rosa nodded and then to her husband, "She's upstairs, probably scared to death."

Diaz took the initiative. "Hola, Mrs. Marroso. My name is agent Larry Diaz. I'm a friend of your cousin's. I'm with the US government, here to help protect Miss Hamilton."

Rosa looked the man over. "What can you people protect?" she spat back.

"Come with me Mrs. Marroso. We'll get her," The agent said, ignoring the sting.

Rosa looked over at her husband, who nodded.

Just as they left, Jack came around the corner into the restaurant. He saw the uniforms and froze. Deni signaled him in and made the introductions. "Jack St. Julian, meet my wife's cousin, Captain Heraldo Suarez of the Federal Narcotics Department."

Jack held out his hand and received a firm, but non-threatening handshake, and a calculating appraisal. He glanced at the scars on the side of Suarez' face.

"Where's Jan?"

"She's okay. Rosa has gone to get her," Deni answered.

Jack looked from one man to the other. "What's happening?"

"You know these men?" Suarez asked.

"No, but I know what they are."

Jack looked up as another suited man came through the kitchen door. He had US cop written all over him. Behind the man was Rosa with Jan in her embrace.

Jan had been crying. As she entered the room Jan saw the men. Her back straightened, she patted Rosa's hand to let her go, and walked over to Jack's side.

"Please Senorita, have a chair," Suarez said.

Jan complied.

"My name is Captain Heraldo Mexia Suarez," he stated officially. "I am with the Federal Narcotics Department. This man is Special Agent Larry Diaz from your United States Drug Enforcement Agency. He is here as a guest in my country."

Both men handed her cards.

"You're looking for my brother, right?" she cut to the chase.

"Miss Hamilton, we would like to talk to you. Do you mind?" Diaz asked gently.

Jan looked up at Jack as he interrupted the authorities. "You didn't answer the lady's question," Jack looked intently from one cop to the next.

Neither was used to having to answer questions but this man's voice spoke of authority. "And you are, Señor?" Diaz demanded.

"Jack St. Julian, and you still haven't answered the lady's question."

"Yes. Yes, of course we are," Diaz spoke first.

Jack then turned on Suarez and waited for a response.

"Si, Señor. We are looking for him and many more. That is why we are here."

Jack evaluated the pair. "This was it," he thought. "Once you start, these are the guys you have to go with." He turned to Jan and nodded.

Diaz mentally registered the name St. Julian.

Jan started, "I could see him coming up the stairs. I hid in the bathroom. I heard the screen rattle, twice. I heard voices, then nothing. When I peeked out he was gone. What happened?"

"We got there just as he was at the door," Diaz stated.

Jan looked at him. "Thank you, officer."

Then out of the blue she smiled at Jack and said, "The lock worked!"

Jack cracked a smile. "We'll have to get a patent."

"Why do you think these men are after you, Miss Hamilton?" Suarez asked seriously.

"I do not know." She looked from man to man, then finally surveyed Suarez squarely, "I really don't know, but I want my brother back."

Suarez said. "Miss Hamilton, your brother works for the Vegas family of Mexico City. You knew that did you not?"

"Yes. He is their chief financial officer of Vemexa. He is very good at his job. They just opened the Maria Elena hotel here. Why? What's that got to do with anything?"

"Well, Miss Hamilton, we seriously believe the Vegas family has recently become very deeply involved in drugs and other things," Suarez said bluntly.

"I don't know anything about that, and Todd told me that he had nothing to do with drugs. I asked him straight out. He swore to me he only worked on very legal things. He's a lawyer, too, you know," she added defensively, realizing that she was not being entirely truthful.

Suarez paused, "We don't know entirely what is going on, but something big has taken place. The night before yesterday, Ernesto Vegas and his bodyguard were assassinated. You know that."

She nodded.

"Yesterday, north of Tepic two men died trying to evade a police road check. We strongly suspect they worked for the Vegas family. There was a considerable amount of cocaine in their vehicle. One died in a shootout. The other died in the hospital last night."

"Bad day for the Vegas boys," Jack said with no pity.

Suarez looked at him before he continued. "It has been a strong rumor that there was some kind of a double-cross within the family, and that a very large shipment of cocaine has been stolen, worth hundreds of millions of dollars. Until now, we have not known who stole what from who, but with all this activity it would appear that something is happening. And as Mr. St. Julian so aptly put it, this has been hard on the drug dealers, which is fine with me, so long as innocent people do not get involved or harmed. That is why I have to ask you again Miss Hamilton, what is your involvement?" His tone just a little firmer than earlier.

"Wait a minute, Captain, they tried to kill us!" Jan screeched.

"When was this?" The cop asked.

"Yesterday! They tried to run us off the road. They crashed and we escaped."

"You left the scene of an accident, Señorita?" Suarez demanded.

Jan's mouth slammed shut. Silence filled the room.

Suarez turned on Jack. "Why, Mr. St. Julian?" he threatened coldly.

Jack looked the man square in the eyes. Time stood still.

Then Jack calmly stated. "You gentlemen have two choices. Get your information quickly, with our cooperation or make threats. Maybe you'll learn something, maybe you won't. I wouldn't bet on the latter."

For a long minute Suarez held Jack's stare. The Mexican could see there was no fear. Reason and discipline finally won out. "We ask your cooperation."

"Thank you. We are on the same side, officer," Jack said. "Go ahead Jan."

"I don't know what is happening. My brother invited me down here for a vacation, to show off his new hotel—he thinks of it in that way. He never said anything about what goes on, other than he is this rich family's financial manager, and he has made them a lot of money. He always says how happy they are with him. He never said anything about drugs or illegal stuff, honest."

Suarez and Cruz absorbed this like good cops. They were weighing how "the subject" spoke with what she said. Jack watched them doing it.

"Tell me about yesterday," Suarez said.

Jan went on to relate all that had happened to them.

To Jack, both men appeared satisfied that she had been telling the truth and that she was not involved in drugs. Her belief in her brother's innocence on the other hand was simply naïve. Everyone also knew ignorance wouldn't protect her. For whatever reason, Vegas wanted to get to her and whatever he wanted her for wouldn't be healthy.

As the telling of the events unfolded, Jack watched the two men exchange glances.

"Miss Hamilton, I have to tell you, it would be best if you went home," Diaz stated evenly.

"She is in danger whether she goes home or not. Vegas reaches into the States," Jack countered.

"I'm not going anywhere until I have my brother back. He's my family," she stated firmly.

Suarez thought for a moment. "We can offer you protection."

"What can you do?" Jack snapped. "Put her in prison so Vegas can run around until you catch him? What have you got on him anyway? I hear he's a billionaire. If you could pin something on him you'd have done it."

"This has to be done legally, Mr. St. Julian."

"Yeah, and he's got more lawyers than you do, politicians too, I'd wager," Jack shot back.

"I understand your frustration, Mr. St. Julian, but what does that change?"

"Nothing changes. Both of you have priorities." He stared

hard at each man. "Miss Hamilton's safety is not at the top of your list. You want this doper; you both see bait." He looked hard at Jan.

"Mr. St. Julian, that is not the way the US government conducts business," Diaz responded sharply.

"Bull!" Jack snapped. "Both of you and your governments will use whatever is necessary to achieve your ends. Now, if you want to discuss a mutually-acceptable arrangement maybe we can get somewhere."

"Like what, Mr. St. Julian?" Suarez countered.

"I'll keep an on eye her," Jack stated flatly.

Jan looked at him. She had hoped he would intercede in her defense, somehow she felt safe with this man.

Jack saw her look and turned to her. "Your call."

"What would we do? Where would we go?"

"Let me take care of that," Jack answered cryptically.

"Captain St. Julian, I do not need to tell you that as a tourist, a guest in my country, military or not—you have no authority," Suarez stated gravely. "Deni has told me a little about you. What you have done in the past may be one thing, but this is very different. Do not get too involved in this."

"No problem," Jack retorted, with the most innocent of smiles. "I just want to keep the lady safe. No crime in that is there, Captain?"

The Mexican didn't look convinced.

"This is what I have in mind," Jack continued, as he briefly laid out his plan. The officers didn't like it, but Jan was adamant she wasn't leaving, and she wasn't going to trust the Mexicans to protect her. She threatened to scream to the press if they forced her.

The compromise had been that Suarez' bodyguard would stay at Rosa's until Jack and Jan cast off. Suarez reluctantly agreed and eventually they pulled out leaving the bodyguard behind.

Once alone Jack said, "I have got to get organized. Jerry has us about ready to go. We'll be on the water for at least two, maybe three days before the *Juan de Fuca* gets here. By then, the harbor patrol is supposed to be all over the dive site." Jack turned to Jan. "Is there anything else you need?"

"I don't think so."

"I'll help Jerry get his stuff off the boat. Shouldn't be more than an hour," Jack said to the armed officer and Deni. "You going to be okay?" he asked Jan.

She nodded.

Before Jack left, Deni ran upstairs and brought down his old .303 Lee-Enfield rifle, loaded it and placed it behind the bar, under a strip of cloth. He phoned Angelo to come in early and let him know about the rifle. The cop watched but said nothing.

Jan came and sat beside the Deni. "Tell me about him," she probed.

Deni smiled, "Hasn't he told you anything?"

She shook her head. "He said he was married, but she was 'gone'?"

"She died about eight months ago. He is still pretty messed-up."

"Oh."

"He's been coming down here a long time. He is younger than me, but we sort-of got along. Jack and his dad were different from other tourists. They didn't just come to get drunk and, well, you know." He paused. "They treated us as real people, not servants. I remember Jack's dad..."

Jan saw a faraway look in Deni's eye.

"He's dead too?"

"Si, Señorita. Anyway, Señor St. Julian's Spanish was terrible, but he was, as you say, 'game.' He tried to speak it. Papa appreciated the effort. Papa never went to school. His English was no better than Jack's dad's Spanish." Deni grinned. "They would teach each other, old drinking songs. They would sing together, each in the other's language. They did this especially when coming home from fishing. It was very terrible.

Jack and I would take shelter in the front of the panga but there was no escape," he gave a melancholy wince.

"Your English is very good," Jan said.

"Papa was a hard man but made us study in school. I spent two semesters in California taking business courses in college. I guess that put the American in my English."

"Deni is an unusual name, where did you get it?"

My grandmother was French. It's supposed to be Dennis, but everyone calls me Deni.

"So you guys have been fishing buddies for years?"

"Yes, but there was more," Deni gave her a conspiratorial smile. He waited until his wife walked past, busy with the duties of the kitchen.

"And…" Jan waited.

"Well, it happened a long time ago. Jack's ship visited the naval base in Puerto Vallarta. He was a young naval officer. There was, as they say, an incident."

"Wait, his ship?" she asked.

"Of course. Navy or Coast Guard, one of those. I don't know the difference." He shrugged. "I think it was a destroyer or something like that. Did he not tell you?"

Jan shook her head again. "Just that he was in the military, some special service he said. I don't know anything about the military."

"Then that is something he will have to tell you about. You must ask him and then tell me." "What do you mean by that?"

"When Jack was in the service, his papa came down by himself a couple of times. He would tell us of the exploits of his son. He was very proud. It is not that we didn't believe Señor St. Julian, but…" Deni paused. "It is only… well, the stories, they seemed so impossible. Then one day Jack arrived at our door. He had bullet holes in him." Deni stopped for dramatics. "He was weak. He spent a month with us. Carmen and Rosa fussed over him. He would come out in the launch—sometimes just to sleep, and later as his strength came back he would help out. You know, fish a

226

little. That was before he was married. Before he left, he told me only a little about what happened. He was in the South China Sea. Apparently some terrorist tried to take over some little country, and Jack and some others stopped them somehow. Things got pretty rough I guess. Anyway, Jack helped get everyone back safe—everyone but himself."

"Who's Carmen?"

"My baby sister. She too is a nurse, a health nurse, she works for the government. She wants to be in love with Jack, always has."

"But…"

"Jack is not in love with her," he shrugged.

"Why? What happened?"

"I go too far, you must ask Carmen this. I can tell you a story about Jack that is really… well…" he paused again for effect, "… a legend," he said in a low, conspiratorial voice. "I was saying he visited us here in Puerto Vallarta when he was a young ensign. This is many years ago, of course. It was some joint naval exercise or something. Anyway, the whole crew got shore leave, so Jack and I got together and 'did the town' in an ancient naval tradition."

"You went out and got hammered," Jan interjected with a straight face.

"You have a way with words, Señorita. Toward the end of the evening we got split up. I think our navigational gear had not been working 100 percent. Sailors were all along the Malecón— you know, the boardwalk downtown?"

She nodded.

Deni stopped again as Rosa walked by. "…As I was saying, it was getting late. I decided to head back to La Cruz. I had been walking back to my truck when I heard this awful scream. I ran to it. It was coming from down a back alley. I ran and there were several sailors. They were all drunk and were being rough with a young lady. The light was poor, but I could see her dress had been torn and she had been knocked to the ground."

"They hadn't…?" she asked tentatively.

"No, but it didn't look good. I walked in and started knocking heads together. There must have been eight or more of them. Things weren't going well when all of a sudden Jack showed up. We had a lot of fun—bodies were bouncing off walls and falling to the ground. I think some were smart enough to run. It was over very quickly."

Jan looked up. Deni's wife quietly stopped behind his chair. "Then what happened?" Jan asked.

"I went to see after the young woman. She was okay—just scared. About then the shore patrol showed up. I heard later that although no charges were laid, those young sailors suffered greatly under the hand of Ensign St. Julian. But in the end, it was I who suffered the worst," Deni concluded somberly.

"Why was that?"

"Well, I helped the young girl home, to be sure she was okay. Before I know it I am married. So you see from that affair—I have been sentenced to life."

Deni suddenly yelped as Rosa's kitchen towel came snapping down hard on the top of his head.

"Ha! All lies!" she barked, jumping back with practiced ease out of the grasp of her husband's thrusting arm. "How many did he tell you there were?"

"Eight or ten," Jan answered, a smiled racing across her face.

"Ha! Not 20 or 100? The number increases with each telling," Rosa looked at Jan and gave a wink.

Deni grabbed again this time capturing her arm. He swung her around into his lap his arms encircled her in a bear hug.

"I'd have been better off going to the boat with those boys, rather than to be trapped for life by a smelly fisherman," she laughed.

Deni squeezed her waist burying his face in her hair and growled as he bit her neck. With the practiced ease of generations of Latin flirtation, Rosa wriggled out of his grasp. As she escaped he delivered a crisp slap on her departing rump. She responded with another snap of her towel. As a snake he grabbed the towel forcing her to let it go. Rosa shot something at him in Spanish. Deni responded with a bright smile. Jan did not need to know the words to get the meaning.

"Well, you see what I mean?" he asked with an innocent grin.

"It looks as if the suffering has been mutual," Jan smirked.

"Perhaps so," he gave wolfish smile.

19

Vegas stoically took the Ferret's information on what happened in La Cruz in silence. He filed the revenge on Marroso under future projects. Right now he had a shipment of drugs to find. He had loyal police in the states of Sinaloa and Durango stopping any trucks that fit the description of his errant vehicle.

Santana and the helicopters were combing over the swamps of San Blas but had nothing to report. A Cessna had been covering the sky north of Bucerias to Las Varas. Now that the shoe was on the other foot, Vegas got a sick satisfaction from the difficulties the narcos had trying to find the farmers and shippers of drugs.

Santana called, just after noon. He had been in San Blas for nearly 24 hours, checking with those who were with the family. Offering olive branches to any willing to come forward with information, he was beginning to bear fruit.

"Garcia has contacted me," Santana said. Garcia was the head honcho for the area and had been one of Ernesto's main men. "I gave my word there would be no retaliations to anyone who cooperated in finding the cargo."

"It will be so," Vegas confirmed, "only if we find the cargo. Has he heard anything?"

"Ortega had contacted him, saying there had been some complication. He never got back to Garcia with anything more, but the knowledge of the truck is becoming public. I am hearing some of the other families are sending people into the area to look for it."

"I'm hearing the same. It will be news soon, we must be very careful." Vegas related what had happened in La Cruz.

"You want me to visit this fisherman and his wife?" Santana asked.

"Once this is over, consider it one of your first tasks. I want it dirty—attitudes like theirs must be discouraged. Right now, all assets must be on this truck."

"So be it. I will get Garcia to scour everywhere."

"See to it," Vegas commanded and hung up.

For the hundredth time, Vegas looked at the maps before him—aerial, marine, topographical, government and road. "Where did you put it, brother?"

*   *   *

The sun was past its height when they finally cast off. Jack slowly pointed the *Heavenly Daze* in a west-southwesterly direction out of the harbor; the course got them away from land in every direction as fast as possible. Once they were a good two miles out he yelled that it was safe to come out. Jan arrived with a pair of beers between her fingers. Jack continued to motor straight out into the middle of the bay then set a course due west for the true Pacific.

As the sailboat left the harbor, Suarez' guard reported in. "He has taken the woman out of the harbor."

"All right. I want you to stay in La Cruz, close to the restaurant and the Marrosos," Suarez commanded. "Vegas may try revenge to distract us. Stay visible. I will send some backup."

"Si, Señor."

Before noon, Suarez had received authorization to take whatever measures necessary to find the shipment, and if possible, pin it on Vegas. He decided an anonymous tip was in order.

*   *   *

Jerry spent his afternoon at the wharf helping a Mexican fisherman repair an outboard motor. He watched as a tall young man, with a sun-bleached ponytail, ambled down the deck. Jerry recognized another beach bum when he saw one—this one looked nervous.

"Hey man. What's happening?" the man asked.

"Not much," Jerry said, wiping his hands on an oily rag.

"Look, I want to rent a sailboat. It's called *Heavenly Daze*. I met a chick, light brown hair, at the Maria Elena hotel the other day. She said this guy rents out his boat to private parties."

All this was said in one quick, well-rehearsed burst of dialogue. Jerry looked at him for a long moment before answering—Deni and Jack had told him the bad guys were going to come looking for Jan. Jerry threw out the bait. "light brown hair, like shoulder length, right? Pretty good looker, nice legs?"

"Yeah, man, that's the one."

"Man, I don't know what's going on, but she was here yesterday," Jerry said. He saw the man's eyes light up.

"She was?"

"Yeah. It's all over town. She'd spent the night before on that boat, if you know what I mean?"

"Lucky guy," the young man grinned.

"Yeah. Well, I don't know who she is, but it looked like the guy got caught or something, 'cause there were cops all over the place yesterday morning. I heard they took her and put her on a plane back to the States. The guy took his sailboat out of here like the devil was after him."

The young man stood silently taking this all in.

"I figure she must have some big-shot husband who found out and was looking for blood," Jerry added.

"So, she's gone?"

Jerry nodded his head.

"Did the guy say when he would be coming back?"

"He didn't talk to no one, man. Like I said, he just jumped on his boat and took off like a scared rabbit. He didn't worry about breaking the speed limit, either. There are a couple guys who want to talk to him about that, too." Jerry forcibly stopped himself from saying more. What he was doing was fun, but he didn't want to overdo it.

The man stood there, indecisive. Finally, he said, "Okay," then turned and walked away.

An hour later, the Ferret had the regrettable task of telling Vegas more bad news from La Cruz. Vegas listened intently. "You believe this?"

"I do not know, Señor. We are checking with the airlines now, but will take time to get past security and find out if she was on any plane."

"Continue and report back immediately."

"Si, Señor."

*   *   *

The news broke: "$400 Million USD in Drugs Lost. Suspected To Be Somewhere in the State of Nayarit."

The TV announcer related the assassinations and the two traffic accidents, doing a good job of tying all three together. The police would not comment of course, it was the sort of journalism Vegas hated.

It was going to be a gold rush, people would be all over the place. He had to find the truck quickly and the woman was the key.

Vegas picked up the phone and called the pilot of the Cessna. "I want you to change your plans. There is a sailboat I want you to find."

"Okay. Can you describe it?" the pilot asked.

Vegas grimaced—he hadn't really paid that much attention. He knew nothing about sailboats. "It has a single mast," he paused. "The sails were white."

"That narrows it down to about 95% of the sailboats in Mexico," the pilot thought, but wisely kept his mouth shut.

"Its hull had a grayish coloring. It looked like it was made of steel rather than fiberglass."

"That helps," the pilot said diplomatically. "Which way you think it might be headed?"

"Supposedly west, toward Cabo."

"I don't have the range to get there and back and stay airborne."

"Just get out and find it," Vegas hung up.

The pilot picked up some maps and started plotting potential courses. "Talk about your needle in a haystack," the man said to himself, sighing in frustration.

20

Jack anchored between the two Marieta islands. The water was calm as a lake. As Jan watched the rocks and sand bars slide past well beneath them. Jack stopped at a spot where the water was deep blue.

"We'll be okay here tonight I'm sure," Jack said. "Have you ever worked a gas stove?"

"Yes,"

"If you don't mind handling the galley, I'll get the boat settled for the night."

"I don't mind."

They warmed up some chicken mole, rice and refried beans from Rosa's. Jack offered her wine, she drank a little. Charlie thought poorly of smelly bitter chocolate sauce on chicken and settled for dry cat food. They enjoyed a gorgeous sunset over the edge of the island and ate under the stars as Jack pointed out different constellations.

"I can't keep my eyes open," Jan finally confessed.

"I'll clean up. Thanks for helping." Jack grabbed for their plates. "Oh, by the way, the boat is alarmed. I forgot to tell you last night because I was staying outside but I've got to get some sleep tonight. Let me show you how to arm and disarm the keypad."

Jack had her practice twice to get the idea. As tired as she was she tried to watch and understand the combination. Shaking her head, she sleepily looked at him and asked, "Why not just use a rubber band?"

Jack gave her a wry smile. "Never mind. If you need to go outside just wake me."

Jan gave him a final smirk, turned and headed for her stateroom.

Jack sat at the helm scratching the cat's ear, reminiscing on past nights he had watched the stars, Pat in his arms. He set his watch alarm for one hour and drifted off.

During the night he got up several times and scanned the horizon with his floodlight. There was nothing. Each time he came in, he shut and locked the companionway door. Charlie was not used to this but complied dutifully with indoor guard duty.

Jack had the boat moving at first light. He brought Heavenly Daze around so she faced into the wind. Wasting no time he worked his way to the bow and positioned himself just forward of the main mast. He strapped himself to the mast with a safety line then took the mainsail winch handle and inserted it into the ratchet of the winch. Jack deftly cranked the winch, hoisting the mainsail to its full height. He cleated off the main halyard and hurried back to the cockpit where he released the main sheet, setting it to take advantage of a fresh, steady beam wind.

They were well out to sea when Jan poked her disheveled head out the companionway door and looked at him sleepily. "Don't you ever sleep?" she asked.

"Good point. But right now, how'd you like to try your hand at breakfast? Coffee first."

"Aye, aye, captain," she smiled, turned and vanished.

Not long after, coffee arrived, strong and black.

Jack set a course that took them south, past the Morros, through the wide channel in the south of the bay. This was the passageway that all the big cruise ships navigated. Jack was relieved to see that there were no boats anywhere near the Morros rocks, perhaps the professor's secret had been holding safely.

Jan eventually reappeared with an ugly looking mess of scrambled eggs, chopped ham and melted cheese. "It's supposed to be an omelet, but I'm not used to cooking on a moving ship. Sorry."

To Jack it was hot and tasty. "Whatever it was supposed to be, it's good," he said, finishing it all.

South of the Morros, Jack steered due west out into the open Pacific. The mountains of the Sierra del Cuale range, the spur of the Sierra Madres that flanked the bay, soon slipped into the eastern horizon. They sailed peacefully. The only sounds were coming from the sails that snapped briskly in the crisp offshore breeze.

After Jan returned from cleaning up, Jack asked, "How about you steer and I'll get a bit of a nap?"

"If you think I can." She looked at the big wheel apprehensively.

"Sure. The wind's constant. All you have to do is keep us going straight. I'll just be on the deck here. We have autopilot, if you want."

"I'll try," she gave a shrug of insecure excitement. She really did want to try.

"See the heading, 260° west?" He tapped the compass. "Keep us pointed in that general direction. You don't have a lot to worry about. Normally, after sunrise, the prevailing wind out on the ocean remains pretty steady but a sailor needs to keep a sharp eye so that the sail doesn't begin to "luff" or flutter—a sure sign that the vessel is falling off wind. But if you make a small adjustment to the tiller, you'll be able to keep her under sail.""

"260 degrees west. Aye, aye," she saluted and added a cheeky smile.

Jack lay out on cushions on the deck. In short order, Jan could hear he was asleep. Charlie climbed on his chest and made herself comfortable, soon joining him in slumber. Jan watched him, with his cat's head hanging off the edge of his upper arm— the picture of tranquility.

She drew a deep breath and surveyed her surroundings. From behind the wheel she got a new point of view. Her mind began to wander: fantasies of sailing the seven seas, nothing but her and the wind. "And maybe with that man—that wouldn't be so bad," she thought. He had been awfully nice and obviously very capable. "Yes, sailing the seven seas might be quite the life."

Thinking of Jack turned her mind back to Todd and she saddened. She'd only agreed to go with Jack as a way to stay down here. It was that or go home, they had made that very clear. Now she realized she was still unhappy, being so far removed from the search.

Jan maintained their course for nearly an hour, lost in daydreams. The sound of an engine startled her. Turning, she saw a big cabin cruiser coming up fast. Frightened, she yelled to Jack. He shielded his eyes, took one look at the fast approaching vessel and lay back down.

In short order the cruiser was on them, Jan saw Deni waving his arms in greeting. The close proximity of another craft made her nervous. She kept one eye on the compass and both hands on the wheel.

Deni pulled alongside, much too close for Jan's liking. One of his sons expertly matched their speed. Two couples, Deni's fishing clients for the day, leaned over the side and watched the exchange. Jack looked at the audience.

"They're from Quebec, Canada. Don't speak much English. Their Spanish is better," Deni hollered.

Jack nodded and gave them a friendly wave. They all waved back.

"So," Deni called over to Jan behind the wheel. "He's already made a galley slave of you?" He laughed. "Probably got you doing the cooking." Deni looked at Jack. "How are things?"

Jack gave him a thumbs-up. "How about you?"

"We had a visitor yesterday," Deni said, "Jerry saw him on the wharf. He asked to rent your boat. Named it and everything. Asked about Jan."

"What did he tell him?"

Deni laughed. "Basically that the cops had come and whisked

Jan away and that you hot-footed it out of town in your sailboat. I think he said something about an angry husband."

Jan looked at the pair. "What?"

Deni's laugh strengthened. He gave her an innocent shrug then that wolfish smile. "Anyway, Suarez called. So did Diaz. They say they are searching everywhere—but no luck."

"Yeah," Jack said.

"Diaz says the airline cooperated, J.H. left Puerto Vallarta yesterday afternoon, American Airlines. She arrived safe in Dallas with a connection to Indianapolis. It's all on the records, he said."

"Well, that's as much as we can do," Jack said. He turned and looked at Jan.

She bit her lip. "Nothing about Todd?"

Deni's face darkened. He shook his head. "Sorry, Señorita. Well, I got to make a living. You need anything?"

"What about the Professor?" Jack asked.

"Oh yeah. He is coming in tomorrow by plane, and your ship is on its way. What do you want to do?"

Jack thought for a minute. "Probably best to meet them at sea."

"Maybe." Deni waved and ordered Israel to pull away. "Headed for Corbetena."

"Doesn't Deni have a CB or something to talk to us with?" Jan asked after he had gone.

"Yeah. Everyone uses VHF, but it's open channels, and I'm a little concerned at who might be listening. Just being careful with the cargo. Cell phones don't work out here." Jack straightened himself out. "I arranged with Suarez that, if anything really urgent comes up, they'll risk the VHF, but cryptically. In that case we'll get more protection too."

She dropped her eyes and said no more. Jack stepped down into the wheelhouse and joined her at the helm. "You okay?" he asked.

"I guess," she muttered, the tranquility of the sailing now lost. "Do you think something bad has happened to Todd?"

Jack kept a poker face. "There's no way to know. There's always hope."

Jack had an idea. They changed course to 315° north and west. They passed another traveler, a giant green sea turtle heading west. Jan laid on the edge of the deck looking over as Jack sailed to within twenty feet of the turtle, before it popped its small head up and dove out of sight. Later, two pods of whales accompanied by dozens of dolphins passed, heading east into the bay.

The morning melted away into tropical perfection, the offshore breeze stayed fresh and true. Sailing was easy and lazy.

As the sun passed its zenith a small rock grew on the horizon to the northeast. "What's that called?" Jan asked.

"Corbetena. It means 'the corvette' in Spanish,"

Jack said. "There's some good fishing here. The bottom shallows—with sandbars, and some rock outcroppings. On the east, there's a huge sand bar—extremely good spot for red snapper—up to a hundred pounds. We call them hachinago in Spanish."

"I've had that in a restaurant at the Malecón. They served the whole fish, eyes and everything," she grimaced. "How could something that small get so big?"

"Well, they do. I have pictures below. Deni, me and a guy from New York—catching the things; the snappers are monsters. Deni gets a good price for them."

"He would sell what you caught?"

"Sure. What were we going to do with about 400 pounds of red snapper? All the fishermen do it," Jack smiled. "The customer pays for the boat for the day. If they have a good day, they catch a bunch of fish. They're happy and tip the captain and crew. Then the captain takes the catch and sells it." Jack chuckled. "So, when fishing is good, it is very good for the captain. How do you think Deni bought the restaurant? You should ask him about the land holdings he has out by Punta Mita. The guy's a land baron!" Jack laughed.

Jan just shook her head and smiled. Deni's charter was nowhere to be seen.

"What say we catch a little supper?" Jack asked.

"Fishing?"

He nodded. "Have you ever used a hand line?"

"I've never been fishing."

"Oh? Well this is a good way to start." He stepped below and returned with an old gallon plastic water bottle that had a wad of fishing line wrapped around it. On the end of the line was a stubby, pencil-thick lead weight. Two different-sized treble hooks were attached to the line at approximately 12 and 24 inches above the weight.

"Isn't the hook supposed to go on the end?" Jan asked as he un-spooled about six feet of line.

"We're going to jig for bottom fish. That means the weight hits the bottom first, then you jig." Jack slipped small bits of bacon onto both sets of hooks, and threw the line into the water. He held the plastic bottle so rounds of line peeled off by the weight. The line stopped on its own accord. Then with the line between his thumb and forefingers, he lifted up in a quick jerking motion, about a foot each time.

"See?" He demonstrated a couple times before handing the rig to her. "Just wait for it to sink back to the bottom. You'll feel the line go slack, then jig up a couple times."

She took the jug in one hand and tentatively held the line in her other as Jack had done. She gave a quick pull up but the line gave a bigger pull down. "Oh, it's stuck," she sighed.

"No you got a fish. Hold on."

Her hand was taking on a life of its own as the line jerked and pulled. "What do I do? What do I do?" she yelled excitedly. "Here, you take it!"

"No, you got it. Reel in."

She looked down at her hands. One held a plastic bottle, the other the line. "How am I supposed to do that? Oh!" she shouted louder. "It's taking off!"

The line pulled out of her hand, forcing her to squeeze hard on the bottle. She watched the line head under the boat.

"Pull up or you'll get caught in the rocks."

She obeyed. She stood bouncing on her tiptoes and lifted the bottle over her head.

"Reel in." A big smile cracked his face.

Charlie recognized the action and joined in by clawing at Jan's leg in an offer to assist. The woman jumped as the claws found traction. "Charlie, stop that!"

"Reel!" Jack repeated.

"How can I reel? I haven't got a reel!" she snapped. The line kept trying to pull itself out of her hand and the cat wouldn't leave her alone.

"Wrap it around the bottle," he laughed.

"Oh! Why didn't you say so!" Still standing on her tiptoes, she used one hand to loop line around the bottle. What she got was a mess. Long curls of loose line got entangled around her fingers. She stopped for a second, looked at the mess and scowled. She decided not to worry about appearances and kept winding line. The bottle was soon attached to her hand, engulfing her in a bird's nest of fish line. She lowered her hand but kept winding and looked at the Jack. "You have a smug look."

"Just enjoying the view."

In short order, the fish showed. Once out of the water, it offered little resistance. Jack watched as Jan gave a disgusted look at the raised fish. "Ugh! It's ugly."

The fish was stubby, blotchy, and orange and grey in color, with long wavy-like fins and a big mouth. It couldn't have weighed more than two pounds.

"Here, I'll take it now." He grabbed the line and gingerly grasped the bottom of the fish just behind the gills. "You got to be careful with this little guy, they called him a 'scorpion fish,' for good reason: He has poison on the tips of his dorsal fin. They're quite sharp and painful." Jack carefully removed the fish from the hook, using needle-nose pliers. He lifted up the cushion on the seat and dropped it in a box underneath. "They are, however," Jack gave her a big smile, "good to eat."

He handed her the hook and then stood back, giving her an appraising look.

"What are you looking at?" she asked.

"You know," he assessed slowly, his hand on his chin, "you're about the prettiest fishing pole I think I've ever seen."

That got him a scowl. She held out the offended limb. "Just unwind me, Captain. St. Julian."

"Yes ma'am," he complied.

She looked at him as he held her arm, unwinding line over the side. "That was fun."

"Try again?"

She nodded enthusiastically.

Once the line was free Jack reeled it back on the bottle. He slipped another piece of bacon on the empty hook and commanded, "Just unwind until it hits bottom."

She followed orders. When the line hit, she gave it a jig. On the third jig she got another strike. This time she was ready. She twirled the line around the bottle and pulled up another one— different from the first, dark and uglier, if possible. Again she let Jack deal with the fish.

"Good! I think she's got it," Jack said to Charlie.

The cat took up guard position on the top of the cushion above the fish box. Each time a fish showed up Jack had to lift her out of the way, under protest of course. Once the cushion was back down, Charlie returned to the same spot.

The final count was half a dozen. Jack threw some back and kept others. He explained the superior meat qualities of one type over another. To Jan it seemed that Jack was saying: "the uglier the fish, the better the eating would be."

"So, this is what you men call deep sea fishing?" she laughed.

Jack pan-fried the filets with shaved almonds, browned butter and garlic. He poured a chilled glass of a crisp, white wine for both Jan and himself. They ate under the shade of the wheelhouse dodger, the canvas cover provided escape from the tropical sun.

"This is good," Jan commented. "You like to cook?"

"You sort of get into it when you are out here. There is often little else to do. Although often ingredients are limited. And then there is the very particular tastes of some of the guests." Jack scratched Charlie as she crowded his plate, having already finished her share.

"You love the sea, don't you?" Jan asked.

"Yeah. I guess it's kind of a family thing." Jack looked out over the horizon. "We've been on the sea for several generations. Grandpa and dad were smart, the family business grew with Puget Sound and Washington State. Grandpa got his start as a kid in the Yukon gold rush, if you can believe that. Dad kept it up through the Second World War, and after that he did salvage work around the sound. But, back in the '70s, he invested in a kid named Bill Gates and his silly computer idea. 'That young pup,' Dad called him. Dad knew the family a little and took a chance early on. We have a firm that manages all the finances now. I check in from time to time," he trailed off.

"Do you have any family?" she asked, trying to keep the conversation going.

"A brother, he manages the foundation. What about you?" he asked, changing the subject, just as quickly wishing he hadn't.

"Just Todd and Mom. She's fading to be honest," she said sadly. "She doesn't really know me anymore. I kid myself to think that she does. We talk a little, but there is no connection. Alzheimer's is going to kill her, and she doesn't even know it." She paused. "I guess maybe it's better that way but it's hard to be around."

Jan sighed and tried to relax her shoulders. "And Todd, he's been so generous to us. He built a rest home where mom and other victims can stay. We have an administrator. I don't really have to do anything but take care of mom, but there are so many others who are all alone. You just can't help yourself from caring."

Jack nodded but remained quiet. He was touched by Jan's connection with her mother and brother, even if Todd privately irked him. As the boat gently rocked, Jack realized it was the first time he had opened up to someone, even just a little. It felt good.

For several minutes the pair peacefully watched the horizon. The day finally began to wane. Jack weighed anchor and set sail back towards the Marietas. The afternoon onshore breeze coming from the north, freshened—usual for the time of year. *Heavenly Daze* held nicely—the wind filled her sails and gave her a pace she loved. The rock quickly sank into the western horizon.

Soon after they left Corbetena they were escorted by a school of bottle-nosed dolphins. Jan was delighted as they swooped past, and under the boat. She raced to the bow and leaned over the side, mesmerized by the way they kept perfect time with the edge of the sailboat, trading places with each other as one and then another took the lead. A dolphin would vanish only to reappear moments later on the other side of the bow.

After a time the sea mammals drifted away. Jack watched as Jan dreamily walked back toward him running her hand on the side of the cabin's smooth teak railing.

Jack had seen the same look on Pat under almost the identical circumstances. They had been out on the ocean, not far from here. He had intentionally sailed through a school of feeding tuna and dolphins. They had watched the show for several minutes. "A ballet of the sea," Pat had called it. He would never think of it any other way.

Later, when Jack and Pat got back to Seattle, she told all her friends, it had been the highlight of the trip.

"Funny," Jack thought sadly, "how little things that only last a short time, mean so much." They had only six years together but they'd been perfect.

"They were wonderful!" Jan said excitedly as she approached.

"I've seen TV shows where they do that. I didn't think I'd ever get to see it for real."

"Not many people do, especially in Indianapolis," he laughed. "Treasure the memory," he added softly, giving her a sad but genuine smile.

"I will," she responded enthusiastically. "They were diving and jumping right under the bow. I was afraid they were going to get run over, but they always seemed to get out of the way just in the nick of time. They are amazing! How can they do that?"

"We forget they are flying, and we are practically an inanimate object—like a bird flying by a tree."

She looked at him. "I didn't think of it that way. But of course, we're in their world here, not the other way around."

"That's right. Man forgets that sometimes, most of the time," he corrected himself. "We mostly just travel on the top of their world, but so much of what we do to it, and under it, affects them. That's always got to me. I guess my dad showed me the love of the sea." He stopped himself. "I sound like some kind of activist."

"Why shouldn't you love your home?" she stated frankly, closing her gaze on him.

Her honesty took him back. He gave the woman a quick glance.

As the oncoming shore began to affect the ocean, long slow swells lifted them as they approached. After each rise, the sailboat would lazily glide down the gentle banks. Jan laid in the shade of the sail, trying to sleep under the gentle undulation of the boat. Charlie had taken a comfortable position on her stomach. Jan looked at the cat. "What am I going to do about Todd, Charlie?"

The cat's only response was a lazy blink from heavy eyelids. Jan reached down and scratched behind an ear. "He's always cared for us. Now what?" She stopped and looked up at the sail. "Where are you Todd?" The cat offered little in the way of counsel. She just closed her eyes and purred heartily. "If they kidnapped him or something, they'd want money, but why? If he knew something he'd tell what he knew. I know he'd never risk me or mom in anything."

Jan looked at the cat. "Quite the life," she sighed.

Jack wandered by on the other side of the boat. Jan's eyes followed him until he vanished down the companionway. "What about that one?" she asked the cat. The eyes opened a fraction then slipped closed again. "He's been a life-saver, literally," she said. "He seems to know himself. I haven't known that many guys, but he seems, just so, so confident. Of course you know that." The cat didn't acknowledge.

Jan lay back looking up at the mast swaying back and forth gently. The US and Mexican flags fluttered in the breeze. Under different circumstances she would have been about as content as the cat on her lap. She'd met a great guy. They were out on his sailboat, sailing in the tropics. "They made movies about that sort of stuff," she thought, "but this wasn't like that at all." She looked at the approaching mountains on the eastern horizon. "Over there people had died. Terrible things were happening and I've entrusted my life to a virtual stranger. Nice going, Hamilton," she thought and drifted into sleep.

After a short nap she joined Jack at the wheel.

"You can take the helm again, if you like."

"Sure," she said. "It's a great way to daydream."

"It is, isn't it?" He smiled back. "Just hold 110° east and call me when you're close enough to see surf break on the islands."

"Aye, aye, captain." She stood beside the wheel.

After half an hour the Marietas came slowly into view. "I see white water," Jan called.

Jack brought up cold Pacificos.

"Sounds good. This steering is hard work," she laughed, reaching for the cold beer.

Jack sat down on a cushion on the ledge, to the right of the companionway. Charlie jumped up beside him. He let her lick a taste of beer out of his palm.

The trio sat in quiet tranquility, watching the wake as they slipped through the water. "Are there flying fish down here?" Jan asked.

"Yes, why?"

"Well, twice now I saw a couple of funny looking fish jump out of the water and they seemed to fly alongside us. They must have been able to stay out of the water for 15 or 20 feet."

"Those were probably flying fish. My lazy companion here," Jack looked at the cat, "has a special taste for them." The cat looked up at them as if she knew they were talking about food. "Her favorite is prawns. I practically have to double the portion when I cook them. Even then, she'll tear my leg up, trying get my share. But she also has a passion for flying fish. When we are running at night—especially in heavy swells—the fish will be attracted to the running lights. They actually fly onto the deck. It's not unusual for three or four of them to end up stranded." Jack stopped to scratch Charlie's ear. "I swear her ladyship knows when the conditions are right. She will prowl the deck several times a night to get the poor fish. When she catches one, she has to bring it below to show it to you. She's so proud of herself."

"When I was a kid, our cat did that with birds. It was disgusting," Jan said.

"There is nothing like a live fish dropped on your face, at three in the morning." He gave Charlie a crisp head rub. She reacted by giving him a swat then grabbing at his hand to bite. "Oh no you don't!" Jack whipped his hand away in the nick of time.

He finished his beer while the cat tried to entice him into a fight. Jack got up to escape and looked at the approaching islands. "It's about time to lower the sails and head for the barn, as my old daddy used to say."

Jack brought the boat around so she faced into the wind. He secured the mainsheet, the rope that allows the large sail to move from side-to side, into a midship cleat. Next, he quickly vaulted back to the main mast. There he allowed the main halyard (the rope that makes it possible to haul the main sail up-and-down the mast), to slide evenly over the winch by way of a three-loop circle. By looping the halyard around the winch barrel this way, the friction makes it possible to control the descent of the sail, even in windy conditions. As the mainsail began to drop, Jack fed the falling Dacron sheet into even folds, in between the "lazy jacks"—the guide wires on either side of the sail. He arranged the folds neatly on the boom in an accordion-like fashion. Once the entire sail was down, Jack secured it with nylon ties.

During the day they had seen only a couple of other sailboats and charter fishing cruisers in the distance. Jack had intentionally changed course to avoid contact, but once back to the bay there was little he could do. He planned to get back late so all the day-trippers would be gone.

Earlier in the afternoon as they were heading back, a small Cessna had circled them and then headed north towards Punta de Mita. Jan had been below at the time. Jack had not liked the way the plane had circled but there was nothing he could do.

21

Vegas' problems mounted. He received word that as of tomorrow, Captain Suarez would be closing the entire northwest coast of Mexico to all but regularly scheduled air travel or charters with prearranged flight plans. Casual flying and flight training were grounded. Vegas already had his lawyers on that one but it would take time.

Late that afternoon his luck changed. The Cessna pilot reported in.

"I think I spotted him, Señor. At least the hull had an odd, grey steel look to it."

"Where?"

"About twelve miles west of the Marietas, heading east at 110° degrees into the bay."

"Was he alone?"

"I could see no one else, but…" the pilot left the answer open.

"What time?"

"Exactly sixteen thirty-eight. 4:38 pm." The pilot had jotted down the details. "He was under sail. I didn't want to stick around too long and make him suspicious, so it was impossible to get a speed. But if I were to guess he is either going to moor between the islands this afternoon or Punta de Mita. He could try to make for La Cruz under darkness."

"Good. Go and see if you can spot him again, so we can find out exactly where he is."

There was a long pause. "Señor, I cannot, not without

permission from the police. Do you want me to do that? They know I have been flying all over the place for the last two days." A confrontation could cost the man his license, or worse, his plane.

Vegas thought for a minute. "No. I have another idea. Stay available—I may need you under any circumstances."

"Si, Señor." The pilot was relieved to disconnect.

Vegas thought for a minute. "So you think you can just come back do you gringo? At least I'll fix that arrogant one and his pretty boat." Vegas lifted the phone and called the Ferret in Puerto Vallarta.

*   *   *

Jack approached the Marietas from the south. Jan looked further south where white water was breaking on the Morros.

"What do we do when the research ship gets here?" she asked.

"Well," Jack chuckled. "If I know the Professor, there'll be more action than a three-ring circus. I'm going to keep *Heavenly Daze* as a base of tranquility. At least that's the plan." He pointed towards the white water of the Morros. "We are diving just over there." As if reading her thoughts, Jack added, "You're welcome to stay."

She gave him a weak smile and a nod, turning away.

Again they navigated between the two islands. The swells of the ocean settled. Inside the calm, between the islands, was another sailboat at anchor. It was a nice navy blue, 45-foot sloop. Through binoculars, Jack saw a Canadian flag. Two pre-teenaged kids were jumping off the back into the water. Nearby a woman was floating lazily on an air mattress.

Jack pointed to the flag. "No trouble there." Jack dropped anchor in the same spot as the day before. "I'm for a swim. What about you?" he asked.

"Sure."

Jack dropped through the companionway to change. By the time he was back, Jan was already in the water. He climbed onto the rigging and executed a perfect swan dive. Under the water he turned and came up under her, grabbing a leg and pulling down hard.

She resurfaced spitting water. "Buster, you only get to do that once!" she laughed. She reached up with both feet and used his chest as a backstop and pushed off hard driving him under. She was off doing a fast, hard breaststroke. Jack recovered quickly and gave chase.

She was a strong swimmer. It took all he had to catch her. By the time he did, they were on the opposite side of the boat. He thought about grabbing a leg but then thought there was a good chance he would catch the other one in the head. He poured it on and pulled up beside her. He saw that she had seen him, and waited for an evasive move. It came an instant later as she somehow came to a complete stop. He stopped too. Each floated, breathing heavily as they caught their breath.

"You're a good swimmer," he acknowledged, breathing deeply. "And nasty."

"I was the only girl on the swim team. I lost my top more than once and had to learn to defend myself," she smirked and caught him with a splash in the face. This time he was ready and captured her hand. He pulled her to him and tried to plant a kiss. All he got was her forehead as she pushed him under with her legs. He kicked powerfully underwater. When he came up she was a good ten feet away. He decided that was enough and headed toward the ladder and relative safety.

Jan hadn't given chase. She had been stunned by the failed attempt at a kiss. She'd realized too late what he was trying to do.

She watched him climb up the ladder. For the first time she had seen him without a shirt on. He was very fit. She noticed the straight-lined scar on the back of his left arm, just above the elbow. Higher up by the shoulder, was another long scar. Jan figured they must be part of the stories Deni had been telling her about.

He turned to face her when he got to the top of the ladder. Another deep scar ran across his abdomen matching the one on the back of his arm.

She suddenly realized her concept of "rugged looking" came at a price. She called, "What's the matter buddy—afraid of the sharks?"

"If you want some more lady, I'll be right…" he stopped in mid-sentence and looked out toward the other island.

"What is it?"

"It's okay. Just a minute." He disappeared from view.

She looked out across the water. A black wingtip suddenly sliced through the water, thirty feet from her.

She kicked hard for the ladder. Just then Jack reappeared with fins and snorkels.

"It's a shark!" she cried as she reached the first rung of the ladder.

"No, no a manta ray, and a big one."

Her hand rested on the first ladder rung. "That's good?"

"Yeah, they're fun. Quick, get these on." He handed her down the fins and mask. "What you got to do," he instructed, "is float over it until it turns its back to you. Then you dive hard and grab its shoulders. Get a good grip fast, 'cause it will take off on you like a rocket. Are you game?"

She spun and dove in one motion.

From the deck, Jack dove flat, holding his mask secure. His momentum put him beside her. He handed her a mask as they made for the ray. The animal arched, slowing under them. It was cruising, ignoring the disturbance above, totally at ease in its environment. As it came under them, Jack gave a robust kick downwards. Above, Jan watched in amazement as he got one hand on each shoulder of the manta. Unconcerned, the ray effortlessness curved out and down in to deeper water.

Jan watched as Jack held for the longest time. He finally

peeled off and headed for the surface. He broke the surface, a good thirty yards away, and idly began swimming toward her.

Jan put her face under the water. Two other rays were gliding along in deeper water, between her and Jack. Suddenly one of them headed for the surface. Jan watched as it cleared the water by its full body length, and returned with a great splash.

Jan began swimming out to meet Jack. Halfway there, a ray slowly circled under her. Quickly, she imitated Jack's move and grabbed the shoulders. She was stunned that the hide felt like the hair on a wet Labrador. She suddenly felt the propulsion as the ray took off. The watery world flew past, and as she watched the ocean deep grow closer, the pressure in her ears began to increase.

The ray made a slow arch, leveled off, and came around— near the rock below. Finally Jan's lungs demanded attention, and she let go. The ray continued its lazy arch as if nothing had happened.

Jan kicked toward the surface. Breaking clear, she came up only dozen yards from the boat.

Jack, off to her left, waved and both headed in the direction of home. She hesitated, keeping her head submerged, hoping the ray would return, but apparently the rules were: only one ride per customer.

Jack was already on deck when she arrived. She handed him her fins. "That was wonderful! They are magnificent."

"All part of the service," he smiled.

She remembered the kiss and smiled to herself. "That part of the service needed work."

Jan quietly lay in the sun to dry. The cat tickled her by licking drying salt off her belly. She idly studied the caves and crevasses of the shoreline. The few sandy beaches looked inviting.

"Why am I beginning to think I'm being taken advantage of?" she asked Charlie who had no response.

In the main cabin Jack was kicking himself: "What was I

thinking? …You weren't," the answer came back immediately. He stopped and consciously got control of himself.

After a few minutes, Jack came up on deck. "That makes a guy thirsty. Would you like a beer?"

Jan lifted her head. "What I'd really like is to learn how to make those pina coladas they serve down here."

"Okay. I'll show you."

In the galley Jack showed her the recipe. "Okay. First, you're in Mexico, right?" Jack said studiously.

"Okay," she agreed, not sure of the joke, but beginning to know him well enough to figure there was one.

"Okay. So instead of white rum, we use tequila—the white stuff. Besides, I'm out of white rum."

Jan nodded with a smile.

"So pour already," he encouraged.

"You want me to do it?"

"You wanted to learn."

"Right." She poured a shot of tequila into the blender.

"Ahem," Jack coughed.

"Sorry." She added another shot.

"Now, it's downhill from here. One part tequila, one part coconut cream, one part pineapple juice and ice." Jack gave her a look again to see if she was getting into the spirit, and to judge what his advance had done to the relationship. His emotions were in a turmoil—try again, risk rejection. And there was the burning thought of infidelity to Pat.

Jan sensed something, but let it ride. She really did want to know how to make a pina colada, there was time for other things later. She followed Jack's directions to the tee, doubling each ingredient.

Jack continued. "One trick I've been told is 'don't skimp on the ice.' Of course, I was told that by a bar owner, so… I don't know. Ice is the cheap part."

To follow Captain's orders, Jan dropped in more ice.

They stood watching the blender grind away. After it settled down to a smooth roar, he nodded. She stopped it and poured them each a big plastic glass full of the frothy mixture.

"Umm, that's good," she decided as she took a health swig.

"I've never been much for those kinds of drinks. I prefer it straight."

"Sure, a tequila and rum guy? You were in the Navy right?" she chided him.

"Yeah. Retired. It's a long story. What would you like for supper?" He changed the subject. "I could crack open the barbecue and grill a steak outside, or we have leftover chicken."

"Let's do steak. A boating barbeque sounds fun. I don't mind waiting."

"Steak it is then. I'll get the barbie going." He turned and headed up stairs.

After thirty minutes of effort and a quarter can of lighter fluid, Jack got up and looked at the briquettes, a few were just beginning to glow. "This mesquite is wet. That makes it hard and slow to light."

"That's fine. I think I'll try another one of those pina coladas."

"Sure. You want me to help?"

"No. I'll go solo. You want one?" she asked with a touch of a wrinkled smile on her face.

"No, I'm fine," he answered.

Jack fanned the few glowing coals with his hand, cursing the mesquite and reminding himself to get a propane barbeque.

In the galley, Jan soon realized that the first batch had used up most of the ice, so she replaced it with an extra shot of tequila for taste and a bit more pineapple juice. Again she got a frothy concoction that tasted quite good, but she had made more than her tumbler would hold, so she sipped the last bit out of the blender. "Waste not, want not," she thought.

Jack was standing over the barbecue watching the coals do their thing. Jan came up behind him and rested her cheek on his arm for a brief moment and looked down on the fire. "Is the steak ready?" she asked.

"No, as a matter of fact. It's still in the fridge."

"I'll get it," she said and headed back down the stairs.

Before Jan headed back up she looked in her glass, half empty. She decided to top it off, adding a touch of pineapple juice and shot of tequila.

Jan was secretly pleased with herself as she succeeded in negotiating the stairs with the steak in one hand and the tumbler in the other, even though the boat seemed to be moving back and forth. With great concentration she set the platter down and celebrated her achievement with another sip.

Jack was bent over, still trying to get the briquettes to cooperate. She watched as his lungs filled, the muscles in his back tensed. He gave a mighty heave. His power and strength had saved her once and his care and concern had kept her that way.

There was such a sadness about him, but as a woman she was sure she understood. She set the glass down and felt herself standing a little unsteady. "Poor man," she thought. "He needs someone to care for him." She stepped behind him and reached around his broad shoulders.

Jack was slightly taken back as her arm came over his shoulder and gently turned him into her tender caress. Jan looked up at him in a most meaningful way. She reached up and kissed him heartily.

The warmth of her body came to him as a wave of hot passion. He pulled her close, his arms engulfing her as he pressed her breasts and hips closer. The kiss was almost painful at first, then he warmed and realized he had to go on. He kissed her back with all the passion he could muster in that startling moment.

Their embrace lasted and lasted. Suddenly Jack realized he was kissing her but there was no response, her body had gone limp. He loosened his embrace slightly and her lips fell off his mouth and slid down his chin. Her head flopped onto his chest.

He gently grasped a handful of hair and pulled her head back, she was out like a light. With a deep sigh, he lifted her off her feet and carried her to her stateroom. He pulled a sheet over her, looking down at the beauty of her slumber. He shook his head, turned and flicked out the light.

When he returned on deck, the first thing he saw was Charlie enjoying the steak she'd dragged off the plate and on to the deck. As he walked up, the cat shot him a look that said, "Well, if you're not going to eat it…"

Again, Jack spent the night at the galley table, leaning back on the bench seats. He had shut and locked the companionway door and set the alarm, much to the disdain of Charlie. Several times he had to get up to accommodate her. It was comply or have her use his leg as a scratching post. Each time he had let her back in, Charlie showed her gratitude by jumping up on his lap and letting him be her mattress. That gratitude saved their lives.

22

The first hint of morning was coursing along the tips of the eastern Sierra Madres. Inside the cabin it was pitch dark. Charlie's sixth sense felt something. Her head popped up and she jumped off of Jack's lap aggressively, pulling Jack out of his slumber. In their time together Jack knew the cat's actions, he was fully alert before his eyes opened. "It's just Jan, you fool cat."

Undeterred, the cat scratched at the companionway door and waited. Jack lay there listening for Jan's movements, but heard none. Then he sensed as much as felt, a bump below somewhere on the hull.

The Ferret waited in the inflatable Zodiac. He had seen the light of the diver from time to time as he swam towards the sailboat. Then it had gone out. Time passed slowly—too slowly.

The diver surfaced once and confirmed his heading. He switched off his light and proceeded underwater by the headings of his luminous instruments. He approached the boat, just forward of amidships. He worked his way to the back in under a minute, tied the remote detonator charge to the cleat supports of the rudder. As he surfaced to confirm the location of the Zodiac, his air tank bumped the hull. He dove immediately and reversed his heading, staying well underwater.

Jack knew every squeak and twist *Heavenly Daze* made, that was not one of them. He listened for another minute in the darkness but there was nothing more.

Slowly and very deliberately, he picked up the cat and shut her in the closet. He unlocked the companionway doors and silently eased them open.

The moon's reflection off the water provided enough light to see the deck. He stayed low under the cabin deck line to prevent anyone from seeing his silhouette. Everything seemed to be in order. He scanned the shoreline and saw nothing. He looked into the water, the darkness gave nothing back.

He quickly slipped back down into the cabin and retrieved his mask and dive light out of the closet. Charlie escaped at the same moment and raced up the stairs before he could grab her. Ignoring the cat he picked up his dive knife.

Jack slipped silently over the side and into the water. He headed to the rear of the hull and immediately noticed the plastic ties. Rounding the rudder he found the package. He recognized the remote charge and quickly cut the zip straps. He watched in chagrin as it slowly fluttered back and forth—sinking at a snail's pace. He gave it a kick with his foot. That pushed it a few more feet away before it again returned to its leisurely descent.

Jack broke the surface, pulled himself on deck, raced to the bow, set the anchor winch on automatic, then ran to the stern. He reefed the key out of his pocket and turned the motor over. Forcibly willing himself to wait until he was positive the diesel was well and truly turning over, before throwing the motor into gear.

The diver heard the sound of the engine and knew that he was in trouble. If the fool on the zodiac pushed the remote detonator, the concussion would blow his eardrums and probably kill him. He shot for the surface.

The Ferret heard the sound of the engine and reached for the detonator. He knew the detonation would kill his own man, but Vegas' order had to be obeyed. Then suddenly a hundred feet from him, he saw the splash and light of his diver. He pulled the switch.

In the wheelhouse, Jack caught the sight of the distant light and rammed the accelerator. The propeller was put in a full spin, the boat lurching forward. It had only gone a few feet before the ocean erupted, but that few feet spelled the difference between disaster and safety.

The ocean ballooned like a silent giant boil. Then the sound came as the blast wave broke the surface, spraying water thirty feet in every direction. The boat bucked violently as if kicked in the rear. Guy wires and stays strained to their maximum. A couple let go, sending killing whips of wire through the air.

The impact threw Jack forward onto the top of the canvas wheelhouse canopy. He landed on his hands and knees, did a quick roll, grabbed the steering wheel and was on his feet before water stopped raining down.

A light in the distance caught his eye. There they were; a Zodiac with one standing silhouetted rider.

The ringing in Jack's ears prevented him from hearing the Zodiac's outboard engine kicking over, as it high-tailed away--as fast as the propeller could bite water.

What Jack did hear was the pathetic cry of a cat.

Jack grabbed the dive light and scanned the deck and water around the boat. Dead fish began floating belly-up to the surface. The cat cried again, this time Jack got a fix on two paws sticking out of the water, but no head. Jack ran to the side and cleared the lifeline, coming up four feet away from Charlie. He grabbed the sunken back of her neck roughly and lifted the limp rag of a cat out of the water and swam back towards the boat with one hand.

He regained the boat and realized the ladder was gone. He couldn't get up with one hand. As cruel as it seemed, Jack realized he was going to have to throw Charlie on deck. He was just lifting his arm to get maximum pitch when Jan appeared and reached out to grab the animal from him.

Jack was on deck in no time.

"You know the Heimlich maneuver for a cat?" she asked unthinkingly.

"Here give her to me." He took the cat and gruffly lifted her by her tail and hind legs, her head hanging lifeless. With the palm of his hand he delivered a sharp blow to Charlie's abdomen. Nothing. He tried again.

This time water dripped out of her nose and mouth. Encouraged, he delivered several more, until a tiny gush of water poured out and the animal spasmed. He flipped her over and holding her jaw open with two fingers he blew into her nostrils.

"Come on!" he yelled as he took another breath. "Damn you cat!" He blew again. In that moment Jack felt Charlie make an effort to take her own breath. With Jack's next breath, he felt movement.

Charlie's paw came up weakly as if to ward of a blow. She coughed, bringing up more water. She feebly tried to get Jack to stop blowing in her face. She rolled over, trying to get up. Jack let her go, figuring nature nurtured a strong sense of survival. The cat heaved and coughed several times, emptying her stomach all over the deck. She stood there on wobbly legs for a moment then made an almost comical imitation of a drunken sailor as she staggered along the deck, dignity totally shattered.

Jack and Jan couldn't help but laugh at the sight. Jan saw an unmistakable tear in the man's eye. She reached over and gave him a hug.

"What happened?"

"Vegas sent me a message," he said.

"Why?"

He turned and looked her squarely in the eyes. "For daring to get in his way."

"Oh Jack. What have I gotten you into?" She hugged him harder.

"I wouldn't worry about that." He gently ran his fingers through her hair, but his jaw was hard set.

Their conversation was interrupted by the sound of an outboard. Coming up on them was a man from the other sailboat.

"Are you guys okay?" the Canadian called as he reached the edge of *Heavenly Daze*.

Jack caught the man's line and helped him aboard. "We're fine."

"What happened?"

"It's a personal thing. Someone wanted to buy my boat and I turned them down."

"You're kidding."

Jack shook his head. "No. He wanted it real bad. Now he's going to get it."

After the man left, Jack went below deck to survey the damage. After checking the interior he went over the side.

Jan dried off the docile cat and gave her fresh water to drink.

When Jack returned he reported, "The rudder is a little loose. We lost a couple guy wires and have a small leak which the bilge pump can handle. But we have to head in. I have to get her out of the water to make sure everything is really okay. If we have pump problems out here it could get interesting."

Jan nodded.

They got under way immediately. A little after seven o'clock Jack risked using the VHF to contact Deni.

"Where you at?" Jack asked.

"Just leaving the wharf. What's up?"

"I had company."

After a long pause, Deni asked, "And?"

"I'm okay but have to head in for some repairs, pronto..." Jack let the sentence hang.

After another long moment, Deni responded, "That's a shame, but this old donkey has to work. I'll talk to you tomorrow, normal time." With that the line went silent.

Jan looked crestfallen as Jack hung up. "He won't help?" She couldn't believe it.

"Oh no. We are to meet at Punta del Burro." Jack gently increased the speed on the throttle.

A little over two hours later, they rendezvoused off the

Burro's Point. Deni took Jan on board *Carmen II*. The two men who had chartered the boat had no objections to the detour, especially when they saw Jan.

23

Jack tried to unravel what had happened as he motored into Puerto Vallarta. All he could figure was that Vegas was getting even. If he had known Jan was on board they would have tried to take her.

Perhaps they didn't need whatever they thought she knew. Maybe the drugs had been found which might be too bad for the dopers up north, but could mean Jan was off the hook. That thought didn't last a second. Jack had just learned a graphic lesson in Vegas' style. If Todd Hamilton had done something to get on the wrong side of this guy, Vegas wouldn't rest until he got even with as many people as possible. That put Jan at the top of the list. This would mean Deni and his family too, which meant that Jack had to repay the lesson before it was too late.

As much as he hated to do it, Jack contacted Diaz. The DEA agent was waiting when Jack docked in the repair yard of Puerto Vallarta's municipal wharf next to where the ocean liners dock, only a few blocks from Zillia's harbormaster's office.

Jack surveyed the crowd of four well-armed Mexican cops and two police cars accompanying Diaz.

"I hope you're not coming for me?" Jack asked, only half kidding, as he threw a line over to the DEA agent.

"No. Two are for me. I am usually undercover, but right now all gloves are off. The other two are for you, courtesy of Captain Suarez. He doesn't want anything to happen to either of us. I wouldn't be the first DEA agent murdered down here."

"Works for me," Jack said.

When Diaz stepped aboard Jack filled him in on what happened. While they were talking, Jerry showed up.

Jack had contacted him on the way into Puerto Vallarta and asked him to come and look after the repairs, and keep an eye on Charlie. Jerry looked at the law enforcement entourage and smirked. "Maybe that BS I sold that guy yesterday was closer than I knew."

"You just keep an eye on the repairs and two eyes on Charlie."

Jack went on to relate the results of the attempted bombing.

"Man that sucks! I'll walk over to Walmart and get her some shrimp for a treat," Jerry said.

"She'd like that," Jack said.

Before stepping into the back of the rear police car with Diaz, Jack announced, "I have an errand I must do."

"Your archeology professor, Captain?" Diaz gave a smug look.

"Doing a little checking up, have we Agent Diaz?"

"Umm. Impressive record, sir."

"Let's keep that to a minimum around here, okay?"

"Aye, aye," the DEA agent smiled. "Your professor arrives in less than an hour. You'll want to meet him I'd guess?"

Jack thought for a minute. He'd told the professor differently, but things had since changed. As much as he didn't want the professor involved in his problems with Vegas, there didn't seem to be any options.

"Yes. Let's head over there."

In the car Diaz filled Jack in on some other details. "The University of Washington research ship has still not been cleared."

Jack turned slowly to stare at Diaz. "You're serious?"

"Yep. They were supposed to be here last night, out at the Morros, but there were still hang-ups."

Jack couldn't believe Zillia would still be dragging things. Had the big ship been there, the attempt on their lives wouldn't have been possible. Zillia's stupidity was starting to create serious problems.

Jack, Diaz and two of the police officers, met the professor at the baggage claim area of the airport. A group of four young, very fit graduate students accompanied the professor.

"Hi Professor," Jack reached to shake the professor's hand.

"Hello young man. I hope you have my ship ready," the professor said bluntly before shaking hands.

"Well…" Jack started.

The professor stopped. "What an old fool I am. I'm terribly sorry about your loss. I will miss your dear wife. You must be… Well, I'm sorry," he trailed off.

Jack just nodded. "Thank you."

The others accompanying the Professor introduced themselves. The men were all experienced divers. Jack could see they were itching to get a chance to work on the underwater site. One of them offered, "We want to congratulate you on your discovery, Señor St. Julian."

"Don't thank me," Jack said. "There's an old lobsterman that deserves the credit."

"The *Juan de Fuca* is here?" the professor asked.

Jack looked him square in the eye. "Not exactly. From what I understand, they are about a hundred miles out, waiting." Jack looked up at Diaz for confirmation.

"And why is that?" The old man tensed.

"They still haven't been given permission to enter the bay, nor to conduct any research in this area, for that matter."

"The reason?"

Jack tried not to smile. "You know the answer, sir."

"Zillia," the professor snapped.

Jack watched the instant transformation in the professor's demeanor.

Legs and back straightened and his chest surged, raising him up to his full 5 feet 4 inch fighting height. "Well, that's one major domo I've had just about enough of. I still remember him, lazy and worthless. Had family connections; the only reason he got anywhere. Well, they won't help him now," he threatened, marching toward the exit.

Before the professor reached the exit he looked at Jack. "You have arranged transportation?"

Jack paused for a second a wicked smile crossed his face. "Oh yes. We have transportation and a little cooperation."

From Diaz's information on the *Juan de Fuca's* inability to enter the dive site, Jack knew there would be a confrontation. Jack had rented a black stretch Lincoln Town Car limousine, in which they loaded their research and diving gear. One of the grad students volunteered to drive. The professor sat in the back with Jack. A police officer sat up front on the passenger's side, riding shotgun. They sandwiched the Lincoln between the two police cars.

So it was that the three-car procession drove slowly and officiously into the parking lot of the harbormaster building; lights flashing and sirens blasting for a mile before they arrived. The cars sat wailing away in the parking lot for a full minute. A crowd gathered. People in the harbormaster's building looked out windows. Two policemen finally jumped out to shield the entourage. The other policemen opened doors for the dignitaries.

The police and students formed an impressive perimeter as they entered the building. The professor led the senior trio with the grad students following. The last two policemen brought up the rear. All had stern, official looks on their faces.

Diaz put on his best bureaucratic attitude, a scowl affixed to his face, his nose high in the air, aloof to all around him.

To the credit of Zillia's secretary, she tried valiantly to deflect the assault but she was totally out-manned and out-flanked before she knew what hit her. She had been in the midst of sputtering that Mr. Zillia was in an important meeting when 110 pounds of academic tiger barged through Zillia's private door. The professor left the door open for Zillia to get a good view of the audience.

He caught the bureaucrat on a phone call. The professor reached over and killed the receiver in middle sentence.

It is widely believed that the Mexican government does not possess nuclear weapons. However, anyone in the vicinity of the offices of the Puerto Vallarta Harbormaster would have had grounds to think otherwise when Professor Antonio Garcia Torres lit off. He took Zillia to places he didn't know existed. Screaming that the US State Department was here to file an official complaint, the professor heaped scorn on Zillia at "…snubbing the American's generosity. The government in Mexico City was trying to keep this thing from blowing all out of proportion. Irreparable national face was being lost. The Mexican archeological community will become the laughing stock of the western world—all of this because of one Gilberto Capilla Jose Zillia."

With a seamless transition of a seasoned professional, the professor then demanded to know why. Why hadn't his calls been returned? Why had his representative—one very influential and recognized American research scientist, Captain Jack St. Julian, United States Navy, a decorated hero no less—been ignored? For effect, the professor pointed to Jack through the open door.

Jack just glared and bit his lip.

"And this other man," the professor pointed at Diaz. "Do you think the police are here to protect me?" he yelled.

"Do you?" Not waiting for an answer, he continued.

"This man is with their State Department. Way up. Washington, D.C. He has people that he has to answer to—big people—and answers are what he wants. And he wants them from you, Zillia. You! Why is this not happening, Zillia? Why? These police could just as easily be coming for you. That may happen yet. I can only protect you so far, Zillia."

Zillia remained stunned at what was happening.

"You are the one everyone is looking at," the professor continued his abuse. "You will be remembered for this. Maybe you will never be forgotten, or maybe you will never be heard from again—I think that is more likely, don't you?" He stopped for a microsecond for breath. "Well, don't you?"

The harbormaster's face had grown whiter and whiter with the telling. He saw the crowd of people staring in at him; his staff in the background doing the same. He began to pull papers and forms out of his desk, pounding stamps on them, signing wherever his pen hit.

"I think it's more likely you will be counting coconuts in some mosquito-bitten, backwater seaport in Chiapas. That's what I think."

The professor pulled out some paperwork from his pocket and handed it to Zillia. "Sign these," he ordered smoothly.

Zillia kept stamping and signing.

"You still haven't had the decency to tell me what you are going to do, Zillia. Everyone is watching you," he pointed again to the men crowded around the door. "What are you going to do?"

The man finally got a chance to answer when the professor grabbed a quick bite of air.

"My staff…" he started with a shrug.

Anticipating the stock excuse, the professor cut him off. "It is a weak man that blames his staff, Zillia. I would have expected more of you. I thought, worse…" he stopped in midsentence, staring at the man. "…No! I am positive your superiors—all of Mexico City—would have expected more of you. Madre Dios! What is going to happen when this gets out?"

Jack shook his head. From his point of view, the harbormaster was melting into his chair. The professor would have made any Chief Petty Officer proud.

Zillia handed over two fists full of forms.

"These better be in order, Zillia. After all this time you'd think you could fill out a form properly." Professor Torres snatched the forms, crushing them in his fist.

He then leaned his knuckles on the deck and his face closed on Zillia's shivering figure. "If you have done something to that site, if the sand has been disturbed, I will personally spend what life I have left making you wish you had none."

With that he spun on his heels and marched out the door, the crowd separating as if by divine intervention.

As they exited the building, Jack gave the professor a smile. The professor scowled at him but winked.

In the Lincoln on the way to La Cruz, the professor hummed as he went through the paperwork. "Well, that was nice," he said in complete tranquility.

He handed Jack the forms signed by Zillia. "The good harbormaster has signed an authorization that all expenses for the expedition will be paid out of his budget."

"That was a thing of beauty, Professor Torres. I commend you," Diaz laughed.

*   *   *

It was shortly after noon when the entourage quietly pulled into Rosa's. A policeman stood by the entrance.

Jack got on the radio to Deni. "My ship has finally come in," he said.

"That is good, amigo."

"Yeah. They should be having lobster at the market late this afternoon."

"You want me to stop by?" Deni asked.

"You could do that. You might have some good-looking fish they would like."

"Roger."

Deni spent the day chasing schools of tuna. His charter never realized the search was continually in a north and south direction. It was just after four o'clock when a large vessel came into view. Deni made for it.

As the two vessels approached, Deni explained to his clients that the ship was coming to pick up Miss Hamilton. *Carmen II* pulled under the shadow of the massive dark blue hull of the

270-foot MV *Juan de Fuca* that towered 60 feet over the fishermen. A crowd gathered on the open aft staging area of the *Juan de Fuca*, as they craned one of the large inflatable service vessels into the water.

The charter fishermen were a little concerned as they helped Jan over the side and down into the inflatable, but the big ship flew both American and State of Washington flags, and the crew on the launch were all uniformed in University of Washington colors.

A grey-haired, uniformed officer met Jan as she stepped aboard the *Juan de Fuca*.

"Miss Hamilton, Captain Erikson at your service." The Captain offered his hand.

"Thank you sir. I appreciate your hospitality."

"It is nothing. I understand you are having some difficulties."

"Yes sir. It is good to be on American soil again, so to speak. Have you heard from Jack?"

"Captain St. Julian is in Puerto Vallarta. I understand he has picked up his professor and company. They will be headed out shortly. In the meantime, let me show you to a stateroom."

24

Professor Torres had been incensed when he heard about the attack on Jan and Jack. As official leader of the expedition, he agreed that she could stay on the *Juan de Fuca*, but acknowledged that it was the ship captain's call.

"I'll like to get out there as soon as possible. This whole thing has got to have Jan on edge," Jack said.

"You must have protection out there," Diaz demanded.

We will have at least one harbor patrol vessel with us the entire time," the professor said. "I will see to that." He smiled gravely.

"They are armed?" Diaz asked.

"Si," The professor answered.

Diaz nodded his approval.

"I'll get Deni's boy to take us all out in the panga," Jack said.

With Arturo behind the wheel of panga *Carmen I*, Jack and the archeology group waved Diaz good-bye. Twenty minutes later they met Deni heading back to shore.

"We'll radio if there is any need for supplies," Jack called across the water. "Otherwise we'll see you and the lobsterman tomorrow."

"Early," the professor yelled.

Deni nodded and gave his young son a fatherly look before heading home.

When they got to the *Juan de Fuca*, the professor stepped over the side of *Carmen I* and onto the dive deck. Jack was right behind him. The professor accepted a firm handshake from Captain Erikson.

Jack made the introductions. "Professor Torres, Captain Erikson of the research vessel *Juan de Fuca*."

"Captain Erikson, on behalf of the University of Guadalajara and my country, thank you for your generous offer of this research vessel," the professor said.

"Professor Torres, the honor is ours," the Captain replied.

As they finished making introductions all the way around, Jan quietly came up and stood next to Jack. Both the captain and the professor looked at the pair.

"This is the young woman?" the professor asked of Jack.

"Jan Hamilton, Professor Torres," Jack introduced.

"Señorita, young St. Julian has told me a little of this terrible harassment you have experienced." The professor took both of Jan's hands and squeezed them. "How can one explain the despicable acts of some people?" Professor Torres turned to the Captain. "You know this young man?"

"Oh yes, professor," The Captain nodded his head solemnly.

"I knew his father. This young pup is a rascal." The professor shook his finger at Jack with a good-natured smile.

"Well put, professor," the Captain agreed, enjoying Jack's obvious discomfort.

Jack raised his hands in defense. "All right. Don't we have a mission to run?" he interjected in an attempt to change the subject.

Jan smiled, reading the dynamics.

Jack asked, "Jan, have they got you squared away?"

"Yes," Captain Erickson interrupted. "She's in the room you were supposed to be using before you ran off and played hooky. The few things you left are in the galley. You can sleep there tonight."

"Yes, sir," Jack saluted with a grimace. "Okay. Let's consider the mission?" he repeated.

Finally the professor took the bait. "Yes, let's see where we are at."

The professor's grad students and the rest of the party gathered around the table in the main wardroom. Nautical maps of the area covered its surface. Jack took out his GPS and began relating the story that Deni had first shared, along with the experiences of the dives. This was his first opportunity to coordinate his GPS readings on state-of-the-art maps.

"We started here," Jack's finger traced a trail on the map. "And this is where we found the musket ball and here, the egg."

All eyes followed as he pointed to the spot where the egg was found.

"This is where it goes deep," he said, pointing just beyond where the egg had been located.

They leaned forward to read the depth gauge of the canyon. The map showed that the canyon serpentined in a westerly direction, dropping steeply to averages of 250 to 350 feet, over a distance of a mile.

"These areas should provide us with plenty of SCUBA exploration." Jack waved his hand around the rocks and shallows that constituted the Morro Islands. "We have a side scan sonar on board that can be towed behind a boat. Gives us a great view of the bottom. Deni's cruiser, *Carmen II* can handle that easily. I've never used one, but the chief mate can show us how it operates."

"I figure the Newtsuit should start at the edge of SCUBA depth and head deep, professor? Too bad we don't have any rebreather equipment. The Newtsuit is overkill, but what the heck, the Navy wants it tested." Jack looked up for confirmation and to acknowledge the project's rightful owner.

"I do not understand this suit thing you talk about," the professor noted.

"It is like a deep-sea diving suit from the old days—only very high tech. It's made of cast aluminum, and is very strong. This new prototype allows a man to go to depths of over 1000 feet— that's 300 plus meters—with no concern for decompression."

"And you know this suit?" one of the students asked.

"Yes. My father knew the inventor. As a teenager, I got to practice in it while they were developing it."

"Figured you were expendable?" the Captain deadpanned.

"As a matter of fact, that's exactly what they said," Jack laughed. "More than once. The Navy learned of my experience, I been checked out on the new generations they now use for Naval rescue operations. It's one of these new prototype's we have on board. And, if I recall, I would have not been in the Bay of Banderas and found those artifacts if we hadn't needed parts for the suit over in Cabo."

The captain smirked and nodded agreement.

"The man's right," the professor realized. "And we are glad for it."

Professor Torres turned to his students. "All right. Let's set up some grid coordinates, plot depths and calculate bottom times."

Jack watched the old professor question and guide the students. Everyone shared in various possibilities and probabilities, before coming to any conclusions. The old professor was a pro.

"What time do you anticipate your friends will be here tomorrow?" the professor asked.

"I would think around eight," Jack said.

The professor turned to the Captain. "May we take a look at the gear you have offered?"

"Certainly, let me get you the chief mate."

As they were walking out of the wardroom, a steward approached the Captain and quietly spoke into his ear.

"Jack, come with me," the Captain said. To the rest, Captain Erikson stated, "Wait here and the chief mate, the officer in charge of the work deck will be right up and explain the routine."

Jack and the Captain walked outside to see the approach of a large inflatable craft heading their way at full speed, the words *Harbor Patrol* boldly printed in Spanish on the sides. Jack could see a uniformed officer standing "at the ready" of the mounted machinegun on the bow.

"They radioed they were coming and would be with us for as long as we are here."

Jack watched the oncoming vessel. "Maybe this harbormaster nonsense was over," Jack thought.

*   *   *

It had taken 30 minutes for Zilla to stop shaking. He didn't know what felt worse; the fear of reprisal on an official level, the humiliation of the dressing down or his hatred for the irritating old man.

"That the wiry little two-bit academic could come into my office and treat me so in front of my staff was not acceptable," he fumed.

His jaw clenched in determination, he picked up the phone and dialed Vegas' number. "Señor Zillia for Señor Vegas."

The secretary again gave the stock reply: "Please leave a message. Señor Vegas is busy at the moment."

"I am no one's messenger boy!" Zillia screamed into the phone. "You tell Señor Vegas that Jack St. Julian was in my office not an hour ago. I know where he is and what he is doing. I warn you Señora, this is important and when Vegas finds out you are playing games, it will not be my head, do you understand?" He screamed, slamming the phone down.

Less than ten minutes later Vegas called Zillia from his temporary headquarters in Tepic. "What have you got?"

"Ah, Señor Vegas. I informed your secretary that Jack St. Julian was here an hour ago." He let the statement hang.

The line went quiet for an uncomfortably long pause. Zillia started to sweat, the game of making Vegas wait was just too dangerous.

"Why?" Vegas finally snapped. St. Julian was supposed to be dead or at least in the hospital somewhere, but the peacock bureaucrat was not supposed to know that.

"That archeological expedition I told you about last week, well there is a research vessel right now nearing the Marietas. The Federal Department of Antiquities has authorized some exploration of the area. I do not know why but it came from the very top. St. Julian is part of it somehow."

Vegas racked his brain. He knew no one in any government department associated with these things. Zillia would have to do. "Tell me more."

"The ministry has ordered us to provide protection for both the site and the vessel while in the area. It is a direct order. I must obey."

There was a long silence. Zillia's head began to pound. His ears were ringing.

Finally Vegas responded. "Excellent. You should do just that. I only want to know one thing."

As Zillia listened to the demand, his blood went cold.

The phone, hardly back in its cradle, rang again. "What?" Vegas snapped.

"We found something," Santana stated. "Not the truck but something."

"What?"

"There's a marijuana shipment here, near the coast, fifty kilometers from where you are. Garcia's people want our favor and are willing to betray another."

"This a set-up?"

"I don't think so. I'll have Garcia covered when you arrive in case there is anything."

Vegas thought for only a moment. "I'll meet you there."

Within minutes and in separate vehicles, Vegas, his driver and four bodyguards were on their way to meet Santana. An hour later Vegas' group slowly ground to a halt in front of Santana's Ford SUV and two pickups, each with four men in the back.

Before stepping out of the car, Vegas reached into his jacket and slipped the safety strap off his shoulder holster and loosened the Browning. All heads turned as Vegas stepped cautiously out of the car behind a bodyguard. This was the first time any of them had seen their new master. This would be a night to remember, if they survived.

A short, wiry man in a black tee shirt, black jeans and cowboy boots, stood beside Santana in the headlights of his truck. Benito Aquaria Garcia had nominal control of much of the illegal activities in the area. He had long been loyal to Ernesto Vegas but as a practical man, he understood the new realities.

"Señor Vegas," Garcia extended his hand.

Vegas nodded and shook the man's hand. "What have you got?"

"There is a warehouse not far from here—the Lopez family of Juarez uses it. They have been making threats to us all week since…the news," Garcia paused looking into Vegas' eyes. What he saw was a deadly, cold stare that Garcia could not hold.

Vegas looked at Santana. "Trap?"

"He says they have been watching the building for weeks," Santana nodded toward Garcia. "We have only been here for a couple days, but there has been nothing suspicious. There are four men, little activity."

"Tell me about this place," Vegas commanded Garcia.

"It is a tobacco plantation. One of the warehouses stores marijuana. From what we can determine, it is full, waiting pickup."

Vegas thought for a minute. Taking out a rival's stash would spread the violence at a time he didn't need any more distractions, but the value of the cargo would help with the expense of the search. Then Vegas thought of Suarez. He turned to Garcia. "We will take this gift now, right now. You will do this, but you will ride with him, unarmed," Vegas nodded at Santana. "I want no one to escape. No one, you understand?" Vegas looked hard at the man.

Garcia snapped to attention. "I understand. It will be done, Señor Vegas." The man trotted off to inform his men.

Turning to Santana, Vegas said, "Go with them and see this done. I will come just behind you."

The killer nodded.

Garcia returned and stepped into the backseat of Santana's pickup with the killer beside him. Santana slapped his driver on the shoulder. The driver positioned them behind Garcia's two pickups as they all moved out slowly. Vegas' driver and his bodyguard's truck followed a hundred yards behind.

After eight kilometers the lead truck pulled off the paved road onto a crude, gravel path. They worked their way up a narrow draw for another kilometer, away from the coast. Vegas surveyed the terrain as he followed at a distance. It was an excellent place for an ambush, but nothing happened. As the ravine began to widen, they pulled up to the other trucks. Four armed men jumped out of the back of one and headed into the jungle in either direction. In the growing dark, the rest and waited in silence. After about ten minutes Garcia's pickups took off.

In Santana's pickup, Garcia barked, "Go!" to the driver.

The three vehicles moved rapidly in darkness, past the thick brush that was growing along either side of the road. In the dusk they saw the abandoned old farmhouse and the open-air tobacco sheds—long leaves drying on poles, hung high in the shed. The storage building lay just beyond, an old pickup sat beside it.

At the first crack of automatic rifles Vegas, signaled his driver to move. The attack was sudden and vicious, the occupants never had a chance.

When Vegas arrived, one man lay dead in the doorway. Another limp body was being dragged into the light from the back of the building. Two other men stood in the glare of headlights. A couple of Garcia's men covered them with automatic rifles. One man tied their hands behind their backs. The rest searched the area. In under a minute everyone gathered around the captives. Santana walked up to the two shivering men and held a knife on one of them.

Vegas watched through the darkened windows of his car. These ex-Ernesto men must understand the new order. Besides, the tiger, the merciless animal that ruled the very core of his being, needed to be released. After a tense minute, Vegas stepped slowly out his door.

All action stopped. With a quick, knowing glance to Santana Vegas casually walked up to the captives. Vegas buried his switchblade into the first man. Simultaneously Santana stabbed the other.

In a nearby field under a crude shelter covered with palm branches, a young teenaged Indian girl cradled her new baby. As she listened to the screams, tears rolled down her cheek. One of the men had been the father.

Later that night a car sped by the Tepic office of Suarez' Federal Narcotics Department. As the car passed, a filled, bloody sack was thrown onto the doorstep. About the same time Garcia's men were putting torches to the tobacco barns.

25

Jack and Jan stood on the helicopter landing pad at the bow of the ship enjoying the distant lights of Puerto Vallarta.

"The captain was showing me around the ship today." Jan said. "It's really amazing. There are all kinds of laboratories. Your whale research is going 24 hours a day. It's over my head, but they sure take it seriously."

"Most of its over mine too." He laughed.

"There's this brass plaque on the wall of the bridge."

"Umm." Jack gave her a guarded look, knowing what was coming.

"It says this ship is owned by the St. Julian Foundation of Seattle Washington. Captain Erickson said technically you own this ship." She said with no little admiration.

"Well, that's not exactly true." Jack countered.

"But not exactly false."

"It's owned be a foundation, a group of concerned people. The university leases it. We have to know more about the ocean. We are in trouble as a society, without this knowledge we will be even worse off."

"So I take it that, that is a passionate yes." She gave him a disarming grin.

"I told you dad did okay in investments."

"Very okay apparently." Jan teased him. "Money's worthless Jack, unless you do something with it." Suddenly she dropped her head in sadness. "I told Todd that only the other day…"

"Yeah, I've heard it before too." Jack swallowed hard. The memory of the Greek restaurant and reaching for Pat's hand across the table flooded his memory.

They stood, each lost in their own worlds, silently looking out over the ocean.

"This thing you are doing is safe?" she asked, not wanting the conversation to end. "This diving suit…?"

"Yes, relative to anything to do with underwater."

"And you actually think there is treasure down there?"

"I doubt it, maybe some artifacts that will add new knowledge to their history. Mexico's history isn't a particularly peaceful experience. The Spanish made a point of destroying anything that had to do with the cultures they found, and those previous cultures were none too kind to their predecessors either. They built pyramids that rivaled the Egyptians, you know, but almost everything about their pre-Columbian cultures has been lost. Besides, it is a big ocean—a needle-in-a-haystack example doesn't come close."

Jack looked down at the harbor patrol boat as it bobbed 50 yards away. The men on the craft were looking up at the couple.

During the night, the ship had been abuzz with activity. The *Juan de Fuca's* crew had taken the initiative and tracked the ocean bottom with their state of the art multi-beam sonar. This gave the divers a precise layout of oceans floor.

Those involved with the whaling research had worked out a system with the "treasure hunters"—as they had been named, much to the professor's chagrin. The three small inflatable rafts of the *Juan de Fuca* would take off early in the morning in search of their mammals. Deni's *Carmen I* would act as a remote for the divers.

The Newtsuit was brought out onto the dive deck and prepped. Jack climbed up onto the loading platform next to the suit and stepped down onto the ridged metal crotch of the lower "legs" half of the suit. He maneuvered his legs down the inside of the suit and settled his backside onto the crotch, just to get comfortable. Jack adjusted to the absolute rigidity of the cast aluminum frame, which would be the guardian of his life while he was underwater.

By 8 am everyone was busy on the gently rolling lower dive deck of the *Juan de Fuca* as Deni, Ivan and the lobsterman in *Carmen II* and Israel in *Carmen I* approached. The harbor patrol boat stopped and cleared them with the research ship before allowing them to proceed.

As the fishing boats bobbed in the water just off the *Juan de Fuca*, the lobsterman looked in amazement as he surveyed the bustling rear staging platform of the research ship, located just off the waterline. It was the most sophisticated technology he had ever seen, complete with racks of all manner of diving equipment, stainless steel shelves arrayed with plastic-coated electronics, gauges and all forms of gadgetry.

"They have a space suit?" the lobsterman whispered to Deni.

"And a spaceship." Deni smiled looking over at the side scan sonar that resembled a 15-foot torpedo with gull wings hanging over the ocean on a crane.

The pair watched in amazement as an assistant mechanically raised the arms of the upper half of the Newtsuit, so they pointed spread eagle into the air. The crane operator then swung the upper half over and slowly lowered it on to Jack. He lifted his arms and the upper half of the casing consumed him.

Deni and the lobsterman looked at each other in disbelief and then back to the ship-board action.

Jack smiled to himself as the suit closed over him. The familiar, claustrophobic feeling always reminded him of Buzz Lightyear from Toy Story movies inside his space suit.

Jack quickly reacquainted himself with the gauges and controls. He rubbed his back on the interior of the suit. He flexed the controls for the arms and hands.

Inside the suit, with practiced ease Jack slowly pulled his right arm down and out of the arm slot. He scratched his nose and then slipped his arm back into position. With his big frame the whole suit was a tight but manageable fit.

The hand controls inside the gloves allowed him to smoothly insert and release the selection of tools attached to the suit's forearms and belt, into the external hands. The hands had greater dexterity than a human hand, with them he was able to turn full 360° circles to screw and unscrew objects.

Jack maneuvered the right hand to pick up a piece of rope with brass locking clasps at either end. The two finger-pinchers of the hand deftly lifted the rope. With his left hand he grasped the brass clasp, flicked it open and closed over the other clasp, making a loop. Using both hands he undid the loop and reattached the special piece of cord back on his suit belt.

"Testing, testing," Jack said over the mike.

"We read you, five by five sir," the assistant on the headphone announced.

"Fine. I'm ready when you are. Let's get me out and we'll convene, then get to it."

"Aye, sir."

The team opened up the suit and Jack stepped out, all to the wonder of the lobsterman.

Deni flipped a rope to one of the research vessel's men as he docked against the side of the dive deck. The lobsterman's reverie was broken as the professor came bounding up to introduce himself.

"Hola, amigos," the professor greeted them as they stepped up on deck.

They led the lobsterman to a makeshift table on the dive deck. In short order he was pouring over maps, telling of his experience with the bottom around the Morros. In truth there was little he could tell them about archeological finds, but he enjoyed the notoriety.

Jack approached Deni as the others were gathered around the table. "We want to use the *Carmen I* for divers and the *Carmen II* to tow a sonar device. Is that okay?"

"Sure. What do they need to do to my boat?"

"Nothing. The side scanner uses a tow cable that has its own bracing system and the laptop computer hooked up to it. It records the two-dimensional picture to the laptop screen. They have techies to run it. All you have to do is run the boat. The *Carmen I* will follow and dive if anything is found.

Deni shook his head in amazement.

This being the first chance Deni had to meet the professor, he asked straight out, "So, what is all this really about?"

Everyone including Jack, stopped to listen.

"There is a theory—theory, mind you," Professor Torres repeated, "that there were Spaniards in the Bay of Banderas before Buenaventura sailed in. When Buenaventura came somewhere between 1525 and 1530, he was met by an army of angry natives, some say 10,000 strong. On their spears they had banners, like flags. That is how the bay got its name—Bay of Flags it would be in English. Anyway, he wisely concluded that a tactical retreat was in order. The thing is there have been rumors of another party before him that came and pillaged the area. That is why so many natives came out to challenge Buenaventura."

The professor reached into his valise and pulled out a thick leather binder, wrapped in heavy protective plastic. "In here are the shards of an old diary of Heraldo Santa Anita Alzarro." Torres looked up at Jack, "You and your father were with me when we found this." He gave Jack a fatherly smile.

"You see," he looked up at the Americans, "It was known that after Cortez penetrated Mexico City and had taken the king, Montezuma, captive; priests had taken many of the remaining members of the royal family and much of the temple treasures the Spaniards hadn't yet seized, and headed west. It was also known that rival tribes hated the cruel yoke of the Aztec. These tribes betrayed the priests and caused the end to all that was the empire of the Aztecs. Other conquistadors—Sandoval, Alvarado and others covered the plains and highlands of Mexico, exploring, conquering and searching for gold. The early records of this time are thin and sketchy; evidence of other explorers has faded into history. I believe Alzarro was the first Spaniard to come to this area. But I have no proof, other than this diary.

Maybe this expedition will find something, likely not, but we will see. And for sure, we will not find it on this wonderful ship." The professor clapped his hands. "Vamanos, let's get moving."

On his command all parties got into gear. Jack and Deni shared a smile as Jack headed for the Newtsuit.

"You don't look so good amigo" Deni observed.

"Was a long night, been thinking."

"Sure."

Once again, encased in the Newtsuit, he quickly rechecked his controls. "Ready when you are," Jack said over the radio.

"Engaging crane in five seconds."

Jack experienced another Buzz Lightyear moment as he hung helpless and as the crane picked him up, swinging him over the side, and slowly lowering him into the water. In the near distance he saw the patrol boat being kept busy as local fishermen tried to get a closer look at the goings-on. As he was raised over the edge of the water, all attention turned to watch the suit submerge.

Jack floated neutrally buoyant. Water lapped over his large bubble-like visor. He and two divers did a final safety check.

Jack was pleased with the action and response of the new generation of controls—everything was quicker and tighter.

Engaging the foot controlled hover-throttles, he maneuvered just below the surface, forward and back—up and down a couple feet.

Over his headset Jack heard, "Sir, we gerry-rigged a more powerful metal detector so that it will adapt to your right hand controls.

A scuba diver placed the detector into the brace of Jack right "arm." Jack fiddled with it for a moment—the oversized controls of the metal detector were awkward but workable.

"I can make this work." Jack confirmed. He could clearly see the meter window on the Fisher metal detector.

"We've recalibrated the Fisher 8X to compensate for your suit. It should be pretty accurate, but remember to keep it pointed away from you."

"Understood." Jack answered.

"We are attaching a tether rope from the detector to your belt. If you need to release the detector, it will stay with you."

"Roger that."

Jack watched the diver release the detector. It gently began to sink. Jack reached for it with his left arm and after two tries, attached it back to his right arm.

"I got it." Jack confirmed.

Finally, all personnel were satisfied. From within the suit Jack gave the divers a nod. To the audience on the deck, he raised his arm in a wave. The last thing he saw was Jan looking down at him, her face tense, arms crossed tightly across her chest.

It only took seconds to reach the 50 foot bottom directly under the ship. From there Jack worked in an easterly direction, following the rapidly-descending ocean floor. He spent the time getting used to the response of the new controls, liking the quickness and improved agility. As he descended, that old feeling of being an aquatic hummingbird came over him as he propelled himself up and down as well as right and left.

It had been agreed that because of the versatility and speed of the suit he would sweep areas below 100 feet. The first pass would be with the metal detector, then he'd come back and search the many pools of sand for non-metallic objects with compressed air.

Although the Newtsuit could cover a lot of territory, the metal detector's limitations would slow them down.

"Okay. I'm at my depth and starting at my first grid point," Jack reported.

"Roger that," Deni answered.

"Hey there, amigo. They draft you?"

"Everyone's busy. I'm going to keep track of Israel and the

professor's divers. They are following Ivan in the *Carmen II*, so figured I could keep up with you too."

"Sounds good." Jack listed off his coordinates and began his sweeps. "By the way, how long will the battery on this detector last?"

"I'll check." Deni answered. A couple minutes later he returned. "Two to three hours."

"Roger. See you at lunch."

Deni was stationed at the radio on the dive deck. He'd been supplied with plastic-covered maps of all the morning's pre-agreed diving sites. As each group reported in, he marked off the areas covered with different-colored erasable markers. The professor hovered around like a mother hen listening to every report.

The twin headlamps on either side of Jack's helmet illuminated the water as darkness grew heavier with depth. A school of bonitos paid him no notice as he moved through them.

Jack decided to cover the eastern wall of the canyon and work in a north-to-south descending pattern. The many crags and narrow chasms made for slow going, but the mobility of the suit allowed him to hover like a hummingbird, making the task easier.

Although life was sparse compared to nearer the surface, Jack was still pleased to watch in the beam of his headlights, the vibrant colors of angelfish and butterfly fish, poking at the sparse vegetation that grows between the gray-green rocks. Jack sighed with contentment—if he had his way he'd live 30 feet underwater on a coral reef.

Back on the deck of the *Juan De Fuca,* the chief mate reviewed the workings of the dive equipment protocol, the computerized console and general safety points. One of the grad students translated it into Spanish for the lobsterman.

The lobsterman tested and retested the diving console they had provided him, turning the computer on and off, in fascination. The grad student tried to explain how the console automatically calculated depth, temperature, current and many things. The lobsterman stood in awe.

Deni said to the chief mate, "He's never seen a computer before. When he runs out of air he simply comes to the surface."

The chief mate just shook his head.

The rest of the team stood ready in wet suits, with buoyancy control devices, and all the other equipment needed for SCUBA. The lobsterman wore nothing but a pair of faded shorts, tank, his new console, and a dive bag for lobsters.

It had been agreed that two of the grad students and lobsterman would go out with Israel in *Carmen I* to a pre-assigned spot, 500 yards east of the rock where Jack had made his first GPS readings.

The *Carmen II* had been rigged with the side scan sonar and was to start its search pattern next to the northernmost Morro rock. Their orders were to radiate out from the rock in a circular pattern until they reached the other Morros rock. Then start again in the same fashion from there. Search all area less than 100 feet deep.

On board *Carmen II*, Ivan, the grad students and two technicians from the *Juan de Fuca* began their search around the Morros.

After two dives, everyone was to meet back at the ship, rest, compare notes and organize for their next move.

They slowly fed out cable. The towed sonar immediately began receiving images on the computer screen. At slow trolling speed Ivan quickly got the hang of what they wanted and turned the steering over to one of the research students, so he could watch the screen.

"How does this work?" he asked.

"You know how sonar works as a depth finder?"

"Of course, all our boats have them. A signal goes out, hits the bottom and comes back, telling you your depth."

"Well, this is just a little more sophisticated. It's called a side scanner, made by an outfit called JW Fisher. It sends out a beam, both down and sideways, for about 8 to 10 meters. We run it about 5 meters off the bottom and it gives us readings that create two dimension images, instead of the single 'depth' image. That way we can make out objects on the bottom."

Having fished the areas many times, Ivan found the opportunity to "see" the bottom fascinating.

Just before lunch they made a find.

Deni and the professor met the two boats as they returned.

Deni was confused as the students passed up to the professor, what looked like a large, oblong Hubbard squash-shaped rock. They all handled it as if it were the Holy Grail.

"What's the big deal? It's a rock," Deni looked from one to the other.

"Yes." The professor agreed. "But what kind of rock?"

"I don't know. Smooth, grey, hard." Deni said sarcastically.

"How many smooth, flat rocks do you find, thirty kilometers out in the ocean?" The Professor asked.

Deni shrugged.

"You see," the professor continued. "In the earliest days, they had no metal for ballast so they used the next best thing— stones. This could be a river rock from where the ship was built, it will help us identify where the ship originated."

"Oh."

After lunch they repositioned the grid search to where the stone had been found. It didn't take long before they located three more. A crude pattern began to emerge.

The grad students and techs on the *Carmen* II marked a number of points where unusual images were sighted. The students organized to dive to those headings.

After noon and the replacement of batteries, Jack headed into the deeper parts of the canyon. He repositioned himself and began sweeping laterally across the path of the ballast rocks. The walls of the canyon became more distant, deepening as he moved to the south. Pockets of sand became more numerous. At 240 feet, Jack began to pick up faint movements on the detector's needle. In a matter of a few feet the needle was pegged, as Jack was able to make out in the headlights, the ghostly shapes of wreckage from a modern commercial fishing boat.

"Deni, I found that shrimp boat on your dad's map. Looks to be about a 30 footer?"

"Yeah. Back in the '40s one went down near here. Three guys drowned."

Jack picked through the wreckage and confirmed the coordinate.

"It's pretty torn up, on its side, bow down in a crevasse, rigging's gone."

The sea had claimed it. Marine growth covered everything, a colony of triggerfish now called it home. Jack spent the rest of the day with no real results, picking up only the occasional piece of modern junk that had been cast over the side.

That night they all reconvened around the dive deck table comparing notes. Jack's and the other parties' many readings were entered into a survey computer for future reference. The river rocks were thoroughly examined, weighed and photographed from every angle.

Deni listened over the CB to the local fishermen's chatter. They were upset at not being allowed to fish an area they felt was their own. Deni knew this was nonsense—the fishing wasn't that good. The reality was, they wanted to know what was going on. Deni and the lobsterman enjoyed themselves, making up lies over the CB about what they were really doing. From mining for gold and oil exploration, they moved on to alien spaceship sightings. The pair decided to sleep on *Carmen II* to avoid the wrath of their compadres.

*   *   *

That evening Jack and Jan stood on the bow looking out over the darkening western sky. The well-lit patrol boat bobbed in the near distance.

"There's been no word on Todd today," she sighed.

"I understand Suarez is running around San Blas up north. Reportedly, there were some murders or something. Wonder if any of that has to do with all this Vegas truck business? I am sure Suarez is giving the bad guys fits," Jack tried to reassure.

"Do you think there is any hope?" Jan continued, looking up into Jack's face.

"You must have hope…"

She waited for him to finish. He looked down at her for the briefest of moments. He quickly looked away and across the darkening horizon. "Beyond hope is what you know is right. Part of me knew that seeing Pat again was… beyond hope," he said slowly then stopped again. "It was totally different, but I lost her too," he confided. Jack grasped the railing tightly.

Jack's mind was a maelstrom of anguish. He wanted to grab Jan and hold her, squeeze her tight. But how could that be right? It was Pat he longed for. He turned and walked back into the ship.

Jan stood stunned. Her hand came up instinctively reaching out for him, grasping nothing but air. The woman in her absorbed the man's pain, as only women can. An unbidden tear rolled down her cheek.

26

The next morning Jack sat alone nursing a black coffee when Deni sat beside him.

"You look like crap," Deni stated flatly, watching for a reaction. Jan had told him what happened.

"Didn't sleep so well. No sweat," Jack shrugged.

"Again?"

In spite of the professor's enthusiasm, the morning's preparations were handled in sullen routine. The scuba divers and the side scan sonar continued their grids.

Jan was not on deck when Jack descended under the waves. He spent the morning touring the canyon's west wall with no success, save for pockets of modern junk.

He in his mind he replayed the seconds of the attack on Pat all through the night. He thought, "Now this woman is coming into my life. What is right? I love Pat, but she's gone. 'Moving on,' they call it." Jack closed his eyes tightly. "This is not moving on, it is just pain. How can I move on? I never even got to say goodbye. You were just gone, my love." A tear rolled down his cheek.

"How's it going down there?" Deni inquired, breaking his reverie.

After a long pause, Deni repeated himself, "You okay?"

Jack regained himself. "Not seeing much, mostly vertical walls. I'll cover them this morning. This afternoon I'll focus on the sandy bottom of the canyon, maybe."

"Hmmm, maybe," Deni answered. "You okay?"

"Let it go, Deni."

"Si, Señor."

Jack took a deep breath, "…hell of a place to have a runny nose," he thought, bringing himself under control.

As the morning progressed Jack's military discipline helped him focus on the task at hand. "Time enough for personal issues later," he kept telling himself. "When?" his mind kept coming back with.

After resurfacing for lunch and a planning strategy, Jack's mood brightened.

Later, as the crane released him from its control, Jack looked out across the ocean. The seas were calm, the day perfect. There wasn't another vessel in sight. Jack wasn't sure if he would rather be on the surface or under it—either was perfect on a day like this.

At the canyon wall where he had left off that morning, the thought struck him. "Deni, is the patrol boat out there?"

"No. They radioed that they were having engine trouble and were headed back in. Another boat is on the way out."

Jack didn't like it, but there wasn't a lot he could do about it. "Keep me posted."

"Roger."

An hour later he was at 220 feet, hovering over a large, jagged cliff that extended beyond his sight. He worked horizontally along the edge of the cliff when he picked up a faint movement of the detector gauge. Working down, Jack found the movement increased. Below him was a 50 yard bowl-like shelf, cut deep into the side of the cliff. The bowl was filled with sand.

"I have another faint metal contact, dropping to 240 feet."

He identified the most intense point of contact under the sand without difficulty. The needle pegged then let up. After a pass over the entire bowl to confirm the location, he landed next to where the needle was the most active. He removed the detector from his arm, selected the compressor tool, and went to work blowing away the sand. The coarse sand melted back in a cloud. The light ocean current took the cloud away like smoke in a gentle breeze. Suddenly at the bottom of a three foot cone a ray of light flashed up from the earth, reflecting off his powerful headlights. Surprised by the flash Jack stopped digging, the light went out as sand cascaded back down. Starting again he widened the hole from the top creating a much wider bowl. This time when he began clearing sand from the lowest part of the bowl, a blazing arch of a golden crescent began reflecting out of the sand.

"Oh baby!" Jack exclaimed.

"What was that?" Deni asked.

"Oh nothing. Just doing a little digging," Jack smiled and started to hum.

Jack had to widen the hole one more time as the sand walls kept collapsing. At eighteen inches the diameter of the disk began to decrease. It was perfectly round, like a giant coin. In the very center was a square opening, roughly two inches wide. Jack extended the suit's finger probe into the square hole and gently lifted. He felt the strenuous weight of the object resisting his effort as the disk slowly emerged out of the suction of the sand.

With the probe acting as a Herculean finger, Jack examined the disk. He was blinded from its brightness when his headlights caught it at just the right angle. It was nearly an inch thick and covered with hieroglyphic writing. Jack recognized the object as an ancient sundial used by the Aztec.

"I'm heading up," Jack stated. He laid the orb back onto the sand and peeled off the short length of rope with the brass clamps. Looping it through the hole, he attached rope to the disk and the loop to his belt.

"Why, what's up?' Deni asked.

"I'll explain when I get there." Jack began his ascent.

Sixty seconds later, Deni asked "How you doing?"

"Just coming up. Why?"

"We got company."

"How so?" Jack asked.

"There is a Zodiac coming our way at full speed, it doesn't say "*Harbor Patrol*." You said your friends from the other night took off in a single outboard Zodiac, right?"

"Yeah."

"Well, my guess is they are back."

"How long you figure we got?"

"Couple minutes, probably less."

"Okay," Jack said and stepped on both thrusters full blast. Things had just been going too well.

"You got a plan?" Deni asked.

"Working on it. You got anything up there to repel boarders?"

"I'll see what I can do."

"Before you go, let the Captain in on what's up."

"Roger."

Jack quickly came up under the hull of the research vessel, near the anchor chains. "I'm directly under the ship. How's it coming up there?" Jack asked.

The crusty voice of the Captain came over the headset. "What's going on, St. Julian?"

"Captain, these guys want Miss Hamilton."

There was a long pause. "That won't happen on my watch, mister."

Jack watched above as the wake of the Zodiac circled the vessel.

"We are mobilizing as we can. Israel's got the .22, but has divers down and can't leave them. Anyway, he'd never get here in time," Deni said.

"Roger. I'm directly under the dive station. How many are there in the boat?"

"It's our two friends from the other day. I recognize the guy who stuck a knife in my back."

The sight of his half-drowned cat crossed Jack's mind. He watched the raft angle straight for the ship, directly above him.

"Where are they sitting in the boat to my position?" Jack asked, ascending closer.

"One guy's in the front, about five feet back, in the middle, sitting," Deni listed off. "The driver is three quarters of the way back, port-side standing at the wheel."

Suddenly Deni came back, "Jack, the front guy just raised a rifle at us. The driver's got a pistol."

"Showtime, amigo." Jack closed under the Zodiac.

"Professor Torres is out there telling them off."

"Deni, get him out of there fast. He'll get hurt."

"They just tossed a rope at him, told him to take it. He told them what they can do with it and threw it back. They are yelling now. The lead guy is standing, trying to get a loop on the ship. The professor's pushing them back with a grappling pole."

"I'm moving. Make your move, Deni," Jack instructed and advanced under the rubber bottom of the raft.

Jack engaged the razor-sharp, scalloped edge of his slicing tools into both mechanical hands. He ascended until his helmet was touching the bottom of the Zodiac. Jack spread his arms out spread-eagle and in a grand-scythe motion, slid the knives through the back half of both inflated sides. The scalpels tore through the fabric like through soft flesh. Compressed air exploded out of the openings, blowing his arms away. But his thruster kept his body in place. He quickly brought his arms up again and sliced the rear secondary air chambers. Instantly the weight of the outboard motor buckled the stern; the raft folded in half and into the sea.

That same instant Jack felt the concussion of a loud roar directly above his head. The surface of the water opened up beside him. Through a curtain of dense bubbles the body of a man appeared.

"What's going on?" Jack yelled, but got no answer.

When Deni saw the water boiling under the zodiac he'd made his move. The Mexican bravely charged the rifleman. In one great swoop Deni expertly cast an old-fashioned, hand fishing net over the raft. Along the outer edge of the net was a series of little lead weights that made it expand like a giant netted Frisbee; the net formed a perfect circle that descended on the unbelieving front occupant of the raft.

Just as the net hit him, the Ferret fired at Deni, but the loss of balance from the sinking raft and the net spoiled his aim. The shot narrowly missed Deni and rang off the bulkhead of the ship above. The net caught the rifle barrel, twirled down, and pinned the man in a tangled mess.

When the outboard folded under, the rear man was bowled backward into the ocean. The man struggled through a torrent of bubbles to reach the surface, but something pulled him down. He opened his eyes only to see an alien monster staring back at him.

Jack watched the man open his mouth to scream. "You better get someone to take this guy. He just breathed in a lung full of ocean," Jack radioed. "Where's the other guy?"

"Everything is under control," came the voice of the Captain. "But you better get up here."

Jack broke the surface just in time to catch Deni standing in the Zodiac, his big fist plowing into the rifleman's face. The Ferret went down like a sack of potatoes into the floating remains of the Zodiac.

Several crewmen jumped in the water around Jack, they took the semi-conscious man and dragged him to the ladder while others assisted in getting Jack lifted on the crane. As he rose above the deck, Jack saw Jan kneeling over the professor. When she looked up at Jack, he could see her shirt was splattered with blood.

By the time Jack was out of the Newtsuit, everything had settled down. Jack recognized the Ferret, now tightly looped in yellow polypropylene rope, blood still leaking from his broken nose. The other attacker had his hands tied behind him and was vomiting on the deck. The crew stood over him. One held a flare pistol at his face.

Jack immediately came over to Professor Torres, who was

now sitting in a deck chair. Jan was putting the finishing touches on a bandage around his head. Blood was caked on his neck and down the shoulder of his shirt. He looked pale but spry.

"You okay, professor?" Jack asked.

"Oh yes. In good hands. The young lady says the shot just grazed me. Nasty headache though," he winced.

Jack looked at Jan for confirmation and she nodded. "A nasty scratch, took off a piece of ear, too. He should get stitches."

"Bah!" the professor said. "Must have caught the ricochet."

"Are you okay?" Jack looked at Jan.

"Oh yes. Just a little messy."

Captain Erikson stepped up. "I have radioed in. They are sending out a chopper."

Jan looked into Jack's eyes for a long moment. Tears starting to swell in her eyes. "They won't stop!" she pleaded.

"We will see it stopped," he stated coldly, "but one thing at a time."

Jack helped the professor to his feet. "I have something for you." Jack picked up a length of rope from the deck and handed one end to Deni. "When I give three tugs get ready to pull, but be careful."

Holding the other end of the rope, Jack took a lung full of air and dove into the sea.

Startled, everyone stepped to the edge of the deck as he vanished under the ship.

Jack kicked hard to the anchor chain and threaded a double bowline through looped rope. He gave three quick tugs and cut the rope that held the disk to the anchor chain. Jack quickly propelled back to the surface.

The disk swung out through the water like a giant pendulum. For a moment it started to sink, then just as quickly it began bobbing toward the surface.

Jack broke the water just in time to see the sun flash off the gold for the first time in nearly 500 years.

Everyone froze. The disk hung motionless. From Jack's

vantage point in the water the look on the professor's face was priceless.

Suddenly everyone came to life and jumped at once. Others joined Deni on the line. The professor started barking orders, warning not to let it touch the side of the ship.

By the time Jack was back on deck, everyone was standing around admiring the treasure. The professor was on his hands and knees, his face almost touching the disk. He lovingly passed his fingertips over the writing. After a long minute of examining the one side, they carefully turned the disk over. To one side of the square opening was a nasty gash in an otherwise perfect object.

"Oh, what a shame," Jan said.

Fingering the gash in the treasure, Professor Torres closed his eyes for a long moment. "No, young lady, it is no shame." He looked up at Jack. "You, young man! What were you doing endangering such a priceless object? How dare you act so fast and loose!"

Jack pointed to the man's head.

"Oh yes, of course." The professor's hand ran across the bandage. He then laughed and grabbed Jack's hand, shaking it furiously.

Quickly things got themselves sorted out. Everyone followed as they moved the treasure into the wardroom.

Deni approached Jack and quietly whispered, "You should have told me it was heavy. I almost dropped it."

Jack smirked and slapped the fisherman on the back. "Don't tell the professor." Then his expression turned cold. "We have some unfinished business."

Deni nodded solemnly.

"Let's go see the Captain," Jack said.

"Their Coast Guard is sending a helicopter out to take back the injured passengers and the prisoners," Captain Erikson informed them as they approached him on the bridge. "They have asked us to head into the naval station. They want to know what happened."

"That makes two of us, Captain," Jack said. He looked squarely at the man. "We need a little privacy with our two boarders back on the diving deck. Do you have a problem with that?"

The Captain's eyes narrowed as he read their meaning. "None at all."

With the treasure in the wardroom, the dive deck was deserted. Deni dragged both men out of the storage locker where they had been caged and laid them on the dive deck.

Jack fixed his gaze on his friend and said in Spanish, "It's time to get some information."

Deni smiled slyly. "Si."

They looked hard at the prone pair.

"We meet again, amigo," Jack stared into the Ferret's eyes.

The Ferret stared back defiantly.

"This one first," Jack said.

"Si, amigo," Deni agreed heartily.

"You can't do anything to me," the Ferret snarled.

"Watch me." Jack grabbed a handful of the Ferret's shirt and dragged him to the edge of the deck. He loosened the cable of the Newtsuit boom and attached the hook to the rope behind the man's back.

The Ferret started screaming profanity in Spanish and English.

Jack ignored him and punched the controls, lifting him into a standing position. The action drew an even louder response from the thug. Jack walked around the protesting man and checked the strength of the connection, then came around beside Deni who was facing the man.

"Maybe we are making a mistake," Jack said.

Deni gave him a quizzical look.

"We are in a hurry, right?" Jack reasoned, looking at Deni.

"Si."

"Let's do this a different way. Let him down."

Deni complied, not sure of his friend intention.

Jack unhooked the cable.

The Ferret sneered at Jack. "I told you, you could do nothing to me."

Jack returned a cold smile. He bent down and attached the hook through the rope securing the man's feet. The Ferret's smile vanished and he started cursing again.

Deni gave a sharp bark of laughter as he realized what was going to happen next.

"Enough," Jack said. Deni pulled the lever and the cable tightened. The Ferret went down hard on the steel deck. The crane lifted him upside down and out over the ocean. Jack began to lower the squealing lowlife toward the ocean's surface.

The Ferret lost his nerve. He pleaded with Deni not to do this.

"Why have you been chasing us?" Jack asked.

Silence.

Jack got on his hands and knees close to the man's face. "You will talk to me or you will talk to the fish," Jack snarled.

The man's cold eyes said nothing. Jack gave the thumbs down to Deni. As the Ferret's head slipped under the water, his body spasmed as he tried to lift himself. After 10 seconds Jack gave the thumbs up. As soon as the Ferret's head cleared the surface his stomach emptied. He gasped for air.

Jack looked him in the eye and simply stated, "You understand of course that when your friend sees what we have done with you, he will tell us what we want."

Everyone turned and saw the other man staring in wide-eyed horror.

Jack returned his gaze to the Ferret. "So, this is it pal. Frankly, after what you've tried to do to me, the woman, my boat and my damn cat, why should I even want you to live?" Jack smiled and stepped away from the edge. "Take him down."

As the cable lowered the man's head to the surface, he broke. "Stop! Stop!" the Ferret cried. Deni quickly pulled him up about a foot above the water's surface. "Please let me up! I'll tell you anything, please!"

Jack looked hard at the man. "You don't answer once and we'll drown your sorry ass. Comprende, amigo?" Jack spat.

The man stared at Jack's face. He knew he was looking death in the eye.

Jack signaled Deni, and the Mexican laid the man onto the deck.

"What are you doing here?"

"The woman," he panted.

"What about her?"

"Vegas wants her. She knows something."

"Why?"

"She knows where the truck is."

"What truck?"

"The one stolen by Ernesto Vegas and her brother."

"Vegas ordered the hit on his own brother, didn't he?" Jack asked.

"Si. For the robbery of the truck."

"Where is Miss Hamilton's brother?"

The man's eyes flashed to Jack then to Deni and back again.

"He's dead, isn't he?" Jack demanded.

The Ferret saw the look in the gringo's eyes and knew his life hung by a thread. "I did not have anything to do with it," he pleaded. "He tried to escape and was killed. They didn't want to kill him because he knew where to find the truck."

"Where is he?"

"In the hills, in a farmhouse. I will show you," he bargained.

Jack walked behind the man and undid the hook. Together, they dragged the Ferret and his partner back into the locker.

Jack and Deni walked slowly back to the wheelhouse. They met the Captain's eyes and nodded.

"We just got a message for you two," the Captain said. "Some guy named Captain Suarez wants to talk to Deni. He also wants Jan to come in to Puerto Vallarta. Suarez has some news and more questions for her."

Jack reviewed his options and nodded.

In the distance they heard the thumping rhythm of helicopter blades. They found Jan at the helipad, watching it approach.

"No point in telling her about the brother. Not yet at least," Jack said.

"Roger."

Jan turned and saw the expression on the men's faces as they approached. "What?"

"We need to ask you a couple things," Jack said softly.

"What?" she repeated, anxiety crossing her face. "Something about my brother?"

"Sort of yes and no. Those guys were looking for you."

"Why?"

"One of them repeated what Suarez told us the other day. There was a big heist of some kind and your brother was involved."

"No. That's not possible. He just wouldn't be involved with anything like that. You have to believe me," she pleaded.

Because of compassion for the woman's image of her brother, Jack continued: "Jan, your brother was a big shot with the Vegas family. By all appearances they had gotten into drugs."

Deni added gently, "They are very bad men."

As Jan listened in silence, her face paled and her hands began to tremble.

"We know one brother was killed by the other, that's how brutal they are. Todd must have been mixed up somehow with the losing brother. He was supposed to be at that party that night wasn't he?"

With her face in her hands she gave her head a small nod. "You'd have been there," Jack said flatly.

She lowered her hands, tears spilled down her cheeks. "He had been acting so tense for the last few days. I think he stayed out all night, the night before. He was really tired the day we went for a drive. That morning I saw filthy clothes in the laundry. He wanted me to go home. We argued." Jan looked up at Jack. "I've been cooped up for so long, looking after mom.

This was the break I had wanted so badly. We compromised. He agreed to doing no work and spending just one day with me and then I'd go home the next day." Her hands covered her face again.

"What did you do that last day?" Jack asked.

"He was on the phone, even though he promised not to do business. Something was going on. He said they were in serious negotiations on some big land deal." She looked at the two men, "Why shouldn't I believe him?" she pleaded.

"No reason," Jack responded evenly. "So what did you do later?"

"We drove out to Punta de Mita. We went by La Cruz. I thought of you when we drove by." She blushed, the tears under control as she concentrated. "We stopped at some road where there is a gate. I was surprised when he got out and unlocked it. We went down to this beautiful beach. There was a couple of old, knocked-down buildings. I asked him about it, and he said it was a place where they were going to build a magnificent resort. It was a beautiful beach—sort of a crescent bowl, with perfect sand. We played in the waves. It was really a lovely spot. He said the whole coast had been re-zoned and developed. He talked a lot that afternoon about how there was going to be a second wave of more development."

"Do you remember the name of the place?"

"It was a funny name. Two words in Spanish, something about paradise."

"Paradisio Escondido?"

"Something like that."

"'Hidden Paradise' in English."

"Yes, I think that was it. When we came out he was talking about how much money they were going to make. He told me we, too, would be rich. I didn't say anything to spoil it, but I didn't care about being rich. I just wanted him to come home. We went back on the main road. He was still talking about land and making fortunes..." she paused. "As we pulled back onto the

main road…" she stopped, then backed up and started again. "…
I remember we drove by some other gate on the other side of
the road. He was just saying how valuable the land was going to
be. He slowed and said something I thought was odd. He
pointed at another other gate and said 'up there in the hills was
the most valuable piece of ground around' "

Jack looked at Deni.

"I've hunted up there," Deni said. "Which way were you
headed when you drove by this other gate?"

"Towards Punta de Mita. We finished the day there and then
went home. We had dinner in Puerto Vallarta, at a place called
Señor Mister Pepe's. After dinner we were both really tired. It
had been a lovely evening." Tears were starting to swell again.
Jan looked at Jack. "What can we do?"

"Right now, nothing. We are going back to Puerto Vallarta,
but don't tell the law any of this. This Vegas is evil. If he finds
out we've told the police we'll still be in big trouble. After
we're finished with the cops, we gotta smoke this sucker out,
one way or the other," Jack finished.

They all watched as the big Naval helicopter descended to
the heliport deck at the front of the ship. After securing the two
attackers in the helicopter they called for Jan and Deni.

Deni said quietly to Jack as they approached the helicopter,
"I think after today he will not stop coming—whether he gets
his dope truck or not. We are in deep now. My family, too. I
am a simple fisherman." Deni looked his friend in the eye.
"Something else is needed."

Jack silently put his hand on his friend shoulder and
nodded.

"I will go with Jan," Deni continued, "You must get home
and prepare to do those these your military has taught you. I will
go with you when we return."

*   *   *

Miguel Vegas stood in the harbormaster's private office and listened to the Naval dispatcher confirm that Jan Hamilton was on the helicopter.

"We have work to do."

They marched out together. Zillia wiped sweat off his brow as Santana led him out of the building.

27

Jack said his good-byes to the Captain and the professor, loaded onto *Carmen I* and quickly outdistanced the research vessel.

The sun was tipping toward the western shore by the time Jack passed the breakwater at La Cruz. On his way in he had set his plan. First, they had to locate this legendary truck and then get that information to Vegas, but not until Suarez was ready.

Jack cautiously approached the rear of the restaurant. Rosa gave a start when he materialized in her kitchen. She began to speak but he raised his finger to his lips. He scanned the modest, early evening crowd. The surfing musicians were nursing Coronas over in a corner; their surfboards leaning against the wall behind them. The rest of the crowd looked like the usual collection of lovers and tourists.

Jack turned to Rosa and saw the anxiety in her eyes. She unconsciously continued pounding a roll of tortilla dough in slow cadence.

"Where is Deni?" she asked.

"Suarez called Jan in. Deni went along to keep her company. They should be back soon."

"There is something wrong, Jack," she stated gravely.

"Why, has something happened?"

"No. I can feel it."

Jack looked her straight in the eye. Nothing but the truth would do. "Yes, something bad is happening. They tried to kidnap Jan off the ship today. For some reason Vegas wants her."

"What are we going to do?"

Jack took her hand. "The Navy trained me to do things." He lifted his left elbow, exposing the scar across the back of his arm. "You remember this?"

A tear came to her eye.

"I love you people for letting me come here and heal; not just that time but now, after Pat. You have never asked and I really never wanted to talk about it, but I want you to know that I am going to solve this problem. I swear it with my life. I will do everything I can to protect your family."

He looked her straight in the eyes and said, "After today, when we realized what was going on, we're not going to wait for them."

She reached up and patted his cheek.

"I have to change. As soon as Deni gets back we will get this matter over and done with. I promise," he smiled, "but right now you have work to do, there are hungry people out there. Which reminds me," he mentioned, changing the subject, "I could go for some of your chilies rellenos."

As he turned to head upstairs, the phone rang at the bar. They both froze as Angelo picked it up and looked their way. They headed for the bar.

Night was coming on when Deni and Jan exited the Federal Law Enforcement office. Deni stepped up to the first pay phone he came to.

"Where are you Deni?" Rosa asked anxiously.

"I'm fine. Is Jack there?"

"Si. You be careful." She handed the phone to Jack.

"You guys okay?" Jack asked.

"Yeah, but I smell a rat. Suarez never showed, they said he got tied up with something."

"You get back here. I'll be ready. I'll try to find Suarez and put a fire under his butt, calling you in like that could have put us all at risk."

"We'll get a taxi and be straight there." Deni hung up.

316

*   *   *

The cab passed the airport. Jets were bathed in spotlights, waiting to return to the north.

Jan thought about Todd. "Should I have gone home? Would things be different somehow if I had? Have I done something that got him in trouble?"

The taxi slowed in the thick traffic north of town. A few cars ahead, they could see police lights flashing.

"Must be an accident," the taxi driver said.

Deni watched as they pulled up to a police car. A uniformed policeman raised his hand to stop them. The cop slowly walked over to the driver. Everyone followed the policeman's approach.

Suddenly both passenger doors flew open. Deni never had a chance. The barrel of a pistol stabbed viciously into his ear. Out of the corner of his eye he saw Jan being hauled out by a cop who also had a pistol at her head.

The man with the gun snapped, "Anything foolish and you die."

Deni allowed his antagonist to pull him out of the car and lead him to the side door of a police van. Just as they tried to pull Jan into the van she screamed. The cop slugged her in the stomach, canceling any breath she had. Deni moved on Jan's attacker then everything went black.

Deni awoke to the splash of tepid water pouring over his head. As his consciousness increased, he realized he was in a sitting position. He felt a tight rope around his chest, confining his arms behind him. His vision slowly cleared. Jan was tied to a chair on his right. She was staring at him. Deni shook his head, only to confirm a fire alarm going on in the back of his skull.

Deni scanned a crowd of men watching him. Three were mere mortals—he could take any or all of them in a fair fight, but there was nothing fair about this. Two of the men were cops, both had pistols aimed at his head. Another was well-dressed, with the look of authority. The big one that had pulled him out of the cab held a sawed-off shotgun. That one was going to be a problem.

"Señor Marroso?" The well-dressed one said.

Deni heard him through a fog. Deni' eyes settled on the voice.

"Señor Marroso," the man repeated. "My name is Miguel Vegas."

That name brought Deni to full consciousness.

"Good. I see you recognized the name." Vegas walked directly in front of the tied pair. "We can do this with you or without you," he said in Spanish. "I'll speak English so Señorita Hamilton understands," Vegas continued. "Miss Hamilton knows the location of a truck. I want it returned. We can do this easily or I can be quite forceful," he said with a cold smile.

Deni, finding his wit, responded, "You'll kill us either way."

"That is not true," Vegas answered with a frown. "I have no beef against you people. I just want to recover my goods and be on my way without trouble. Killing makes trouble." Looking at Deni, Vegas stated calmly, "I cannot imagine Miss Hamilton wanting to see any harm come to you," Vegas turned to Jan, and finished the sentence, "and the rest of his family."

Jan's lips trembled. "I'll tell you anything, but I don't know what you want."

"It is a large truck, Miss Hamilton, worth many hundred millions of dollars. Someone took it, I want it back."

"I know that. I just don't know where it is."

His eyebrows rose, "You know this, do you? And where did the information come from?"

Jan's eyes involuntary flashed toward Deni. Vegas' attention turned to back Deni. "The two fools you sent to the boat today told us," Deni said.

"So, you know of this, do you?" Vegas said to Jan.

"Yes," she said, a tiny fragment of confidence building in her voice. "I know that much, and… and where's my brother?"

Vegas looked at her in mock confusion. "You do not know where your brother is?"

"No. I've been trying to find him for days."

"We have your brother, but he is in no condition to talk. You will tell us what we want and then you can have him back." Vegas paused for a moment to let this information sink in. "Now, Senorita Hamilton, Jan, tell me what you do know."

"He's lying!" Deni yelled. A fist from the giant crushed into his eye.

Vegas paid no attention and continued reasonably, "Please continue."

Jan stared from Deni to Vegas. She had never witnessed such violence. "Please, stop. There is some road Todd told me about; how it was supposed to be worth lots of money." She tried to think. "Towards Punta de Mita…"

Everyone froze as they waited for her words.

"Off the main road. There's a gate. Got a lock on it," she stumbled.

Vegas looked down at the woman. She was soft, innocent. He exchanged a look with Santana. She did not understand the meaning of deceit. He was going to enjoy teaching her.

"When did he tell you this?"

"The other day when we drove to Punta de Mita. On the way he pointed out some road. It was a dirt road."

"You can find this road?"

"I'll try." She looked up at him with doe eyes in an effort to resolve the situation amiably. The rope under her chest highlighted the tightness of her breasts against her blouse.

"I'm sure you will." A flicker of a smile twitched on Vegas' lips as the tiger growled within.

Vegas turned to Deni, in a harsh tone he said in Spanish, "You are coming, walking or being carried. Anything funny and your guts will be opened, comprende amigo?"

Deni's left eye was starting to swell; his field of vision narrowing. He had to wait for a chance. Right then there was none. Staying healthy was their only hope. He looked up at Vegas and nodded.

"Vamos!" Vegas commanded.

Santana walked behind Deni and slipped a fine wire loop over his neck. For an instant Deni thought his chances of survival were past. But even though the wire was snug, it did not choke him. They untied him but the moment he was freed the wire noose tightened slightly. The pressure brought Deni up out of the chair.

The two uniformed gunmen swept into action. One opened the van doors while the other confirmed Jan's hands were secured together with plastic ties before freeing her from the chair. With his gun in her rib cage he escorted her to the van.

They forced Deni to lie on the floor behind the front seats. The other bodyguards piled in on the seat around him; their feet on his body. Jan was led to the passenger's front seat. Her seat belt was secured to her and locked with a nylon tie. Vegas got in behind the wheel.

*   *   *

Jack checked his watch. He had plenty of time to get ready before Deni arrived. After calling and leaving an urgent message for Suarez to contact him he walked over and joined the two musicians.

"Hi guys. How did you do today?"

"Great," Willie answered. "Join us?"

Jack pulled up a chair. Angelo came over and handed him an uninvited beer. He declined and asked for bottled water instead. Rosa delivered the chilies rellenos.

After eating, Jack made his excuses and headed for his apartment. Inside, he noticed the faint scent of Jan. He showered with no soap and got into an old pair of black pants and a navy-blue long-sleeved tee shirt.

Downstairs he grabbed the keys to Deni's pickup. Rummaging through a couple of toolboxes he grabbed a few things.

Rosa called him in. "Suarez is on the line."

"What is going on?" Jack demanded of the cop.

"What do you mean?" Suarez countered.

"You called Deni and Jan in."

There was a long pause on the line. "No, I did not."

Jack's blood froze. "Someone did. They are heading in from Puerto Vallarta now."

"Don't move. We will be there in under two hours." Suarez hung up first.

28

Crammed in a fetal position on the floor of the van with men's boots all over him, Deni couldn't budge. The ride was agony. Although he couldn't see, experience told him where they were.

He recognized the reflections of lights as they traveled north, the feel of the bridge over Bucerias, the cloverleaf at the turn off to La Cruz. He gave a sigh of relief once he was sure they had passed the turnoff that would have led them into La Cruz. They covered another few miles before Vegas began to slow. The winding, narrow road was even more uncomfortable for Deni as the van swayed back and forth, around the sharp curves.

"There's the one turn off," Jan almost shouted with relief.

Vegas pulled off the paved road. "Down here?"

"No. A little further and it will be on the other side."

A hundred yards ahead they found the road. Vegas pulled the van up to the gate and illuminated the lock. One of the policemen jumped out. He took a toolbox from the rear of the van. Everyone sat in tense silence as the man picked the lock. In short order, he loosened the chain and threw wide the gates. After Vegas drove through the cop closed and locked the gate.

They traveled cautiously along the rutted dirt road, which was no more than a wide path. When they came to a Y, the lock-picker got out and searched the grounds with a flashlight. He finally signaled a direction. They searched different old roads for over an hour finally coming to the riverbed. Following the riverbed for a couple hundred yards, their headlights lit up the small hut.

"There," Vegas said. Everyone saw the big diesel.

The men jumped out of the van, leaving Santana with Deni.

When the trio came to the back of the Dina, they saw that the gates that closed off the back cargo area were swung wide open. The heavy canvas cargo cover was still tightly in place, covering all but the bottom two feet. Cartons of tile were spilled out onto the ground, as if some giant carrion bird had begun devouring the entrails of its prey.

"Get the branches off," Vegas commanded. "You," he looked at the lock-picker. "Get it started."

The man returned to the police van and grabbed his box of tools, leaving the back doors open.

Vegas walked back to the van. He cut the tie securing Jan's seatbelt with his switchblade. "Move to the driver's seat," he commanded.

He took Jan's tied hands and secured them to the steering wheel with another plastic slip tie.

"Get him out," he ordered Santana.

Pressure on the looped wire forced Deni to rise and step out of the van. Santana marched him thirty feet from the van.

Vegas took the 12 gauge shotgun from Santana. "Untie him," Vegas commanded.

The two men knew the routine, Vegas stepped back to cover Deni with the Browning in one hand and the sawed off in the other, while Santana removed the plastic ties holding Deni's wrists. Santana then took the noose from around Deni's neck.

"You can help me decide what to do with the woman, amigo. It can be quick or it can be slow. I have business here," He noted as he gestured his head at the truck.

Deni looked at the man with contempt. "You know what you're going to do."

Santana took the shotgun from Vegas.

Just then the lock-picker cop returned. "Señor Vegas, there

is no key and I do not know how to hot wire it. I know nothing of diesels." The man fairly shook in his boots.

All froze.

"I'll do it." Santana snared.

"Here, cover him." Santana handed the cop the sawed-off. Vegas walked back to the van and pulled out a short-handled shovel.

"Dig." He commanded, throwing the shovel at Deni's feet.

Deni stood there, every fiber in his body screaming to run or attack. Yet he knew that either option would be futile. He took a deep breath and tried to focus all his energy on maintaining his composure. Even though the evening was cool he was sweating. He bent over and took the shovel. He was disappointed when it bit easily into the soft, sandy soil.

From the front seat of the van, Jan stared in horror as she comprehended what Deni was doing.

*　　*　　*

It was another picture perfect evening in La Cruz. A light breeze moved gently off the hills back to the ocean. The sounds and laughter in the restaurant were familiar and at peace. Jack stood outside the kitchen, trying to absorb the mood but it was hopeless. Combat nerves had taken over. "Another mission," Jack thought, "...that was supposed to be over. Pat was supposed to be here and we would spend the evening with our friends." That was supposed to be reality, but his longtime friend and a new woman were in trouble. That was the new reality. Pat was no longer his.

An hour after talking with Deni, alarm bells were screaming in Jack's head. Driving from downtown Puerto Vallarta to La Cruz shouldn't take more than forty minutes, tops. But in Mexico, anything can happen—an accident, traffic jam, whatever.

After another fifteen minutes Jack had had enough. Something was seriously wrong. Suarez wasn't going to get there in time, and Jack could wait no longer. As he walked through the kitchen Rosa was furiously trying to keep herself busy. The salsa was chopped exceptionally fine on this night.

Jack walked over to the side of the mesquite grill. He grabbed a handful of small pieces of carbon out of the bag of charcoal next to the stove and put them in his pocket. "I'm going to head out. Deni must have gotten stuck in traffic or something," Jack said to Rosa.

The words meant nothing to her. "Where are they?" she pleaded.

"When he gets back," Jack stated calmly, "Let him know I went to find the truck, okay?"

She nodded stoically and continued chopping.

Jack looked at Rosa, she had been part of his extended family for so long. Jack thought about how wise these Mexican people were, they had an understanding of events that were out of their control, and had the ability to adjust. He thought of willows blowing in the wind, strong, but willing to bend when the need arose.

Jack powered Deni's pickup as fast as he dared utilizing the entire narrow road. Tires squealed as he muscled the truck around the hairpin corners. He relied upon his experience of the road and trusted that the night traffic would be light. His luck held. He soon passed the old gate that was the turn-off to the beach at Paradisio Escondido. He saw the gate on the opposite side of the road. In his headlights, he could see that a vehicle had recently used the dusty road.

Jack examined the lock and chain. They were of good quality—it would take him a while to saw through. He paced back-and-forth, in front of the fence. In his flashlight's glare he caught sight of a patch of vines that had recently been trampled by tire tracks. Jack walked over to the shallow ditch and realized he could easily make the crossing in the truck.

He followed the dirt road for about half a mile, heading up hill. He turned off his headlights to adjust to the darkness of a half-moon. Rolling down both windows, he listened as he crawled slowly forward.

He reached a second turn and judged that he had come far enough in the truck. He pulled it off the road into a thicket and stopped. Before he got out, he blackened his hands and face with the charcoal.

Jack froze as a diesel engine suddenly broke the night silence. He quickly strapped the sheath of his hunting knife to his belt and trotted into the darkness towards the sound. It wasn't long before he saw the glow of headlights through the thickets. He worked his way up onto the riverbank, keeping inside the dark shadows of the bushes.

The first movement he saw was a policemen working at the back of a big, rumbling, diesel truck. A police van illuminated the men's efforts. "So, the police have already found it," Jack thought as he waited and watched, deciding whether to announce himself. He was about to move when two other men walked in front of the van's headlights. Jack immediately recognized Vegas.

With the stealth of a blackened ghost, Jack worked his way to the back of the open van. From his vantage point behind the van, he picked up the sound of digging. He crouched under the chassis and saw Deni knee-deep in what was obviously going to be his grave. Another cop was holding a shotgun, bringing the count up to four.

As close to the van as paint, Jack began to rise. He suddenly felt movement within the vehicle. Rising to full height, he looked in the corner of the rear window. Jan sat sideways on the driver's seat. He could see from her silhouette that her eyes were transfixed on Deni, hypnotized by the unfolding horror.

Jack gave the van a push. It rocked imperceptibly. He looked for Jan's reaction, but she hadn't noticed. Again he pushed. This time her head moved, perceiving something. Pushing again, he watched her head turn; she was looking around to see where the motion was coming from.

"Okay Jan, now just stay cool." Jack thought. He slowly slid his face into view. Her eyes widened as she recognized him.

Jack raised his finger to his lips. To Jan's credit, she slowly swung back around to see if anyone else had seen her sudden movement and was making a move toward the van. No one was. She tipped her head, signaling Jack to enter.

Like a snake, Jack expertly slid smoothly over the rear seat. With the side door open, Deni and the cop were positioned parallel to the door, either one could have seen him. Jack snaked down onto the seat and along the far side of the van. From his position, he could see Deni to his right. Even though he moved very smoothly through the van, he couldn't stop it from wiggling slightly. The motion caught the attention of the guard.

Out of the corner of her mouth, Jan whispered, "He's looking this way."

Jack froze, a black lump lost in deep shadow.

Deni saw his guard's attention shift. He stopped shoveling and prepared to make a move. The immobile Deni brought the cop's attention back to him.

"Dig." The cop stepped back another pace for safety.

Just as he brought the shovel to the dirt, Deni thought he saw something moving in the side door of the van.

"Don't stop," the man snarled again.

Deni waited as long as he dared, then started again—slowly working closer to the gunman.

After the sound of digging settled to a rhythm, Jan whispered, "He's not watching this way."

"How many are there?" Jack asked from behind her seat.

"Four. A big one, Vegas, and two dressed like cops."

"How are you tied?"

"By those plastic strap things—one around my wrists and another through the steering wheel."

"Hold your hands as far away from the steering wheel as possible so the plastic is tight when I cut. Do not move your hands after you're loose. Got it?"

She nodded. From his low vantage point on the other side of the seat, Jack looked up and could see her face. It was stained with dust and dried tears but her eyes were sharp and alert.

"I'm going to get you out of here." He reached behind her and freed the ties with his knife.

"We're going to be okay, but we have to save Deni, right?" he asked, searching her eyes to see that the words registered. All too often, Jack had witnessed civilians crumble in the face of terror. He prayed Jan could hang on just a bit longer.

She nodded, her jaw set in total determination.

"I need your help to save him, okay?"

Jan gave a more aggressive nod this time. Jack knew he was burning time he just didn't have, but he had to get her under control.

"I'm going to free Deni." Jack nodded his head toward Deni.

"I want you out of the van through this door," he pointed at the driver's door, to be sure she understood. "Understand? When you see me make a move, you run and keep running."

Jan looked down at him, her face hardened, alert. In her eyes Jack saw a warrior. "This woman had steel within fire," he thought. He knew she would be okay.

Just then, they were distracted by the increased RPMs of the truck and the grinding of gears, as it began to move.

Jan jumped at the action. She turned to ask Jack where she should go but he was out of the van.

The diesel started moving back down the path of the bank it had come up. The moving lights of the truck sent shadows dancing through the trees.

Jack crouched by the back tire of the police van. He picked up a small stone, as slow as sunrise he moved away from the van and into view.

Deni's eyes only flinched for a second, the cop saw nothing. Deni bent over and picked up a small scoop of sand. Deni kept his rhythm as he watched Jack raise his arm to throw something.

The rock hit the cop squarely in the back and he winced and turned. Deni's shovel came at him before he knew what hit him.

The shotgun went off sending pellets just inches from Deni's feet.

Both Jack and Deni descended on the cop. The three men wrestled for only a moment, but it was a moment too long.

At the sound of the blast Vegas drew his gun and raced to the van. In the shadows he saw men grappling and fired a wild shot in their direction.

Jack instantly realized Vegas was after Jan.

The cop held a death grip on Jack's shirt until Jack buried his fist in the man's face. Jack pulled the unconscious man over and grabbed his pistol. Deni went for the shotgun.

At the sound of the first shot, Jan reached for the door handle. She saw Vegas coming, firing his gun. When the pistol exploded she cringed low and swung the door open, only to run right into Vegas' grasp.

Her scream was stifled by a back-handed slap to the face. Vegas clutched her arm and dragged her back toward the slow moving diesel. Without looking he fired another shot toward the van.

Even though she was totally outmuscled, Jan fought like a wildcat. She brought her free hand up and reached for Vegas' eyes. She couldn't reach them, but her nails dug deep into his face. He winced and shook her violently. By the time he had dragged her to the back of the truck, she was on her third attempt at taking an eye out. Vegas pistol hand came down on the side of her head, knocking her senseless.

The other cop had loosened his pistol and was looking for a target. Something moved by the grave. The cop fired.

After grabbing the first cop's pistol, Jack had broken too late for Jan. By the time he got within range of the van's door Vegas was dragging her to the back of the diesel. Try as he might, there wasn't a clean shot that didn't risk hitting Jan. Jack fired a shot high toward the retreating drug lord and then raced to the hut to get a closer look.

Vegas realized he couldn't carry her dead weight and return fire. He grabbed the woman and bodily threw her in to the back of the cargo bay, under the canvas cover with the drugs. He slammed the matching tailgates shut and dropped the locking rod down. Satisfied that this would hold her, he raced to the passenger side of the cab.

"Go! Go!" He yelled at Santana.

Santana steered with one hand and held his gun in the other. He simultaneously punched the accelerator and reaching out the window and fired twice.

"Cover us and follow!" Santana yelled as he passed the remaining cop.

The cop realized how vulnerable he had suddenly become. He fired wildly into the night and bolted for the police van.

As much as Santana wanted to move, the truck would only tolerate so much of the rough slope. He was forced to steer cautiously down the sandy bank.

No one saw Jack race for the back of the diesel. He grasped a rail of the tailgate and pulled himself up.

From his grave-cum-foxhole, Deni clutched the shotgun and waited for an opening. It came as the cop bolted for the van. As the man was entering the driver's door, Deni was coming in the side of the vehicle.

The cop saw him coming but couldn't bring his gun to bear before Deni caught him upside the head with the barrel of the sawed-off.

The cop fired, missing Deni but catching the stock of the shotgun. The impact twisted the sawed-off out of Deni's hand, numbing him to the elbow. The concussion within the cab was deafening and stunned both men. Before the cop could get another shot off, Deni grabbed the man's wrist and arm-wrestled for control. Deni had superior strength but the man had the better position and two good hands.

Deni slowly gained control and the gun dropped to the floor. Using his numbed right hand like a club, Deni brought it down on the side of the man's head, pitching the cop half-way out of the door. Deni grabbed traction with his feet and dove over the top of the man; both rolled out of the vehicle.

Once free to move Deni finished the man off with a vicious blow to the throat. The cop crumpled to the ground.

Deni looked up to see the diesel's taillights vanish into the darkness.

He jumped into the police van but found no key in the ignition. Pounding the wheel in frustration, he jumped out and started searching the cop's pockets to no avail. He raced over to the other cop who also had no keys.

With the strength of his wrist he gave the ignition a mighty twist. The plastic casing snapped. He quickly pulled wires out and hotwired the van and slammed it into gear.

*   *   *

Hanging onto the outside of the tailgates Jack tried to reach down and pull the iron locking pin out. But the bouncing and twisting of the truck jammed it tight. With his knife, he cut away the heavy canvas cover above the tailgate. Using the rails as a ladder Jack slowly climbed over the gate and through the canvas slit.

Jan sat in between boxes marked "ceramic tiles," rubbing her face. She looked up groggily and gave Jack a weak smile.

"You okay?" He asked.

"Sucker hit me." She brushed her hand across a blood stain in her hair. "But I got some of his face." She looked at the blood under her nails. She handed Jack a feral smile.

The truck rolled over a bump and both heard the cargo noticeably shift.

"We got to get you out of here. This stuff's coming loose. If they slow down enough, think you can jump?"

"Better than staying. Where's Deni?"

"I left him with the shotgun."

She nodded.

"When you hit the road, lay flat and dead-still, hopefully they won't see you."

"What are you going to do?"

"I'm going to stop them."

"How?"

"Haven't figured that part out." He gave her a cock-eyed smile.

"Jack this is serious, just get out."

"Oh, it's serious." His smile turned cold. "But there is no point in worrying about it."

In the cab of the truck Santana began to relax. "Haven't driven one of these in years, no big deal."

"We'll get back to the 200 Highway and Tepic." Vegas said. "We'll store this thing in our warehouse and reload."

Santana nodded.

They slowed as they approached the gate to the road. "What do you want to do?" Santana asked.

"Just go through it. It's not that solid."

"Si."

From his vantage point Jack realized they were coming to the gate. "Get ready."

With Jack's help, she climbed over the rail and hung on to the edge of trunk.

"Remember to lay flat and don't move. Once we're gone, get into the bush and wait. We don't know who will be coming up behind us. They don't want you dead."

"I'd rather be dead." She snarled.

When Jack figured the truck had slowed as much as it was going to, he whispered. "Go, go!"

Jack held Jan as long as possible and then she stepped down onto moving ground. Their luck held as the truck actually slowed a little more, giving her a chance to lie down and freeze.

Jack pulled out the cop's pistol from his pocket. He breathed a sigh of relief when the truck surged forward. He heard the metal of the gated fence giving way. As darkness enclosed upon Jan, Jack saw she had done perfectly, not moving a muscle. The truck never slowed.

"Showtime." Jack crammed the pistol back in his pocket and unsheathed his knife. He felt the fabric of the canvas cover. It was tough. High up on the back of the cover he cut a slit and lifted himself up. The fabric held.

Jack used the tailgate as a ladder and reached up to the top edge of the cover. He cut another slit and pulled himself up. On the top of the load, he cut slits and pulled himself forward.

When the truck got onto the pavement the ride smoothed out and speed increased. For Jack, speed was a problem, the momentum of the curves created such a swaying motion it almost flung him off. He quickly established slits for his feet as well as his hands. At each straight stretch he "frog marched" forward, gaining on the cab. From his perch atop the cargo, Jack heard the faint sound of sirens in the distance.

He made it to the back of the cab when the truck was about a kilometer out of La Cruz. Sheathing the knife, he pulled out the pistol.

The cargo truck was using the entire narrow road.

From his vantage point, Jack could see the lights of the approaching cars. Just before they broke around a sharp corner, Jack fired into the top of the cab, empting the pistol. The bullets' energy was absorbed by the metal roof, but concussion turned the windshield into a fog of fractured glass. As if on cue, a police car came around the sharp corner. The car driver slammed on the brakes too late. The car bounced off the truck like a toy.

With the impact, Santana instinctively swerved hard to the right and off the road—right at the corner, hurling them into space. For a long second there was nothing in front of them but small bushes and branches of larger trees, being smashed out of the way by the 5 ton flying missile. Suddenly, a massive rock outcropping appeared through the thick bush. The truck was almost vertical when it smashed into solid rock.

The impact drove the steering wheel into Santana's chest. Their seat belts held each man as their necks snapped like twigs. A hangman's noose could not have done a better job. If that were not enough, nearly 5 tons of ceramic tiles and cocaine crushed down on them like a giant battering ram. Boxes exploded from the cargo bay. The area was instantly covered with a cloud of white powder, like snow.

The police car careened into the shallow ditch on the other side of the road and came to a sudden stop. Suarez and Diaz struggled to free themselves from their seat belts and airbags.

The two trailing cop cars screeched to a halt, sirens and lights blazing. Men jumped out and ran to the edge of the road; others ran to assist their commander.

Cocaine dust choked everyone. All quickly donned masks from their emergency medical supplies. The cloud slowly floated away with the night air but not before coating the area with a fine dust.

The first vehicle from the opposite direction was Deni and Jan in the police van. They slowed and pulled up to the wrecked cop car. Deni looked around the dash and flicked on the flashing lights.

Jan ran to the road's edge. In the shadows of light and the snow of powder, she could see the undercarriage of the truck fifty feet down in the ravine, its rear wheels still slowing rotating.

She stood stock-still in disbelief. Deni came up behind her and wrapped his arm around her. They looked at each other, unable to comprehend the reality of what they were seeing.

Once freed from the car Suarez strode up and down yelling orders. Men got flares burning up and down the road. Others threw ropes down the steep cliff.

Someone realized there was no need for the sirens and turned them off. The silence was deafening.

Men yelled to each other as they began climbing and macheteing their way down the ravine. Others shined powerful flashlights down; the beams reflected off the white powdery haze that covered vegetation, giving the whole area an eerie ghostlike quality.

The US DEA agent recognized the couple and came over.

"What happened?" Diaz asked.

"He's gone." Jan looked up at Deni, tears filled her eyes.

Deni gave a ragged breath and pulled her tighter, fighting for control.

"This was the truck?" Diaz asked.

"Si."

Just then Suarez came up to them.

"What's happening." He commanded.

"That's the truck we've been looking for." Diaz said.

"Then it is good." Suarez said somberly.

"Jack was in it." Deni said limply.

"Madre Dios! What happened?"

"Jack said he was going to stop them." Deni said.

"Why did you insist on getting involved!" Suarez snapped.

"Because he was a trained solder and his wife was killed by druggies." Deni snarled right back, daring the cop.

"I am so sorry amigo, Senorita. He was a brave man." Diaz broke the tension.

Jan buried her face in Deni' chest and sobbed.

The first searcher reached the truck. For a long moment there was a pause in the yelling and noise, as others worked their way toward the cab.

Deni was the first to hear something strange.

"What was that? Listen." He looked down over the area.

Jan got control of herself and pulled away. She tilted her head and tried to hear anything unusual.

Deni retrieved a flashlight out of the police van and scanned the area around the truck. He and Jan walked back down the road where the diesel had traveled.

"I swear I heard something besides those guys. But can't see anything through this bush."

They walked further back from the accident and the strange noise became clearer.

On a whim, Deni scanned his light through the tops of the stand of huge huegra blanca trees that covered the cliffs between them and the ocean. There, straddling a branch the thickness of a telephone pole was Jack. When the beam hit him he gave a hardy wave.

"Jack!" Jan screamed.

Others searchers turned their attention toward the pair and the flashlight beam. Soon the area around Jack was lit up like daytime. He was 40 feet up from the base of the tree.

"Are you okay?" Deni called.

"Been better. Nothing broken, I think. My hands are a mess." He showed his palms. Even from a distance they could see that his hands were raw and bleeding.

"How'd you get up there?" Deni asked.

"Got caught in the vines and made it to this branch." Jack grabbed a vine that was hanging from above the tree, and gave it a wave.

"You're kidding?" Jan said.

"Tarzan!" Deni gave a hearty laughed.

"Wouldn't want to try it again." Jack said, sardonically.

Jan hugged Deni out of sheer excitement and laughed up to Jack. "Okay Tarzan, how you going to get down?"

"Keep a couple lights on me."

"Wait a minute." Deni yelled. He handed the light to Jan and jogged back to the van. In short order, he had the headlights positioned on Jack.

By now, traffic had piled up on either side of the wreck. When the crowd saw a man up in the tree and caught the drift of the story, several drove up to the edge of the cliff and added their headlights to illuminate the area under Jack. Others grabbed machetes from their vehicles and started clearing a path from the road to the base of the tree.

Jack gingerly took his knife and cut strips out of the legs of his pants and made padded bindings for his hands. He tested his grip by pulling on the vine, to ensure it would hold. Then gradually, with the vine in one hand and the tree in the other, he began working his way down the tree.

By the time he reached the ground several pairs of hands were waiting to ease him down the final few yards. A cheer went up from the crowd on the road. His rescuers helped Jack up the cleared path and into the waiting arms of Jan.

Jack looked like a refugee from a war zone. His clothing was ripped half-off his body. His face and arms were cut and bleeding, but he stood tall as his hugged his two companions.

The trio supported each other as they walked to the waiting ambulance.

The US DEA agent stood by the ambulance. "What happened?"

"We'll talk after we're fixed up." Jack demanded.

As the ambulance pulled away the trio heard over the radio that the two men in the truck were dead.

Jack and Deni's eyes met. In spite of their pain, they couldn't help smiling.

EPILOGUE

A couple of flying fish darted out of the water, gliding parallel to the sailboat. Charlie started at the sight, breaking Jack's reverie. The azure-colored water flashed by in a hypnotic rhythm. Jack heaved a deep sigh and slipped back in his thoughts of the past few days. In his mind's eye, he saw Jan's face, eyes red and saddened, but resolute.

Only this morning, she was standing with him at the airport, away from the crowd of fellow travelers. Agent Diaz and two Mexican policemen stood at a discreet distance.

"So, this is goodbye?" he had asked, suddenly realizing he wasn't ready for her to go.

She'd looked into his eyes giving him a gentle smile. "I have responsibilities back home. And, I have to take care of Todd." She'd swallowed hard.

Jack nodded.

The night of the action, everyone had met up at the clinic in Bucerias. Suarez and Diaz had been breathing fire and brimstone at Jack's actions. They wanted to know what civilians were doing with firearms and insisted that this whole affair was a matter for the police.

Jack nearly got arrested for pointing out that the weapons were all the property of Mexican drug lords and that the police were, in fact, on hand.

Then the real fireworks started. Jan started yelling in English and Rosa in Spanish about innocence, women, rape, dirty cops and men's idea of protection. The two cops were defenseless in the face of the feminine onslaught. Jack had started laughing. That almost got him killed by both sides.

Later the next morning, Deni and Jan had directed the police to the farmhouse just north of Puerto Vallarta where Vegas had held them hostage. There they found Todd in a shallow grave.

Both Diaz and Suarez wanted Jan out of the country for her own safety, but she would not leave without her brother's body—which the police would not release. That had been when Professor Torres weighed in, packing serious political muscle. Given the incredible gift Jack had found for their country there was nothing he couldn't ask for. It had been agreed that she could leave and take Todd with her. Forensics would be done in America and reported to the Mexican authorities.

The professor proved game as a fighting rooster. The top of his left ear was missing and he'd never hide the scar across his scalp, but the stories he would tell would be priceless. Jack almost pitied his students.

The press had a field day. One of the biggest businessmen, turned drug lord in Mexico, "had gotten his." The story of the fallen family was classic Mexican tragedy.

Jack was pleased that he and Deni had not been mentioned— better to just fade away than make a splash as a drug-lord killer.

The night after the accident, back at the restaurant, there had been quite a reunion. The *Juan de Fuca* cut a regal picture out in the harbor. The golden artifact had been unceremoniously brought into the restaurant, accompanied by four heavily armed guards. Professor Torres, Deni and Jan were each sporting skullcap bandages. Jack had white padded hands but they all toasted along with the rest—to the Aztecs, the beauty of the bay, the whales and just about everything else. Willie and Lobo put on a show. It was some party.

*　　*　　*

Jack's thoughts returned to the morning at the airport. The intercom squawked "final boarding." Diaz motioned that it was time.

"You know," Jan said, looking Jack squarely in the eye, "I think I'm owed one more night on that sailboat of yours."

She reached her arms up, placed them around his neck and planted a strong and eager kiss. "I seem to vaguely remember some unfinished business."

He'd looked down and gave her a wide, lopsided smile.

"If you ever get to Indianapolis sailor, you've a little thank-you coming," she'd flirted, giving him a wicked look.

A stewardess had approached them, it was time to go. Diaz and the cops had moved in and spoiled the moment.

Jan had given Jack one last desperate kiss and hugged him tightly. "Thank you," she'd whispered in his ear.

Then she was gone.

Jack came back to the present. He looked out across the bay. He loved this place and these people, but he knew in his heart it was time to get back to the rest of his life. Jan had shown him he was still capable of feelings. There was a very big ocean out there and he was in a position to make a difference. There was a life left for him, the right thing to do was live it. He knew Pat would agree.

Charlie jumped on his lap, circled and settled down. He gave the cat's ear a scratch.

"I wonder if there's any decent sailing in Indianapolis?"

THE END

ABOUT THE AUTHOR

HORATIO STREET

Now semi-retired, Horatio spends much of his time aboard his sailboat *Heavenly Daze*. He cruises the Pacific coast from the Alaskan Panhandle; south to the Baja peninsula and beyond the Bay of Banderas in Mexico, researching places for his many unfinished manuscripts. Born in Scotland, educated in South Africa. He has been a forensic investigator in the United States and Canada for decades. He draws upon this work and the many interesting and unusual people he has encountered for his interpretation of human nature.

A particular hobby of Horatio's is mastering the fusion of local foods and wines accompanied by eclectic music. Greed's Poison is Horatio's first work of fiction. Watch for his next novel — "*Trapped*"; the tale of three strangers struggling to survive in the remote wilds of British Columbia.

TRAPPED

BY HORATIO STREET

The morning sky glowed red. Claire Avery pounded the steering wheel of the pickup with her fist. Tight-lipped and determined, she negotiated the crude, narrow, gravel road that was flanked by sheer, gray rock on one side. A steep precipice fell away on the other. The bank was so steep, that the tops of great Alaska spruce trees below were nearly level with the road—yet only yards away. It would be possible almost to jump to the treetops. At this moment, Claire could certainly think of someone she would very much like to push over the edge.

The first rays of the mid September sun painted the tips of the western peaks; this only deepened the gloom in the canyon forest below. The path Claire drove had been punched in only that year; its sole purpose was to get the gold exploration equipment in. The rocks under her tires were the size of footballs—raw and sharp. The rocky road fought the pick-up every step of the way, buffeting Claire back and forth within the cab. It threatened to twist the truck off into the nothingness of the canyon below. Claire's head and shoulder repeatedly bounced off the driver's door as the 4x4 crawled along; but she remained focused. She was getting out of this god-forsaken, rain-soaked, fog-enshrouded corner of the earth—no matter what the risk.

Claire felt like an escaping hostage. She'd been trapped for over a week at her husband's mining exploration camp on one of the Alexander Islands, off the southeast coast of Alaska. The camp was nothing more than a collection of beat-up trailers, dug precariously into the mountain slope. It was inhabited by twenty men and three women; women who were rougher than most of the men. At least they drank more, swore better and spat further. "Yeah," Claire thought, she'd "been a hostage." Maybe "prisoner" was a better word for it—and in more ways than one. She even felt guilty for her crime of running away—not just from the camp, but from her marriage and the pain of her husband, Frank's selfishness. Now, if only I can get a plane out of here.

*   *   *

So began Claire Avery's "escape." But before the sun would set this day, she would lie battered and bruised in another man's bed in a remote cabin in Northern British Columbia. His name was Ryan Neville. She would be trapped with two hunters she had never met in her life.

For their part, Ryan Neville (38) and Chris Seltzer (19) had returned to the lake once more—as they had for many years. Only this year was different …very different. Frank Seltzer, Chris' father and Ryan Neville's best friend and long-time hunting partner, had died the previous summer. This would be their first trip back and both men knew the experience was going to be emotionally painful.

For both men, Frank had been a rudder in their lives. To Ryan, Frank was a best friend; the one who helped him adjust to the desertion of his wife. He was also the man who helped him start a new, fulfilling career as a wildlife photographer. To Chris, Frank was a loving father and mentor in life. Now he was gone and Chris was going to have to face the rapidly-approaching responsibilities of manhood— without a father.

Suddenly now, what was going to be an emotional experience anyway, took an impossible twist as this woman literally fell into their lives.

Now all three were going to have to adjust to new realities, new responsibilities. And like it or not, they were going to have to

346

live together or die. As well, any creature in this part of British Columbia lived by only one rule: "Kill or be killed."